OVER THE PLAIN HOUSES

JULIA FRANKS

# OVER

## *the*

# PLAIN

# HOUSES

*a novel*

HUB CITY PRESS
SPARTANBURG, SC

Cover and book design: Meg Reid
Proofreaders: Beverly Knight &
Rachel Richardson
Cover painting: J. Chris Wilson
*Spillway at Highlands Country Club*, 2005
oil on canvas
*in situ* Highlands Country Club, Highlands, N.C.

Library of Congress
Cataloging-in-Publication Data

Franks, Julia, 1964–
    Over the plain houses / Julia Franks.
        pages cm
    ISBN 978-1-938235-21-4 (alk. paper)
    1. Married people—Fiction.
    2. Farm life—North Carolina—Fiction.
    3. Fundamentalists—North Carolina—Fiction.
    I. Title.
    PS3606.R422575O84 2016
    813'.6—dc23
        2015032618

 HUB CITY
PRESS

186 W. Main Street
Spartanburg, SC 29306
864.577.9349
www.hubcity.org

## HER KIND

I have gone out, a possessed witch,
haunting the black air, braver at night;
dreaming evil, I have done my hitch
over the plain houses, light by light:
lonely thing, twelve-fingered, out of mind.
A woman like that is not a woman, quite.
I have been her kind.

I have found the warm caves in the woods,
filled them with skillets, carvings, shelves,
closets, silks, innumerable goods;
fixed the suppers for the worms and the elves:
whining, rearranging the disaligned.
A woman like that is misunderstood.
I have been her kind.

I have ridden in your cart, driver,
waved my nude arms at villages going by,
learning the last bright routes, survivor
where your flames still bite my thigh
and my ribs crack where your wheels wind.
A woman like that is not ashamed to die.
I have been her kind.

—*ANNE SEXTON*

# PART ONE

*End of March*

## CHAPTER ONE

·

IT WAS THE WEEK BEFORE EASTER WHEN THE LADY agent first showed up to church. When the gray coupe rolled past, the first thing Irenie Lambey noticed wasn't that a woman was driving but that a sculpted angel leapt straight out from the grill, her head raised and her back arched, silvery wings sweeping behind her as if she were about to take flight.

Later, after the agent and her husband were dead and the Department of Agriculture had closed its extension office for good, there were those who held out that her first day had been sometime in the summer.

But Irenie knew different. She knew on account of the birds. It was that moment in the year when winter still tightened the earth but spring snuck in from overhead. Robins and warblers and purple martins were back, and the flax birds had switched out their gray feathers for yellow. The trunks of the sassafras and sourwood ran wet and black with sap, and the fingers of the service trees had swelled but not budded. It had to be the Last Supper service because her sister wore her blue muslin, and there were those who turned out for the first time since the fall, and the whole fray about how close was too close to park the automobiles to the horses and mules started up all over again.

And Irenie Lambey felt alive, unfurled.

The deacon Haver Brooks must have seen that the lady agent meant to park the motorcar and that there was no room for her to do so, because he waved her on just the way he would a man, and Irenie knew he meant to show her the place where the road bent and widened enough for a pull out. Moments later the two of them came slow-picking their way over the frozen ruts, Haver with his hat in his hands and circles darkening his armpits despite the cold, the USDA agent craning up at the trees, pressing the top of her small-brimmed hat with one hand while shielding her eyes with the flat of the other. Haver followed her gaze as if her curiosity had already infected him some too.

Irenie's sister Elizabeth leaned in to her ear. "Four churches in Eakin and she comes up *here*?"

It was true. Other women wouldn't have done that way, especially not without their husbands.

Elizabeth jogged her infant up and down on her hip. "I wonder what it is she wants."

Irenie didn't say a thing. If she had, it would have been something like this: how in the world did it feel to drive your own automobile to a place you'd never set eyes on and arrive there full of wonder and questions and not caring one whit what the people there said about you?

Her sister shifted George Junior from one side of her pregnant belly to the other. Without thinking, Irenie raised her arms and took him, the infant miffling against her collarbone until the wet soaked through the cotton to her skin. She was glad he wasn't hers. She had raised one and buried one, and now, at thirty-two, it seemed enough.

Her son had told her something of the lady agent, how she'd visited the school at Christmas time, handing out a donated toy and a bristled toothbrush to each child in the class, how she'd taught a reading program after school. She was the new wife of Roger Furman, who also worked for the Department of Agriculture. But today she looked for all the world like she'd stepped from the pages of a catalog, her suit cut to the shape of her plumpish body, her hat tilted over her forehead, a wave of pretty dark hair curled against her collar.

George Junior pushed his arms against Irenie's sternum to examine her face.

Across the yard, Haver was introducing the newcomer around, sweat shining across his forehead and chin.

But George Junior had noticed that his mother was out of sight and began to lean away, twisting his head and torso in an effort to locate her. To distract him, Irenie opened her eyes wide and mouthed, "Wah, wah, wah," until the baby's attention swiveled back to her. She extended him a finger, and he wrapped it in his own, his eyes searching her features.

She looked to check the newcomer again and caught up her breath. Mrs. Virginia Furman from the USDA extension office was already studying *her*.

She panicked. Dropped her eyes to George Junior' red red face. The stranger knew. Of all the women in the churchyard, she'd picked her right off.

But what? What could she know? There was nothing *to* know, save that Irenie Lambey wondered what it was like to be her.

The proper thing would be to nod or wave or make her way through the clusters of churchgoers to introduce herself. But Brodis was somewhere behind her now, perhaps watching, perhaps not. Her husband didn't think much of the government extension office. And the fact that they'd sent a woman up the mountain on her own...Well.

Now the lady agent stood by herself among the clusters of worshippers that broke and shifted and recombined. The youngest Hogsed boy stopped to talk to her, and the woman stooped down so that her face was the same level as his. And when he wandered off, she stood up, alone again, examining the outside of the clapboard church or brushing her hands against the naked branches of the ninemark bushes. Or looking at Irenie Lambey.

Irenie put on like she didn't notice.

Now the woman bent at the knee and sat right back on her heels to make herself as short as the Hackett twins, who were both turned out in red scarves. The two little girls seemed to have plenty to tell the government worker, and she let them, nodding at something one of them said, or knitting her brow and holding an index finger against her chin, as if sorting out the best points of the conversation. The twins' presentation gathered force, and soon they were interrupting one another and throwing their stick arms and shrieking with wild laughter, little girls still young enough to blurt the truth without questioning the way the world would receive it. (When, Irenie wondered, had she and her sister and the rest of them lost that freedom? Was it something their parents had taken away, or a thing they had given over of their own accord?)

The lady agent was laughing too, throwing her head back to show white rabbity teeth, and then slapping her hand on her thigh, really and truly slapping it, the way only old men ever did. And then one of the Bledsoe boys ma'amed her and touched his hat, but none of the adults shook her hand nor waved in recognition. No one made room for her in their conversation, and soon she was by herself again.

Irenie made up her mind that one day she'd introduce herself to the new agent from Eakin, whenever the earth had warmed and people went to socials and singings, whenever Brodis had left off standing behind her, and things were easier between them. When the time was right, she'd introduce herself as Preacher Lambey's wife, and Brodis would be glad to see her neighbor the newcomer.

The sound of the bell lolled through the yard. Irenie's sister Elizabeth lifted George Junior from her arms. The clusters of churchgoers loosened and drifted toward the entrance. Once inside, Irenie's eyes and ears adjusted to the dark and the din. The coal stove at the front glowed hot, and the new electric bulb illuminated a circle above the sinner's bench, the wire serpenting along the beam of the ceiling. Behind the pulpit box, Jesus at the Last Supper spread his arms, portraits of the church's elders at either side of Him. Below the bench sat the twenty or so saved members of the church, facing the congregation.

Then the woman from the Department of Agriculture was at her side, quiet and brimming with intention. Irenie gave a little nod and moved toward the platform behind the pulpit, where she always sat. The woman kept pace with her. Irenie willed herself not to turn her head. She was halfway there. Then, unbelievably, a touch on her arm, insistent. The woman spoke, but not to introduce herself. Instead she pronounced the name of Irenie's thirteen-year-old son.

"Matthew. He's yours?"

Irenie stopped. So that was it. A problem with Matthew.

"Yes." Her voice came out more brittle than she'd intended. Something had happened in the school. He'd disappeared during recess or daydreamt in class. Or the other boys had stolen his lunch bucket or peed on his composition book. Or the woman had noticed that her son wasn't included in marbles or climbing trees after school. That he walked on his own. She braced for the pity-heavy comment or the too-polite question, marshaling the regular defenses. Or maybe the woman was wanting to talk about his bodily frailty. Years ago there'd been ladies from another brought-on organization who'd staged lectures in the county courthouse about nutrition. But Matthew was never short of food. Even in the worst winters, Brodis put meat on the table. There was no one could say her husband didn't provide.

"I'm sorry to intrude. I'm Virginia Furman." The woman was even younger than Irenie had figured her for, her face unlined and flushed, her lips and nose full, her eyes as big and brown as a spaniel's. Except she wasn't a spaniel. Anyone could see that. She was a woman who kept her own privilege.

"I know who you are," Irenie said. "I've got to—my husband is the—excuse me." Dee Dawson brushed past her. Elizabeth watched from across the aisle.

The other woman touched her arm again. Her voice was urgent. "I'm sorry to be so forward. It's just that...he's so intelligent, so much keener than anyone else in his class..."

Irenie felt an unbidden rush of affection. People didn't describe her son that way. What they mostly did was describe his peculiarities.

Then, if the speaker were feeling charitable, she might say, "But he *does* seem clever."

Mrs. Furman kept talking, her words coming fast and unbroken. "The boy knows the Bible like the back of his hand—he found every passage he heard, and he found them within seconds—he kept handing me the book with his finger on a line."

It was true. Matthew had learned early on that the best way to please his father was to study on the scriptures. Like many people, he could quote chapter and verse, but unlike most, he had an uncanny ability to link the passages to other stories he'd heard. It was a certain kind of skill, even if it wasn't useful in the way people thought of useful. Her father had it too, that ability to collect ideas from lots of places and then put them together to build something new and unexpected.

But Mrs. Furman had noticed it.

Irenie wanted to hear more about her son's talents, but the two of them had followed the flow of worshippers toward the pews. The other parishioners were settling in, shrugging out of coats and scarves. She extended her hand. "It was a pleasure to meet you, Mrs. Furman."

But the other woman ignored her hand and kept talking. "Mrs. Lambey, I don't think your son is getting what he needs from that school."

There were only a few people standing now. Irenie was supposed to make her way up to the front of the church, where the saved members sat behind the pulpit box. It was certain that Brodis was watching her now. No doubt he was already seated, waiting for her. She heard the deacon Haver Brooks step up. Everyone in the church, sinners and saints alike, had begun to quiet.

Virginia Furman whispered, "Mrs. Lambey, please, there's a new school in Asheville, for exceptionally intelligent children."

Irenie stopped. Mrs. Furman's face was inches from her own, her cheeks flushed red and her long front teeth as straight as board and batten. "He could get in. I just know it."

For once Irenie didn't want to sit in front. She wanted to hear what the woman from the Department of Agriculture had to say.

For once she couldn't recall a good reason not to sit with the regular congregation. There, in the pews, her own mother sat among the sinners—now catching her daughter's eye and patting the seat at her side. How long had it been since she'd spent the day with her mother's full hip against her own, the squeeze of her hand upon her knee, her sister's gossip chittering past her ear? Irenie cast a quick glance toward the bench behind the pulpit, where the saved sat, rock-faced and proper. On impulse, she took a place next to her mother and sisters and motioned Virginia Furman into the pew beside her.

Mrs. Furman leaned into her ear and whispered, "There are *scholarships*."

The choir commenced singing, "I Heard my Savior Speak to Me." Irenie picked up the other woman's hand and squeezed it in her own.

Brodis glanced to the raised platform behind the pulpit where the saved members sat in U-formation, the women in calico store dresses, their hair fastened in biscuits at the napes of their necks. She wasn't there. He turned toward the congregation. There, at the door, two women filled the dipper at the water bucket—but not her. People were settling themselves, the men next to the window in the square of morning light, the women on the other side of the aisle shadowed in gloom. And Irenie. Right there, in the pews among the sinners. She was supposed to be sitting on the platform behind the pulpit. She was supposed to be sitting among the saved. She, more than anyone, belonged to the Lord.

Why wasn't she sitting among the saved?

But there was no time. Haver Brooks was making his way to the front of the room. Brodis stepped up and found his own place among the church members and the fellowshipping preachers. His wife didn't look at him. In place of meeting his eye she untied the strings of her bonnet and stared at the pulpit as if her behavior didn't matter a thing in the world.

She had an obligation to the congregation, especially on this day, the sacrament of the Last Supper. It was her mother's habit, this sitting among the congregation, not hers.

But his wife was an inside-herself woman. Even when he'd first met her, and told her about the accident that had crippled his foot, she'd listened without saying a word. She'd looked *at* him and *in* him, as if she had the self-experience to understand the lull and fester of despair. But she'd been younger than him by ten years, narrow-shouldered and slim, her hair the color of ancient pennies. The big freckles on her face and arms were coppery too, and he'd wondered right away how much of her body did they cover.

But these days her private thinkings vexed him, like a walnut a man carried in his pocket. He couldn't leave off touching it, rolling it between his fingers, worrying and working it until the thing loosed itself and the two halves fell away as they'd been meant to do all along.

Now Irenie's mother leaned in and said something to her, both of them laughing in response. Next to them, a raft of aunts and nieces whispered and giggled.

And something else. The woman from the extension office was sitting at her right. Why? And why had she come all the way across the river to get into this church, and by herself?

Furman, that was her name. They had two agents to work at the USDA office now, two men and now the woman. The men had come five years ago, in '34, then commenced holding meetings and visiting farms in both counties. From the get-go they'd been selling the idea of tobacco. And there were people that had switched. Rickerson was the first to get shed of his wheat and rye and cane. Brodis was the last, even though he didn't use the tobacco for himself and had to sell every leaf. After that, the push was for separate pens for the animals. Build more fences and paddocks and leave the crops free in the open, they said. Never mind that the deer and raccoons would get them.

Not that any of the agents had ever farmed a day in their lives. And you couldn't trust their interest. It was the looking-down kind, the kind that made a body to take in a stray dog or an idiot child. The kind born of vanity.

But Isaiah had told that the crown of pride would be trodden under feet. And it was sure Irenie believed that way too. She wouldn't be swayed by a stranger come from across the river for some kind of charity visit. Most likely the outsider was happenstance. Just that his wife had for some reason chosen this day to cozy up to her mother.

When Haver ran out of announcements, Brodis stood, his bad foot prickling in his boot, his mind overstrung. He said, "Let us pray," and the sound of fifty heads bowing was like a communal sigh, or the swing-out of a gate. He felt something inside him give way then too. The first voice, Mary Higdon's: "Dear Jesus, be with my mother..." Then another voice joined in, a man's. "Lord, I know..." And then another and another, each with its own plea. The jumble of sound rose above them until it was a needful cloud kept aloft by the pleas on either side, a communal swell of voices, some soft and insistent, some shy, some strident, all rising together in a bubble of hope, and then floating up toward the ceiling, where it dissipated in a scattering of *Amens* and *Thank-yous* and faded in a murmur and a sigh. The room had warmed, and the prayer evaporated in the smell of burning wood and warm bodies. Then the voices of the choir spilled over their heads.

Haver strode out and began lining the words.

"I heardan-old-oldstory."

The congregation sang the words back majesty slow. *I Heard an Old Old Story....*

"Howasavior-camefrom-glory."

*How a Savior. Came From Glo-ry....*

Haver led the swaying congregation through three times, the chorus at first mournful and rich as the droning of bagpipes, but each rendition more vigorous than the last, until the singers pounced on the final notes. *Beneath the. Cleansing. Flood.*

With the last word hanging yet above them, Haver boomed, "Let us join hands in fellowship." Women hugged, men embraced, and sound bubbled up again. Brodis turned to Haver, and for a moment, their caviling and jockeying fell away. For a moment all he saw was a vulnerable old man with a ring of fat around his belly and sweat mizzling the armpits of his white shirt. Brodis squeezed the deacon's shoulders in a tight bear hug and Haver Brooks squeezed him back. It would be a good service, he could see, never mind his wife's shenanigans.

He hadn't planned what he was going to preach on. He never did. To do that would have been to rob the Holy Spirit of an opportunity. Every time he'd ever stood up without a pre-thought sermon, the Lord had given him the words. The trick was to step aside and get out of the way, to lay down whatever other thing you figured needed saying and let the Spirit through. Now he gripped the pulpit block and surveyed the congregants. His mind was a blank. He listened. The room was still, expectant. The lady from the extension office was sitting very close to his wife. She regarded him with no expression at all, but he had an idea of her thinking. Like every other person from every other brought-on organization, she saw them as curiosities. That's how come she kept her hands folded careful in her lap and her face unlined. She was young, even pretty, her hair full and auburn-colored, gold light winking from her ear lobes. She was the only woman in the room to wear jewelry. Even the sinners left their fancy things at home on church day. The lines that came to him then were from Peter. *Let it not be the outward adorning of plaiting the hair, and of wearing of gold, or of putting on of apparel.*

But that wasn't from the Spirit. That was him. He set it aside and kept his mind loose. The faces in front of him seemed pure and childlike, and in that moment he too felt peeled-back, young. From somewhere inside him the sermon rose up.

"The Jews," he said, and the words were a gift, the surest proof he had of the Lord's favor. "The Jews were waiting for a king with a fancy gold crown to sit above everyone and rule the people and tell them what to do." He paused to let the picture lay down in people's minds. "But that ain't what happened."

There was a shift of appreciation in the congregation.

"Instead the King came plain. Wearing rough clothes and talking simple talk." Just like you and me.

The audience said yes without saying yes, all eyes on him, a few nods. "And on that last night, He knew that someone He loved would betray him."

Irenie and Mrs. Furman were sitting straight up now, alert, brows slightly raised. There was something similar about their posture that Brodis found troubling, even though they didn't seem aware of one another's presence. Only him. Only Jesus. But there they were, among the sinners, where they both of them had chose to sit, even for some reason his own true wife, as if she didn't know how that choice would cast a doubt on the status of her soul.

He willed his mind back to the image of Jesus. "He knew His neighbors and His loved ones would pierce His flesh with nails and spit upon Him while His blood soaked the earth." He paused to let the image take. Then he bellowed. "And what did He do about it?" The question suspended itself above the congregation, an enormous glass balloon that would either float or crash, depending on what Brodis said next. "He *lowered* himself, that's what. In place of getting angry, in place of shouting and making threats, He *lowered* himself, ladies and gentlemen."

The room was perfectly still. The little boys in the last row had stopped passing whatever object it was they'd been sharing. Next to them, his son Matthew stopped looking out the window. He'd grown up ten inches over the winter, gangly and loose-jointed and full of the Kingdom of Heaven.

"And what did he say to those gathered around him? And what did he say to the fellow who was going to betray him? He said, 'Let us give thanks.'"

"Now." Brodis scanned the congregation. "All are invited to take part in the washing of feet." At his side, Haver Brooks had prepared two trays, on each a row of saltine crackers and a glass filled with grape juice.

About half the adults stood. The woman from the extension office moved her legs to one side to let Irenie pass, and it seemed to him that there was some acknowledgement or comment that passed between them. Then the congregants and the members were milling at either side of the pulpit. Haver broke in, "Will the older members be seated first." There was nervous joking about who might be considered older. Brodis let the jitters and awkwardness settle some, until the grayhaired had seated themselves in the front pews, women on the right side with their feet crossed at the ankles and tucked under the pews, men on the left with their feet planted block-like in front of them. Most of them were farmers. A few, like the Rickersons, had bottomland, but most were like Brodis: tilling the watersheds and the ridges and every slope in between. The people who owned valley land anymore went to the Free Will church in town.

Brodis felt calm. There was no one made a move to touch his footwear. Instead, faces pointed toward him, waiting for the instructions they heard every year, the silence stuffed with an energy that would have embarrassed him under other circumstances. Haver gave each of the standers a terrycloth cutting. Some of the men tucked it into the galluses of their overalls, and some draped it over a shoulder. There was no one looked at the enameled pans resting on the oilcloth on the table next to the pulpit. The two Hogsed boys stood next to it, waiting. The kettles steamed on the coal stove, and the hiss was the only breath in the room.

Lem Thompson took the pulpit, his skin creased and lined as an old saddle and his gaze pointing in two directions at once. Since birth, the wandering left eye had empowered him with seeing and knowing more than he saw and knew. Now the old man set to reading with an energetic chant, each phrase punctuated with an intake of air that in another preacher would have been a rest but in Lem was the tightening of a ratchet wrench. "'Now-when-Jesus-knew-that-his-hour-was-come, ah." Each quick breath cranked the sermon up. "He-began-to-wash-the-disciples'-feet, ah." The sentences constricted, sped, tightened, until Lem stepped away from the pulpit and from the printed word, and his eyes drilled down on the congregants and the foot washers both at the same time. "And-do-you-think-he's-feeling-shame?"

The voice of the congregants was immediate, members and sinners alike. "*No!*"

Brodis stole a glance at his wife. She had closed her eyes the way she did when she was trying to figure out what she was feeling.

Meantime Haver raised up the hymn, and Lem didn't even acknowledge it. If anything, the old man began shouting louder.

"Jesus-Christ-got-right-down-on-his-knees!"

*Blessing and honor, glory and power. . .*

"And-bowed-down-before-the-disciples!"

*Bow unto the ancient of days. . .*

"And-took-up-their-feet-and-bathed-them!"

Spontaneous voices rose up from the crowd, as if cheering Lem on. That was the way it started. Always with Lem. A sudden resentment bared itself naked in Brodis's soul, a rusty artifact uncovered of its own accord. He willed himself to look at it and dust it off, ancient and corroded as it was. Then he willed himself to set it aside.

The music swelled. "The-scriptures-say-that-a-Christian-is Christlike, ah. But-what-does-that-mean?"

Murmurs from the congregation. Brodis saw that Joe Rickerson was crying.

Meanwhile the older Hogsed boy took the first kettle from the stove and began pouring the hissing water into the pans. The younger followed with a pitcher of cold.

Now Lem spoke with deliberation. "Brothers and sisters, all who are seated, as you are servants of the Lord, you may remove your shoes."

It was the instruction they'd been waiting for. Eleven heads and eleven torsos moved forward to untie eleven pairs of boots. Each man's full attention went to the unlacing, as if the task were new to him and required his full concentration. None gawked down the row at his neighbors' feet, blue-veined and exposed like genitals. None joked about ugliness or fust the way they would in the logging camps or any other place where men lived together too close. But Brodis knew these men. Like him, they worked on the mountains, uphill, through creeks and branches and snake-infested forest. They worked for every piece of food they put on the table. And yet, they had come here, of their own accord, in their puniness, with their feet naked and red-wrinkled, looking to be better men. And he was kin with them.

He glanced at the women on the other side of the aisle. Irenie's feet were pale and freckled. He turned his head. Did his wife submit her soul to the Lord? What was she thinking about right now? Why hadn't she taken her rightful place among the saved?

Lem's voice: "Let us commence to washing the feet of the Lord's servants." The younger men dropped to one knee, and there, like suitors, knelt before their elders. Without thinking, Brodis kneeled at the pan of water in front of Haver Brooks, as his conscience had called him. Haver's feet had troll-like knobs at the sides of the toes and sprouts of black hair at the center of each digit. Brodis had forgotten how they appalled him. It wasn't his own filth, but worse, the wretchedness of someone else's. But the feet were also old, and the heels had cracked so deep that he could spy the red insides, like the split hooves of horses. It had to hurt. Brodis cupped a fissured heel in his left hand and scooped the water in his right. Embrace the ruin of the physical. A fellow had to pass through it to get to the other side. The lighter grace-lit side.

Lem called for the washers and the washed to switch places, and now the elderly knelt before their younger neighbors. Then Lem Thompson stepped in front of Brodis, steadying himself with one hand on Haver's shoulder, grunting. He rested on one knee, and Brodis found himself looking at the top of Lem's bowed head, his white hair transparent, the pink scalp showing beneath. The old man breathed heavy. Brodis wondered had Lem seen the corrosion of his childish resentment. Lem lifted his foot and began washing. And maybe it was the warmth of the water that started it. The swell came from his toes, an effulgent good will like the effect of block-ade whiskey rising up his legs, energizing his thighs and into his torso and his heart.

And there. Beyond Lem's bent head, the lady agent sat pin-straight, her head cocked to one side, as if she were watching a pair of rabbits japing. And the Spirit rose right up and spoke through Brodis. "There may be some who haven't let Him into their hearts. For those people, now is the opportunity." The government agent didn't blink. He let his gaze sweep the rest of the sinners. "Is there anyone here who is ready to walk the aisle?"

There was a movement in the back, near the boys, a slight figure in overalls. Howard Gooch. No obvious signs of drunkenness this morning. Today Mr. Gooch walked steady, then eager. Then he was throwing himself at the mourner's bench, his knees hitting the wooden floorboards so hard that the chair Brodis was sitting in quivered too. Mr. Gooch looked straight up at the electric bulb. Brodis stood then, never mind his wet feet. Mr. Gooch was breathing, "Aaahh, please help me, please help," the loose skin of his neck trembling. Brodis reached for the man's hands, the skin light and crumbly in recent years, as if his body were sloughing away. Mr. Gooch had come under conviction years before, but the Lord had not yet seen fit to save him, probably because he hadn't succeeded in changing his life for more than a couple weeks at a time. His backsliding was famous. To Brodis, the man's temptations seemed puny. For Brodis, giving up music and swearing and drink had been easy. But that was him. He pressed Howard Gooch's flaking hands and understood that if he was to squeeze them too hard he would crush them. The man was weeping and muttering for help.

"Lord grant it," someone called from the men's side, and others echoed with prayers that threaded among and across them, the weft of them supporting the slight weight of Howard Gooch. Leastways for now.

Haver began singing, "Just as I am without one plea, but that Thy Blood was shed for me." The other voices joined in, "And that Thou bidst me come to Thee, O Lamb of God, I come."

Mr. Gooch closed his eyes and muttered something, but Brodis couldn't make out the paper-whisper. Then, out of the blue, he did. "Oh, Lamb of God, I come." And the sound was so frail that some part of Brodis that had been frozen loosened, and he forgot about the leprous feel of Howard Gooch's skin and raised their four hands aloft, and his own soul rose up too, breaking a little free from the beastly shape he'd been born to, and from that small height he saw that his own challenge was different. He saw himself for what he was, a man who figured to outsharp the God that had made him. His task was his own: to lay down the questions and the pride because here was Howard Gooch, a drunk with a mountain to climb, willing to throw down his body and his soul for God. Again.

The congregation held them up, the voices welling as if in one accord, and soared, and glided, the cadence rising and falling in waves of sound that carried away pettiness and grief, now weaving together again, now carrying the promise of the Holy Spirit, and the richness of life, and the nearness of joy, and Brodis became once again his younger stronger self. Here in the church, among these white enameled pans and this tender flock kneeling in the blanched light, he was his best self. This was the meaning of Grace. These were his people, and this was what Heaven must be like.

# CHAPTER TWO

IRENIE PAUSED ON THE PORCH TO LISTEN. IT WAS PAST midnight. She pulled shut the door and held her breath against the likely of whining hinges. If he was to rouse, she could say that her bowels had run away with her and she was headed to the privy.

She eased the latch into place.

The night air was an ally: sharp, alive, alert. She stretched her hands into the army overcoat and pushed the eagled brass buttons through the holes.

Best to wait one, two, ten minutes, in case he had waked. Ice skinned the washing tub, and frost dusted the stacks of wood, the cut and the uncut, both of them outsized by the great frosted pile of coal. And the new school glowed up hot in Irenie's mind. Though she'd kept it to herself all day, she hadn't for a moment forgot it was waiting, like a live fire hiding under a heap of ash in the morning fireplace. You slid the shovel under the gray until you heard the grate of iron on stone. Then, when you flipped it, the coal kindled up orange in the dark.

She listened. But there was only the ghost of her own breath hanging in the stillness, and beyond that the persistent march of water from the springhouse to the branch, its hurry to the base of the mountain, to the place where it joined the river under the white arms of calicoed sycamores. Scram and Lacy and Stomper opened their eyes and watched, but it was the redbone Fortune who lifted her head and cocked her ears. Irenie considered the dog for a moment but motioned her to stay. On warmer nights, yes, but not now.

Winter didn't need dogs. The earth was packaged yet, drum-tight. Its creatures still slept, the white-footed mice curled into the cracks of the barn, the voles buried beneath the beech leaves, the yellow-painted box turtles drawn up tight under winter-rotted logs, the snakes like hairballs in the roots of trees. Likewise the bears suckling their newborns high in the silver-lichened beeches—and her son sleeping his odd, fitful sleep, clutching and unclutching. The world was hers, at least for an hour or two. Brodis was safe accounted for in their bed, under the quilts she'd sewn, dreaming virtuous dreams.

It was strange. She'd married him in part because he'd seen the world, and she'd thought a life with him would open her up too. But somehow the opposite had happened. They'd set up house-keeping so close to home that the land was part of her great grandfa-ther's original parcel, and to this day she hadn't figured out how the wide place that had been her growing up had shrunk so tight that she found herself lonely in it. She'd come to hate the root cellar. All winter she'd inventoried there, sitting in the dank with the fust and the mold nudging at the door. Cull the apples, unwrap the sweet potatoes, put the potatoes by, set the squash out for cooking before it was too late, all the while Brodis roaming the ridge to gather and salt the stock, or chasing game and checking rabbit boxes and tak-ing the saddle horse into town for shoes. But she was the keeper of the house and the yard and the fields. She'd cooked and put up all manner of food. In the root cellar, in the weak air, the lamp gut-tered and the flame bowed and whickered. Only the bluest center stayed constant, low between the lamp's brass thumbs, and on days when she overspent her time there, she found herself staring into its gentian eye.

She was tired of being inside.

The walks were the only part of her life that belonged to her alone, when she wasn't obliged to chores nor mothering nor livestock. Matthew was old enough to take care of himself, and the black of night had become a time of possibility. If she didn't spend it sleeping, well sir, that was hers to say.

Or maybe it was curiosity, a dare to herself to see could she get away with it.

And what would it mean if she did?

Now she stepped from the overhang of the porch into the paleness of the yard, where the full moon shrank into the branches of the blue-gray beech, its hair tattered with last year's leaves. The outlines of its arms reached full across the chicken pen and into the yard to touch her broganned feet.

I'm here.

Behind her, the house squeezed itself shut like a fist.

Her feet found the path uphill without trying. Frost crystals grew up like mushrooms, and frozen puddles crunched beneath her feet, loud on account of the metal landscape. It was the same ice and water that had carved the mountains, the ancient seep and trickle of it under and into rock, its freezing and unfreezing, the cracking of granite, the insistent chiseling, water that found out the crevices and always moved downhill.

As soon as she cleared the level of the house she felt her lungs expand and relax and expand again. There in the blued clearing before her was the bowed outline of a fox, his back curled against the whitened earth, his nose intent and pointed at something in front of him.

I see you.

The animal arched up, hopped forward, and slapped his front paws against the frost-tight ground. Then he gave a vigorous shake of his head and was gone.

It'd been two years since she'd found the skeleton of that other fox, the bones bleached clean and so beautiful and sorrowful that she couldn't bear to leave them. But when she'd brought them home for Matthew to reassemble on the porch, Brodis had stood apart and watched the two of them puzzling out the pieces, and not more than a minute had passed when he'd asked about the stew, and was supper on its way or not. And she'd heaved herself up from the floorboards and said it was true that she'd left off starting the cornbread too long.

The fox had been the first thing she'd taken for herself. But the way Brodis looked at it made it silly. That night she'd woke wide-eyed in the dark. It'd been easy to creep from the bed and pack up the fox and take it up the mountain. It'd been instinct that had taken her to the crevice in the side of the rock, the same overhang she and her cousins had played in as children. Except that this time she was alone, and grown, and it was dark. And there was no one looking to find her. There she'd set the lantern, and there she'd unwrapped the bones and puzzled them out, the skull an empty box, the ribcage a shell, the backbones precise and stacked like threaded bobbins. In the months that followed she'd brought other things too: river stones, and snail fossils, Matthew's first teeth rattling around the bottom of a jelly jar, a Cherokee pot, programs from school plays and camp revivals, locks of hair and baby clothes, and whatever was unlikely and surprising that she could call her own. Other women she knew hosted weddings and infares or designed quilts and baskets and flowerbeds. Other women she knew planned. She didn't. In place of planning, she preserved, with mason jars and jelly jars and the battery casing that kept her daughter's baby blanket from the moths. And she held those glass moments close. That way you knew that whatever happened, you could always go back to that Christmas play program spread on your lap, that moment whenever they'd just darkened the theater and the audience had hushed of a sudden single accord, and your son stepped onto the stage. Whatever happened, you would always have that. You pulled those moments from the garbage and they were yours to own. They were proof you had lived. And they were enough, mostly.

Leastways for her. Where her son stashed his moments she hadn't figured out.

On the mountain she knew her way without trying. There in front of her was the silhouette of the grandfather oak, its giant arms cradling the sky, there the rhododendron branch blocking the path, there the granite outcroppings where she'd hid as a child, there the grayback boulder spattered with lichen and festooned with laurel. She and Matthew had found arrowheads in its overhang. Now a movement caught her eye—the fox ribboning against the base of the boulder. Then he was gone. She stopped and smelled. Underneath the clean smell of ice was something hot and alive: the musky-coffee smell of pups, curled under the boulder maybe, blind in the dark, a secret sealed from the world.

She stored this information among her private collectings. Sometimes she kept these for herself, and sometimes, like the arrowheads, she gave them to Matthew as gifts.

Around her the pillars of the tulip trees vaulted up the sky, the moon throwing their columned shadows before them. The new-built classrooms seemed close, the dining hall and the dormitories all electrified, the books issued to each student for him alone.

There are scholarships. The lady agent had said it. She had a way of opening her eyes up wide when she meant to make a point.

It was certain Brodis wouldn't like the idea coming from the outside. Not after the trains and the tobacco and the teams of city boys in shirtsleeves building national parks and kicking people out of their homes and damming up rivers. Not after the big game hunter who moved to Tennessee and imported magic Russian boar with tusks like elephants that could gore a man to death. Or the Baptist missionaries that poured in from Atlanta because the church in that city was *affiliated* and turns out there wasn't any call for a mountain church to call itself Baptist unless they were affiliated too, and a whole group of them telling Brodis and Haver Brooks they couldn't just call their church whatever they wanted unless they got it in with the national organization, and the national organization had its own preachers thank you very much, and when Haver and Brodis ignored them, here they came knocking on doors, their hands stacked with pamphlets.

And now this. It would need finagling. You had to take care for the timing. Tomorrow before bedtime might make.

On the ridge the hemlock crowded out the tulip trees. Old chestnuts twisted like the red carcasses of tortured ancient kings, their massive spiraled torsos lifeless and naked, their ghosts sifting among the castled evergreens. They had their secrets they weren't telling either, and they remembered the ones that had left, the peregrines and the otters and the wolves and the beaver. And then the woods turned laurely, and the tree line dropped away, and the top of the mountain opened like a fairytale ballroom big as the horizon.

Across the clearing a pair of slanted yellow eyes stared at her, and even in that first moment she marked that they were narrow-set, intelligent eyes, bigger than a bobcat's or a dog's. But not a bear's either. Then another pair and another. Rustling followed, but not the kind that signaled a charge. More like she'd invaded a jealous private party, and the participants now made ready to hide their illicit activities. She couldn't see them, but she sensed that they studied her. There was a snort, and a single big-chested outline commenced to show itself: a wedge-shaped head with an absurd snout, small pointed ears and great tusks that curved toward the moon, tusks that spoke of jungles and exotic forests, of Mowgli and fairy-tale dragons that burned your house to the ground in a single breath. Behind the beast's head bristled a silver-tipped collar, as if it was wearing a cape. Below that, its body and hindquarters dwindled to an absurd smallness.

It couldn't be a pig. The legs were too long, the ears too pointed, the hooves too small. And yet there wasn't any other thing in the world it could be.

It was them.

The beasts began a great shuffling, and within a second, the caped one turned and followed the crowd toward the west and the Tennessee ridge.

Irenie hadn't known pigs could move that fast.

The bald was quiet then, but changed. Rooted-up turf lined the earth around her, and the air breathed sharp. Her foot landed in something soft. She lit the lantern to find a segmented mound of scat. It was still warm. But it didn't smell like the shit of the hogs they put up before slaughter to harden the fat. It smelled like sulfur and decomposing flesh.

How had they come to be here?

The look of the yellow eyes in the night, the intention of them, meant something. They had judged her and found her meaningless, as if they'd been the ones to discover her instead of the other way round, as if whatever change they brought was already here, already bigger than her or Brodis.

She wrapped the pig dropping in a leaf and carried it that way between her thumb and finger. For now. Later she'd find a jar and store it in the cave with her other moments, the ones she'd saved for good. She didn't tell Brodis about the pigs. It was only a matter of time before he'd know. Besides, it was her story to own, not his.

## CHAPTER THREE

THAT EVENING IRENIE SCRAPED THE LEAVINGS FROM the dishes and promised herself to do it. There was no good in waiting. She didn't even have to mention Mrs. Furman.

Brodis was leaning against the back of his chair, a penny already gripped between his thumb and index finger, now tapping absently against the tabletop. For years, he'd been paying Matthew a cent for each passage, though she and he both knew it wasn't the money that mattered. It was the ceremony the boy wanted, Brodis taking the coin from the glass jar, his hand holding Matthew's while the other pressed the penny into the boy's palm, Brodis peering all solemn into his son's face.

Good job.

This evening her husband seemed relaxed. He was even humming, tapping and humming. Then out of nowhere his mind seemed to circle back to something he'd forgot to be curious about. But his question was loose. "What did you and that agent talk about yesterday?" From the sound of his voice, he hadn't even turned around.

Irenie stopped scraping plates. Then, before she had time to make a plan, the answer slid right out of her. "Matthew." As if she'd been telling fibs all her life. "We talked about Matthew."

Her son yanked his head in her direction, waiting for more.

"She said you were one of the most intelligent boys she'd ever met."

Did her son really and truly straighten or was it something she couldn't help but imagine? Either way it was a great new pleasure, this ability to bequeath to him a stranger's admiring words.

Brodis grunted. "We didn't need a outsider come from another state to tell us that."

The boy flushed from his collarbone straight up to his hairline.

Brodis didn't seem to notice. "Besides. It only struck her that way because it wasn't what she expected to find here." It was only one sentence, but somehow it made everything she'd tried to do smaller.

"You think she's judging us."

"I do. She may know how to teach reading and toothbrushing, but it don't mean she knows how to live better than other people."

And she might have said it then, fertile ground or no. But it didn't seem fair to bring it up in front of Matthew. There was never a time when he wasn't paying attention.

Brodis wasn't finished. "And she's going to want the same as ev erybody else from a distance, same as the missionaries or the census takers or the regulators or anyone else from the government. Every single one of them wants you to change in some way."

As if he already knew what Irenie was going to ask. As if he were closing the door before she even got to the threshold. But there was still time. Wait until they'd both undressed and slid under the quilts. She could bring it to him then, like a gift she hoped he would receive. And he might. He might.

Now Matthew folded his arms behind his back and lowered his head, his eyes watching his father from beneath his lashes. His hair was so fair that his brows blazed white against the pink of his skin. And already he was tall. Already the floorboards jumped when he walked across the kitchen to lift the lid of the stew pot and ask what was for dinner.

Brodis cued him. "All right."

Irenie turned back to the sink and reached for the next plate on the stack.

"In my Father's house are many mansions." Her son's voice was as slim as a girl's, flinching when it stood before Brodis. Tonight it seemed especially thin. "If it were not so, I would have told you. I go to prepare a place for you."

Her husband was still, a man who was never in a rush. He was preaching in three churches each month now, with tent revivals and camp meetings in the summer, and there were those who came specific to hear him. But a strange thing happened when a man reached the place he was trying to get. His thinking set, like a churn of milk gone to butter. It took the shape it was going to take, and there wasn't a thing in the world that was going to change it short of melting or breaking into pieces either one. It was what it was. Only a man whose believing had hardened to certainty would turn in his wife's cousin for making stump whiskey. Only a man who was sure of his place next to Jesus would have drawn a map and marked the location.

Matthew's voice floated toward the ceiling boards above his father's head. "And if I go and prepare a place for you, I will come again. And receive you unto myself."

Brodis grunted the way a man did when the evidence in front of him confirmed everything he already thought. And when she'd said it was only a bit of liquor and that it was more hobby than business, he'd told her she'd do better to stay away from the issue on account of her moral judgment being clouded anymore.

That was years ago. It was the first time she'd noticed herself receding. Even then it was more like a recognition of something that'd been happening for a long time, a kind of drawback, the way a lake sank down in a dry spell, shrinking into itself bit by bit, and so slow that you didn't notice it—until one day you looked up and there was your husband, the same beautiful and forthright man he'd always been, but so far away up the bank that his shape could be the shape of anyone. And him not noticing how wide the distance had become.

Instead she stayed alert among other women, hoping to hear that the shrinking wasn't happening to her alone. But most of them talked about other people, not themselves. If they had a name for the hurt she felt, they weren't telling it in public. Or maybe they didn't have the energy to ask questions, whenever every bit of effort went to the feeding of mouths. And maybe one day they looked up to find their lives had fled them.

Matthew's voice quavered and rushed. "I am the way, the truth, and the life." But something was different, as if some other task urged him forward, as if he'd already seen the new-built school. As if he knew too that every boy there would have read *Treasure Island* as many times as he had, that they too had stashed the book under their pillows for months before returning it late to the library. "No man cometh unto the Father but by me."

Irenie turned from the sink.

Brodis seemed to sense a difference too because he nodded and said something that sounded like, "Getting too easy for you now."

And perhaps it was that break from routine that gave their son permission to say it, the boy taking the opening that his father had given him. "Daddy?"

"What." The word that ought to have ended on an upswing finished flat as a command.

"I have a question." Her son looked bright and quick, the same way he'd looked whenever he'd discovered the arrowheads, impatient to show her the thing he'd spied half buried in the earth. And for a moment, she felt it too.

For a moment. But she'd already pre-planned the conversation about the school. She didn't want to wait another day. She gave her son a hard look, but the boy's attention was on his father.

Brodis's tone was bored, as if he'd already heard every question there was to ask. "What is it."

Her son seemed to straighten. "When he says no man cometh unto the Father except by me, that means that you got to have Jesus in order to get into Heaven, right?"

"Unh huh."

Matthew's eyes skipped from his father to the table and back. "What I don't get is the part in Luke where the lawyer—."

"What part in Luke?" Brodis's voice quickened. Irenie couldn't see his face, but she could guess the walled expression there.

"Chapter ten, I think twenty-five or twenty-six, where the lawyer asks him how to get eternal life." Matthew's eyes swept the table now, and Irenie willed him to change his mind. The desks in the new school would be golden with linseed oil varnish, their surfaces uncarved and unblotted. Whatever the question was, it wasn't worth it.

But Matthew didn't check himself, and when he opened his mouth to speak again, she felt alarm, but also pride. "And Jesus answers that the way, the way to get to Heaven is to love God and your neighbor. He doesn't talk about how you have to, you have to go through Him to get there."

Brodis didn't move.

Uncertainty flickered into Matthew's eyes. "Through Jesus, I mean. How come He didn't tell the lawyer that he had to go through Him?"

A moment passed and Irenie realized she was holding her breath. The kettle on the stove hissed, and she poured the water too fast into the dishpan. The steam rose up in a cloud.

Matthew pressed ahead. "Or likewise whenever Mark says, you know, that he, that he who believes in God and is baptized shall be, shall be saved, and he that believes not..."

The sound of Brodis's sigh cut him off, then the thud of his boots hitting the floor, the creak of the chair as he came to his feet. Brodis reached into his pocket and withdrew an object Irenie couldn't see but guessed to be his pocketknife. When he held it out to his son, she saw that she was right. He opened it with his thumb and turned it handle up. "Take this."

Matthew took the knife, hope and confusion raising up his features.

"And go on out there to the edge of the yard and cut you a switch."

For the first time, the boy looked at Irenie. Her response came unbidden before she thought to make it, an immediate and tiny shake of the head. *Don't say no.*

Matthew's features collapsed, and he didn't look her way again.

But Brodis must have noticed, because he stood and looked around. Irenie turned back to the sink so that her husband wouldn't spy the anger in her face. Nobody said anything.

Then the door opened, and the cold blasted into the room.

"Come back here," Brodis barked.

The door widened and Matthew's face appeared. "Sir?"

"Get your coat."

Matthew did. The latch clicked shut behind him. Only then did Irenie seize the minutes. "Brodis..."

His stare made her tiny, his answer immediate and swift. "Foolishness is bound up in the heart of a child, Irenie."

There'd been a time she'd tried to tell him about the receding, and the way the lake shrank into itself. But he'd looked at her so squarely that she'd stopped. "You're keeping the bad," he'd said. "You're nursing it." And it might be he was right. Maybe she was saving the wrong things, like the memory of the little girl buried in the tiny pine box. Either way, she couldn't see confiding in him.

But now she made herself say it. "For asking a *question?*"

His eyes pinioned her to the drain board. "His heart ain't right, Irenie."

Irenie stared back. It wasn't true. There wasn't a thing in the world wrong with the heart of Matthew Lambey. But before she could say so, the door opened, and her son entered, a look of woe on his thin features. He laid the switch on the table.

Brodis sat down. In place of looking at the switch, he spread his knees and put his hands on them, bending his face toward the floor as if lost in contemplation. After a moment, he looked at his son. "Look here, Matthew. You've been grubbing potatoes ever since you was this big." He held his hand parallel to the floor. "You know that whenever the furrow is cracked good and deep it's something there. So you dig. And you might get a fair size potato or might be a medium one or sometimes you get only a small one. But you dug it up and now you got it. Can't put it back in the ground. Can't say, 'I don't like this potato because it's too skinny or too round or too ugly and got too many black spots.' No. You take that potato because that's where your sustenance comes from. That's your food. You take it and you're thankful because without it you'd die. Only a stupid man throws the ugly potatoes away."

Matthew was still standing, eyes sliding toward the wood stove. "Yesser."

"And only a prideful man refuses the potato with the blackened eye."

"Yesser."

"But that's what you're doing with God."

"Yesser..." Matthew didn't sound convinced. His eyes skipped from the stove to Brodis to Irenie and back again to this father. "Sir?"

Brodis cut him off in a dead level voice. "No. You wanna take the parts of the gospel that are fat and smooth-skinned and pleasant and keep them for yourself. And you wanna throw the disagreeable parts away."

"I don't wanna throw them away. I just thought they were supposed to—"

"And you're finding disagreeables because you're looking for them. You're grubbing in that potato patch expecting to find black ones. Looking to find something ugly. God's word is like anything else. If you expect to find something you don't like, that's exactly the thing you'll find." Brodis scrutinized his son's face.

"Yesser."

"There is a way that seemeth right unto a man, but the ends thereof are the ways of death."

"Yesser." Matthew's eyes flickered from his father's face to the floor and back again.

"The Kingdom is set up in the heart of the people."

"Yesser."

"Not in their heads."

"Yesser." Eyes on the floor.

"I know that there are some like your Papaw believe you have to bend your faith in order to get along in the real world. He calls it compromise. But that don't hold water with the Lord." Brodis paused and reached for the switch. Then he waited for his son to look up. "You see this?"

"Yesser."

Brodis flexed the switch. "Bends, don't it?" He pulled the ends closer to one another.

Matthew looked worried.

"Bends pretty far, don't it?"

"Yesser."

"The more you bend it, the easier it is to bend a bit more." The stick was almost doubled now. Brodis touched the two ends. "What was once straight now goes both ways. A direct contradiction."

"Yesser."

Brodis squeezed the two ends together. The stick made a cracking sound and began to splinter. "See that?"

"Yesser."

And still Brodis flexed. "Just about broke in two but it still bends." More cracking. The green fibers resisted until they couldn't. The pith split. A thread of bark held the two pieces together. "Come here."

"Yesser." Matthew stared at the splintered stick, an expression of alarm on his face.

Brodis proffered the fractured limb and peered into his son's face. "There's all manner of people out there who'll tell you how to believe." He almost sounded as if he was pleading. "But you gotta understand. The thing you're compromising is your own soul."

The features in Matthew's face had widened and spread. "Yesser."

"Comes a point when a man can't tell the difference between a bending and a breaking."

"Yesser."

"And you know and I know that the scriptures come from the Almighty. If He was to be mistook about Heaven, then He could be mistook on anything. And then why would we believe His gospel at all?" Brodis gripped Matthew by the shoulders. "If a man can't hold true to his believing on the small stuff, how can he hold true on the stuff that really matters?" There was an undercurrent in his voice that Irenie couldn't name, something that in another man she might have identified as fear.

Matthew didn't answer.

"If you can't accept the details on faith, what's gonna happen whenever the Lord asks you to do something difficult? You're gonna start asking Him about the particulars?"

Matthew said nothing. These were not questions for answering.

But Brodis seemed to want to hear the answers anyway. He set them out without apology. "You'll never become a firm kind of man, that's what. You'll be one of those fellows who can never decide. And no one will ever trust you to make a hard choice."

Irenie turned back to the sink, slid the scraped dishes into the dishpan without making a sound, poured the bucket of cold well water into the dishpan. The steam dissipated instantly.

The linseed-oiled desks seemed a long way away.

*CHAPTER FOUR*

THE FIRST TIME BRODIS CLUCKED THE MULE, IT
snorted white breath into the morning and took a reluctant step, just
enough to tighten the traces between it and the plow. On the second cluck, it commenced to tramp forward grudge-slow. One step,
then two. The spewed frost crunched under hoof, the plowshare bit
into the earth and inched forward, and the soil parted, turned, rose
up and rolled over the dust of white in a soft brown ridge. Brodis
swung his crippled foot around and up the new-turned furrow, and
then again, and again, and it wasn't long before sweat damped his
collar and slid down his spine. He leaned on the hickory grips, and
the dense grain of the wood told him of the rip of the share, and the
upboil of earth, and how the soil resisted a man's effort until it had
no choice but to yield with a sigh of mud and mold and rot.

He'd been at it since '24, the year he'd quit the logging drives.
He'd had a permanent limp after the accident but also a bank account at Asheville Savings and the profits of fourteen years on the
river, to say nothing of his new soul. He'd considered himself a
rich man, so rich that he'd ignored the feeling that Irenic Raines

wasn't meant to be his. They'd married and set to farming, and he'd learned to plow a straight furrow in the static earth and to clear a stump with a plug of dynamite, to salt his stock in the summer and gather them in winter. There was a repetition to it that river work didn't have. But it was heavy. A piece of land could never do anything but wait dumb and fallow for the imprint of a man. But his wife moved along it like she'd been born for it, like she had a direction, away and away, and a fellow had to be nimble to stay with the flow of her. And in the evening, she was there, coming out of the spring house or bending to feed the fire in the cook stove, a damp patch of sweat at the small of her back and the cotton fabric clinging to her body, in the house that he'd reframed, on the land they'd sown, and he felt he'd discovered an unclaimed world and made it his own.

But now she'd become a fittified spring that dried up and disappeared on you. Two days ago she'd chose to sit among the sinners. Just sitting with her mama for a change was what she'd said at supper, and he'd let it lay. Let it lay because he was full of good will and Mrs. Dawson's fried chicken and Mrs. McCurdy's pie and a dozen congratulations.

Just then the grips of the plow kicked him in the ribs. The blade had caught. The mule stopped, stiff-necked and bored. Brodis pulled up and heard the gray slide of steel on granite. He reached under the share to prise up the stone. The soil was moist and cold, the rock immovable and fair-size enough to need the shovel. He lifted out the blade and stepped past the steaming mule toward the barn. Inside, among the post-hole diggers and fence-stretchers and wire cutters, hung a long handled shovel. The implement was as tall as his chest, and he swung it forward like a limb and planted it in the ground with each step, noting the halo of light at the top of the mountain that meant the rising of the sun. Step, plant. Step, plant.

His eye might have seen it first, but his mind didn't record it right off. Then it did: an oval print amongst the spears of frost.

He stopped. For a moment he considered going back to the plow, returning to this spot only after the sun had burned the mark away. Ten minutes was all it would take. By then warmth would settle across the field, and the white-cauled earth would brown again. Just walk away.

But no. That wasn't the promise he'd made to himself whenever he'd taken up with the Lord. He'd sworn to confront the truth head-on. Brodis shifted his weight and swung the bad foot around.

The print was smaller than his fist, too small to be from his own boot. Next to it the heel mark was shallow, hurried. Inside the oval was the word *Sear*, backwards, no final *s*.

For some reason he thought of the lady agent. No, not for some reason. For a very particular reason. For the reason that here came a woman driving an automobile up somewhere she didn't belong and not two days later he, Brodis, was finding the footprint of a woman where it didn't belong. The closest homeplace was Irenie's parents, two miles distant by the drovers' road.

The only woman for miles was his wife. And right now Irenie was washing up the dishes. She hadn't been out but to go to the privy. There was no way she'd trudged up to this field in the pre-dawn. No way at all. There was no reason on earth for her to be up here.

But why had she sat with the sinners on Sunday? And how was it he'd let it go as if it was nothing?

Somehow he'd let his guard drop. He'd done the same thing he'd done every spring before. He'd gotten comfortable and then he'd gotten old.

But Irenie wasn't old. She didn't have a gray hair on her head. And what was it had passed between her and the Furman woman? And why was the Department of Agriculture sending the wives of its agents up into mountain churches?

Every day the outside world crowded further into the valley, and with it forces that were bound and determined to steal away the God-fearing thoughts of right and true people. Every day the devil rallied his legions.

He swung the shovel up above his head until his whole body extended toward the coming day, and the effort of it increased and livened him. Then he bent at the waist and whipped the blade straight down. It slammed into the furrow, incising straight and deep. He left it upright and shuddering.


In a previous life, he'd wanted for resolve. That was a different time, before trains and trucks had replaced the last of the river men. Back then the drives always ended in music and cards and drinking and sworping, and even though he'd sometimes been in outfits that set up revivals and prayer meetings, none of the preaching had ever hit, even after he'd been in the business for ten years. True, the knowledge rode heavy on his mind, always there, along with the sense that there was a thing that needed doing, that was indeed imperative above all else, but that somehow was too distant to actually do. For more than a decade he hadn't been adequate to it. But after the accident, his life had changed. Lyman and Colter were the ones to find him, naked and facedown at the edge of the water. Brodis remembered being rolled over, the weight of his body a thousand pounds against the dirt of the shredded bank. The only thing he recalled with certainty was a moment when the earth became so white that he was looking at a burned spectacle of the log boom and the river crew, like a photographic plate, the human figures glowing against the blackened sky. Colter loomed over him with fear-struck eyes, and Brodis knew the man then for what he'd always been. He was an angel. Even Lyman, who he hated, looked like an angel. The next seconds changed his life. The concern in the two men's faces became a visible light, then a bodily sensation, then a fire that burned from the inside.

His body too. His torso that had a moment before been heavy against the earth now weighed nothing at all. He leapt to his feet, vaguely marking that his foot wasn't behaving the way it ought. But there wasn't any pain. He shouted with glee, and it was as if all the energy and love he'd ever produced in a quarter century of living were erupting without his consent. Later, the drivers told the story of how he'd run up the bank naked as a baby, waving his arms and shouting to beat the band, embracing anyone who'd let him. No limp.

But Brodis didn't remember. What he did recall was the sense that a lifetime of pride and hiding-away had vanished, that his heart had broke open, making room at last for that which was bigger than itself. It had taken a near-killing, but something inside him that had been chilled for ten years in the mountain headwaters had at last warmed. He felt love for people he'd once looked down upon and pity for those he'd despised, and the hard pride that he'd lived with since before he could remember thawed to make room for the word of God. He never drank nor played cards nor entered a rough house again. The old habits dropped away, and he lived a clean life. That part was easy.

What bothered him were the questions. That first day, before he'd even got back to camp, Satan had wormed into his head, whining to Brodis that the white light and the angels couldn't have happened, that it wasn't realistic. Use common bay-horse sense, boy. You were just scared and excited from the accident, that's all.

And right then he'd faltered. Already. Not a day had passed, and the devil had succeeded in hardening his heart. Brodis hadn't rested a moment since. Satan always came in the same sly guise, with lawyerly arguments and rabbit-trap questions, all of which began with the same word: How? How could such-and-such happen, and how did a certain feature make sense, and how come this other had happened? But he'd learned to recognize them for what they were: distraction, illusion, cowardice.

All he had to do was wait until she took the brogans off. Just wait.

In the meantime, fence-mending. It took him hauling the cut planks from the barn and her testing the old ones for rot. Brodis crowbarred the broken palings and kicked them free, surveying the rotten wood for salvage nails. Inside, crabgrass and horsemint feathered across the furrows. Among the weeds, blades of corn furled up stingy as fists.

"Set up that one there," he told her.

Irenie held the plank against its neighbor and pressed it flat against the weather-gray cross support, leaning in with her full weight.

Brodis drove two nails straight in. The top of the plank snugged up against the crossbeam, but the bottom sprang towards them.

Irenie bent and rested her weight on one knee. The sole of her right boot pointed straight out. Now. Brodis stepped back to get a look, but it wasn't far enough. He stepped again. Irenie glanced over her shoulder at him. "Not straight?" Just then a rabbit bounced out of the furrows, and the dog Stomper erupted into flopping and yelping chase. During all the noise Brodis backed up again.

*Ears.* The word on the bottom of her right boot was *ears.* But he hadn't seen the left one.

Irenie spoke over her shoulder. "Matthew did a good job training them dogs."

Brodis replied without thinking. "Yep."

His wife's too-soon answer: "You were better to tell him that."

"Did." But when he tried to lay his mind on the where and when of the conversation, he couldn't get but so much. He tapped the bottom of the plank. "How about getting lower."

Now his wife rested on both knees. Both soles pointed at the sky. And there, right there it was: the oval, the backwards *Sear,* the last *s* worn away.

Brodis drew up beside her. It made no sense. Her features hadn't changed: same transparent lashes, same strands of hair loosened from the long braid, same patchwork of freckles easing up the tender skin in front of her ear. And before his brain thought to think on it, his hand went there, his thumb brushing the unblemished skin. Surprise turned her toward him and raised up her features. He didn't plan to trace the line of her jaw with his index finger, where the skin stretched smooth across the bone. He didn't plan to ask her the question right then and there. "Tell me what it is that's got into you."

Her eyes scouted his, then found a resting place somewhere beyond his shoulder. "Nothing particular." She pursed the side of her mouth in a way that made it clear there was indeed something very particular. Then she seemed to wrest her attention back towards him as if returning to the world of the here and now from another one peopled by spirits and demons. The transition seemed to pain her. And right then, in place of answering his question she took it into her head to bring up the woman from the extension office again, if you could believe it. "Mrs. Furman says there's a school in Asheville for very intelligent children. She says the classes are specialized."

Anger welled inside him. How had they got back to talk of the government? He closed his eyes and breathed slow. It was possible that all boots wore out the same way. It was possible that every woman in the county had a pair with the same pattern on the sole.

Possible. Not likely. His wife was talking now about a new school. Brodis muttered a response and put two nails between his lips. He listened without listening.

The print had been from a small boot. A small foot.

Irenie talked on. Her voice was careful, planned out, and it was this tone more than anything that finally caught his attention. "She says they have *schol*arships for mountain children. Some of the smartest ones go for free." She splayed both hands upon the springy wood without looking at him. The veins in her arms testified to the effort involved.

Only then did it occur to Brodis that they were having a conversation about his son's future. And that his wife was trying to sway him to do something she didn't think he'd want to do. "How come?" he asked.

"How come what?"

He pinched one of the nails from his mouth and positioned it against the wood. Because of the other one between his lips, his words had to squeeze out sideways, making his voice come terse and low. "How come they to go for free?"

Her voice was casual, falsified. "To get them to stay in school. To get them to a place where they can find jobs as teachers or businessmen or leaders. Someplace where they can use all the parts of their minds."

"But not working on a farm."

"No," she allowed. "Not working on a farm." Her hands splayed above and below the nail head, long-fingered and slender and traced with a blue-veined filigree that put him in mind of the tiny skeletons the plow turned up in the tousled earth, the white-laced surprise of them.

Brodis grunted. "Charity then." He bent forward and positioned the nail between her hands. He brought his hammer arm up. Then he stopped. "Nope. Move your hand."

Her voice came on faster than he expected. "Not charity. Scholarship." She widened her grip on the chestnut paling, pushing the board flush against the cross timber, close in against the others, the heels of her hands white with the pressure. "So that mountain children can grow up to be leaders in their community."

It was the first time he knew for certain that the argument wasn't just a matter between him and her. "Whose words are them?"

Now his wife looked at him full on. Her eyes were belligerent, lawless. "Mine. Those are my words."

Brodis swung the hammer, and the steel arced strong and true and slammed into the head of the nail, and the chestnut paling cinched up against the cross support. He drew the implement toward his temple for the second stroke. Her words, his left hind foot. They had the mark of the government all over them. Again the hammer dropped. Again it hit the nail true, now flush. He stood, slid the tools into his pocket. "It's a pretty come-off when a town like Eakin can't school its own children. There ain't anything wrong with that boy that he needs a special education from the government." Behind Irenie, the straw man turned with a whine, his torso impaled upon an axle, each arm a raised wind-paddle. A crow coughed, and the others flurried into the air. It was the only scarecrow in the county that moved. Matthew had conjured and built the thing himself.

Irenie was still talking. "He hates school. He wants to quit."

Brodis was quiet. His wife didn't account for the fact that teasing could be good for a boy. Plenty of men had come up stronger for it. "It's more work here than can be done alone."

The scarecrow turned back toward them, and the crows scattered like chaff. Brodis picked up the palings and moved down the fence.

Irenie followed. "We could get a hired man."

Brodis fitted the crowbar behind another damaged paling and put his weight into it. The board moaned toward him. There was a time when his mind had a picture of his son grown strong. But now he couldn't feature Matthew leaning into a plow or reaching into a bellowing cow to pull out a breached calf. Farm life seemed to splinter his son: the horse that died in labor or the quick wring of chicken necks, the hot slaughter of lamb and pig. Yet here his wife had given Brodis the picture of his son grown powerful again, this time as a leader, and after so many fallow months, the image burned with surprising strength. For the first time Brodis envisioned his son at sitting-down work, at a desk in the courthouse or the school, his hair the same ruffled color as the light on the river in the late afternoon.

His wife kept talking. "A hired man would make. Clabe Ingles would do it."

Brodis grunted. It wasn't the point. "It's fine and good to send a boy for a education, but first you've got to ask yourself is it the education he needs." He turned the rotted board over and examined it for nails.

His wife studied his face. Behind her, the crows hung in the whispering air, waiting. "Mrs. Furman said some of the students go into business. A good portion of them go to college."

College? Last night his son had asked why Jesus gave three different people three different requirements for getting into Heaven. "I'm not talking about that sort of education. That's books and reading and arithmetic. He's already good at that."

Irenie seemed to consider this. She didn't argue. "You mean church."

He turned to her. "You know and I know there's no point studying history and algebra when there's no ensuring he's going to church."

His wife stood the next replacement board before her like a shield. Her voice came out small, but it didn't back away, as if some part of her that had been submerged all these years were finally breaking the surface. "They have churches in Asheville." Maybe the same part that sneaked out of the house and left footprints in the frost.

"Yep."

"He can go to church without us."

"Could. If you're willing to bet his soul on it. I'm not. You saw him last night." He reached for a new board. "Eternity is a long time, Irenie. A good portion longer than a little unpleasantness here in this world."

Incredibly, she kept at it, her voice wobbling but still coming at him. "Mrs. Furman said that the—"

"The boy has enough."

"But he's—"

"Enough."

Finally, silence. Or almost. His wife turned her face toward the fence and made something that sounded like a squeak.

He shoved the new board into place. The hammer arced through the air and met the nail head with a loud crack. A man hadn't ought to suffer a woman to teach, nor to take authority over him, but to be in silence.

## CHAPTER FIVE

(

HER HUSBAND HAD SAID NO. NO WAS NO. IRENIE leaned her weight into the handles of the wheelbarrow and pushed. The single rubber tire cut a deep groove in the mudded earth.

Worse, she hadn't stood against him. Not that time and not the time he'd told Matthew he'd never be a firm kind of man. Her son had given her the one look that night, the one beseechment. He must have seen it in her face, that she'd not help, because he didn't turn around a second time. And he hadn't in the days since.

She hadn't figured herself for the kind of person who knew a thing to be wrong and sat by and watched it anyway. She wondered was this the person she'd compromised herself to be or had she always been this way and just never stepped outside herself enough to see it.

The lady agent was younger than her, but she'd dressed up in a fitted suit and driven by herself up to a town full of strangers for something she knew to be right. That fact unsettled Irenie, not because of what it told about Mrs. Furman but because of what it told about Irenie Lambey.

She set the wheelbarrow by the tobacco frames. Ahead, a jay watched, tapped the ground twice with his beak, then jerked his head up to check her, just like the chickens did. *Peck, peck, look. Peck, peck, look.* Very same waltz. Blue liverleaf flowers starred the grass. The service trees bloomed on the mountains like puffs of fog, and the branches of the redbud curved and wingled against the naked forest. A wren's voice see-sawed the morning air. *Teakettle, teakettle, teakettle.* It had been two weeks since she'd seen the pigs. Since then, they hadn't intruded into the talk in town or in church or in school. But Irenie knew what she knew. They would be back.

She sank the shovel into the manure in the wheelbarrow and emptied two loads onto each plot. Then she began working it in with a spading fork, using the tines to break up the red earth and separate the greenish-black clumps of compost until each frame was a rich uniform brown. She tamped the tops with the back of the shovel. After the last one she set the blade in the ground and leaned on it. Each box looked the same, dark brown, fecund with nutrients, a promise. She spread the page of newsprint, nicked a corner of the waxed seed pouch, and tilted the contents onto the center of the paper. The seeds were small as sugar grains, and she pressed her index finger into the pile, rubbing her thumb against the pad so that the grains fell from her skin and scattered somewhere on the brown compost, though she couldn't see where. Even after three years of tobacco, it seemed impossible that something so invisible would grow.

The preacher birds had returned and taunted without stop. *Over here, whaddya want? Tell him no. Whaddya want?* It was the sound of planting. Another winter had passed. Another summer would begin. *Pretty bird, tell him no. Whaddya want?* The pallid seasons of the future stretched before her.

Then the songs went quiet, and a jay took flight. A shadow glided across the tobacco frames, the spread of its wings a broken jag against the pine-walled boxes. The outline flapped hard against the sun and cut across the sky. Vultures didn't do that way. They spiraled in the updrafts, lazy and effortless and beautiful. But this bird was working hard. It flexed its wings once, then twice, and drew itself up on a wooden fence post twenty feet away. A red-tail. Irenie held her breath. The bird was sizeable, the band around her waist and the feathers on her back the color of brick. She folded her wings, hunched her withers and puffed her chest with quick energy, her white breast pulsing and her yellow eye unafraid because she knew that she'd soared across a valley on her own and that she could take to the air again at any moment. Somewhere she had a nest, with young ones, and somewhere responsibilities to them, but that didn't keep her from sitting here now, magestical in her survey of everything that belonged in her territory. Then, as if deciding that Irenie was no threat, she shifted her interest to the yard below, now empty of chickens—then to the unsprung wolf trap balanced atop the nearby gatepost, the jaws dropped below the level of the wood. Irenie held her breath. There were two traps, each with a wide mouth on a spring lever. If a wolf was to step on the plate, the spring would trigger, clamping the device around the animal's leg. No amount of thrashing or biting would loosen it. But the rusty traps had hung in the back of the tool shed as long as Irenie could remember, ever since her uncle had owned the land. She'd never known anyone to use them. There were no more wolves.

But last winter Brodis had discovered the contraptions and set to scraping and steel-wooling and oiling. Underneath the orange, the metal was gun-barrel gray.

And when he'd told her they were for the hawks, she'd shaken her head and said it was too much trap for a bird. It was the only thing she could think to say that sounded reasonable, though she knew when she said it that it was no reason at all.

"No such thing as too much trap," he'd countered. "Dead is dead."

"But you can't kill all of them. There'll be another one to move in when that one's gone."

He jerked his head up. "Which is it. It's either too much trap or it's no sense doing, but it ain't both."

But it was both, and it was neither. He watched her, the steel wool immobile between his fingers. "I don't know," was all she could muster.

He didn't move. "Then say what you mean, and quit coming up with side reasons."

"All I know is we never did it that way before." He had resumed his steel-wooling. "And I'm asking. Maybe you could leave off on my account."

He stopped scrubbing and gave her a look. "I might do. If you were rational about it."

She had nothing to say back.

Now she propelled herself toward the hawk and waved her arms. "Shaaa!" Without seeming to see her, the bird stepped off the fence, flapped two deep-sweeping flaps, and sailed capably across the yard, gliding to a stop in the walnut tree, then retreating further to the new-leafing oak.

It hadn't always been so. He hadn't always been so. In 1924, there'd been lots of boys. She could have had a choose and pick. Whether it was for her red hair or for her father's 500 acres of rolling orchard either one, she never knew. Neither had a thing in the world to do with who she was. The land had come to her great-grandfather from the Cherokee at three dollars an acre, and the hair was a matter of luck. Yet they were hers and she'd gotten used to them. As a girl, she'd played in the orchards and grown accustomed to the idea that one of the Eakin boys would someday persuade her to leave them. But they bored her, those boys: Frank Pruitt who was so sure of himself because he could wrestle the others to the ground, Hallie Crisp who never missed an opportunity to talk about his father's store, Freddy Smith who met the whole wide world with his chin tucked in like a bull set to charge. There wasn't a thing in the world wrong with them, any of them, but all of them tried so hard to please it reminded her of her least siblings. When she imagined a life with one of them, she knew what it would hold, each day visible years before it happened, like standing in the middle of a row of apple trees. If you were to line it up just so, a corridor opened before you, and you could see further and clearer than you ever thought possible, the length of the view making each tree uniform, each gnarled trunk distilled into sameness, no twists, no surprises, no new. The view unsettled her.

That spring the train engines had huffed down the single gauge railroad track, hauling oak and hickory and birch down the mountain, the timber stacked high on the flatbeds. But even then some of the wood came down the river in flotillas, and with it the log drivers, stepping from trunk to trunk as quick as squirrels, each with his pick pole held loose across his thighs, now and then tipping the end against another log to push it away or steady his balance. The men were grizzly with whiskers, and they shouted halloo whenever they passed schoolchildren gathered on the banks, the expectations of the crowd hanging in the air with the smell of the men's cigarettes and sweat. Some of the drivers whooped at the girls or touched their hats or hollered pretty things. Brodis never did. He was furthest away, his gaze on the river ahead, as if he was bored by the schoolchildren or spied something downstream the others had no knowing of. In those days he had a mad look about him: red woolen shirt flapping loose from his wide shoulders, hair hatless and wild and swept from his forehead like the crest of an owl. Most of the drivers were small agile men, but Brodis was tall and long. He had family near her sister's husband, and once long ago, had grown up there. Now he lived in the camps.

When the river rose, Irenie and her classmates carried their lunch pails past the bridge to the falls and watched the logs roll over the ledge and skirt the rocks below. The boys argued back and forth about how much skill was required to drive the timber. Frank said the cleated boots made walking on the wet wood as easy as walking on a floor. Bill Hicks said Frank didn't know his ass from his elbow. But both watched the logs float through the rips and the slides, the noise of the whitewater silencing their shouts and distancing them from the men on the river. Each driver approached the pitch the only man alive, bent at the knee and feet spread, pick pole ready, eyes reading the water in front of him until the log nosed itself over the edge down and down into the boil, burying itself and the fellow's knees, and then bobbed up at the edge of the foam pile. And when a driver lost his balance in the chute, he pushed against the rocks or another stick to steady himself, sometimes hopping to another piece of timber altogether. Irenie never saw one fall. But some of them did. Some of them died. But when she spied them at the bottom of the drop, they were forever laughing, Brodis too, as if he made a pleasure of stepping so close to the afterlife and then away again, as if he knew something of his own mortality that she didn't know. And maybe that was the attraction. Or maybe it was the thousand other things the drivers knew that she'd only heard rumor of: the logging camps in the wilderness, the waterfalls on the peaks, the fires in the Smoky Mountains whenever the trees exploded before your eyes, and the whole enduring journey to the mill towns, to Waynesville, to Canton, to Ohio.

She found herself jealous of girls she'd never met who lived in places she'd never seen. It might be he had someone in one of those towns. Might be she was prettier and smarter than Irenie. Did she eat the same vegetables? Did she study the same books in school?

Then one day he was back. He appeared without warning at a Friday night singing, all stringed sinews and knobby knuckles, too tall for his surroundings even when planted in a straw-backed chair. With anguish on his brow and a wooden cane resting across his thighs, he seemed unplaced, like a carnival bear on a chain. There was no one sat next to him. His eyes vigiled the other cake eaters, skipping from one to the next in vexation. They lit on her but didn't show a flicker of interest, and she wondered if he was the only unattached fellow in the county who didn't have a thought for her father's acreage.

The next time she saw him was the July camp meeting. It was the same four day affair she'd attended every summer of her life. She'd just spread the canvas tent on the grass and was pushing the wooden stakes through the brass grommets. A pair of hobnail boots stepped in front of her, above them a splitting maul balanced across a shoulder.

"Want help with those stakes, Irenie Raines?" His eyes were the color of the furthest ridges, his forehead a cliff, the bones below it jagging forward like bedrock. From the side of his nose to the corner of his lip, ravines. She wasn't prepared for that kind of hand-some, and it caught at her throat so hard she had to look back to the wooden stake. When she stood up, her legs trembled, but there wasn't a thing in the world for it but to peer into the blue wilderness of his eyes and ask, "How come you to know who I am?"

He watched her evenly but didn't smile. "Everybody knows who you are."

She thought on that fact. It wasn't flattery, the way he put it. It was more like stating the colors of the sky or some other thing they could both lay their eyes on and agree to be true. And once it was pointed out that way, you couldn't put on that you didn't know. So she just nodded. "Aren't you gonna ask if I know who you are?"

He smiled now, and his smile was white and wide-spaced, and the way it landed square on her warmed her so much it alarmed her to consider her old life without it. "Do you?"

There wasn't any other thing to say. "Yes."

"And how come you to know that?" He swung the maul from his shoulder and set it at his feet as easy as another fellow would a hoe.

"I know all kinds of things." She willed her voice calm. "You work on the river. You come from over near Mars Hill. You don't like to wear a hat."

And then Brodis Lambey tipped back his head and laughed into the sky so that the muscles in his neck shimmered with sweat, and she thought then that she could say anything she wanted to him so long as it was true.

In 1924 she'd had the steam to make decisions that stuck. She'd taken it for granted it would always be so. That she would always be so.

A year later they'd both changed. God had taken their first child but saved her. Then He'd called Brodis to preach. It had seemed unlikely at first. Here was a man who didn't spend words cheaply and didn't savor the company of other farmers, much less a crowd. Here was a fellow who was too young or too handsome or too keen on himself, one. It was years before the town of Eakin gathered to his preachings, and longer still for other places. And nowadays there were those that followed him from street to church to revival, and it seemed the most natural thing in the world. But there was a difference between a man who was working to get someplace and a man who was working to maintain the place he was in. Something about the maintaining had made him hard when there wasn't call to be so, each year more beetle-browed than the last.

And in the meantime Irenie did her best to think on crops. Better to schedule the future by slicing it up. A growing season was a period of time you could get hold of. Potatoes needed setting in the ground by the end of the March moon in order for them to make by September; corn during the growing of the April moon when the whippoorwill sang; squash, cucumbers and mush melon in the May bloom days of Virgo. If you paid attention, you had it in your head the way things would turn out. There would be lettuce and rhubarb in May, radishes, peas, and onions in June, beets, cucumbers and melons in July, corn, tomatoes, peppers, and lima beans in August, cabbage, apples and walnuts in September, and then, in October enough squash, collards, sweet potatoes, and rutabaga to last the winter. Each was the next thing, that was all.

But in the past three years, it had been all about tobacco. And Irenie had learned to focus on the moments she already owned— the choices preserved in glass or stowed in the recesses of a mountain. Now she stretched the cotton sacking taut across the tobacco frames and secured it with paper-string, imagining the green shoots unfurling, the roots stretching timid and dark into the black compost. In two weeks or more, the seedlings might show themselves as clusters of green dots against the soil, and she might have to thin them with a pair of tweezers. Might. Or a hard frost would fur up the sacking and she would open the boxes one morning to find the shoots exhausted and limp.

*Pretty bird, pretty bird.*

Then a sound like a dead pop, metallic and flat, and she couldn't lay her mind on the meaning of it. Until she did. After a long second, the hawk's scream split the air, followed by a spastic beating of wind that flapped and flapped and stretched time out of its track until it flagged and halted as if to take a long breath and gather up the will to move forward. Irenie ran toward the scream, but the bird was a blur of wings and white air, and then all at once somehow in flight, a miracle, pounding her great way into the sky, trailing drops of blood across the dust of the yard all the way to the white oak, her outrage careening up the valley in a high wail. Then she did a queer thing. She bumped into the mid branches of the tree, pitched forward and toppled into the new leaves, took flight again and was gone.

Leaves trembled. Chickens shrieked.

The trap was still balanced on the fence post, the metal jaws clenching two yellow and brown twigs—except they weren't twigs. They were jointed and hinged and precise. The long toes reached out across the metal plate like fingers grasping for a purchase. For some reason they didn't bleed.

She scanned the sky but didn't see the hawk. Somewhere up there she was beating and beating the skinny air, through the up-drafts or down the valley. Or maybe towards another tree, one with a nest lodged high in its crown where new hatchlings flopped and squealed. Maybe she watched their open mouths, circling.

Without stopping to study on it, Irenie found the second trap and pressed the point of the spade into the center plate and knew in that instant that that was how you found your earlier self, with-out planning whatever steps you'd thought needed planning. In the same instant the steel jaws leapt together and grabbed the blade with a violence that jolted straight up her arm and into her spine. When she pulled the shovel away, the steel teeth rasped down the blade and etched four jagged parallel lines into the metal.

And Brodis safe in his place in the world, certain-sure that he could teach the birds a thing or two if given half the chance. He'd leave for the river soon, a week, maybe two. The creeks were ris-ing. Even with his limp, they'd hire him to work the stationary flumes and the sorting booms whenever the waters peaked. And when he returned, his spirit would be as ragged as his feet.

## CHAPTER SIX

(

A BOY GOT THE SAME KIND OF EDUCATION NO MATTER how it fit him. That's the way the county did it anymore. But it had been different once. When he was Matthew's age, there'd been a war on in Europe, and boys coming up a few years before him were boarding trains, and all the young men he'd ever looked to had disappeared in one season. All of a sudden Brodis was one of the oldest children in school, and the teacher set him to tutoring younger pupils, never mind the fact that his father was paying two dollars a month to send him there. But there were trains leaving town three times a day, and after they'd hauled out all the young men of the county, they went to hauling out the minerals and timber. And on the way back, they brought flossy fabrics and refrigerators and cast iron sinks. The world busted in, and the general stores filled with flower-painted china and factory dungarees and orange-colored crackers wrapped in cellophane. And Brodis, at the age of fourteen, went to logging.

He'd stepped off the company train into the Quinlan-Monroe camp with a letter in his pocket and a bedroll slung over his shoulder.

Straight off, he'd stopped and stared. In front of him opened acres and acres. The only thing between him and the ridgeline were stumps, slash, deadfall, broken limbs, and treetop lops. Above his head, a machine with an enormous arm swung an oak trunk like a toothpick while a fellow in a wide-brimmed hat shouted curses and instructions, a gaggle of others craning their necks to follow the timber's progress. It was a masterstroke of human industry.

But he'd been skinny then, and the foreman told him he was too green to work with the skidders or the road crew. Same as he would have told Matthew. Both father and son skinny and smart. The difference was that Brodis didn't have what it took to conjure up a new straw man or train a pack of hound dogs to do half his chores for him.

The foreman had just grunted, assessing him with his eyes the way a fellow did a horse or a woman. "Dewey's the only one wants youngsters. It don't work out with him, then you come back next year and we'll find you a place with the teamsters. Right now you're too small." Brodis stood as tall as he was able. "Can you swim?"

Swim? Brodis nodded on habit, though he wasn't sure it was the right answer.

The next morning Dewey Lister searched him out as he was sitting down to table in the camboose. "You. New boy."

Brodis turned.

The man was no bigger than him, spare and tight as a knuckle-joint, the growth on his cheeks flecked with gray. His shiny pate overcame the features of his knobby face. "Are you Brodis or are you Fletcher?"

"Brodis, sir."

Dewey stepped back and gave him the same look the foreman had. "Can you swim?"

"Yessir."

Dewey Lister made a dismissive sound in his throat. He was missing one of his front teeth. "Where's Fletcher?" He reached into the front pocket of his shirt and withdrew a piece of oilcloth, unfolding it to reveal skinny papers and a tiny canvas pouch.

"I don't know him, sir."

"Well, find him. Then both of y'all meet me here in twenty minutes." He tapped a pile of tobacco onto a paper and glanced quick at Brodis's feet. "And get you some wool socks."

Brodis watched him roll his cigarette. "Yes sir." He wondered if he'd been dismissed.

Then Dewey Lister plugged the cigarette between his lips and jogged away in a queer forward-pitched gait, and Brodis saw that the man's boots were thick-heeled and raised from the floor with something that looked like barbed wire. Gouges in the pine planking marked his leaving.

Fletcher turned out to be a diluted-looking boy with red-rimmed eyes and a light brown fur growing on his chin. Brodis never did ask how old he was. He didn't want to give him the pleasure of saying, "I'm sixteen, how old are *you?*"

Dewey Lister was the walking boss, and he didn't talk to either of them.

They started with two other crewmen at the bottom of Allen's Creek. The bed was wide but the water a trickle. In place of picking their way up the bank, Dewey and the other crewmen clomped right up the middle, their cutter boots making spiked prints in the sand that caved in upon themselves the moment they lifted their feet. Brodis wondered how come they chose to be wet, but he didn't ask. Instead he followed in the pooling impressions, and the cold of the water soaked straightways through to his feet. Behind him, Fletcher leapt from rock to rock and soon lagged behind.

The creek was like none he'd seen. What you marked most was the litter: the broken wood and twisted deadfall. Draped in the crooks and branches were clumps of wet-looking leaves, as if the stream had flashed high and then receded quick. The foliage on both sides had been swept clear and the laurel and rhododendron cut back twenty feet. The naked earth baked in the sun, and sumac and weeds and poison vine had already set root. A few young hemlock and walnut still stood, but most had been toppled in the mud. When they came across a beech tree fallen into the channel, Dewey and the other regulars took their packs off, and Brodis did too.

Then Fletcher. Brodis couldn't see what had caused the tree to fall, only that it seemed to have tired of holding onto the loosened earth. Now the roots tipped upward all naked and spindly against the sky, like a girl who'd tumbled from a porch and flipped her skirt to expose everything. It was exciting and disturbing at the same time. Dewey laid a band saw across the trunk of the tree and motioned for Brodis to take a position on the other side. "Here." Brodis scrambled across the log. Then Dewey handed Fletcher the ax. "Get as many of them top branches as you can." For a half an hour they chopped and sawed at the beech, the smell of wintergreen whanging the air.

In the afternoon the creek rounded a sharp bend. A manmade wall of cedar and chestnut planking stood just inside the curve, upright in the dry bed as if by some accident of planning. Brodis couldn't feature its purpose, even as the crew set to replacing one of its planks. His eye searched upstream and tried to imagine the creek with rushing water. Without the wall, the current would be forced to the outside of the bend, wouldn't it? After a while that water would make an eddy, a dead place where you could wade or fish. So the wall—the *boom*—was supposed to get rid of the eddy and move the sticks along. Because... Brodis saw it then: dozens of logs piled up in the bend that in turn would trap more logs. A jam.

Fletcher was running his hand along the side of the boom. It was two board-widths taller at the deepest part of the curve than it was at either end. "What's the wall for?"

Jackass. "*Boom*," Brodis corrected. "A boom is something that makes the timber to go where you want."

Fletcher ignored him and directed his question toward Dewey Lister, who was driving a nail into one of the bottom planks. "Sure, but what's it *for*?"

Dewey Lister never looked up. He seemed not to hear.

Brodis answered louder than he needed. "Keeps the logs from piling up."

And that was the difference right there. Matthew wouldn't have done that way. Matthew would have figured it out just as quick if not quicker, but he would have covered for Fletcher. He would have made sure the other boy understood everything he did without rubbing his nose in it. He would have brought the other boy with him.


"Watch," Dewey told the two boys one afternoon after they'd worked their way up Allen's Creek to the splash dam. The new-formed lake was a depthless gray, the statues of broken stumps protruding through its mist, a field of timber floating motionless on its surface. Bracket booms like stationary rafts channeled floating sticks toward the sluiceway. "Don't do nothing else either." Dewey commenced unbuttoning his woolen shirt, and for a moment Brodis thought he was going to take a swim. Then he stepped onto a slanted rock and, without checking his pace, onto a peel-slick log. The wood dipped with his weight, but then he was in the middle, and then he'd already stepped onto a she-balsam. Now he footed from timber to timber, as nimble as strolling through a meadow in the morning gloom.

Fletcher shouted, "Hoo boy!"

Brodis said nothing. It couldn't be as easy as it looked. Dewey's feet never slipped, and his arms never waved at his sides for balance. Brodis tried to unriddle the secret. Both of Dewey's knees were bent, always bent, that was one thing. Nor did he seem to reach out with the top of his body, not once, not ever. His chest was perched right there, just atop his hips. Dewey made a little leap from the log to the shore. It was the first time he'd extended any effort. The log bobbed once in the water and was still. "Who's first?"

But Fletcher was already unbuttoning his jacket. He started from the same granite outcropping Dewey had, took a confident step onto a cucumber tree, and as he transferred his weight, the wood moved away, leaving him to straddle the open air between the moving timber and the rock. Then his rear foot crashed into the water and he fell.

Brodis laughed. But not too hard.

"Hold on," said Fletcher. "Let me try again."

But Brodis had already planted his hindquarters on the get-in rock, both feet firm on wood. He drew the log as close as possible and eased his body over it. The timber didn't give much when he transferred his weight. And then he was standing, edgy and parlous, yes, but standing. He took a step, and the wood spun under his feet. He looked to correct with the other foot, but it was too late. He leapt free of the log, and found himself standing in three feet of water. He chanced a glance at Dewey, but the man was already buttoning his shirt and didn't look up. "Don't drown yourselves."

Brodis and Fletcher looked at each other. How?

Dewey picked up his rucksack. "And don't get anywhere near the blessed dam." He turned away and began walking up the bank, throwing out one more tidbit as he went. "Suck you under so fast you'll be dead before you know what happened."

When the rains began, the camp by the railroad tracks came to a halt, and the crews came to restless rest, gathering in the steel cars that served as camboose and bunkhouse, playing cards and rosining string-fiddles and arm-wrestling and rumpusing. But Brodis left his dry clothes under his cot and hiked back up to the headwaters in his woolen underwear. Wet was wet, and the air was cold enough that when he waded into the lake, the water felt warm. He pulled a hemlock trunk to him, still barked, and it was the surest purchase yet, scratchy under his palms. He hoisted himself to a sitting straddle, then to a shaky stance, feet wide, knees bent, not too stiff, and not too still.

All day the rain drubbed the surface of the lake, and all day he practiced. The idea wasn't to stay put. It was to ready yourself to move. Now, whenever there was no one to show off for, he learned the textures of the trees, the wide easy plates of pine bark, the stringy slip of cedar skin, the striped grip of poplar and hemlock, and the sure fissured purchase of the bee tree. And yes, he'd done it because it was a job, but that wasn't all. There was something in him did it for the same reason Matthew kept a notebook for pencilling the names of the plants and the salamanders. Just that Brodis didn't believe in list-making. His notebook was in his head.

At night he listened to the patter of water on steel. On the fourth day, Dewey Lister appeared in the door flap with a fourteen-foot spruce pole. Attached to the end was a pipe like a large screw, at one side a hook.

Something in Brodis's chest leapt up.

Dewey also brought a bundle wrapped in a rubber blanket, which he set upon the cot. "You're gonna need these."

Brodis unwrapped the rubber blanket. Inside was a pair of woolen pants, the same kind Dewey had worn to clear the creek bed. Everything except the pick pole was brand new. "Hot dang!" was all he could manage.

"Don't get lumpy on me. They've took it out of your account already."

"I'm gonna drive on the creek?"

"Hell, no. You're gonna walk the creek, same as everybody else. This watershed don't open till we get down to the Pigeon."

"I'm gonna drive there?"

"Hell, no. But as soon as you got the money you get yourself some Chippewa boots from supply, and tell Callahan you want the ones with the caulks. And get you some Neatsfoot oil too. Case you want them waterproof."

They always did the splash dams in the mornings, whenever a ghosty mist hung above the water and the thousands of sticks of timber clogged the surface of the lake and stretched way to hell and gone into the steaming gorge. For some reason you always positioned yourself next to a group of other men, either standing at the edge of the lake or hunkering on an outcrop high above the splash dam. Two massive crossbars held a gate of wooden scantlings in place, while freshets of water shot straight out through the gaps in the timber and onto the rocks below. There, at the bottom of the creek bed, the powder man waded in, his woolen pants turning dark to the knees, a solitary figure in the shrouded air. The powder man did everything slow: attach the rust colored bundle to the crossbar with a piece of wire; then pack something—later Brodis knew it to be fabric and cardboard and waterproofing sulfur—around it. Then the powder man stopped and dragged a match across a rock. He lit the fuse.

The spark mesmerized you whenever you saw it up close, a spit-ting, fittified flame that wasn't a flame at all but a live energy that danced and popped up the string. The powder man had already begun his climb out of the gorge by then, and you were torn, want-ing to watch the dam for the moment of explosion, but unable to keep your eyes off the fellow hand-over-handing on the rocks below. Whenever he gained the bank, he put his fingers in his ears, and you did too.

The explosion slammed straight up the gorge and into your spine. The gate's crossbar buckled inward, and then the whole dam flung itself out and out and up and up in a torrent of splinters and water that leapt and crashed straight into the air before it stopped and hung, suspended, and then slowly, as if against its will, spumed toward the creek below. Logs rammed and bellowed their way through the sluice and then kept coming, thousands of them, some of them snapping like twigs whenever they hit the creek bed and some of them disappearing like pine needles in the great white foam. The torrent bucked and writhed with the force of a raging animal escaped from its captors so that you had to remind yourself you were standing far above it. After several seconds you realized you were covered in a thin mist, but by then you didn't care. By then you were overtaken by the sheer audacity of men moving massive objects from one location to another without the aid of train nor skidder nor mule. You got it. Allen's Creek had gathered itself from the ridgelines and the springs which in turn became rivulets cutting their way through gullies, one parallel to the next. It was a built-in transport system that Quinlan-Monroe was only improving. Nature was the one had invented it. She used gravity.

And at some point in there you realized you were grinning like a fool.


The water didn't slow until it reached the bottom of the watershed. The drivers on Brodis's team kept the timber moving. The pick pole was for balance first, for moving timber second. You didn't plant, or you'd push yourself right off. Instead you used it like a finger to touch on a piece of wood or a rock. The banks and the bottom rushed past, and you couldn't hear a thing but the sound of the river. Below, the water shifted and eased, flexed and thinned, contracted itself into a knot or disappeared into spray, moving like the muscled back of some giant serpentine beast. Brodis got to the place where he could separate himself into two parts, the lower half that attended to the contractions and flexions of the water below him, that steered and moved the vehicle he stood upon, and the upper half that stayed loose, controlled his weight, centered always over the place he wanted to be.

But it was the not-talking he liked most, same as it would one day be for his own son. You looked up the steep bank where a creek-branch tumbled from a mountain crevice, the water sheeting and leaping from the rock above, and the cascade so white and alive that you wanted to lay claim upon it, on this place and this moment, whenever this certain kind of freedom poured from the rocks above. Each day more wood floated into the river, bee tree and poplar and cucumber magnolia that the loggers called wahoo, from streams worked by other companies in other watersheds. They passed roads and houses, and the people waved or touched their hats or shouted hello. And then Quinlantown floated into view, the wooden structures yellow with newness, the mud streets crowded with young men. A giant flume dumped wood into a manmade pond at the side of the river. Beyond that was a steam-powered loader lifting still more timber from rail cars.

"They don't use the river?" Brodis was dismayed that he'd asked the question before trying to sort it out for himself.

For once Dewey didn't seem to notice. "It don't work for every kind of tree. Some kinds waterlog. Your oak, for a sample, it likes to sink after a few days."

"Same with your hickory?"

"Ash. Cherry. And anyway, it's all about the trains. Everybody loves them some trains." He sounded bitter. "In five minutes they'll be using Shay engines to pull up their pants in the morning." It was years before Brodis would understand that kind of unhappiness.

The mill paid the crew in cash. There were forty-seven dollar bills for thirty-two days' work. For years after, Brodis had as much money as he wanted, and he lived in the camps where his needs were few. It was the kind of work that brought you to the top of your senses and then beyond, to a place that soaked you up into a bigger sort of grandeur. And a curious thing happened when the timber dropped over the edge of a pitch. If a fellow did nothing, the front end of the log dove straight down into the pile of foam, then straight out from under him, launching his body forward into the water like a slingshot. But if you shimmied straight back to the upstream end of the log fast enough that the front of the stick still looked over the ledge, then for a moment the back-weighted log sailed in the air, and you had to step back to center right quick to level the log as it hit the water flat and gentle with a pillowed *boof.* If you did it right, you had the timber and the air and the river by the balls. And, for a second, you flew.

But the industry had changed. Now they used the trains for everything, floaters and nonfloaters the same. Besides, a man couldn't crouch without bending at the ankle. He couldn't nimble from one stick of timber to the next, nor flex his feet against the plated bark, nor feel the live roll of water beneath him and pit his wit and his timing against the heave and boil of it. A man with a lame foot needed staying on land.

)

## CHAPTER SEVEN

BRODIS WOKE TO FIND THAT HIS WIFE WASN'T IN the bed beside him. His body felt her absence before his hand touched the empty mattress.

It was dead night. The fire in the stove had died down but not out. He listened for her step in the next room, but the silence there felt permanent. A minute passed, then two. Nothing. He threw back the covers. His feet hit the floorboards, and the cold grabbed him. Below the window, a square of light stretched across the floor, and that was where his legs took him. On the other side of the glass, the moon set down atop the privy. The building leaned over the creek branch. The door didn't open.

*Sear.*

In the kitchen, familiar objects surfaced up from the shadows: pickling barrel, strings of hanging vegetables. The door of Matthew's room had gapped, and Brodis treaded past, on habit lifting his lame foot against the possibility of splinters.

The lantern still hung by the door, but her brogans and coat were gone. The fingernail moon offered little light. He opened a lamp and struck a sulfur match. When the wick had finished guttering and flaring, he turned it down until it wasn't but a yellow wing. Then he set to dressing.

Up the hill, the new-plowed field was barren, the furrows shadowed like the surface of some false and stagnant river. The barn was quiet but live, in the shifting breathing manner of creatures in repose. He slid open the stock door: manger and barley box, barrels of meal and sweetfeed, the bin of corn tops. He held the lantern aloft and peered into the mule box. Still there. Next door, the saddle horse whickered too. Wherever she was, she'd gone on foot.

*Sear.*

He peered up the stairs to the loft. "Irenie?" Nothing but the shadows of harness and plow lines, hames and singletrees, coils of rope.

Below the barn crouched the house, the mountains vague and hulking on three sides. He listened without knowing what for. It was as quiet as the first day of the world. She was out there somewhere, her slight form wrapped in the too-large coat, maybe nothing but a nightdress underneath. It was a good coat, an Army coat hand-me-downed from her brother. It came fair to her knees, but its blackness wouldn't show against the night, wherever she was.

Or she wasn't alone. Maybe there was somebody to walk beside her, someone lowhatted and slouch-shouldered, one hand buried deep in a pocket, the other at her elbow, touching.

The devil didn't ever quit looking for a way in anymore. First the lady agent and the school, now this.

He stepped onto the porch, lifting his bad foot so as to stifle the sound of the drag. When he turned to ease the door shut, the latch slid down without a hitch, though he couldn't remember the last time he'd oiled it.

The rack over the door held two guns. He touched the octagonal barrel of the Winchester, then lifted it from its supports and pushed the clip up from the bottom of the stock until it clicked. He checked the safety before he pulled back the bolt and then eased it forward, watching the bullet slide into the chamber, the sound of metal against metal cold and definite as daylight. With his thumb, he touched the safety again and stepped onto the porch. The yard looked the same, but darkened, stilled, waiting. He cradled the rifle across his torso, the heft of it solid against his chest. Nothing.

He checked the privy, though he knew before he opened the door that it would be empty. The same went for the smokehouse and the springhouse. He even leaned over and peered under the porch. The dogs raised their heads and regarded him with curiosity. Scram thumped his tail upon the hard-packed earth.

Brodis returned to the house and fitted the gun back into the rack, then surveyed the kitchen again, as if he'd somehow missed seeing her there the first time. He put his hand on the door of Matthew's bedroom and commenced to shut it. But the quilt on the boy's bed had fallen to the floor, and Brodis paused. Light silvered the bony jut of his son's shoulder and the white of his hair. Brodis bent to pick up the blanket, and Matthew turned over onto his back. His father paused, the blanket suspended between his hands. At any second, his son would open his eyes—and ask, and ask. The questions that began simple would lengthen and grow, tendriling through the room and curling around the doorframe until the livid roots insinuated through the floorboards and wrapped the poplar footers and colonized the hearts of father and son.

Brodis let go the quilt. It crumpled to the floor.

Back in his own bedroom, the stove had burned down. He reached for the tongs, selected a medium-sized piece of coal from the scuttle, opened the iron door, and tossed it in. It flared yellow, and he tossed in another. Then he shut the door and stared through the isinglass screen at the flickering light. On instinct he reached for the Bible at the bedside table, the leather softened by years and hands. But he was too distracted to open it. In place of reading it, he held it solid and bulky against his ribs.

The shotgun and the deer rifle were not the answer. They were the solution a man reached for on instinct because he couldn't shed the habit of guarding his flock and doing for himself. But whatever there was that bore the name of evil required more than buckshot. Whatever there was that bore the name of evil required prayer.

He lowered himself to his knees, and the front of his dungarees pulled tight against his thighs. He closed his eyes and waited for the almond-eyed gaze to level down at him. The sense of woe he'd been fending off all evening filled him now and quickened his prayer. Look over her. Keep the animals and the vagrants away, for sure she is a woman little in stature, with small hands and slender neck not built to fight nor outrun. And sure she is loyal and biddable, a modest woman who guards her body and her thoughts, who cares more for the grace of her eternal soul than any other thing.

The eyes of Jesus were moist, long-lashed, appraising.

Amen.

She wouldn't have walked to her parents' home at this hour. She wouldn't have walked anywhere unless it was in her mind to deceive him.

He undressed and laid himself on the mattress. In the corner of the window the pale eye of Venus gauged him. For a long time he stared back. He didn't hear the lift of the front latch, but he heard it click shut. The sudden thought that welled in his soul was *thank you, thank you*, and in his mind, he leapt up to certify she was sound and whole and safe.

In his mind.

But the shy scrape of metal didn't fit, nor the nothingness of her step, nor the way the door shut without the dryness of metal on wood. The worser part of his soul reared up and doubted. The moon had long ago sunk behind the ridge, and the house was black. But then she was there in the doorway, the nightgown floating around her shins, brogans in hand, a bare-felt pressure of air. And there was habit in the way she set the boots on the floor without a sound, the practiced way she eased into the bed without disturbing the blankets.

Her breath was light, ragged, the flush of the outdoors rising from her skin. There was something else too, a breathless heat that rose from deep inside her. A woman didn't get that heat from going to the privy.

For a long time he lay awake and listened to his wife breathe, preparing himself. He was a patient fellow. He could hold off, could follow, could sly-foot. He stared at the ceiling. The devil had his own job to do, sure. And he did it with whatever tools he could find, be it USDA agents, or wandering missionaries, or teams of New York City boys wearing CCC shirts. Satan wasn't blind. He was more clear-eyed than any man alive. And he had his ways of drawing souls to his side. Brodis remembered too well the whine and pull of his temptation.

But that didn't damp the anger that had kindled up in his heart.

The next morning Irenie filled the shovel at the hearth and shook the live embers into the stove's firebox. A handful of tinder, and the ash flamed yellow. A few pieces of loose coal, and the fire leapt up hungry, a pall of gritty black smoke leaking out. She clicked the steel door shut. Maybe it was a matter of practice. You practiced letting another person make decisions for you long enough and pretty soon that was what you got used to doing.

From outside came the double thud of Matthew's buckets on the porch planks, then the slap and rub of hands, the pivot of a heel as he turned for the chicken house. She opened the door to fetch the buckets, and the yard was gray with the edge of daylight, the smell of apple and cherry blowing white and pink. She poured the water into a cauldron, lifted the iron lid from the stove's central eye, and set the pot on the coming flames. She scooped a cup of water into a ceramic bowl and dusted in the flour, kneading the lumps through her fingers, then rolling the dough in a sheet. The oven popped and cracked with heat.

But what if you practiced something else? Something like springing the trap yourself?

Her husband stamped in the doorway, set the milk bucket by the stove for scalding, and pulled off his coat. By the time Matthew came from the chicken house, Brodis was at the window with a safety razor, peering into a glass propped on the sill and tilting his head to study his chin. Here was a man whose jaw was as cleanly drawn as it had been at twenty-five, whose teeth hadn't yellowed, whose face and body had become tighter, not looser, whose shoulders carried no sag—and who paid these things no mind at all. Irenie had never known him to look into a glass except for shaving, and even then, even now, he didn't seem to see himself. Yet he ended each day asking his God to keep him away from pride and vanity.

Maybe people set up a picture for themselves when they were young of the kind of person they wanted to be. But a lot of them seemed to forget what it looked like as they got older. Either that or they couldn't help but to slip further away from it when life got difficult. But Brodis never did. He never stopped bringing his real self closer to his picture self.

They ought to all of them do that. Practice.

Matthew hadn't brought any eggs. He stood just inside the door, as if he couldn't figure what to do next. "Daddy? I... I expect you better come look at this."

"Look at what." Brodis drew the razor from his ear along the line of his chin without a flicker.

"I reckon we've had a fox to break into the chicken house."

Irenie slid the spatula under the biscuits and onto a plate without a sound.

Brodis's hand had stopped, the blade poised in mid-air, a single path cleared through the soap on his face. He turned his head toward his son. "Tell me."

"They're all ruffled up, sir. And there's a hole, underneath, dug out last night." Matthew's hands fluttered in the air like birds. "I'm pretty sure it wasn't there yesterday, sir."

How long ago was it Irenie'd seen the gray ribbon slip under the boulder? How long since she'd smelled the vernal musk of pups? It couldn't be much more than two weeks.

"How many did he get."

"One, I reckon. I'm sure. Just one."

Brodis turned back to his glass. He dipped the razor into the shaving mug. "As long as it wasn't the new Barred Rock."

Matthew jammed his hands into his pockets and looked at the back of his father's knees. Irenie knew what her son meant to say and held her breath. "Sir. It was."

"Was what."

"The Barred Rock, sir."

Brodis sighed and bent his head over the basin. He scooped the warmed water over the lower half of his face. "Well, you know what to do."

"Yesser." The boy started to go but turned back again. "Daddy?"

"What."

Brodis's face was buried in a towel.

"Bettern I bring Scram or Fortune?"

Brodis hung the towel on a nail over the sink and sighed again. "You make the decision, Matthew, and take it for your own. Then stick with it."

"Yesser." Matthew seemed to drive his fists deeper into his pockets. His shoulders hunched around his neck. Again he turned to leave.

"And Matthew."

"Yesser?" The nerves were naked in the boy's voice.

"Go to the barn, at the steps to the loft, where the hames and traces are hanging. Then look up. It's a old oak bucket hanging there. Climb up and get that bucket and bring me out one stick of dynamite."

"Yesser."

"One stick."

"Yesser." The boy's voice carried the recognition that he'd been trusted with something new and adult.

"And a spade."

"Yesser."

By the time Matthew came back, Brodis was drinking a cup of coffee and staring out the kitchen window. The boy stepped onto the porch and rubbed his hands and small-talked the dogs. The redbone looked up at him and thumped her tail on the wide boards. Scram, the blue-speckled, loitered at the edge of the clearing and followed the proceedings with mournful eyes. Matthew threw the door open and handed Brodis a spade and a rust-colored stick in waxed paper. Brodis stood in the doorway and turned the nitroglycerin from side to side in his hand, then smelled it for what seemed to Irenie an overlong time before fitting it into his pocket. He started to slide the spade in as well, but stopped. He examined it, frowning at the four teeth marks etched into the length of the blade. He turned the implement back and forth.

Irenie could feel the pounding of her own blood, the hot flush rising from her neck. Practice, yes. But not now.

Matthew watched his father, seeming to sense that the delay had nothing to do with him. "Daddy?"

Brodis jerked his head up.

The boy watched his father nervously. "What's the matter?"

Brodis glanced at the spade one more time. "Pffff." Then he slid it into his coat pocket. "Some beast that yet walks the earth."

Whatever that meant. It didn't matter. So long as he didn't ask about the traps.

He reached for the rifle above the door then bent to leash the dog. "Fortune. Yep." He handed the leash to his son. "Good choice."

"Yesser." The boy's voice carried expectation. The dog hung close at his thigh. Then the three of them, father and son and dog, stepped from the porch into the lightening yard, past the yellow-leggy forsythia and the blue-flagged iris and the dewed webs cupped in the crooks of the shrubs. Fortune cast back and forth, her eyes and nose eager on the ground. Then she opened up a track and they set out, Brodis and Matthew walking side by side but not together, their attentions separate and focused on the thing that lay ahead of them.


Father and son followed the hound. Brodis felt extra alert, never mind that he'd spent half the night vigilant as a cat while his wife pulled the air in and out and in. The sleepless hours had sharpened his senses instead of dulling them, had charged him with electric strength. And now, this very morning, his son and his wife would see what real school looked like.

Ahead the dog took to barking. And there she was, aside a granite boulder on the creek branch, pacing and tracking, her nose glued to the ground. Sure enough, the base of the rock had a hole the size of a mush melon, the soil worn smooth by the passing of furred feet. Fortune thrust her nose in as far as it would go, haunches high in the air. Matthew called her off.

The feel of the dynamite was the same as ever in his hand, velvet wax. There'd been a time when he'd always had a half dozen pieces in his rucksack. He liked the burnt-sweet smell of it, the condensed potency. It was a thing that turned you around, that inverted the place you were in and made it something else. On the river it was magic. He handed the stick to his son.

The boy held the thing as if bewildered.

"Feel it," Brodis said.

Matthew shifted it to his other hand. "It's heavier than I would have reckoned," he allowed.

Brodis read his son's mind. Like a stick of unseasoned kindling. "It ain't that."

"Ain't what?"

"Ain't what you think. Ain't a stick of firewood."

"Yesser." The boy studied the cylinder in his hand. His presence on the earth was slight. He called you sir but avoided your gaze, like a salamander that melted into a hole when you approached.

"Smell it."

Matthew lifted the rust-colored rod to his nose.

"Smell that."

His son's features seemed to wrinkle against his will. "Yesser."

"Remember that. That's the nitroglycerin. That's what makes it explode. You smell that ever, and you're on the lookout. It's a thing more powerful than a rifle or a shotgun, either one. You can't control it the same."

"Yesser." Matthew tried to hand the dynamite back to Brodis, but Brodis made out not to notice. Instead he bent to leash the dog.

"You ain't never gonna use it when you're in a hurry nor when you're not sure it'll turn out the way you want. Hear? Never."

Matthew's eyes were huge. "Yesser."

"Always picture out the chain of events that could happen. Right now is how you want it. That boulder ain't going nowhere because it's too big. But a rock could shatter if you was to have enough dynamite. And if it does, it's moving fast as a bullet. Fast as a hundred bullets. Remember that."

Matthew dragged his eyes away from the boulder in consternation. "Yesser."

"The first thing is to crimp the cap." Brodis showed his son the charge of powder in the closed end of the blasting cap. He slid the fuse into the open end, then, with a pair of pliers, bent the metal tight around it. "See that. That ain't the main thing. That's just gun powder, and it makes a small explosion, like firing off a shotgun."

The boy was attending to each word. "Yesser."

"It'll blow that cap."

"Yesser." Matthew nodded, more confident now.

"The shock from that little explosion is what makes the dynamite go, not the fire."

"Yesser." His son was as sharp as they came.

Brodis handed the leash to the boy, opened a knife and began cutting a hole in the side of the dynamite. Matthew looked concerned. "It ain't the cutting either." He pushed the blasting cap into the cut. "Except if it's a fluid coming out. Except if it's weepy. Then it's old and you don't do one thing with it except burn it. All of it." Brodis remembered the way the river boss had tiptoed around a can of ruined explosives, eventually burning the whole stash because it had become too unstable to keep.

"How come?"

"Because. It won't take a blasting cap to make it go. Could be just a little shock, like dropping it. Maybe even a clap of thunder." Brodis wrapped the cap with black friction tape. He fingered the fuse. "See that?"

Matthew bent in. "Yesser."

"That's sixty seconds."

Brodis watched his son measure the length with his eyes. "Yesser."

"You ready?"

The boy nodded and stepped back. "Yesser."

"Put it in the hole."

"Me?"

"But not too far. That fuse has to be above the ground."

The boy held the dynamite between the tips of his fingers as if it were a dead animal. He squatted and placed the end in the hole, but just barely. It stuck out from the earth like a birthday candle.

Brodis leaned in. "Further than that. Get it all the way in there."

Matthew pushed the cylinder further into the hole.

"Now pack some of that dirt in there around it. Good and tight." Matthew spaded up the moist soil and pressed it into the opening.

"See, because the force of the explosion's gonna go where it's easiest. Not into the rock or the ground, but where the open space is."

Matthew packed more dirt.

"Now. Come over here." He led his son around the other side of the boulder and into the branch bed. He tied the leash around a sapling. "This is the place we're gonna go to. But not run. We're not gonna run. We're gonna walk here steady. Got it?"

Matthew exhaled a deep breath. "Yesser."

"Let's go light it then." Matthew's footsteps dragged in the leaves behind him. The boy seemed always to want to follow behind instead of beside. At the mouth of the den Brodis handed the matches to his son.

Matthew opened the box and paused. He looked at his father. "Just light it like a candle?"

"As soon as it takes, we're gonna walk, not run, into the branch."

Matthew's hand shook, and so did the match. But the fuse caught right off, and the sizzle whispered up loud and insistent, a sound that comforted and excited Brodis at the same time.

Matthew was in the branch before he was, his breath so fast and ragged that it obscured the buzz of the fuse. The color had drained from the boy's cheeks, and in the slant morning sun he seemed almost to be made of silver light, or white, a thread of energy so slender that it alarmed him that he, Brodis, had been given him to shepherd in the world.

Then something punched Brodis in the chest, and the ground jumped. A flume of dirt blew out the backside of the rock. Matthew made an "eee" sound. After the silence had returned, Brodis held his son's shoulder for a long moment. He listened. A turkey chobbalobbed in alarm.

He let go the boy's shoulder. "Go."

Matthew clambered up the bank and around the boulder. Dust hung in the air. By the time Brodis rounded the rock, his son had come to a stop.

The base of the cliff was a churn of dirt and bone and meat and fur. "We got him," Brodis announced. A paw, then another, blue organs, the lower half of a tiny jaw.

Kits.

There was the sound of something falling. The box of matches. Matthew had dropped it next to a tangle of viscera. The boy stared at the head of a kit, its eyes open, its mouth ajar, the teeth elfin and white as filament.

"Pick it up," Brodis said. He meant the matches.

But his son turned to him a face of such aggrievement that he couldn't figure what to say. Then the boy bent over and threw up. Brodis set his hand on the back of his son's hunched shoulder, and there wasn't but fabric and bone underneath. His body contracted again, and it was the loudest sound in the world, far more violent than any word he could have said against his father. It wasn't a willful decision to spurn him, but in place of that a bodily rejection that disobeyed the desire of the mind and refused that which the constitution could not abide because it poisoned and sickened. Matthew stopped vomiting, but he didn't look up. His hands rested atop his bent knees. He didn't straighten.

How many foxes had Brodis hunted and killed in his life? How many deer? And yet these particular foxes had shown themselves indecent—and in the process shown him indecent too. He didn't understand how it could be, but it was. There was nothing for him to say. He'd brought his son to this place knowing that the boy was different from him. Whatever words he might think up shrank in front of that fact. So he did the only other thing he knew. He reached for the other words, the best words, the ones that could pacify when nothing else did because they came from a place that was larger than him and anyone else. "God made man after his like-ness." Six words landing solid and true. "And let him have domin-ion over the fish of the sea, and the fowl of the air." The cadence regular and predictable.

Matthew swiped the back of his hand across his nose and looked away in shame.

"And over the cattle, and over all the earth, and over every creeping thing that creepeth upon the earth."

Matthew's hands jerked and twitched like disobedient puppets. He whispered. "Yesser."

"Replenish the earth, God said, and subdue it."

"Yesser." Still whispering. His son did not look at him.

"And have dominion over the fish of the sea, and over the fowl of the air, and over every living thing that moveth upon the earth. To you it shall be for meat."

Matthew untied Fortune's leash. He held her head between his hands, brought his face to hers. The dog reached out a pink tongue and licked him.

Brodis gathered the spade and the matches and nodded at the boy to turn for home.

In front of the coal pile, Irenie straightened up, scoop in one hand and scuttle in the other, her eyes landing first on Matthew and then on him and then on her son, never coming back to him at all. Bro-dis put the judgment out there before anyone else could. "Matthew did a good job."

His son's eyes were still wide, his shoulders tensed. His eyes didn't settle but skittered instead to some point in the air beyond his mother.

Still Irenie didn't look at Brodis, and he had to remind himself that this woman was not without her own secret, her own sin. And there had been a point to all of this, remember that. "We won't have foxes in the henhouse tonight." But Matthew's nervousness shone like a bright slick thing, something wet and appalling to the touch. "We got them."

"I know." It wasn't until much later that Brodis heard the devil in that sentence. *I know.* Her exact words.

Irenie hauled the coal scuttle to the front of the house and with two hands tussled it up to the porch. Still she didn't look at Brodis, this woman who had somehow learned to rise from the bed beside him and float up out of the house like a specter. He didn't understand it. Nor did he understand this sense that he, Brodis, had chose evil over good, that he was the one God was calling upon to make amends. Hadn't he guarded his flock? Hadn't he protected the lamb and vanquished the wolf? He could not, did not, see a path more righteous.

And yet here the Spirit was sending him this whelming guilt. It couldn't be for nothing.

He stepped past her and into the house. He fitted the .22 into its brackets. Then he stood in the doorway with his arms folded and waited for his wife. What he was meant to say to her he didn't know, only that it somehow featured his own mischoosings.

Irenie stopped, set the scuttle on the floorboards.

"About the school," he said.

Now she looked up quick, and he was the one couldn't meet her eye. In place of looking at her, he watched his son. Across the yard, the boy knelt beside Fortune, his hand massaging the dog's ear and holding her head to his.

"I changed my mind." Then, before she could open up a conversation, he brushed past her.

Let it not be said that he, Brodis Lambey, hadn't done his best to rectify his sins. His wife would do better to worry about her own. He stepped from the porch and into the yard.

# PART TWO

*End of May*

## CHAPTER EIGHT

BRODIS KNEW HE OUGHT TO WAKE IF HE WANTED TO discover his wife's secret. But instead he was dreaming. He knew it was a dream and knew too the way the dream would end no matter how he fought it. But he fought it anyway in the hope that this time the story might veer away from itself and become something new.

He'd been holding his breath for days. And there was something terrible wrong with his foot. Around him the river swirled silt-brown with the secret he would discover there.

It was the same as ever. He'd been shunting timber near the island, just past the tin boom that steered it to the narrows. But something downstream had snagged, and wood had begun to pile against the obstruction. He was only knee deep when he stepped his foot out and felt the boot pause, then, before he could pull it back, slip and wedge. A crevice. He'd begun to work the foot out the same way it went in when something large struck him from behind and pitched him face down into the current. The pain in his foot was instant, but he couldn't bring his face out of the channel to breathe, and the boot could no longer be made to move. Within seconds, he'd braced his free foot against a rock and pushed until all the air in his body had bubbled out his nose and something in the bones of his trapped foot gave way. This time the pain was distant and unconnected. But he was free. He had two gulps of air before the current swept him into the jam and he went under.

Rocks slid past. On instinct, he lifted his legs from the river bottom. Above, a crack of light penetrated the canopy of timber, and ahead, another. He swam toward the second. There the light and air burst upon him like a miracle, and he lunged for the trunk ahead of him and hoped it was small enough to get his arms around. His hands found each other and registered the flaked bark that was sycamore even as his legs and torso were swept downstream before him. He pulled down on the timber and was able to keep his head above water, his lungs loosing and gulping the sweet May air. Above stretched a patch of cloudless sky, on either side the crush and groan of hundreds of harvested trees, woeful, ancient, deafening. If he was to stay put, he would be crushed like a grain of corn in a grist mill.

The only way was to swim through the narrows toward the jam and hope to hell it was enough room to pass under. The current would be on his side unless he snagged himself on a branch. A shirt or a cuff would catch, and there he'd be, streaming like an underwater flag until the waters dropped. He had to drop his clothes. He pushed the toe of one foot into the heel of the other, and his five dollar Chippewa boots fell away. He unhooked his overalls and the current pulled them clean off too, shooting a blade of pain through his right foot. Then he took a great breath, loosed the tree, and dropped into the opaque brown, willing his strange new limb to frog kick, sweeping his arms past his torso in mighty arcs, pulling at the water as if he were hoisting himself up a rope in some barren landscape in which he was the sole occupant. He exhaled selfishly, parsimoniously, until there were no more bubbles to breathe out. The surface of the water was black, shot through with cracks of white. His lungs retracted into themselves. Brown inanimate shapes loomed into his field of vision and brushed against him. His lungs shrank to pinpoints and disappeared. In front of him was a forest of wood. He pushed toward a gap. His lungs turned inside out. Then, against his will, he inhaled. Water coursed into his windpipe and he was at first fulfilled by the burn and rush of its passage, that and the secret that had taken him such an enduring long time to find.

He was a leaf. It was true he'd imagined he could control what happened to him on the drives. He'd fancied himself an athlete with the skills to bend the waters to his will. But that wasn't the way it worked. The river had gathered itself from a half dozen creeks turkey-tailing up a hundred hillsides fed by branches in a thousand gullies that had been born of tens of thousands of springs. It had reinvented itself every moment of every day for a million years, and now it was already on its way to the next place it would be. It would decide did it want to suck him into its depths or did it want to spit him to the surface. There wasn't a thing he could do about it. His chances weren't any better than a leaf's. The same was true for every man on his crew and every man who'd ever been.

And he was alone, just as he'd known he would be, his own self in the dark. It saddened him that his death was nothing special, because now it was *him* dying, and it ought to have been different from other men's dying. It ought to have mattered. But in this version of the story, there was no one took note. The Holy Spirit didn't lay on his heart, and Brodis wasn't overcome by the glow of brotherly love. In this version he was alone.

The next he could tell he was on the ground, face down and naked, his toes lapped in the water of an eddy. The mudded bank was warm against his face. A rock pressed into his left rib, but he didn't care. It was Brodis and the rock and the earth, and no one took notice. His body was weightier with sin and earthly cares than ever it had been before, a thousand pounds of iron or more, and he couldn't move.

No one came. No one saw.

In this version of the story there was no warm glow of light, no Jesus, no backslaps from the other men. In this version of the story the secret he discovered wasn't the Christ. It was the other thing: futility. Death. Impotence in the belly of the river or, if not the river, then the falling forest, or the brilliant fires, or the manmade swipe of skidders and engines, or the tumbling offload, or the slow slack of disease. In this version of the story Brodis wept into the riverbank and became a part of the red clay, and he drowned all over again in the earth, sinking and sinking until he was face down on the way to Hell itself. Only it wasn't Hell. It was red clay. The discovery was unremarkable. No demons and no sinners, just this. He knew now that solitude had always been his state and that it was fitting and natural that he should be alone for eternity, but even as he recognized this fact, he was filled with a deep and terrible sense of loss.

He woke in a pool of sweat. The room was dark, and the stove was out. He reached to his wife's side of the mattress, to the shallow depression where she ought to be.

But no. She sat on the end of the bed turning a sock right side out, and he knew as sure as he knew his name that she wasn't preparing for the day but rather just returning from somewhere else. Where had she been? How had she come to leave him? And why did she pretend that everything was as it ought to be? With the clarity of the newly wakened, Brodis saw that if she was to leave this bed, he might never lay eyes on her again. He propped himself on his arm and reached for her elbow. She turned with feigned surprise. Or dismay.

"Where have you been?" he asked, his voice flegged with left-over sleep.

"Where have I *been*?" Her face showed real surprise, but under it, something else she wasn't telling. She lifted her arm free.

"You ain't said a word about leaving this house."

"I ain't left the house." She put the sock on over her stocking and felt around the floor for the other one.

Brodis was sitting up now. He sensed that his argument wasn't proceeding the way it ought, but in place of slowing him down, the knowledge spurred a desperate need to continue. "Where did you go?"

She found the other sock. "*Brodis.*" The tone of her voice was a lecture, the way she spoke to Matthew whenever he chewed his food with his mouth open. It wasn't the way to talk to a grown man. It wasn't the way a wife talked to a husband.

For the first time, he saw the pitfall of his married life: the years he'd spent converting the souls of strangers, when his own wife walked a skinny line between salvation and mortal sin. "Do you love *God*?" Once the words were out of his mouth, he knew they were right.

Irenie bent to lace up her boot. She didn't turn to him, didn't come to him. She hadn't come to him on her own go-ahead in years. But he knew her, knew every part of her, every rise and fold of skin, the hollows above her collarbones, the crease under her small breasts, the curve of her hips full and round like an unshelled peanut, the spread of her buttocks and the soft unmuscled flesh of the inside of her thighs. They were familiar as his own limbs because he had claimed them fifteen years earlier, after he'd emptied his savings account to make this homestead on this land her father had sold him. He'd built the smokehouse and the outbuildings and the roof above them. He'd built the bed they slept in, the same one Irenie was bent on abandoning. A wife was meant to submit herself unto her husband as unto the Lord, for the husband was the head of the wife, even as the Christ was the head of the church.

He lay his hand on her waist in the signal that had been theirs since the first day they married.

She gave her boot-strings a final yank. "Brodis, *don't*. You're not your own self." She pushed off the edge of the bed to stand.

He grabbed at the swing of her hair without expecting to catch it, but by some miracle he did. She stopped. He held to the hank of hair. She was wrong of course. He was more himself than ever. This was him. This was Brodis Lambey, logger, preacher, farmer, land-owner, husband. Self-taught, self-made. A man had an obligation to gather to himself all the things he owned because he was responsible for them and to them. He, Brodis Lambey, was responsible for *her*. All this time he thought she'd been saved. But he knew that when salvation took true, it affected every aspect of a person's life. You submitted to the word of the Lord because it was the word of the Lord. You didn't pick and choose. If you did, if you were to hold something back from Him, you were raising up the seed that would bring about your own fall. He saw it every day. A fellow withheld that one thing that was hardest to let go, but in the end that was the thing that kept him from grace. Or a woman refused to come into the fold like Eve, refused to be ruled by Adam.

Brodis held the end of the braid steady, the way he would wait on a horse to gentle. "Do you realize, wife, that we're getting to the evening of time? Do you realize that?"

"What?"

"The Lord said it in Revelations. That there'd be wars and rumors of war and earthquakes and fire and famine. We've had the earthquakes and the fires, and we've had the famine, and now we've got the rumors of war. And it's gonna get worse, wife. We're getting right down to the time of fulfillment. You're the only one knows did you accept, *really* accept, the blood-bought truth into your heart." He pulled gently on the tail end of the braid. Slowly, slowly her head folded back. With his other hand, he cupped her waist.

Then, gently and firmly, he brought her hair and the back of her head to the pillow. He brought his face close to hers. "*Where did you go?*"

She didn't say a word, but he had the sense that she would change her mind and come willing to the fold if he gave her the chance. He had the sense she would reach her arms around his neck. He loosed her braid. Now.

With one sudden movement, she pushed off his chest and rolled away. But he was ready. He grabbed the snake of hair again, and this time her head jerked back and she crashed into him. In one quick motion, he trapped her hips with his leg and rolled her toward him. Then he was bending over her, willing her to overmaster the pride that had taken root in her heart. "Adam worked the soil too, Irenie."

She stared up at him, and her eyes were the eyes of some wilderness creature at the moment the dogs arrived.

Brodis softened his voice. "God gave him Eve, the one consolation he had for his tribulations." The one part of his living that he didn't have to work for. "Listen." He stroked the side of her face, and her skin that had been soft was thinned now by weather and work. How could it be so? Had so much time passed? "A man shall leave his father and his mother and hold fast to his wife, and they shall become one flesh." He fumbled with the cedar-wood buttons on her dress, but they confounded him. He pulled, and the fabric gave with a ripping noise.

"*Brodis!*" Her voice shrilled at him the same way it shrilled at Matthew when he misbehaved.

The front of her dress was open now. He pressed himself against her body, and heard a sound that he recognized as a button bouncing on the floor. And maybe it was that, the button, that gave him pause. Never before had there been buttons on the floor, never before the ripping of cloth, never before this struggling and pinioning.

But she'd refused ruling. The covenant said that a woman would be ruled by her husband, and Brodis had worked and worked while the one thing that was supposed to be his by right had been denied him. The anger rose in him the same as the sap. He yanked at her stockings until he heard again the sound of tearing fabric. The wife's body does not belong to her alone but also to her husband.

The only thing between them now was his nightshirt. He pulled it away.

Somewhere he heard her gasp, but he didn't stop.

*One flesh one flesh one flesh. One Flesh. One.*

*Flesh.*

*One.*

Then it was over.

In the end, there was nothing in it of grace nor glory. It was nothing but a mean wringing of fluids, like spitting on a hot day, or the last dreg of water a fellow coughed from his lungs after choking in a river. Afterwards, there was only the sink of estrangement, and the fear of his own loosening flesh, of disease and putrefaction and the return to the soil. The dead weight of it.

Irenie didn't unsqueeze her eyes. Somewhere far away, the man atop her groaned and collapsed onto the bed. In place of watching him, she fell into a landscape that was black against the light of the moon. The hollow between the mountains tilted away, and the trees trailed naked against the sky, old and intricate as her arteries. The moon slanted up the mountainside, and the voices of night creatures careened through the air. The trees pulsed, tipped toward her, the winded earth naked in the cold, every scream echoing against the iron-froze landscape. The ridge of trees throbbed its veined throb against the sky, above blasted forests and ravaged creeks and springs and cliffs and then her own heart, a slick bulbous thing laid bare on the metal earth, and she wondered without curiosity did it yet beat. The wind reverberated in her ears and it wasn't the wind but instead the sound of her own voice howling upon the naked valley, along the branch bottom, up the draw, into the mountain at the place where the water pulsed up, past the crack of granite and the skeins of ice where it welled up from ancient black nothingness, below skifts of sediment and leaf scurf and the black pad of winter moss. There the howl stopped.

Part of her stayed there, in that moist sediment between the granite cracks of time, in that cool nothingness. And it occurred to her that she could live there if she had to.

In the distance, the sound of dogs.

Irenie opened her eyes. Gloom and long shadows. His denim overalls slouched on the back of a green painted chair. His shoes splayed on the floor. His shirts hung on nails on the wall next to a dresser he'd made with store-bought glass knobs he'd ordered from Asheville. His Bible weighed on the bedside table. A low ceiling sagged at the center. It was a room she'd never quite seen before, though she'd spent a good portion of her life in it. There was a sound, and with it the recognition that it was a familiar sound, something from the normal world she'd lived in before. It astounded her to hear it here, in the lurking shadow, among this mangled flesh.

It was the sound of snoring, like a stomach digesting the silence. It was her husband, and she was in their bed, and it was late spring. Other sounds made their way through: the low thrush of the creek branch, the insects, a vigorous scurry in the walls, *who-who-who-cooks-for-you* somewhere to the south at the tobacco fields, below the first ridge. The dawn was on its way, and something inside her had ripped open.

The man sleeping next to her was her husband. She'd once imagined that he held her in his regard. But the thing that had happened was a thing you feared from strangers, from bandits and highwaymen in strange settlements, from monsters in fairy tales. A very young girl fell in love with a fantastic older man with worldly experience and undreamt-of talents. He was perfect in every way except for the odd fact of his blue beard. But the young wife ignored the beard. And then one day she opened a locked door and as the panels swung away from her, light spilled in and the horror was revealed. It was impossible to say how many the bodies were, or how long they'd been there, or who had been eating them.

*The wife's body does not belong to her alone but also to her husband.* It occurred to her that she'd never really and truly understood that passage before, never even *heard* it before. The wife's body does not belong to her alone but also to her husband. It wasn't their house. Not even their farm, even though it had once been a part of her father's land. It was his. Brodis's. Everything was his. Even her. And whatever it was that was her real self had shriveled so small she didn't know if it lived. She held herself statue-still, the way she might steady a sulfur match to watch a flame catch, give it time to assert itself before piling on tinder or blowing her breath across it. But there was nothing. The indigo flame was gone.

Then the most unexpected sound in the world.

*Keekit.*

The good-luck saw of cricket legs somewhere in the room. *Keekit.* It was too soon in the year for crickets. Thin and experimental and tuneless and young, so pointy it cut across the rumble of snoring, the giant sated in his den, surrounded by the bones of dead things.

*Keekit.* The creature throbbed, tiny and enormous. He didn't stir.

Irenie edged away from him and rolled off the side of the bed. Once out of reach, she didn't bother being quiet. Nothing could be louder than the rub of cricket-thigh.

She wiggled her feet into her boots, pulled a blanket from the shelf, and unlatched the door. Cold bit the morning air.

Below the springhouse, the stream trickled unimpeded, pooling in a shallow bowl before it ran past the privy. On the bank, bleeding heart bloomed droopy and pink and weary and forlorn. She peeled off her ripped clothing, stepped out of her boots, and lowered herself into the water, cold as a slap, and clean. By the time she got out, her limbs had gone numb, and she pulled a sweater over her head and stepped into her overalls and boots. She started up the hill but didn't realize she was running until she heard the sound of branches breaking and clothes flapping. Her breath ran shallow, but her legs pedaled and pushed and accelerated her up the mountain. She didn't stop until her throat was raw with the cold, and the forest opened to the pinking sky.

The bald was empty, the moon a finger smudge. She knew the shape of the horizon as well as she knew the lines of her mother's face. She'd been a little girl whenever she'd first come here. The mountain and the valley and the homeplace below had belonged to her great grandfather then. If you were to walk into that tree line, just to the north, the ground fell away steep until it shelved into a staircase of cliffs and caves, and all the places her cousin Lesley had run to whenever he was a little boy and didn't want to eat cabbage. She knew each of those rocky recesses, which protected you from the wind, which from rainfall, which were inhabited by other mammals, which held her collection of glass memories. She knew them, but she'd never taken him there. Maybe on account of his foot, or maybe because they were a part of the land she'd kept for herself.

But it was his. Her father had sold the land to Brodis the day after they married.

For the first time, she knew that she would leave it.


Brodis finished the milking but didn't scald the buckets. There was no one had lit the stove, and Matthew's spring water sat untouched on the porch. The boy brought in five eggs and without any words set them in a bowl. He didn't meet his father's look, but Brodis sensed that when his back was turned, his son tracked him. Brodis tipped cold water over his face and scrubbed himself dry with a towel. Matthew didn't wash. Instead he took a turn around the kitchen, his eyes flicking from the cook stove to the hearth to his parents' room, his hands stuffed into his pockets. Brodis opened the bread safe to discover three baked potatoes from the night before. "Eat these," he instructed his son, setting two potatoes and a slab of cornbread on a plate and sliding it across the table. The sound of the enameled plate on the oil-cloth was overloud. Matthew stopped pacing and stared at the food. Then he pulled out a chair and sat down, his eyes darting back and forth between the plate and Brodis's legs. Brodis wrapped the third potato in a dishrag and stuffed it in his own coat pocket, a lumpen weight next to his vague and formless unease.

That morning he fellowshipped at a church on the other side of the river. The moment he stepped to the pulpit, the Holy Spirit showed him a vision of flames, and he knew straight away what he was meant to preach on: the place where the worm dieth not and the fire is unquenched.

He grasped the pulpit box with both hands and searched out the eyes of the people. "Brimstone." He let the word sit hard and terrible on the waiting congregation. But he wasn't willing to go there yet. He followed with a question. "How many of y'all know what brimstone really *is?*"

Nobody moved. A little girl in the third row buried her face in her mother's neck.

Brodis backed off, made his voice easy, conversational. "Sulfur, that's what, ladies and gentlemen. Brimstone is sulfur, nothing more and nothing less. It's the smell of that rotten egg that sat hidden in a corner of the henhouse all summer, or the smell of a privy that's too long being redug."

A fellow in the front row blinked warily. No gold-wearing government agents in this crowd.

"And I've heard tell it's the smell of the water on the Tennessee side of the mountains."

A few nervous titters rose up from the pews. He waited for the fidgeting to die, and then he let the silence hang in the church a beat too long, then another. "But imagine *smelling* that sulfur forever. Imagine yourself, naked as a plucked and scalded chicken, with that filth in your nose and on your skin for all eternity."

They imagined, he could see.

"And that's just the smell, brothers and sisters. I ain't even talked about the fire." Silence. Faces blanched back at him. The adults were afraid. They remembered the summer of 1925 whenever they'd watched the coal-fired locomotives and Shay engines loose showers of sparks as they chugged their way up the mountain toward the logging camps, and they'd heard about the sheet of flame that roared up the hillsides, exploding five hundred year old trees. They remembered standing on the roofs of their homes and dumping bucket after bucket of water that evaporated like alcohol. The fear was already there. All Brodis had to do was tender it, feed it, urge it upward, say the truth about the way it started pretty and yellow-white on a thing it took to eating, and then, whenever it got a hold, turned hot and blue and slow for a good while, as if settling in for a meal, until it leapt up, live-licking, demon-flamed, exulting and dancing its victory, until nothing, not water nor wind nor Jesus himself had the power to stop it.

After the fire, the words of the gospel came to him. "I am the first and the last, and those that are with me are called, and chosen, and faithful. I will show thee things which must be hereafter." He preached on progress, and how it rolled faster and faster, like a cut tree skidding down a hill, and he described how he'd seen giant firs roll down the sides of mountains like children's playthings, bouncing and springing in the air, crushing saplings and splintering entire groves on their way, and always gaining more and more speed. He preached about Progress and how it cut the same quickening swath, how in his day, just in his day alone, the world had changed, how it was the surest sign that the end was coming on, how according to the scripture they were in the evening of time already. He couldn't say how many days it would take before Progress was to come to a dead stop and the Lord was to unleash his armies and time would roll backwards, sure, and they'd be killing each other like flies. He couldn't say how much time it'd be before the hour of His judgment was come.

During the altar call, four members of the congregation fell down on the mourner's bench to ask God's forgiveness, and Brodis felt his heart expand some. Whatever his own sins were, whatever his own weakness, he had at least done this. He had shown the truth to come and they had opened their souls. He wasn't perfect, he knew and God knew, knew his pride and the way his own wife turned him weak, but he, Brodis Lambey, had this morning done the people of Walnut this one small service.

He took the long route home, the shoulders of the mare rolling beneath him like machinery, the skin at her withers hot and shuddery. He told himself the route through Eakin was less work on the animal because it was flatter, but the moment she clopped onto the macadam his earlier unease returned. Then the bridge opened before him, the right lane blocked on account of needing repairs. "One vehicle," a wooden placard read. Brodis waited as a green truck rolled slowly toward him. Then, on impulse he turned the horse down Main Street instead.

He tied her in front of Crisp's store. A group of men sitting on overturned milk crates watched from the porch, the air around them thick with cigarette smoke. One of them was Lesley Raines, a slope-shouldered do-less who oiled his hair and had been in and out of trouble with the federal government for as long as Brodis had known him. He was Irenie's cousin, and his eyes watched Brodis while his mouth cudded tobacco. "Afternoon, preacher." The spite in his voice floated right up at the surface. He squirted a stream of amber into the street.

Brodis didn't stop. "Morning, Les," he returned. Irenie's cousin hadn't done a full day's work in his life, and the matter of the corn whiskey had created a hardness between the families. Now Lesley tipped the milk crate back against the wall and chewed, leery-eyed. But Brodis stepped into the dark of the store. It was no point in putting the Lord to the test.

The interior was dusky and smelled of strawberry flats, kerosene, and linseed oil. On the counter were baskets of crepe flowers for Decoration Day, but Mr. Crisp was nowhere in sight. Brodis felt something in him relax. He hadn't yet laid his mind on the thing he wanted, and he didn't feel like explaining to the old man that he'd only a general idea. He ignored the mattocks and axes and hoe handles and made his way through the displays, past bushel baskets of radish and beets, past the stacks of canned goods. He had the impulse to buy her something, some token that showed that no matter how poorly he behaved, no matter how she construed his actions, he hadn't meant her harm, that he had, in fact, the deepest anxiety for the safety of her earthly body and the salvation of her eternal soul. But he didn't know what the thing was.

The bolts of fabric stood against the back wall. Brodis sensed that this was the place. A cardboard sign advertised buttons by the pound, but Brodis didn't have time to sort the box. And he was embarrassed by the colorful spools of thread and the glass case with the bolts of slick shiny fabric in them. He stopped for a moment to finger some pink ribbon but couldn't see her using such a thing. His eye fell on a roll of green material, and he rubbed the corner between his thumb and forefinger and the cloth slipped through like water. He couldn't picture her wearing it. And anyway he had no notion how much would she need to make a dress. Instead he picked up a stack of handkerchiefs, fancy with tiny stitching, the edges delicate with lace. A bit of red caught his eye. He unfolded the square of near-transparent white fabric. Tiny strawberries vined the borders. No lace. This. This was it, the thing he could present to her in a moment of ruthful tenderness. She would recognize in it the great care he had to protect her and keep her in the shelter of his embrace.

And maybe she would tell him about her wanderings.

Brodis refolded the handkerchief as best he could and brought it to the counter.

## CHAPTER NINE

THE ENVELOPE ON THE KITCHEN TABLE HAD COME from the USDA extension office in Eakin, and it was addressed to Mrs. Brodis Lambey. Irenie willed herself not to touch it. It was their custom to open the week's mail together, after supper. She gave the letter a last look before she stepped into the yard.

Low clouds flocked in the north. It occurred to her that now, when the sky was blue as glass, and the first chicory flowers starred the roadside with blue, and the wind blew the apple blossoms across the hard-packed yard, now was the time to shear sheep. Except that there were no more sheep. Nor were there any more lambs to be born. Years ago, she'd stopped carding and spinning and weaving. Nor was there planting of cane or flax, nor cradling of wheat, nor bundling and stacking, nor mowing of hay. In place of it all, the shaggy mops of tobacco lined the fields, row after leafy-headed row, as if all the growing world had put its energy into this one lurid plant. The sameness troubled her. Where once there'd been whispering cane and melon vines, the heads of tobacco pushed up in absurd formation, greedy for water and potash and food. Their leaves grew broad and white-veined and springy. But Irenie knew the lie of that abundance. The roots were shallow and gave up life to the hoe or the wanderings of deer and pigs. Brodis had to set a barbed wire fence and check it every season.

Irenie opened the springhouse door and stooped into the subterranean fog, the ancient cool of the stone creeping through her boots. It was a weak spring, but Matthew had built such a wide basin into the floor that it kept the temperature the same winter or summer, chatter-cold but never freezing. On the bottom shelf a block of butter hardened next to a bucket of milk and a pitcher of cream. On the upper shelves spilled the greens, the strawberries, rhubarb and peas. She cupped the bowl of peas against her hip and returned to the house.

The buff-colored envelope stared from the middle of the oil-cloth, sitting atop three letters and four due-bills Matthew had brought from town. She sat and fitted the bowl of peas between her thighs, sliding the other enameled bowl against the stack of mail so as to block the letter from view.

The pods were well ripe, and the peas came away quickly, the first of them dropping into the bowl with a metallic *pong*.

The script on the letter was round and wide-open, feminine. She looked to remember when if ever she'd seen Mrs. Furman's hand.

*Virginia's.* It was an old fashioned name, and the syllables whispered of cities and unexpected characters, the promise of could-be: another state, another country, east and north beyond the mountains, beyond these hollows and draws, beyond this homeplace, beyond him.

On impulse, Irenie lifted the bowl of peas and set it on the table, reaching for the envelope at the same time, the paper smooth in her fingers. She held it to the window until a rectangle outlined itself against the light. Perhaps it would be best to open it now, in private. It was addressed to her.

But there was that yank on her hair, the snap of her skull to her shoulder blades, the untalkable thing from Sunday morning.

And the "Mrs." could be a mistake. How then would she explain the broken seal? She slid the envelope back into the stack of mail.


That evening Matthew bolted the peas and fried onions as if he couldn't wait for supper to be over, as if he knew all about the thing that had happened, knew too that since then his mother had changed into her nightdress too early, even while his father was in the barn securing the animals, that when the door latch clicked open, and the slap-drag of Brodis's step sounded across the kitchen floor, she was sinking into the bedcovers and making herself invisible, hiding from the unclaimed guilt that had forced its way into the house and settled there to stay.

Now Brodis stabbed at the peas on his plate. He asked what were the worms he'd seen in the fireplace.

Irenie stopped chewing. She'd forgot about the worms. They'd been as big as her pinky and bright green, white striped, the same color as the leaves. When plucked from the tobacco, they squirmed in the palm of her hand, their suckered feet searching for the terrain they'd lost. She'd picked them one at a time from the young plants and dropped them in a gallon tin. Then she'd dumped the lot of them into the fire. "From the tobacco," she answered. "It was a lot more this year."

Her husband looked up from his plate and studied her. "Chickens would eat them."

But she'd already tried that. Sure, the hens had snatched and quarreled for the squirming meat. "Last year they took sick."

"Sick how?"

She'd thought they were dead. She'd never seen chickens do that way. "Just laid down in the dirt and wouldn't get up."

Her husband was silent a moment, further considering the problem of the wasted worms. "That won't do," he allowed. "I wonder if Rickerson throws them out."

The man who'd attacked her couldn't be the same one sitting here now. He wore the same checkered shirt he'd always worn, had the same broad shoulders, the same narrow waist, the same wave of hair swept back from his sharp-edged face.

She'd stowed the strawberried handkerchief in a drawer, to save for good, she told herself. But this morning the drops of color had caught her eye, the red stitching bright as shame against the white pantaloons and the brown woolen stockings. After breakfast she'd wrapped it in a piece of sacking and buried it in the root cellar. It was easier not to think of the man who'd attacked her as her husband. It was easier to think of him as a demon come through the window, a creature who'd appeared at the edge of day for the single purpose of making her small.

Matthew swallowed the potatoes on his plate and seemed to shrink into his clothes, as if he knew the discomfort in the room was none of his doing.

After supper, Brodis spread the mail on the oilcloth. When he read the inscription on the USDA envelope, he handed it to Irenie. Her fingers tore the edge of the paper, aware of her husband's curiosity and of the muscles in her face that hid her fear and hope.

It wasn't a letter. It was a purple mimeographed page that addressed the ladies of the county "and its environs." It said the United States Department of Agriculture was offering classes through their regional extension office. A second page included some twenty possible topics, to be determined by the ladies' interests, each with a checkbox next to it: The Efficient Kitchen, Paint and Wall Paper, The Decorative Flower Garden, Clothes Closets and Kitchen Cabinets, Linoleum Makes Easy Cleaning, Cooking with Electricity, The Science of Nutrition, Mattress Making Workshop, Dress Patterns, Coat Patterns, Suit Patterns, and How to Make a Modern 6-Gore Dress from a Man's Three Piece Suit. The workshops would be held every other week on Saturdays at five o'clock.

And there, at the bottom of the second page, a hand-written note. "Hope you can make it, Mrs. Lambey! Sincerely, Virginia Furman."

"Look." Irenie slid the first page, the one without the handwritten note, across the table to Brodis. "They're free." She couldn't figure why the invitation made her jealous.

Her husband picked up the list and squinted at it without seeming to comprehend. He set it down. "They won't come."

Irenie hadn't thought of that possibility. She kept her voice careful. "Don't you think? Some of them?"

"Not by themselves, not at night." The beast between them stretched its limbs. The mountains were supposed to be full of bandits and ramblers. But as long as she'd been walking the woods, nary a one of them had reared up from the shadows, or called her a thing of his own, or plucked her by the hair from the life she'd thought was her own.

She stood to clear the dishes.

"I can take her," Matthew volunteered. As if he knew.

Irenie set two plates on the drain board. "Papaw has the Chamber of Commerce meetings on Saturdays." Brodis didn't answer. "Be a chance to talk to other women."

Brodis lifted his glass and drank deep. He set it on the oilcloth with a loud tap. "Is it something you want to do?"

"Yes. It's something I want to do."

He raked both hands against his scalp front to back, grabbed the back of his head, and tilted his face toward the ceiling. Then he sighed. "I'll figure it then."

After clearing up, Irenie read the list of classes again. She made a mark in every one of the boxes, even "Cooking with Electricity." The more time she spent away from home, the less chance she would be there when the demon returned.

## CHAPTER TEN

PAP DOWNSHIFTED, AND THE MODEL A'S ENGINE
seemed to seize into itself. A cloud of red dust blew up and into
the open window, settling on the floorboards and dashboard and
Irenie's new-washed dress. He spoke loud enough to be heard over
the truck's engine and the open windows. "Sure you want to go to
this ladies meeting, Irenie? Come to the bridge meeting and you'll
be entertained for certain."

Irenie smiled at the invitation, and for a moment she wanted
to go. "Might be we'll finish early and I'll meet you there," she
allowed.

Her father was a slight man whose interests inclined toward pol-
itics and hunting. Now he slouched back against the leather seat,
left elbow resting on the window frame, fedora pushed back on
his head. He squinted across the river as if making a pleasure of the
view. The cattle had worn terraces on the slantland, and the steps
zigzagged down the side of the mountain toward the river. Below
spanned the wooden bridge that connected his lands to the train
station and Eakin. Years ago, the pilings had begun to shift, but the

legislature could never agree to set aside money for repairs. Now he and other members of the Chamber of Commerce were calling on the state to do something.

Irenie felt his eyes on her. Her lips, she was sure, were smiling yet. And anyway, the rattle of the truck and the rush of air through the open windows didn't invite conversation. Ahead, the road was dry-rutted and spattered with green patties of mule dung, the cutbanks grown up in purple bull thistle and white and yellow pearly everlasting.

"Why the dolesome look?" he shouted. His hand on the steering wheel was narrow, the knuckles covered in wiry gray hairs, like the paws of some loping grass-eating animal.

She shook her head to show that it was too loud to talk. She'd seen those same hands after supper, furred and cupped and curled around her mother's shoulders, or at the back of a chair, touching but not quite, or twined among her mother's fingers in the half dark the way you did on habit. But never grabbing or fisting at hair, never yanking.

Irenie had always known that men and women occupied different positions in the world. Men were the placeholders. They and the things they built were the way a family was judged. Her father had been the one to negotiate the family's position. He knew how to talk to people and get things done. Tonight he would make a speech about funding the bridge repairs, and men would change their minds. Because of him, others would wait in line at voting booths. Because of him, her mother could ask for a line of credit in any store or sit among the sinners in the white clapboard church or hold a shivaree that drew the whole valley. Her father held her place and the place of his whole family, and his wife had only to move in and out of it at will. Her job was the feeding of animals and the planting of vegetables and the putting up of food and the sewing of clothes and the hygiene of everyone in the house. It had long been so. But now Irenie understood a thing she hadn't understood before. Nobody in the world ever said that her mama held the same place as the hen or the mare or the catch dog, but now Irenie knew that it was so because a man had the power to make it so. The question that seemed to matter most was whether God had decreed it or man. Had God meant for Mary to serve Joseph? Irenie had always assumed He'd set the Lord's mother apart, her and all women that came after. But now she wondered was it truly so. Now she wondered if God had left them unsighted and unseen in His creation.

There was a creak and a cloud of dust, and the truck came to a stop in the middle of the road. Her father pulled up the brake lever, turned the switch straight down, and sat back on the leather seat. He turned to study her. "What's eating on you?" The engine idled out and dust blew in the windows. The air swelled with the saw of insects, died away, and swelled again.

She had to say something. "Does Mama belong to you?"

Her father looked uncomfortable. He took off his hat and waved it in front of his face. "In what sense?"

Irenie already regretted the question. She looked past him, through a screen of Queen Anne's lace to the twisted orchard beyond. Above, the sky had quilted up like cotton batting. "You know, as a thing that you own for yourself."

Her father turned to the empty road in front of him. His lips moved, as if repeating the phrase she'd uttered. Or cursing. He opened the glove box, took out a shellcraft pipe and a small drawstring pouch, and tipped the contents of the pouch into the bowl, tamping it down with his index finger. Then he lifted his hips off the seat and reached into his pocket to retrieve a metal lighter. In place of lighting the pipe, he turned to her. "Well sir, I don't know that your mother would agree to that. I expect she'd tell you I belong to her, just like that speckled cat belongs to her. Except that whenever the cat's work is done, he's allowed to sit in her lap. She don't tolerate me trying that." He glanced at his daughter to judge the effect of his joke.

Irenie sat frozen on the bench beside him, hands at her side, knuckles tight against the edge of the seat. It was the worst answer he could have made. She tried to imagine the same words coming out of Brodis' mouth. "What about Adam and Eve?"

He seemed relieved. "What about them?"

"What about the part where God says he'll make Adam a help meet for him?"

"Well sir, the way I believe is that your mother must have been somewheres else the day they taught that page of the gospel."

Incredibly, Irenie felt the rise of tears.

"I don't guess you're in the mood for jokes, but damnit Ire— *dang* it, that's the longest face you've showed in years."

Her father's new seriousness had the effect of pushing her closer to the rag edge of crying. Now she wanted the jokes back. She took a deep breath and regarded the row-orchard above them. The trees had been grafted so many times that their limbs twisted and warped toward the sky like the arms of witches.

"Seems to me, Irenie, that every creature belongs to its own self. Used to be anyway. That chicken eating feed in my yard, I might say it belongs to me, but it don't. It has its own power and its own life just like every other creature. It don't belong to me in the strict sense of the word. Sure, I'm gonna take its eggs tomorrow morning, and whenever it stops laying in a few years, I'm gonna wring its neck. But that's not a belonging, Irenie. Every creature feeds off every other because it can and because it's got to to survive." He brought the lighter to the bowl of the pipe, spun the flint wheel with his thumb, and mutched on the stem. The smoke was invisible and sweet. "But I don't own that chicken, Irenie. It's gonna do its chicken things all day. And if it wants to wander off in the hills, it will. I can't stop it. I can only kill it. Used to be the same for the pigs and sheep. They'd be up there in the hills, getting as much mast as they could stuff down their gullets. Come winter, or whenever they'd be ready for salt, they'd show up of their own accord and trade that wandering for warmth and victuals. They come back, most of them. Except the ones that didn't. He put the pipe to his lip and took a short breath, then another.

"What I'm saying is that they chose the trade off. Warmth and victuals, but with it come the likely that a man would rob them of their life. Take them out just the same as a bear or bobcat. A man's just more devious about it. If a bobcat could lure them in, he would." He glanced at her to see was she still listening. "The chicken accepts the terms of the agreement because she's dumb and she can't take care of her own self. The sheep used to accept it on habit." He stopped, considering. "The pigs, I never did figure why they came back. Maybe they just wanted a warm place to sleep in the winter." He stared at the road in front of them, and Irenie figured him to be finished, but he wasn't.

"Irenie, a man doesn't own a woman. But whether you accept the terms of the agreement seems to me is up to you."

Irenie folded her hands in her lap. The undersides of the bee tree leaves blew silver. "That's not what the scriptures say, Pap." But before she'd finished the sentence, she knew that she was arguing Brodis' point of view and not her own.

"Pffff." Her father turned toward her, as if comfortable again, ready to pick up a conversation they'd begun and ended a thousand times. "The scriptures. You reckon I have some connection to God that your mother don't have? Hell no. If anything, it's the other way around. Isn't there another part in that book where it says that God created man in his own image, male and female?"

Irenie paused. "Yes. God created man in his own image. Male and female he created them. Genesis one."

"I don't know exactly what that means, but I always took it to mean that women were as much like God as anybody else. That he'd made both of them to contain some part of himself." He looked across at the slantland again. "But I'm not a churched man."

A truck clattered on the road behind them. Pap checked the brake and put the car in neutral, reached below his seat and brought out the crank, then stepped to the front of the vehicle, bent over, and gave the handle a smart turn. The engine sputtered up, and he gave a wave to the car behind as he slid into the seat.

The noise put her at ease, and the swell in her sinuses subsided. What her father said sounded true. There was something in her that flamed separate from Brodis and Matthew and the church, weak or strong or indigo or yellow according to her own doings. Maybe that was the only thing that belonged to herself alone. But it was more than nothing. Either way her father was mistaken on one thing. Brodis did have a relationship to God that she didn't. She'd seen it every Sunday when the Spirit filled his mouth with more words and more emotion than he'd spoke the past seven days combined.

But it didn't mean that He wanted Brodis to take his wife into the frog of his hand and close his fingers around her tight. And it didn't mean that He wanted her to let him do it.

The truck clattered to the bridge. Across the river, the railroad paralleled the water, and the town of Eakin stacked itself between the tracks and the mountains. At the entrance of the bridge, her father stopped the car and waited while a man on a mule clopped toward them. The rider wore overalls and a wide-brimmed hat. When he passed, he touched the brim and Irenie's father touched his. The thud of hooves faded, and the truck surged over the planking, the water below like hammered tin in the late afternoon light. Downstream the river narrowed and accelerated through a strew of boulders, then toward the roar of the falls, where the bottom shelved and the water piled fast into the pool below. As a girl, she and her classmates had toted their lunch pails to the riverbank to watch the bearded bent-kneed loggers. It was the place she'd first laid eyes on Brodis Lambey, leaning lazy and unconcerned on his pick-pole. When he'd neared the edge of the falls, he'd not done a thing in the world but bend his knees and lay his pole across his thighs, pensive in the roar of the rapid. Then, as the timber edged its way over the drop, he seemed to dance backward to the upstream end. Before Irenie had realized she was holding her breath, he danced forward again, and the tree and the man were bouncing into the pool at the bottom of the rapid.

But the river drives had ended years ago. Now the tires of the Ford rolled from the wooden planks onto the smooth of the macadam, then lurched up and over the train tracks. Beyond, automobiles lined the entrance to the filling station, where Willis Darby worked the hand crank, his eyes flicking to the petrol in the glass sphere at the top of the pump. A group of boys played marbles in the alcove in front of the department store, and Ruth Haddix walked up the courthouse steps with a covered dish.

Her father stopped the flatbed. To Irenie's surprise, her throat tightened again, as if her grief had been lying in wait to surprise her all along. The sun sagged on the horizon. A swallow sailed through the long-legged light. Before she could pull the lever on the truck's door, her father cut the engine again. She didn't trust herself to speak. Instead she gathered the strings of her cabbage sack and set it on her lap.

Her father's voice was careful. "There's a pack of Raines living in this county, Irenie. Always has been. Don't forget that. Case it ever gets to the place of want-to versus have-to."

Euly Crisp passed in front of the truck and waved a little half wave, her fingers crooking up and down next to her ear.

"You got family out the back door."

"I know that, Pap," she said. "I know it." She leaned over and kissed her father's cheek, then levered the door open. But the picture in her mind was the red-tail who'd taken wing and flown away. Irenie saw her there, above her nest, circling and circling.


The courthouse was close and dark. Ceiling fans whupped. Tacked to the wall above a brass spittoon fluttered a piece of paper with an arrow and the words, "The Efficient Kitchen."

In the municipal room, six women hovered around a long, naked table, their attention focused on the collection of dishes assembled there. A nervous uncertainty occupied the room. Euly Crisp's voice cut across the others. "All of it together?"

Brodis had been right. There hadn't been any other women to come from across the river. Leastways not yet.

"Reckon it's room enough?" someone said, maybe Loesa. Three stacks of manila folders occupied one end of the table. The ladies eyed them with distrust.

Ruth Haddix was the first to notice Irenie. She clasped her free hand. "Mrs. Lambey..." It sounded like "Mazlammy." Ruth's front teeth had turned brown in recent years, and now she spoke with her mouth halfway closed.

Irenie put on not to notice. "Mrs. Haddix." They didn't lean in to touch.

"How is your preacher husband?" Ruth Haddix wanted to know.

"Just fine." Irenie didn't embrace any of the women from town, though she'd known them since her school days, whenever Ruth had been teased for being pigeon-toed and Selby Huff had struggled with multiplication tables.

"And what have you got there?" Ruth asked.

Irenie handed her the cabbage sack with the baking dish of turnips. Ruth peered into the bag and lifted out the red and white ceramic, but there was no more room on the table. Selby Huff took a final look at the manila folders. "These will have to go."

Then she combined the material into one large stack and set it on the edge of the stage. Freed from the constraints of the files, the rest of the ladies began lining up the pot-luck. The smell of butter and fried food wafted from beneath colored cloths. "Do y'all figure supper for before or after?"

Before, Ruth Haddix said.

Just then a new voice joined the group. "You're *here*." There was a sliver of panic in the statement. "The early birds..."

Irenie and the Eakin women turned to Virginia Furman, who was standing in the doorway. Their host wore a green jacket cinched at the waist. Her cheeks were flushed, either from nervousness or bodily effort, one. When she smiled, she used all her teeth, and this, together with the fitted suit and the cinched waist, silenced them. Mrs. Furman's eye fell on the collection of dishes. "Supper!" she exclaimed. "I didn't expect—well, look at this! Isn't this de*light*ful!" She paused, and her eyes scanned the room as if searching for something, and Irenie reckoned it to be the manila folders. Nobody offered up the new location. But then her eye stopped at the edge of the stage. "Shall we take a look at the materials first?"

No one answered. Two newcomers set their dishes on the buffet table.

"Then, over supper, there'll be time to discuss ideas."

The ladies sighed and mumbled and relocated all the dishes to the edge of the stage. The manila folders were returned to the table. More Eakin women appeared, and the greetings and the talking and the exclaiming got louder, and the number of ladies circling up chairs were fewer than the number of ladies lifting dish towels from casserole dishes to have a peek. But at last everyone sat, and Virginia Furman set the manila folders on her lap.

Viola Hayes spoke up from the blue. "Missus, you gotta October birthday?"

All eyes turned to their hostess and the stone at her neck, blank and depthless as the eye of a dead animal. Mrs. Furman tilted her head. "December, actually."

"Oh."

"Why?"

"I just asked, on account of the opal." It was exactly Viola's style. And just like grade school, there was no one willing to explain what she meant.

Virginia Furman's hand crept to her neck and touched the stone. "Oh. Right. It's not my birthstone, if that's what you mean."

Silence squatted in the room. The clock tripped the seconds forward. Irenie tried to feature how, if a person were wanting to do it, she could set up a sentence explaining the luckless stone. But there was no way to do it without sounding superstitious.

Virginia Furman hesitated, then chose to fill the wide space with her own cheerful voice. "Shall we circle closer?"

The ladies pulled in, and the presentation began. Virginia Furman showed floor diagrams of kitchens with counters in the middle of the room that she called islands. She explained how a housewife could use such an island for food preparation without turning her back on her family. She showed how an efficient kitchen had overhead cabinetry and allowed a woman to move from stove to sink with less wasted effort, all the while interacting with her children and husband. There were glossy pictures drawn with pastel colored pens. Each of the kitchens had its own color scheme: red or blue or buttercup yellow. Each had electric stoves and light bulbs. Indoor faucets curled over the sinks. Mrs. Furman said she knew that not everyone had plumbing and electric, but that those things became more accessible every year and that all of them had better be thinking about placement now.

The town ladies fingered the pictures. Their discouragement was grudging and thick, even though most lived in houses with running water and electric. Ruth said the island was too much. Selby Huff said so what if they did have cabinetry in blue. Euly Crisp said she didn't even *want* to interact with her family while she peeled potatoes.

Afterwards, Mrs. Furman put the pictures back into the manila folders, and the ladies spread out the covered dishes and removed the lids and the cloth dishtowels and ate cornbread and barbecued goat and fried chicken and raspberry cobbler on plates in their laps. The placemats and the dishcloths were gray and greasy, the beans and bread thick and rustic. Kitty Mack's enameled pot was chipped at the rim and Irenie's was brown at the bottom. Buena's Dutch oven was old-fashioned and black with fire. But the women were extra kind to one another that evening. Ila put her arm around Irenie and asked about Matthew, and they all exclaimed over the richness of the cobbler and allowed as how Selby's biscuits would float away if you didn't hold them down. Irenie looked out the window at the leavening darkness and the milky evening and wondered what her life would be if she was to live someplace else.

Mrs. Furman looked defeated. She took a second helping of cornbread and exclaimed about the turnips, but there was never a thing in the world to say back. Silence rose up around her and absorbed everything in the room. In no time at all the ladies fitted the lids back onto the pots and gathered their cloth sacks and paper parcels. There was no one offered to help with the washing. Ruth and Kitty Mack were the last to go. From the street, their voices floated into the open window and were replaced by the faraway sound of children. The bridge meeting couldn't be out yet. There were no automobile engines nor male voices nor horseshoes on pavement.

In the municipal room, the fan rotated, lifting the cover of a manila folder and then releasing it. Irenie took Mrs. Furman's hand and told her thank-you, that the kitchens had given her much to study on. But she too wanted to be outside in the soft spring night.

Mrs. Furman sighed. "That wasn't very well done, was it?"

Irenie started to say that it was fine, but there was something in Virginia Furman's voice that stopped her, as if the other woman were seeking criticism in place of reassurance. Irenie couldn't tell her the truth. She couldn't say that Virginia Furman hadn't turned out the woman she figured her for, but that it really and truly wasn't her fault, that it was something of Irenie's own making. She couldn't say that what she'd liked most was the way she'd traveled alone and stood by the ninemark bushes without caring and that she, Irenie, hadn't come all this way to find a wilted flower. Her eye fell on the other woman's hair, curling and pert against her shoulders, and she couldn't remember ever having such short hair. For an instant she wanted to extend her hand and catch a piece of it around her finger. Instead she said, "No ma'am, it wasn't very well done." Her voice was small. She didn't see any other way to answer, even though she expected Virginia Furman to retreat then and withdraw into her own certainties.

But instead the other woman asked, "Would you help me?"

Irenie couldn't say yes. It was one thing to come to the meetings with the rest of the women and find out every single one lived in a house on a street in Eakin. It was another to step out of that circle that wasn't even hers and do something different.

At the same time, she had a terrible need to find out the thing that this girl-woman knew that she did not.

Virginia Furman didn't seem to notice that Irenie hadn't said yes. She plopped herself into a chair the way a child did, never mind that her lovely green suit bunched around her waist. "I don't know what to do different. I do understand about—it's not as if I don't get the—you know, these workshops are actually designed to *save* money." She stared with distaste in the direction of the manila folders. "In the long run anyway." Two spots of embarrassment leapt to her rounded cheeks. "I should have started with one of the pattern classes. I could have shown them how to make a winter coat from a—"

"For now: don't teacher-talk."

Virginia Furman looked surprised. For a moment. "*Teacher*-talk." She grimaced. "Hell, I guess I was." As if in bodily pain, she stared into space for a number of seconds.

Then she turned back to Irenie. "But don't let my *hus*band hear that phrase." And that sentence *don't let my husband hear* seemed to give her cause to smile.

Irenie smiled back, as if she too were in on the joke. "Show me the patterns."

The couple lived the next street over in a stone bungalow wedged against the hillside. The yard smelled of rose bushes and lilies, and Irenie tried to imagine Virginia Furman bent over her gardening and couldn't. When they stepped into the house, a screen door banged shut behind them. Did that extra door really keep out the flies and mice and did they never fling the windows and doors wide to the summer breezes?

Inside, Virginia Furman set the plates and the flatware on the drain board at the sink. Irenie looked about for a place to set the dirty linens and marked that this kitchen didn't have an island either, only a stand of butcher block worn away at the center.

Virginia Furman took the linens from her and set them on top of the icebox. "Just leave them. I'd rather get your opinion on the patterns. Come." She motioned not with her fingers or her hand but with her whole arm like an athlete throwing a baseball, and the motion was something out of Irenie's past, and then it came to her it was the same gesture her cousin Lesley used whenever they were children and he was wanting to show her some new hideout or fort: a wave that started at the shoulder, exactly the same.

Irenie followed the woman's soft, wide figure through a room whose sole purpose seemed to be the serving of meals. "I'll be right back." She hurried through an archway into the parlor. But Irenie wasn't paying attention anymore. There, at the far end of the room where the ceiling sloped down and the air from the little window ruffled the lace curtains, was an upright piano. The keyboard was closed, the cover gleaming and oiled, the wood stained so dark Irenie didn't recognize what kind of tree it had once been. She only knew that if she was to walk over and touch its surface, she would find it smoother and glassier than anything in her own home, like the round center lid of a mason jar or the side of a glass battery case. She couldn't see the keys, but she pictured them intact. Her mother's piano had two keys chipped to the wood, middle C and F, right in the center, like decayed front teeth.

Virginia Furman returned with a stack of fat envelopes she fanned on the table. "Go ahead. See what you think."

The packets featured tall and straight women with their hats perched atop curled hair, some with veils that hung above sultry lips. Irenie reached for a picture of a darted winter coat, but then, for some reason found her hand on the one next to it, a silky green dress with a cinched waist. The model was the only one in the drawings to smile. The envelope's contents were new and slid out easy, the paper so thin Irenie worried to unfold it. She glanced at Virginia Furman.

"Go ahead. That's what it's for."

Machine-printed at the edges of the pattern were the tiny words. "Cut here" and "Baste three inches," and, "Princess seam." Irenie arranged the pieces, the skirt on one end of the table, the bodice on the other, and tried to picture the general effect. She checked the picture on the cover and looked back and forth for a long time. She could feel Virginia Furman watching her.

"Well?" the other woman asked, and Irenie knew that she wanted more than her opinion of the pattern.

Irenie found Virginia's eyes so as to be able to gauge when she'd gone too far. "You could spread three patterns on three different tables," she suggested. "The ladies could set at the one with the pattern they liked. They could bring their own scissors and newspaper and copy however many they wanted."

Virginia Furman bit her lip and nodded, her eyes not on Irenie but the picture she already had of the next meeting. "And tell them what?"

"Nothing."

"Just not talk?" Her voice held hurt, but also a note of laughter at her own surprise.

"Oh, no, they'll talk."

"No I meant me. I shouldn't do any talking."

"Well, no Ma'am. I expect that's best."

Virginia Furman slumped into a chair, her eyes falling on the pattern. "That bad, huh?" But it wasn't a question that expected an answer. Behind her, the piano reflected the electric lamps. The three legs of the stool pinched together into a ring. The feet ended in globes of swirled green glass.

Virginia Furman followed Irenie's eyes. As quickly as she'd sank into the chair, she straightened. "Do you play?"

"Play?" Irenie snapped her attention from the piano. She felt caught out.

Virginia raised her brow and gave a quick nod toward the parlor. "Piano."

"Oh no. It's just—I haven't seen one in a long time. It overtook me."

"You *used* to play." It wasn't a question.

"I used to fool around whenever I was a little girl. My mother plays. But I don't. It's against our church."

"Playing piano?" Virginia Furman had popped from her chair and was beckoning Irenie toward the instrument with that same wide-open sweep of her arm.

"Music from manmade instruments." Irenie's voice trailed away.

Virginia Furman kept moving. She didn't seem to have heard. "What if I played?"

Irenie followed.

"Are you allowed to listen?" But she was already smoothing her skirt against the back of her thighs and settling her weight on the stool. She whirled it to face the keyboard and flipped up the cover with a gentle oiled thud.

"Not really." The keys were beautiful, white and uniform, not the waried yellow of old men's teeth.

Virginia Furman touched the upper register casually, familiarly, the way a body might touch the head of a child, without possessiveness or conscious attention. *Plink.* "Singing is different?" Her fingers walked up and down of their own accord, independent of the conversation.

"Yes, ma'am. Brodis says it's because God gave people voices to sing with and spread the word of the Lord. But not a piano."

"The piano being unnatural."

"Yes."

"But they have a piano at the Church of God." Her fingers drew a melody upon the black keys that was full of longing and sweetness.

"They're Holiness, ma'am."

"And the church across the street."

"Free Wills, ma'am. Brodis says it's not the tools God gave us."

"Mrs. Lambey—*Irenie.*"

"Ma'am?"

"Can I ask you a favor?"

"Ma'am?"

"Please don't call me *ma'am.* It makes me feel old."

"Yes."

"Just call me Ginny."

"Yes. Ginny. I'll do it." Ginny. It was a little girl's name. Irenie felt pleased and nervous.

Virginia Furman stopped walking her fingers on the keys and turned to her as if something funny had just occurred to her. "And Irenie?"

"Yes?"

"Do you know that you begin a lot of sentences with the words *Brodis says?*" She tilted her head, as if just sorting this fact out herself.

"He's my husband, ma'am."

Ginny Furman gave a little nod and spun the stool back to the piano. "But did you know that you did that?"

"No. I didn't know it." Irenie wasn't sure what she was meant to say next. "Ginny."

"Yes." She looked up.

"That's the way I believe too. In God."

"I believe in Him too, Irenie." Now she dropped her hands to her lap. "But sometimes I don't know why He made things the way they are."

Irenie kept her eyes on the piano keys. She wasn't yet ready to meet that gaze.

The agent allowed, "Maybe it's our job to do the best we can anyway." Her hands strayed again to the keyboard, and Irenie closed her eyes and listened. Virginia Furman whose real name was Ginny played the notes delicate and round, like the peal of a dinner bell away far off.

The pattern-making meeting was a success. Afterward Ginny Furman grabbed Irenie's hands and jumped around her in a circle. Irenie rotated around and around and wondered did it count as dancing.

This time she volunteered to help with the dishes. She slid her bread pan back into the flour sack she'd brought it in, careful to face the greased side away from the Vaughn's songbook hidden inside.

At the bungalow, she waited until the last dish was dried before she removed the book from the sack and asked would Ginny mind playing the one hymn, just the one, because she'd loved it as a girl and could no longer remember the way the piano part went.

Ginny's face lit into a grin, and, for the second time that evening, she caught Irenie's hands in her own and threw them into the air. "Hooah!" she called.

Irenie smiled in relief. "Just the one time." She couldn't feature how it was worse than listening to the hymn sung in church. Now Ginny dragged a chair from the table and set it next to the globe-footed stool. She caught Irenie's hand and pulled her to the chair.

But something was wrong. She flipped through the book with a curiosity Irenie hadn't expected. After a long moment, she said, "I hate to tell you this..."

"What?"

"I can't read this."

Irenie looked at the page. The notes were dark and clear, their squares and triangles and circles parading across the page in a single clear line.

"It's just...we have a different system." Ginny whirled the stool to face the bookshelf next to her. After staring at it for a long moment, she extracted a book of music with a pen and ink portrait of an old-time composer on the cover. She opened it to a weather-waved page. In place of a title, the piece had a number, and the markings on the page were all of them circles. They streamed up and down like jump rope. Ginny lifted her hands to the piano and began. The notes rolled up from the lower register in great round waves, the sound of a dozen basses and tenors tripping and leapfrogging one over the other, then weaving together in a ladder of melody that climbed up and up. Unlike a hymn, the rhythm didn't march or step, but swam, and backstroked, and stalled and sallied. Then the middle notes sailed in, delicious and mellow as bubbles, floating up the keyboard and drifting down in fat lazy swoons, until the basses left off for one beat, then two, and at the high register the finest notes she'd ever heard teased weightless and airy over the top, as light as Jesus on the surface of the water.

Irenie held her breath. Inside her, the indigo flame glowed up, then caught the air and spread its wings in a blaze of orange and green and yellow.

## CHAPTER ELEVEN

TEN DAYS LATER IRENIE WAS SORTING MATTHEW'S school clothes when she made up her mind. Later she would attribute it to the journal, but it seemed just as likely it was the packing itself that set her mind thinking on the path it was bound to take.

For a week Brodis had left the supper table early, pushing back his chair and lifting the lantern from the porch hook even as he chewed his last bite, then pitching off for the barn in the dark. Once there he'd sawed and planed and sanded. On Thursday morning he and Matthew had hauled the empty trunk down to the house. Now the smell of its resin stabbed the air. Irenie spread newsprint and pressed the pages flat against the sticky inside walls. When she finished with the paper, she smoothed fresh tobacco leaves along the bottom. They were a good eighteen inches long now, pinched from the base of the plants. They didn't lay as flat as she would've liked, but they would keep the bugs out. She stood with hands at her waist, and surveyed Matthew's room. Most everything would have to stay. A flake-papery hornet nest the size of a ninebark bush hung above the boy's bed. Next to it, the antlers of an adolescent stag spread across the bead board, the horns unsteady and bold at the same time, shed somewhere in the gloam of a naked winter wood. There were other leavings: ribbon-rows of serpent skins, a yellow coffee can filled with calcified snake eggs, a stack of turtle shells, small-boned skeletons arranged to resemble the creatures they'd once been. Her husband had years ago nailed wooden milk crates to the wall above the bed, and Matthew had filled them with categories, each to each. One held salvaged wasps' nests, another wooden cars and trucks, another polished buckeyes and tops made of whittled spools, another a box of Lincoln Logs and painted metal army men, another model airplanes and construction kits. And there, the arrowheads they'd found near the grayback boulder, and next to them a Lone Ranger sitting with his booted legs spread straight before him, his eyes dots of white behind the black mask.

In all of it, there was no catcher's glove nor team shirt, no bat nor basket nor ball of any sort, not even a marble.

But Ginny had said there'd be lots of boys like him.

She pulled his winter clothes first, the long johns and the boiled wool pea coat inherited from his cousin. She gave the coat a shake and held it to her nose. It smelled prickly, like the pennyroyal and tobacco leaves it had been stored in. She shook the garment and examined each section: two moth holes on the left sleeve that had been there whenever the garment came to him. The long johns had been darned at the elbows and around the collar. These too she pressed to her nose until the smell of soap gave way to his smell, which still carried his infancy in it, vernal and subterranean. She pressed the wool into her cheek until the fibers bit her skin.

After she'd folded the woolens into the bottom of the trunk, she laid the rest of the tobacco leaves on top. Then she turned her attention to the books. Most were black and white fleckled journals. Irenie drew one from the pile and opened it. Columns and rows had been penciled across the page with a straight edge, each day of the week printed in block letters down the left side. Across the top were various personal hygiene chores: teeth brushed, face washed, hair combed, bath taken, all in Matthew's tiny controlled print. At the bottom of each table stretched her own spindly signature, followed by the schoolteacher's.

Irenie dropped her son's Bible into the new-planed crate and considered the quilts. Most had been pieced from scraps of sacking and dungarees. She shook out the Jacob's ladder and held it wide. At the same time her hand brushed one of the milk crates, and she heard the fall and the landing: a marbled composition book, pages down and straddling the floor. A pencil whittled to a point lay next to it. For some reason, she picked up the pencil first. Then she picked up the book by its spine and let the pages fall open. Matthew's tight handwriting filled the page.

"*. . . Or if Miss Hackett has never been married does that mean that she has never once laid down with a man? Or maybe she has and she's just not telling. Does God allow for people to go from birth to death without ever. . .*"

Irenie shut the book. She stared at the fleckled cover for a moment. Then she opened it at a different place.

*If Stomper and Fortune don't go to heaven, what happens to them? Do they just stop having thoughts? Nobody's inclined to tell you, or they just can't feature it, either one.*

Irenie shut the book, set it on the bed, and pressed it into the mattress with the heel of her hand, the way she might do if she was gluing something together.

But after a moment, she opened it again.

*I didn't want to give him Nelson. And Nelson didn't want to leave. A snake like that will cling heavy and tight on your arm. That's how they come to climb trees. That's how they come to be the king of snakes. The belly is smooth and dry, and you can feel the rows of muscles working. I didn't want to give him Nelson. But he says Let me see that snake, boy. And I told him how I'd caught him in the corncrib, hunting mice. And he said I had done well, that it took a fellow with fast reflexes to catch one that big. Then he says Let me see that snake again. So I give it to him. I have to. I unwind him, and Nelson clings tight as he can. He doesn't want to go. They don't like hanging in the air. You have to support them like that with one hand under their upper body and the other under their lower half. I was going to say that to him. You have to support it, Daddy. You have to hold it a certain way. But I didn't. I didn't say one thing. He took Nelson around the middle, with one hand, and Nelson didn't cotton to it. You can't treat a king that way. Bettern I had said that then. Or whenever he raised his arm up like he was throwing a baseball. Bettern I had said it then. Somehow I knew what he was going to do, but I didn't believe it either. I reckoned he would throw him. But he didn't. He made like he was going to, but when he brought his arm down, he didn't let go, and Nelson made a sound like snapping a whip. Or like a fish on a line when it slaps the surface of the water, flat and fleshed. And when Daddy handed him back, I took him. But it wasn't Nelson. It was a rope-carcass, heavy as meat. And he says, "That's how you kill a serpent, boy. The Lord cast him out, which is the devil and deceives the whole world." Bettern I said something to him then, but he reached out and put his hand on my head and let it stay there a long time, and I remember how it felt there, heavy but strong, as if he left it there to protect me. And when he took his hand away, I knew I wasn't mad at him anymore, only mad at myself.*

She flipped to another page.

*She doesn't agree. I can see it in her eyes. But she will never say so.*

Didn't agree with what?

*And it doesn't matter nohow. She always does whatever he wants.*

Always.

*I'll bet Uncle Les and Papaw would have a thing to say.*

Irenie closed the book.

Above the bed, a tight window gave out onto the spice garden, its edges bordered with the feathery leaves of Jerusalem artichokes. The air smelled of sage, dill, and mint. *She will never say so.* She will never say. The wind caught the sour musk of rue, and her gut curled in upon itself and heaved up. She leapt up and ran for the front door. As the wave crested, she stepped onto the porch, doubling forward to let the yellow fluid spout onto the floorboards.

She straightened, exhausted and surprised. Fortune had lifted her head from her paws to watch, ears pointing at the sky, a question in her eyes.

Irenie hadn't walked to the mountain since it happened. The thought of him waking to find her gone made her feather-legged with fear.

She touched the back of her head, where the base of the braid connected to her scalp. She felt again the back-snap of her neck, the tilt of the landscape. *The wife's body does not belong to her alone but also to her husband.* One flesh. The water in the branch had been snowmelt cold, hard as a slap.

She set herself down on the step to think. *She will never say so. She will never say.* She wouldn't, it was true, and somehow Matthew had known it though she could not. *I can see it in her eyes.* The woman she saw from her son's outlook was a version of herself that didn't square with the girl she'd been. It was a version of herself she didn't want to claim.

Low flat clouds masked the sky. The weather would come in the afternoon, and the tobacco would drink it up. And if she did the same she'd always done, she and Brodis would stake it, and dry it, and take it to market. The days without Matthew stretched before her, one lined up after the other, long suppers in which she and Brodis sat at table with only the ghost of the little girl.

If she did the same she'd always done.

It was the beginning she couldn't get past, the exit that would move her from this to that. You needed clothes. Start with that.

Under their bed: the cardboard suitcase she'd brought the day they married.

Now she opened it face down on the floor and beat the sides with the palm of her hand until a shower of dust and particles ticked upon the floor. When she flipped it, the cardboard scratched against the grains of dirt and sand. Inside went her Sunday dress and two pairs of pantaloons, the green felt hat with the flower at the side, the lace-up boots with the little heels.

One of these nights she would take up her walkings again, and when she did, she would hide the suitcase on the mountain in the cave with everything else that was hers alone.

The sound of the middle piano keys swam atop the bass notes, rising into a swale, then a hill, then a ridge that ran on and on and on.

When the demon returned, she would be ready.

CHAPTER TWELVE

BRODIS DIDN'T WANT THE CEREMONY TO WAIT. HIS wife had been as a lost sheep, having gone from mountain to hill and forgotten her resting place. A baptism was the only service that might could bring her back, especially one that was performed in the thick crowd of a summer afternoon. It was bound to summon the Spirit, bound to make people yearn for the moment they too became His blood-bought children, their purest selves. The following Sunday the numbers in the pews would surge, and his wife's thoughts might cease to wandering.

The deacon was the one who'd told him. Coming out of the chamber of commerce meeting and what did Haver see but the wife of Brodis Lambey sitting next to the lady from the extension office and both of them hazy-white through a set of lace curtains. He'd not have noticed he said if the music hadn't been pouring out the window, one of them playing on the piano, he couldn't say which, and him wondering was it possible for a woman like Irenie Lambey to grow cold on the precepts of the Lord?

And Haver didn't even know about the night wanderings.

But Brodis did. He also knew the devil was diligent. Same as God, he searched out the best, hand-picked the purest, the meekest, the faithfullest, then made it his business to find the thing that tempted each. It could be a simple thing, as simple as a manmade piano. It had worked for Nebuchadnezzar. A few stringed instruments, and the people fell down before the golden image and went right off to blaspheming the Lord.

Now the water spooled around a wide sandbar where the creek bent and the earth leveled. The cool air fogged, and the rhododendron leaned in so thick and tangled it was like a shut-up room. Two dozen believers crowded onto the sandbar.

Except today the sandbar was partly underwater. There'd been weather, and the creek had opened and overrun the peninsula so that the beach was nothing but a narrow strip. The channel hurled through the low spread heath, the water claiming the pink petals and bearing them fast downstream. It was no surprise that Haver'd wanted to wait. Wait until it was enough room for both the congregants and the curious, he said. But Brodis had countered him. The moment was now. He could feel it. The clearing pulsed with energy, the creek promised to rinse their collective sins, and the pocket pool was bigger than ever, wide and welcoming enough to purify a whole church. In the end Brodis had got his way because of Andy Ensley. It had taken the boy an enduring long time to come to grace, and the sooner the baptism took place, the better, and what if the devil were to claim his soul before the creek dropped?

Now Brodis squinted into a slice of sunlight that broke through the heath. He felt definite. The Lord hadn't spoken to him exactly—but he felt a certainty that was dense and wooded and ominous. Night was galloping toward them. Not this night, this singular June night that would creep up gentle and embrace the congregation as they spread from the creekside on their way home. Not that. But the evening of time. People figured themselves to have all creation to change their minds. But time was rolling faster, twice, three times as fast as it ever had before. The trees had come down. The logging companies were closing. Champion Fibre had turned to paper making and nothing but. Swaths of forest had disappeared or burned. The streams were brown with silt. The chestnut had fallen and the speckled trout were hard to find anymore. The Rickersons and the Thompsons and the Paints had gotten rid of their sheep and their pigs too. They used store-bought cloth and store-bought meat. Girls Matthew's age had no notion of weaving nor carding nor spinning linsey. They bought dungarees and cloth coats from the general store or the paper catalogs, and magazines showed tables with gleaming dishes and white tablecloths. People had brought-on appliances in their homes, but they'd all at once become poor when they'd never been before. And the state lawed that every child had to attend the public school, never mind that each year they had fewer people to come to church. The government didn't law attendance there. And the wife of Brodis Lambey, the uprightest woman in the county, had wandered from the Lord.

Night after night he lay waiting for her to stray. But she slept a lamb's sleep, curled toward the wall, the buttons of her spine against his chest. During the day, her mind seemed bewitched by the notion of a different life. He had some knowing of what that was, and how the devil put conjectures in your head that made you dissatisfied with a life that was full and rich. But he'd learned to resist it. It was two miles to the closest neighbor, three miles by road. How far could a woman stumble in the shadows? People didn't travel at night, unless they were blockaders cooking mash, or, in another time, witches who'd promised themselves to the dark. Old swampers told a hundred winter tales whenever the poteen flowed and the wood stove was the only warm place in camp. Young women were supposed to have cut their skin and their toenails and hanks of hair and roasted them in coal scuttles over the tops of mountains at midnight. They were supposed to have sworn against God until the devil appeared and proffered his deal. Old women were said to have left their bodies and inhabited the forms of deer, or put spells on men by looking in their eyes, or made neighbors to take sick, or rifles to go awry, or cows to dry up, or wells.

But that was another time. Even then the only reason you'd listened to the stories was because they seemed more real than the ones about the men that had drowned in the April drive or lost their hands to the chipping ax or been crushed during offloading. Old people invented stories. It was easier than admitting a fellow's rifle missed because he'd lost his skill, or that a body took sick by the will of the Lord. There were no more witches. If ever there had been.

And the swampers were half the time wrong about anything that came out of their mouths anyway. In the days of the first settlers it was the old men who'd taken it into their heads to swarm a house in the middle of the night, drunk on superstition and fear and power, a dozen faces flickering in the torchlight and clamoring for proof. They'd shouted about a woman who walked in the night, or said they'd heard tell of a coal scuttle and a hank of hair. But Brodis wouldn't have been afraid to lift the shotgun from its pegs. He wouldn't have been afraid to shield his wife from the mob with the broadness of his body. Then, right there, he'd raise his hand and witness to his wife's faithful devotion to the Lord. The old men at the door would have to lower their rifles, and the crowd would soften and commence to peeling away.

Afterwards, Irenie would be grateful and come to him meekly. The inside of her thighs were pale like the moon, pliant, murmur-fleshed.

Now the congregants watched from the narrow bank of the creek, lined up in their white dresses and white shirts, and further back, the sinners and the curious and the passersby in street clothes, some of them already pushing forward to get a better view.

Irenie stood at the end of the row in a plain cotton gown, the first thing she'd sewn the year they bought the Singer, her back curled over the new machine, her copper braid falling to one side of her spine like a live thing, her thigh tensing against her skirt as her foot worked the pedals. Now she held the Bible before her, the ball of her hair tight and proper, but below it the perch of her jaw, and the place where the blood pulsed, and the line of her breasts against the white. Her eyes came to meet his, and in them was something he hadn't seen in months, the message that she trusted the ritual to him.

Brodis raised the Bible in his hands, and the murmurs of the crowd broke and trailed. He called Andy forth. The boy was broad-shouldered and thick in the neck, the meat of his arms twice as wide as Brodis's, but his face smooth and his cheek pink as a girl's. He'd been living at the foot of the Cross for three years, and he'd finally come to grace last week, at his father's burying, sinking to the earth as if smitten.

His father had died a sinner. He hadn't lived to see the boy's salvation. Andy would be thinking of that now. Brodis gripped the young man's shoulder, and the muscle there was like the haunch of a mule. He squeezed and told the boy to relax. Then he addressed the crowd. "Ladies and gentlemen, a baptism is two symbols at the same time. A symbol of death and a symbol of rebirth."

Irenie had raised her head and her gaze to him. Her eyes were the eyes of the group. They conferred power. They enlarged. He opened the Bible to read but didn't need to see the words in front of him. "Jesus came from Galilee to Jordan unto John, to be baptized of him. . . ."

Andy Ensley fidgeted with his shirt, tucking it further into his dungarees. Brodis took the boy's hand. He squeezed it and raised it in the air. "John baptized in the wilderness." The boy's thick fingers quivered.

Slowly, Brodis wheeled himself and the boy around to face the creek. They stepped into the water that was brown with flooding, and the cold blasted through the fabric of his britches. The sandbar extended a long shelf into the water, and he led Andy Ensley across it. The chill rose to his shins and then his knees. He wore the same woolen pants he'd worn during his timber days, but the cold insinuated itself into his long johns until the hairs on his legs stood on end and his genitals and his sense of charity retracted to his very core. But Andy's hand was slippery with sweat. The water reached Brodis' belt. He turned back to the crowd and splayed his feet wide for stability.

Andy's pants had blackened to the waist, his shirt dry and blousoning in the breeze. His pink cheeks had turned white. Brodis drew the boy closer, put his hand at the top of his back, and said low enough that only he could hear, "Relax, son." Andy smiled, and his teeth were wide-spaced like the pickets in a fence, but the muscles at the back of his neck were as taut as chain dogs. Haver Brooks had followed them into the creek and stood thigh deep. Brodis edged further into the current so Andy wouldn't have to, keeping most of his weight on the downstream side, the way he'd learned to do when forging into a river to set a charge. A rock under him wobbled, and he slid his foot along the bottom until the water pushed the side of it into a sloped stone and he knew his position to be solid. Andy's whole body trembled now, and Brodis spoke again to him alone. "When I tell you, you're gonna bend your knees and fall back easy. I'll be holding you up and keeping the water from your nose. Now, I'm gonna ask you to relax and fold your arms across your chest."

Andy folded his arms across his chest.

Brodis faced the boy, but turned his voice to the crowd. "And Jesus, whenever he was baptized, went up straightway from the water: and, lo, the heavens were opened unto him, and he saw the Spirit of God descending like a dove."

Brodis put one hand on Andy's shoulder and raised the other. His voice boomed over the rushing water. "Do you promise to renounce evil?"

"Yes." Andy's answer was thin and fast, his voice higher than it ought to have been.

"To follow and trust God?"

"Yes."

Brodis turned to the bank. "Do you all of you promise to help Andy on this path?"

"We will," the congregation answered back. Behind them, the onlookers pushed forward, women toting babies and men smoking cigarettes and a boy hauling a live chicken under his arm. Brodis felt the weight of dozens of pairs of eyes, belief-full, expectant with the knowing that he was the person with the burden of bringing Andy to the Lord.

Brodis's voice boomed over the water. "I baptize thee in the name of the Father, the Son, and the Holy Spirit!"

To Andy he said, "Here we go, son. Relax. I'm gonna pinch your nose some, and then you let yourself fall back. I got you and the Lord's got both of us." Brodis placed a firm hand against the boy's withers and went to lowering him. The back of Andy's head touched the water, and his dark hair haloed around his face.

Brodis wasn't sure how it happened, but the next moment Andy had unfolded his arms and clinched his shoulders, then his neck, and in that moment some part of Brodis's spine seemed to pop, and he buckled toward the boy. In an instant his downstream foot had lost its purchase, and both legs were cycling to find a grip on the floor of the creek. The rocks kicked away from his whipping feet, and his lower half was pulled away. When his head went under, he resisted the gasp and kept his mouth closed. Andy's wide-eyed face washed toward him in a blur of brown and white. A flurry of bubbles ascended from his nose, and Brodis realized that the boy's hands were still clenched around his neck. Andy's eyes pleaded, but Brodis couldn't lift his head but so much.

Then the bubbles were no longer coming out of the boy's nose, and the hands on Brodis's neck loosed. He gave the youth a mighty shove and was free, but the creek washed brown around him, and the rocks flew past. He kicked to the surface, but even as he did, he saw the mistake. The water had swept him into the main channel. He swanned his arms and brought his face up fair to the surface, but the current curved against the bank and into the gnarl of rhododendron. He clawed at the sprangled branches, his eyes fixed on the light of the sky, but the water pulled his legs away, and something caught in his—

Against his will, his windpipes opened, and the cold scalded the inside of his body in a place it was never meant to be. The sunlight dappled on the surface, yellow and green and diamond-shaped, and Brodis closed his eyes. Jesus. He willed the white light and the image of his Lord to come to him.

But the picture fell away to someplace in his past. Instead he saw his wife's face, the copper-colored freckles and the silvery lashes. Then that face too was replaced, this time with something naked and twisted and unloved. A terrible nothingness stretched before him. You had better be thinking of grace. Whosoever believeth in Him shall not perish, but have eternal life. Whosoever.

But that wasn't how it was going to be, was it?

Then there was a voice, and hands under his armpits, pulling, yanking, the shouting of instructions, a tree limb giving way, and he was able to move. Someone pulled at the front of his shirt, and Brodis knew himself to be in the creek, Haver Brooks' sweaty face as big as day in front of his own. Haver had him by the upper arms like a dance partner, and Brodis choked up a mouthful of creek water that ran down the front of the man's Sunday jacket. He gasped and kept hold of Haver's arms even though it registered that the expression on the deacon's face wasn't wide-eyed terror but something closer to amusement. Brodis coughed up more water. He made to control his own features but couldn't leave off slumping over Haver. On instinct, his eyes looked for his wife. But there was no one there because he and Andy had been swept around the bend. He remembered the animal grip around his neck.

"Andy?" His voice didn't obey, but Haver seemed to understand. "Back on the bank."

Ahead, William Hogsed struggled through the heath, and Haver told him not to bother, that no one had come to harm.

Brodis rearranged his features to make it so, brushed the spittle from his face, and picked his way behind Haver back to the sandbar.

The congregation wasn't especially surprised or relieved to see him. They were none of them alarmed, two dozen people whose faith had buoyed them enough to conquer their fear of drowning. Many had already got shed of their hats and shoes in hope of being reborn, some of them for the third or fourth time. They had come to take part in the sacrament, and they were patient because they believed.

They couldn't all be wrong.

Andy Ensley was sitting on the bank looking dazed. Brodis tested his voice, then did his best to raise up a shout. "Then Peter said unto them, repent, and be baptized every one of you." His voice cracked. "And ye shall receive the gift of the Holy Ghost."

And then, despite everything, the people on the banks commenced to walking into the water, in ones and twos, spirit-led, holding hands and singing "Breathe on Me Breath of God."

Brodis let the water lap around his shins, but didn't venture further. In the moment of death, the face he had seen had been Irenie's, not Christ's.

He'd chosen his wife over his God.

And that was how the devil got in. Because when it came to the Lord, it was all or nothing.

## CHAPTER THIRTEEN

TRY AS SHE MIGHT TO IGNORE IT, IRENIE WAS REMINDED every time she went to the privy. Her course was late. It had been four weeks since the demon, and Brodis hadn't touched her since.

She knew what she knew. Matthew had been born too soon, Hannah sooner still, a child the size of a kitten. Already fourteen years had come and gone since Brodis had held her in the palm of his hand, her skull a red throb against the dark hair of his wrist. Where there ought to have been a nose there were two holes, and Aunt Annie had said just you wait. So they did, and that winter the wind came through the knotholes, the house cracked and popped, and the tiny girl choked on the cold. Brodis cut planks to lay across the ceiling joists and hold the heat, lifting and sawing until late in the night, the dust floating down in drifts. Sometime in there he also killed the cats for fear they'd suck away the baby's breath, but Hannah closed her eyes and her fists and wasn't yet ready to embrace the shadows she'd been born to. The cough started the second month, a dry *tschack* that filled the house and echoed up the hollow. Irenie and Brodis spent nights walking her in circles, but she coughed as if she were trying to expel the whole wide world. And she didn't grow.

And then one morning while Irenie wore a path around the kitchen with the child against her shoulder, she heard the pounding of a soft fist inside the bedroom, *ka-whump*, and she figured, no, it couldn't be, not when the snow laid five inches thick on the ground and all the birds had flown. But when she stepped into the room, there it was, a cardinal red as a flag, alight on the edge of the chest of drawers, now taking flight and throwing itself against the inside of the glass. *Ka-whump*. Hannah coughed against her collar. The bird collapsed onto its side and its wings fluttered in spasms but in a moment it was on its feet, in a moment flying. *Ka-whump, ka-whump*, a knock of dread certainty.

Irenie fled to the back entrance, opened the latch, and kicked the door wide. White cold poured into the house, and for the first time in weeks the bed and the bureau were plain to the eye, and then a furious blur of color flapped past her ear and into the yard, and lit, just there in the snow by the woodshed, a drop of red.

That night Hannah's coughing stopped. And maybe it was the silence that woke her, the kind of stillness that came only under a blanket of fresh flakes, whenever the wind had died and the birds had left and the humans in the little structure kept to themselves to wait. It was on a morning such as this that Hannah stopped coughing.

They'd had to wait to bury her, on account of the blanketing snow and the sky thick as cream, and Brodis building a fire in the yard before he set off to do the milking and returning with a series of ropes sheet-bended all the way back to the barn and a coffin no bigger than a shoe. Irenie lined the box with yellow gingham and rubbed oil on the tiny limbs and draped a scrap of camphored cotton on the walnut-sized face. The tissue eyelids wouldn't stay closed, but there was no coin small enough to hold them. On the third day, when the snow continued to fall, Brodis tied the shoebox to a rafter over the front porch. On the fourth day, when the snow stopped, they buried her on top of the ridge with four generations of Raines. The wind turned greedy then and raced over the mountain with a meanness that snatched the hats from the heads of the mourners and lifted their coats and slapped the hair into their eyes. The new-spaded earth was red and wet and heavy, too cold to leave a baby in, even one that had died these four days hence.

Or maybe it was four years, Irenie couldn't remember.

And Clary Hedrick said to Florence Rickerson there'd been three children to die that winter and didn't death always come in threes and maybe now this one would be the last. Irenie put on not to hear. The red earth and white snow covered Hannah, and the next day Irenie's breasts wept and she bled into the cotton pantaloons. And the next year Matthew was born, healthy in every way Hannah was not. After that, her courses came every month, no matter how often Brodis reached for her in the night. They had no more babies to be born even though she'd spent whole afternoons conjuring the picture of another little girl. Matthew was two, and then he was six, and then he was eleven. And somewhere in there she stopped dreaming of dresses and plaited hair. You took the dream for granted for so long that the knowledge you didn't want it anymore dawned as a surprise, and then a relief, and you understood why, come time for bed, you'd buttoned the nightdress to the neck and stared into the blackness hoping and not hoping for his breath that smelled like tree bark and his hands as taut as rope. And after you understood yourself in that way, you ended each day bidding God not to bring you another child, not now, whenever your oldest was swinging up into the saddle on his own and training the dogs so thoroughly they followed him from barn to gate to house. Not now, after you'd packed his bag for school and then, in secret, packed one of your own.

And especially not like this.

Irenie tried to feature the little girl from her long-ago daydreams, the one with the springing curls and the white dresses and her skin flushed pink and white, but the one she visioned in place of her was the kitten-sized infant with the blood pushing up against her skin and her hair thin as smoke against her scalp, too small to hold out against the storms and the wind that pushed up from Georgia, too delicate for the cow that kicked and the wagon that rolled and the creek that drowned, too weak for the rains that froze and the ice that cracked under feet. The little girl's head against the linen was the color of wild strawberry, and she slept on. She slept on even when the threats became more personal, when the sullen weight of evenings pressed upon her, and the afternoons in the root cellar, and the memorization of Bible passages, and most of all the hope her parents hoped that she could live her own life while at the same time saving theirs. All of it squeezed upon her, and the thousand expectations of a father's zeal and a mother's grudge and the eighteen plodding years it would take before the child could escape them. The little girl slept on, and only Irenie saw the oncoming weight of resentment poised to crush her.

But then the eyes opened and they were pierce-blue as her father's, and certain sure, and the child was a man with a face like scripture.

Listen. A man shall cleave to his wife, and they shall become one flesh.

Listen. Eve shall be ruled by her husband and in sorrow bear children. She shall spend her life disappearing, and the blue flame shall sputter and shrink into its own self for years to come.

There were some things that called for a decision whose sly form left you crippled or changed from now to forever, one. If worse came to worst, there was the recipe. She hadn't laid her eyes on it in years, but she remembered the look of it, her mother's blue self-conscious script, the ink blurred, probably from the way she'd pressed the paper into the palm of Irenie's hand. "Just that there may come a time when you want to space out the births." Her mother's eyes settled on hers. "You don't have to be like Vina Jones." Mrs. Jones had birthed a child every year for seventeen years running. There'd been three to die still in diddies. One had been thrown from a saddle horse, one had set the smokehouse and himself afire, and one had drowned in the well. Four had left home at puberty to look for work. One had died in the war overseas. And Vina was surrounded yet by infants and shirt-tail boys, forever hunched over the stove or laundry cauldron, forever beating dirty clothes on the battling bench.

Irenie had unfolded the page the way you did a letter. Her mother smoothed a piece of her daughter's hair that didn't need smoothing and pressed her collar flat, and Irenie knew then that the page wasn't just the ingredients for apple cake.

On Sunday morning she wrapped two ham biscuits, a boiled egg, and a baked potato in a piece of newspaper and folded the package into her husband's saddle pocket. She hugged a cardigan around her waist while he slipped the check-rein over the saddle horn and swung his long leg over the side of the animal. Then he spurred the horse, and the beast and its rider trotted up the side of the hollow. Irenie watched her husband's broad back, and the lightness in her mood surprised her.

After breakfast, she found the one chair they owned that didn't have a caned seat. Matthew had built it as a child, Brodis guiding his hand to push the saw and bring the hammer down true on the nail. But the green paint had been Matthew's doing, and Irenie had made so much of its being the only colored furniture in the house that he'd offered to paint the rest. The chair was blocky and heavy, and she had to drag it across the kitchen floor next to the drain board. When she stood on the seat, she tipped forward onto her toes to reach the top shelf. Her hand brushed through a layer of dust, and her fingertips touched the cardboard box, but she wasn't tall enough. Matthew appeared in the doorway of his bedroom, in his arms a box of trash. He was cleaning out his room. He'd been carting loads from his bedroom to burn in the clearing.

"Matthew?"

"Mama?" He stopped and looked up at her through his white-blond hair, the same color it had been when he was a baby. And now he was so tall and so thin. Two marbled composition books peeked up from the contents in the box. She wondered if one was the diary. Or maybe it had already been burned. It wasn't her place to ask.

She stepped down from the chair. "Can you reach away up there and bring me down that cardboard box?"

Matthew set his own box down and climbed atop the chair. He scanned the shelf. "Which?"

"The flat one. The boot box."

Above her, the sound of heavy objects sliding across the pine shelving. The air clouded with dust. Then the movement stopped and there was a beat of silence. "Hot Dang!"

Even as the words, "Watch your mouth, young man," came from her lips, she happened to think what the hot dang was for.

"Do you know about this?" Matthew brought forth a twenty-four ounce mason jar and held it at her eye level. The jar was filled to the top with paper money.

"Leave that be. It's your father's."

"But... how?" His eyes jumped from the jar to her and back.

"The money he gets working the sorting booms in the spring."

His eyebrows shot up in appreciation. "My father is *rich*."

"Your father is no such thing. That's not as much money as it looks."

Matthew shook the jar. "How much is it? Can we *count* it?" The idea lit up his features.

Irenie put her knuckles on her hips. "No, we cannot."

Matthew's face fell. "Why not?"

"Because. There's no good to come from it. The more you count your money, the more it waits to leap on your mind whenever you're not expecting."

Matthew set the jar back on the shelf but couldn't resist another long look. "I just wanna know."

"You see? You've only seen it this once, and it's already got you by the neck. Now hand me down that box."

The cardboard scraped across the shelf, and tiny particles dusted the drain board. The box floated into view, tipping forward and back, a few papers and cards sliding out and onto the floor. Perhaps she was too quick to take it in both hands, perhaps too forceful to insert herself between the contents and her son. But he was still beguiled by the money. He gave the jar a shake. "I bet it's more money than Uncle Les and Papaw have." Then he set the money back on the shelf and stepped down from the chair with regret. "You'd never even know it," he mumbled as he made his way back to his chores. He didn't seem to mark the cardboard box at all.

Inside were hundreds of yellowed notes and recipes, some torn from larger pieces, some written on the backs of notices or letters. Irenie looked at each and set it on the table until she came to the one titled "Indian Tea." Under the title was written, "For regulation of monthly courses." Irenie smoothed the page flat.

The first ingredient was pennyroyal. The springy bush grew calf-high at the front gate, the long-toothed leaves filled with a pungent oil she'd sometimes used to keep away insects. Technically, it was the only ingredient in the recipe that was poison. The Cherokee called it squaw mint, and it had never occurred to her to wonder how come. Now she reckoned she knew.

In the afternoon she set off for the other ingredients. Her father's orchards wrapped across the top of the mountain, and the path wingled around the ribs of it. Below, the wood was grown up in hemlock and tulip tree, the floor thick with needle and leaf scurf. The pods of the redbuds drooped like sickles, and mushrooms pale as toes sprouted at the roots. A warbler called *dee dah doo doo day*, and it was the call of a person searching for something gone missing.

If it happened just right, she might be able to get the brewer's yeast from Lesley. It might be she'd see his truck on the drover's road. The sawmill would be closed for the Sabbath, and her cousin was just as liable to use the day for his other business interests.

Meanwhile the snakeroot. She'd seen the white bottlebrush flowers on the southern slope of the mountain. The shrubs were there yet, airy-looking and tall as her hip, the leaves dark-shined and deep-toothed. The plants came up easily, giving up their home in the cool earth with surprising good will. She cut the stems at the base and laid the roots in the flour sack.

After that the trail descended into the watershed, where the laurel grew in tangles and littered the fern fronds with pink-cupped blossoms. A footlog spanned the creek. Below, mayflies swarmed and Jesus bugs walked the surface. In the water, the trout hung motionless, until they didn't, and then their flanks rippled and winked.

But there was something else, something in the odor of leaf mold and moist root that didn't belong, a thread of a smell that drifted down from the headwaters. It was the corn-sour smell of mash. Maybe that's where Lesley was, stooped over his cook fire, stirring or mixing or whatever he did, and even though she pictured him that way, she couldn't make her mind's imaginings real. And she didn't dare go up there.

Instead she turned and followed the creek downhill. The squaw-root would grow in the cove, where the soil was rich and moist and the farming easy, close to ramps and Solomon seal and dog-hobble. She'd once seen the dead-white columns near the Pruitt home-place, in the shadow of a hickory tree. It might could be there yet.

A joree bird sang *Der-ink! Der-ink! Drink yer teeeeaa!* But then it wasn't the sound of a joree bird at all, but rather a sound *like* a joree bird—an imitation in fact. She didn't consider that she might be the cause of the signal until she heard the bolt of a rifle slide to. She stopped, but not before the thought crossed her mind: this is why Brodis doesn't want you going out alone.

Against a tulip tree sat a man with his arms resting on a gun that in turn rested on his knees, his face obscured by a brimmed hat, a cigarette in his lips. Only then did she see that in the shadow stood a second slimmer figure, his weight on one leg, his pelvis slung forward, a fellow who was easy in his skin and in the fitted vest he wore. Even in the woods, he hung a jacket over his shoulder with the crook of his index finger. She knew the tilt of that hat and the slope of those shoulders. His voice was low, almost a whisper. "*Irenieee.*" It was the same greeting as ever, the call from her growing up, the one that came from the set-along child who got stuck in the hay pile, or from the little boy who wanted to be taken swimming, or the ten-year-old who climbed into a walnut tree and pelted her with green-hulled nuts, or the twelve-year-old who was made to stay after school and scrub down the desks with soap and water. Now the little boy who'd grown into a man motioned her forward.

"Les..."

He held a finger to his lips. His hair was oiled with some prod-
uct that smelled of perfume, and his shirt and his smile were white.
He was a fellow who paid attention to impressions. Whenever you
spied him in town, he was surrounded by a small crowd, the men
easy and self-satisfied in his presence because they'd drunk his whiskey before and counted on doing so again. When he spoke in his
honey-drawled voice, his jokes turned in upon his own weaknesses,
and people laughed aloud. Girls and women touched the pins in
their hair or the buttons at their throats and forgot that at twenty-five he was still a runaround youth.

She stepped next to him, where the roots of a hemlock en-
twined around a granite outcropping. He pointed down the hill.
"Look," he announced. Way below on the drover's road, a truck
chugged up the hill. "From here I can spy anything that comes up
this mountain." Even now he gave the impression that he could
hardly keep the lid on the wild laughter that threatened to boil up
from inside him.

"You didn't see me."

"The hell I didn't." His tone was light, teasey, but he kept his eye
on the road below him. "Besides, I don't believe you came up the
hill."

It was true. The only people who might come around the mountain were those who came from her father's place or Brodis's. "Les,
I can't believe you haven't quit this yet."

He looked up into the branches of the hemlock tree and gave
an exaggerated sigh. "You're not gonna get *sanc*-tified on me, are
you, cousin?"

Irenie glanced at the other man, who was watching their conversation with curiosity. "I haven't seen a thing in the world to get
sanctified about. And I don't plan to."

Les adjusted his necktie. "Keep sneaking up on people in the
woods."

"In point of fact, I was hoping I'd see you."

He glanced at her and then back toward the road. "Do tell."

"I was hoping to get your help."

For the first time, her cousin stopped watching the road and looked only at her. "You were hoping to get *my* help? Is it you who's doing the asking or that fine upstanding husband you got?"

"Me."

"Because I'm not inclined to help old Brodis out at this moment." He returned his attention to the strand of gravel below him.

Irenie looked down the hill too. Mayapples spread their leaves like umbrellas, their white flowers tucked up beneath. None had been trampled by the passage of human feet. "It's me, Lesley, and I would appreciate you kept the request to yourself."

Now the laughter buried in his expression simmered to the surface and spilled out into the quiet morning. "Stump whiskey? You?"

"Don't act crazy, Les. He hasn't changed his mind about that and neither—"

Her cousin's face soured. "Is it money? Don't even tell me he sent you here to—"

"Where do you get your whiskey yeast?"

Lesley tilted his head. "Waynesville—if you're up for the trip." He was looking at her queer. "But you can use just about any yeast."

"What's the difference?"

"It depends what you're brewing." He tilted his head. "What *are* you brewing?"

"Not what you think."

"I just wanna know for…let's call it pro*fess*ional curiosity." His eyes creased into a smile. "That and I don't like the idea of competition from the family proper."

"It's for tea."

Lesley raised his eyebrows overmuch and cinched in one corner of his mouth. "You're using it…for…*tea?*"

"Medicinal."

The expression that softened his face was either disappointment or relief, she wasn't sure. "Right. But listen, I don't have it now. I'll bring it by tomorrow or, say…" He glanced at her. "Where's Brodis?"

"Across the river, fellowshipping all day."

"Right. I'll bring it by today."

★

It was late afternoon before Irenie had dried the leaves and crushed the roots. The pennyroyal she'd plucked and spread in a shallow pan, then set to curing in the cooling oven. The squawroot was more of a chore, a knotted mass of yellow-brown fibers, with tubers the size and length of her fingers. She set the cleaver against the knobby surface and leaned, but the blade skidded away and sliced into the wooden countertop. The second time she set the knife between two bulbous knuckles and leaned again. Nothing happened. Then, all at once the plant gave, and the blade sliced through. The inside of the root was pale and hard. She crushed the tubers with a pestle and was setting the mash in the sun to dry when Scram and Stomper and Lacey started up.

Moments later a truck rumbled up the drive. Irenie slipped the paper into her pocket and stepped into the yard, wiping her hands on her apron and trying to peer over the tobacco. But the plants had sprung up to a forest, the spindly tops waving above her head, the bottom leaves already beginning to yellow and curl.

On the other side of the field, the engine cut. A steel door slammed. The dogs stopped barking. Lesley.

Before she'd made it halfway through the tobacco, a long whistle slit the air, then another. Matthew's voice curled up into a question.

When she reached the drive both Lesley and Matthew had their pinkie fingers in their mouths, Lesley looking sideways at Matthew and speaking past them. "Like *dis*."

Matthew moved his fingers in imitation.

"You haf to curl your tongue. Like dis." Her cousin made a show of peering deep into Matthew's mouth. "Den you blow. Like dis." Another whistle sliced through the heat.

The dog Fortune sat down in the dust and looked up in consternation. Scram fled.

Matthew took a great inhalation of air and blew through his fingers. A wheezing sound came out.

Lesley peered into the boy's mouth again. "Like dis." He held the sides of his pinkie fingers parallel to one another.

Matthew mimicked the action.

Both boys brought their fingers to their mouths at the same time and took deep breaths, but Lesley didn't exhale. Instead he watched Matthew blow into his hands. No sound came. Her son removed his fingers and stared at them as if they'd betrayed him.

"For the love of *Pete!*" Lesley exclaimed in alarm so exaggerated it mocked itself. "Hold on, genius." He maneuvered his hands around Matthew's until he had them in the position he wanted. "*Now* blow."

A low-throated whistle breathed out, and Matthew smiled with all his teeth while Lesley threw back his head and laughed into the sky.

Irenie couldn't help but laugh too. "You're pretty pleased with yourself."

Lesley turned, his face still creased with the pleasure of his teaching. He swept the hat from his head and bowed. "As always, Irenie, as always."

"You're quicker here than I would have thought," she said, even though the sun was already sagging over the ridge.

He set his hat back on his head. "Man who doesn't go to church got all kind of free time." Then he reached into his pocket. "Here is your elixir, madam." Between his thumb and index finger was a short squat jar filled with white powder.

Irenie slipped the yeast into her apron without looking at it. She saw that her cousin was watching her and she was suddenly shy. "Thank you, Lesley."

"Just don't get carried away with your... *tea*." He clamped his hand on Matthew's shoulder, even though the boy was taller than him and still blowing through his fingers, trying to reproduce that first low tone. "For some reason the boy genius can't get out a whistle."

Irenie watched her son make several more attempts. "He'll get it if he has a mind to."

Lesley looked at the sky. "And if he don't, well, that'll leave me cause to come over here again." The sun was sitting on the ridge now. "Ain't no good staying here right now."

"You've been a help to me."

Instead of answering, Lesley grabbed Matthew around the

shoulders and tucked the boy's head between his arm and his torso until Matthew said "uncle" and Lesley crooned, "Uncle Who?"

"Uncle Les," Matthew panted.

Lesley let go. "Best figure out this whistling business before you get down to that fancy school. You'll be representing five generations of Raineses there, and one of them happens to be me."

Matthew nodded slowly, as if considering this information for the first time.

Then Lesley opened the door of the automobile, slid into the driver's seat, and handed Matthew the steel lever. "Wind it up, man." The boy fit the device into the socket and gave it a good crank, and the engine caught and sputtered up steady. Lesley reached out the window and took the lever back. He stuck his head out. "Give me a whistle, genius."

Matthew put his fingers to this mouth, but no sound came.

Lesley shook his head in mock disgust and waved and gunned the engine forward until the dust blew up and the car charged hot up the drive.

When the sound of the engine faded, Matthew said, "How come you didn't invite him to supper?"

Irenie considered before she answered. He was thirteen, old enough. "Your father wouldn't like it."

But the boy was unsurprised. "Daddy wouldn't like him being here at all." This time it wasn't a question.

"I expect that's true." She didn't think it was right to ask him to keep the secret, but she knew he would.


After clearing the dishes, she boiled the dried root until the water was the color of river mud. She opened a canning jar and dropped in the mint, now brittle, where the leaves lay like captive brown beetles. Then she poured the boiling root water into the jar and let it set. After a time, the water was an elemental brown. Irenie measured a level spoon of whiskey yeast and tipped it in. In the darkness the glass was opaque. She shook it, and black particles swam into the primitive brown. When she unscrewed the lid, the smell of brittle leaves and dried up creeks leaked from the opening. She poured the murk into a glass. The recipe didn't say how much a serving was, only at the bottom of the page, in capital letters: "DO NOT DRINK FOR MORE THAN TEN DAYS." Irenie held her breath, tipped the glass, and swallowed.

She drank the tea every four hours, that day and the next and the next, rising in the night to pour it. The fourth day, she plucked the early-yellowed leaves from the towers of tobacco. Bend, stand, walk five steps. Bend, stand, walk five steps. The third time she bent, the ground turned slyly away. She reached to steady herself, and leaned into a pillar of green. The plant gave way, and the stalk broke with a sickening snap.

That evening she drank more tea. But her monthly course didn't commence.

On the sixth day the ends of her fingertips went numb, as if she'd been picking peas on a frosty morning.

She drank the tea straight through the final hoeing of the corn and the planting of half runner beans, when the signs were in Virgo, up through the first tassels on the sourwoods, when the bees congregated to the trees' yellow-willowed fingers.

Her course didn't start. The days of her life with Brodis stretched before her. She was joined to him and always would be. A man shall cleave to his wife and they shall become one flesh. There was again the grab at her back, the sudden snap of her neck, the fust of the stranger's midnight breath, the clenched hands. The twain shall become one flesh.

The nights multiplied and pooled like oil.

The ninth day passed and there was no blood. She gathered more roots. She drank more tea. She drank it through the planting of cabbage and the tassling of the corn, when the yellow squash and zucchini grew fair size in the garden, and the beets cracked the furrows with their growing.

And then it was Matthew's last day, and the boy spent the afternoon sitting by Fortune's side with his elbows on his knees, his eyes staring into the corn and his lips moving serious and steady, as if giving the dog advice or telling her a story either one. In the evening he wrestled with Stomper and Scram. Lacy sat under the porch and sulked.

The next morning, Matthew and Brodis closed up the pine trunk and tussled it up to the road for loading in Bill Raines' truck. Hard green balls hung on the walnut trees, and young fruit on the pear and apple trees. The half runner beans had shot up bright green tendrils that twined around the cornstalks.

The sound of the truck chugged across the valley first, a slow and lonely drone that could have been the first cicadas of the day but she knew was not. Already the air swam with heat, and her limbs seemed to flail at the earth to find a place to set themselves. Her toes were numb. The loudness stopped at the gate, then resumed its climb around the valley. After that came the dust, a cloud that climbed over the tree line. The truck came last, with the sun reflecting off the windscreen, where an elbow draped from either window. Two? Irenie couldn't think why there ought to be an elbow in either window. Then the faces materialized behind the glass, and they were the faces of Pap and Les, and she tried to remember had she known that her cousin was coming She glanced at her husband, but Brodis was examining the clasp on the pine box, and Irenie's mind settled on the brewer's yeast. It seemed a year ago Lesley had stood in this spot and proffered her the jar.

Bill Raines stepped from the truck. Lesley seemed to know better.

Brodis nodded his greeting. He kept his hands in his pockets. "Bill."

Her pap took a draw from his cigarette and gestured with his chin. "Brodis."

Brodis indicated the truck with his head. "What's he doing here."

Bill Raines put on that there was no problem. "Well sir, that boy's in the market for a new saw blade. Can't get this one sharpened even one more time. Got to have a new one. Got to be from the machinist in Waynesville and none other. Trip gets longer every day." Despite his complaints, Bill Raines sounded pleased at the idea of spending the day driving around the state. "In five minutes I'll have another one of my offspring telling me no, we've got to scroudge in one more and push on through to Georgia."

Brodis didn't seem to know how to answer. "We appreciate your help."

"Hell, it's on my way now. Besides, I'd like to get a look at the school that's paying my grandson to haul his skinny carcass into its hallowed halls." He reached out his hand and moved the hair from the back of Matthew's head and into his eyes. The boy ducked and squirmed. "If he can't impress them, ain't no hope for the rest of us at all."

Brodis and Matthew loaded the pine box into the back of the truck, sliding it over the metal bed where it sat next to the old saw blade. Bill said let's run a rope over it, and Matthew did, and they tailed it down with double hitches. The saw blade lay flat on the floor next to the box.

Irenie didn't talk to Lesley. Instead she pressed the bag of fried chicken into her son's hands, then the jars of water. When she hugged him, she smelled the musk of a full-fledged man that was still not entirely different from the unguarded smell of his infant hair. His arms around her were quick, full of the excitement and impatience to be off. When he let her go, the earth shifted and she stepped back and caught herself against her husband so as not to fall.

Her son's voice came thicker now. "Daddy."

"Boy." She didn't know whether Brodis had intended to hug him, but there was something in the end of that word *boy* that seemed to say that now was not the time to look into his son's face. In place of it, they embraced, and each of them stared into the space the other had left behind. At the end her husband closed his eyes the way he only ever did in church.

Then her father started the truck, and Matthew got in, and three hands waved as it circled and pulled away. The pine box sat big and white in the back of the bed as the vehicle lurched up the rutted road, growing smaller and then blurring and then melting into the morning sun. The truck pulled around the bend, and the growl of its motor stopped at the gate, then faded down the road. Irenie re-adjusted her eyes and listened to the sound of insects that filled the space where the engine had been. She had expected this sense of loss and relief. But she hadn't expected this fear.

Now the ground turned to water, and the surface washed out from under her. She reached out to Brodis's sleeve for steadiness, and her husband laid his hand over hers and squeezed.

## CHAPTER FOURTEEN

BRODIS WAS AWARE THAT HE WAS DREAMING AND that he was dreaming of sex. Or rather that sex was dreaming of him. The current of it pulled him in, and he didn't resist. A fellow could fight and fight but in the end he just made himself exhausted. Better to let the whelming force of it wash over and through you until you became a part of its pull. Better to give in to the power of the river and save your strength. And anyway, the sex of the dream was the waist-down kind, the kind you didn't look at too closely. The rest of his body was its normal self. And whatever his waist-down was doing he couldn't control but so much. It was building in the rush of white water.

Then it was pulling him under except that he was glad to be pulled under, and the she he was having sex with was in control and wouldn't let him go and he was glad. The she he was having sex with was warm and undulating and demanding, and for a moment he saw her there and was both surprised and not at the look of her, long-nosed and furred and the color of rust. Her canine teeth gleamed in the moonlight. She was laughing, or yipping, or both.

Brodis woke in a wash of sweat and shame, horrified by the

hardness in his body and the baseness of his own lust. Where had he come up with such misimaginings? The picture didn't leave him. The most unnatural thing about the fox's mouth wasn't those canines. It was her tongue, which was a human tongue.

He stared open-eyed and tried to focus on the real-life planks of the ceiling. In the distance, the rise and fall of wild dogs, calling into the night like manic demons. It was July. His son had left the house the week before.

He found the piss pot, and the enameled lid clanged off. Tomorrow he would sleep with a Bible under his pillow.

He crawled back into bed, hoping that his wife might have roused. But she hadn't moved. He draped his arm over her shoulder and pulled himself against her backside. She lay as if in the deepest recess of dream, her arms and shoulders lifeless. Afraid to sleep, Brodis focused on the oak siding in front of him. He'd harvested the wood himself, taken the timber to the mill years before Lesley was the fellow operating the saw. It had been Georgie then who ran the planks through and loaded them onto the wagon.

Now those boards no longer smelled new. Instead the scent of Irenie's hair filled his nose. Outside, a million insects shouted a lopsided hop. *Katy did, Katy didn't, Katy did, Katy didn't*—their voices conjoined to a multitude that battered the walls he'd chinked and rattled upon the roof he'd patched. Irenie didn't stir. Her arm and shoulder were bare, freckles and sun tan darkening her skin to the shoulder, then fading into the pale of her own true flesh, a white that disappeared under the loose fabric of her nightshirt.

He didn't mean to roust her. His fingers found their own way to her upper arm where the sun had thinned her skin paper-smooth, and then of their own accord stroked upward against the fine hairs toward her shoulder, where the skin was plush and moist.

She didn't move. Not a twitch or a stretch or a sigh.

He touched her hair in the place where it curled in front of her ear. He tucked the loose strands.

Nothing at all. He touched his hand to her neck at the place where the blood pulsed steady and low.

He cupped her shoulder and shook.

There was no response in her body and no living save for that pulse.

He reached for the box of matches on the bedside table. The flare of light did nothing save show him a picture of his wife he'd already known in his mind's imagining: pale, flaccid-jawed, eyes nigh onto closed, lashes shadowing the blue moons of her skin. The copper braid reached to her waist, testament to her membership in God's flock. Her lips were parted, her tongue pushed forward like a mongoloid's, a thin line of drool at the corner of her mouth. The match burned down to his fingers and he shook it out, cursing the waste of it. It took another to light the lamp, which he held above the body of his wife, slack as death, emptied of the presence that had been Irenie Lambey.

He put his fingers to her lips again. Her breath was light and hot.

But her body lay too heavy, like a corpse flung from the heavens, or a piece of debris washed onto the bank of some spring-flooded river, the column of her neck too thin to do the work she'd done, her youth already spent in the work of days, her arm bent before her as if in prayer, the fingers curled in upon themselves, the nails like chips of mica.

He didn't know how he knew the spell was broken, because she never woke. Perhaps it was a change in the pattern of her breathing, or the tongue that no longer pushed against the front of her lip, but now when he cupped his hand against her shoulder, she opened her eyes. "What's the matter?"

Brodis peered down at his wife. The moons under her eyes had paled, but nervousness had lit on her like a captured winged creature. "Where were you?"

"What?"

"Just now. Where did you go?"

A certain knowing skittered through her features, but then was gone, sunk into the lake of feelings she kept from him. The question had touched something she didn't want touched, and the answer she gave him had nothing to do with it. "I've been here, sleeping right beside you."

You could tell about people if you looked at them close. "That ain't the way it was, Irenie. You fell into a lull like as if it was death."

And there again that guarded thing in her face, some other realization.

"Don't toy with me, Irenie."

"I ain't." Meek.

For a long time, he lay quiet, turning these new facts over in his mind. All it would take was his own stillness, the holding of it long enough and consistent enough. Then he would find for certain the secret of her absence in their bed and in her heart, and now, too, this absence of the soul, as if she'd left her body behind to roam in way-off places.

And there was Lesley. He knew something too. The two of them nurtured some secret communication that didn't invite him. Lesley, a boy who would never grow into a man, who smoothed his hair in a glass and had his boots polished in Eakin and was thought well of because he was weak. People loved an imperfect man because it made them feel better about their own behavior. It was exactly the opposite of the way they had done with the Lord Jesus Christ. His eminence had shined the light so deep into everyone else's soul that people couldn't stand to look but so much. And for that they couldn't abide him. For that they had crucified him.

When Brodis slept again, he dreamt of making love to his wife in the dusky dark that came at the edge of day, their bodies pressed into one another's the way they had been designed. In the dream, she looked at him through strands of copper hair, and her eyes shone with a laughing light, and when she opened her mouth to howl, the failing light showed the white enamel, the dog teeth grown long and curled as cant hooks.

He awoke as if dropped from a height, eyes bolt-open. He wasn't supposed to have fallen asleep.

The bed beside him was empty.

Where is thy flock, thy beautiful flock, that was given thee to keep?

The house was quiet. Yet he felt certain there'd been some breath or mutter to waken him. Up near the road an owl who-whoed.

Where is thy flock? That was given thee to keep?

And then there it was, as clear as the voice of God: a leaden stumble of sound, followed by the click of the latch.

He didn't move right away, but his senses and his mind girded themselves, making manifest the thing that he'd set himself to do. Then he reached for his overalls and dressed himself quick and quiet until he remembered there was no one to hear. Matthew was at school and Irenie was gone.

The darkness in the kitchen swaddled him. His hand felt for the lantern by the door and tipped it. There was a clatter and the smell of kerosene. He righted it, felt for the matches, and shoved the whole box into his pocket. Two bullets, one in each pocket to avoid the jingle, same as hunting turkey. The third he chambered into the rifle.

Outside the night was brighter, the moon high as a dime, the stars flung like broken glass across the firmament. And there, up the hollow, a figure in white floating noiseless through a section of wood he knew to be thick-brambled. Not to mention the likely of snakes and skunks and every kind of creature. He set the lantern at his feet and felt for the sulfur matches. Then he changed his mind and touched the safety on the rifle. Shapes formed up. Here was the coal pile and the cedar tree with the low-hanging branch, there the stack of firewood, the split and the unsplit, there the apple tree and the cherry trees. All was familiar and strange, yes, the broad outlines, the placement of the outbuildings. But the ground slanted up where there'd never yet been slant. The walnut trees bent to his neck and shoulders, and roots and rocks broke from the ground as if grown up there on the instant. The figure in white slid away, and a dog wove ahead and behind it while the insects screamed in unison, *katy did, katy didn't*, the same pattern repeating itself mile after mile into eternity. He kicked through the brush while unseen creatures skittered at his sides, the entire host of God's creation come to announce they were the ones owned the night. But she was there too, whether she belonged to God or to the lust of the flesh, whether she'd stayed true or gone aside to uncleanness with another, a whiteness that drifted without sound, the occasional blur of Fortune at her feet.

People strayed, but it wasn't because of the Father. It was because of the world. The doings of man were forever bound to rot and fester. He knew about lust, the gross lust of the flesh, and the lust of the eyes, and the pride of life.

But he had been given her to keep.

Fortune paused and tested the air with her nose, wagged her tail and looked in his direction. The white figure hovered, stopped, started forward, a tender sliver in the dark, and Brodis had to still the impulse to call out to her, to reassure her that he was come to take her home. When she stepped forward, so did he, until a growing thing reached up from the earth and hobbled his foot. He shook his boot and then bent to unsnag himself. The air was thick and dewed everything he touched. When he looked up, the sliver of white was gone, evaporated into the cacophonous forest like so much smoke.

And yet he figured he knew its course, the way it had floated straightways toward the ridgeline, as if it had a purpose and a plan. Even as he thought this, his own feet found a path he hadn't known was there, an animal track headed straight up from the watershed. He squinted into the wood, as if doing so would bring the white clad soul into his field of vision, but he couldn't sight it. The walls of foliage loomed black as the walls of Jericho, and there to his left was the boulder where he'd dynamited the foxes, and his fingers tightened in a shame he didn't understand, the same that came whenever he called up other interactions with his son: the obscene blue organs and the wet orange fur, the boy's kicked-in look.

What should he say to these things?

Then he sighted her ahead, taller than before, solid as a pillar of salt in the cloy of the wood, then vanishing behind the shadow of some tree, then manifest again. The pillar stopped. Brodis froze, and in that stillness came a glow from the figure like a low-turned lamp or the sheen of foxfire.

He caught up his breath, rock-still, and the exhalation seeped out slow. The likely was that she hadn't seen him. He couldn't even make out was the figure turned away or staring at him straight on. He rooted his feet to the earth and tried to remember what he was wearing: his work overalls, dark blue, a green shirt. The figure said nothing, but he had the sense it was waiting on him, or waiting for him to leave, one.

But there was a thing that Brodis was supposed to do or not do, an instruction from his God that he knew, that the Lord had sure enough given him, and it was an instruction to look back, or don't look back, go forward alone, he couldn't recall. He stopped and looked in the darkness for the sloe-eyed face of Jesus.

The Lord is on my side, I shall not fear. In the story, Lot's wife had frozen herself in time because she'd looked for something more than the things she was given to keep. Her eye had lingered on that which was not hers to hold.

Except that this was *his* wife because he recognized the long flow of cloth that was her nightshirt.

Now the insects shouted louder than ever, by the thousands of millions, as if they too knew something that had made them to take up this endless screel in the wild hot night. *Katy did, katy didn't. Katy did, katy didn't.* Lot's wife floated on, into the extinguished gloom. The pillar of salt knew something, and Brodis was bound to know it too. He waited. Behind him leaves rattled. He resisted the urge to turn around. Then, whatever beast it was that had made the rattle shuffled on. Brodis thumbed the safety on the rifle and followed.

He entered a grove of fir so dense that the moonlight disappeared. He set the rifle butt on the ground before him, the stock thudding thick into the needle-rot. There wasn't any way to light the lantern without the figure noticing. Wasn't any call to have it with him at all. He thought about leaving it by the side of the trail and picking it up when he came back, but he couldn't make himself do it. He set out again, and the bail of the lantern squeaked in its swinging, the sound nigh onto drowned by the careening rhythm of the insects.

At the ridgeline, Lot's wife turned east to the peak. The path was wide and hard packed now, and the nightgown floated up the side of the mountain without effort. Fireflies drifted like live ash. Behind him, there was a quick movement, a rustle of a thing, a creature, something he couldn't see that could see him.

The forest opened, and Brodis had to allow more distance. The moon cast his shadow on the rocks: long-leggy, arms grotesque and hanging to his knees. With each step, his bad leg swung around the side, an encumbering that separated him from the one he followed. The path climbed steep and straight toward the bald, and something thin and dread settled on his soul. Moses had talked to God on a mountaintop. But he had done it during the day.

Somewhere an owl swooned. Brodis slowed. Among the she-balsam he'd had some coverage, but there would be nowhere to hide on the peak. The bald pate of the mountain stretched before him now, and his weak leg sent a slow message of pain from ankle to knee. He eased himself down behind a grayback boulder and leaned slow against the granite. The rock was cool against his spine and pressed his wet shirt against his body. He waited. Now he would see what he would see.

Five minutes. No voices. The owl sighed again, now some where close enough to hang over the drill of the insects. He waited. Nothing. Two black shapes darted and flapped above him. The boulder at his back sent a chill through his skin that seemed to collect in the ache between his foot and his leg. He rolled forward onto his hands and knees.

The bald was empty. The pillar of salt was gone, the dog too, vanished into the air or clambered down the other side of the mountain. Nothing. The peopled night screamed in wild delight. *Katy did, katy didn't. Katy did, katy didn't.*

Brodis sat back onto his heels, knees pressing into the compost of dead and rotting needles. The thing he was meant to do had yet to make itself clear. He leaned into his heels and tried to look square-on at his ignorance, a lake of questions that stretched unended into a misted gorge. And it was that picture, maybe, that quickened him and opened up the spirit of prayer in him that allowed that, yes, it was right to say this was a thing he did not know. It was good to ask for right knowledge and action, and no matter what else happened it was imperative to ask for the protection of his wife's eternal soul, who was in her heart a pious woman.

The pain in his ankle brought him back from his prayer. He stepped his good foot forward and leaned to bring himself upright. Wasn't any use hiding now. He passed into the clearing, and the moon gleamed like a disapproving eye, the firmament wide and broad and spangled with a detritus of stars. But then a blast of odor smote his nostrils, and he stopped. Sewage. Or sulfur, one. He squatted onto his haunches and felt for the box in his pocket. He set the lantern on the ground and lifted the chimney from its brass thumbs, raked the match against a rock until it flared. The flame circled up blue, and he turned the wick all the way until it was yellow. The clearing stretched out blacker than before, but the sight of his own hands relieved him, the sleeves of his shirt, his shoes, the ground below.

Brodis stared at the soil. Here had been some reckoning, for the grass was feverish with the movement of some great beast. Mounds of earth had piled themselves in lines, but not the way a burrowing creature did. Something greater had raked and furrowed the earth, something with purpose and intelligence. The smell of sulfur cloyed to the air, and Brodis held the lantern up. The pool of light showed the soil lined, trampled, rearranged. And footprinted. There, the outline of a small boot. There and there the worn circle of *Sear*. And there, beside it, the mark of a cloven hoof, plain and clear. Except that the beast who'd made it didn't come to his mind. Not the split triangle of a deer nor the double ovals of sheep nor the matching trapezoids of pig. This hoof turned in upon its self, pincer-like, most like a pig and yet way too narrow, sharper-edged, curved as of a creature far more agile. Stranger still were the dew claws big as thumbs on either side of the hoof, like nothing he'd seen before. And whatever it was, it walked in a straight line, one foot in front of the other, upright, like a—

He could hardly credence the thought.

The patterned earth shuddered, and a blast of brimstone purled into the air.

Jesus in Heaven, save and deliver us.

The wrecked earth groaned, and his skin recoiled and shivered. Some preternatural reflex told him not to move, and so he stood, and waited, hiding in plain sight, cowering in the fingers of some unflinching power. The world was too still. The katydids had been struck mute. From the soil beneath, something naked and ancient woke, stretched its limbs to test their strength, and breathed through the bottom of his boots and into the balls of his feet, sending a weakness like water up his calves and along his thighs and into the jigsaw pieces of his spine, and from there into the dark mysterious place that was his soul. And there it settled, moth-quiet. A dark spot.

His bad leg buckled. He sank to his knees in the tousled soil and fell upon his hands and breathed the putrid smell of brimstone. His stomach lurched into his throat, and a thin stream of vomit rushed out and splatted the violated earth between his hands. Then his own foulness made him gag, and he sickened again at the thing he had seen, and the thing which was, and the thing that would be hereafter.

By the time he stumbled down the mountain, the woods had quieted, but the shadows moved at the tails of his eyes, and a barred owl shrieked its bloodlust in the maniac night.

I will call upon God, and the Lord shall save me.

But for now, he couldn't do it. He'd had enough correspondence with Him for one evening. The moments in his life when the Lord had spoke to him for him alone to hear had been few and far between. The first was at the river, when God had laid on his heart. The second was when He'd called Brodis to the pulpit. It had been in the days of his daughter Hannah, and he'd dreamt that God was bidding him to preach. Even in the dream he'd known the idea was foolish, and when he'd woke, a sound had come from his mouth that he didn't recognize, a mean hard-edged laugh that suited the freezing cabin and the hacking infant at their feet. The preachers he'd known were fiery emotional men, given to fits of joy and passion. He didn't fit the mold.

He'd dismissed the dream out of hand. Truth be told, he hadn't wanted the burden. The girl he'd married and her new baby were dying, and now God had seen fit to put another saddle on him, a job that paid nothing.

The baby died a day later, and the grief that came over his wife sent her to bed for three weeks. Again, he dreamt that God was bidding him preach. This time, when he awoke, he told his Lord that he would find a way to do it. And that very day Irenie had begun to heal. Not three months later she'd announced she was pregnant again. He carried the dream on his soul, but he hadn't told anyone for fear of being laughed at. But a month after Matthew was born, Brodis and Irenie took him for blessing to Brodis's parents. His father was on the down-go then, in bed most of the day, but he turned his paper-white face to him and said, "So. You're going to be a preacher. Well, then that's what you'll be."

Brodis had been stunned. God had spoke to him. At long last he was listening.

But this. It was a thing a fellow did better to set aside until he understood.

When he reached the house, he was alarmed to see the kitchen windows lit with yellow. He wasn't prepared to look into his wife's face, much less to speak to her. What was a man to say after he'd followed his wife in the night and seen her disappear before his eyes? When he'd felt the certain power of the slow Beast? Was he to ask what intercourse she'd had with it? And if he was to ask, how would he know if her answer came from her own heart or from the thing that had entered her?

The kitchen was empty. The lamp burned on the table. Her brogans by the door were red with mud, though the apparition he'd chased in the forest seemed separate from the woman who shared his bed. Brodis turned up one boot. *Sear.*

She was in bed, putting on sleep, her face turned to the wall, the peak of her shoulder hiding her face, the white nightdress pooled about her body. He had no inclination to speak to her. He held the light aloft and searched for the red and blue marks that would confirm what he already knew, but the side of her face shone pale as a baby's, the edge of her cheek confettied with freckles, an unloosed strand of hair cupped around her ear. Her braid lay on the sheet as thick as an animal. In the lamplight, the color was Magdalene red.

When he finally prayed, the words weren't even his own. "The devil taketh them up into an exceeding high mountain. And showeth them all the kingdoms of the world." Irenie didn't move, and the words of the gospel populated the room. "And saith unto them, All these things will I give thee, if thou will fall down and worship me." The words were a bastion against the reechy stench of brimstone, and the patterned earth, and the watery dark thing from below. And then grief washed over him, and he prayed for his wife who had grown cold on the Lord and looked for things that weren't hers to keep, who'd searched out a chance to leverage her soul. He prayed for the wisdom to find help. The strength to take up this fight. The humility to hear His voice.

This time God answered him right away.

Lem. In the morning he would speak to Lem.

He didn't turn down the lamp. In place of getting into bed, he set himself in the chair and waited for the tremor in his legs to still, staring wide eyed at the delicate slope of his wife's shoulder. He had the sense that they were both of them perched at the end of a great precipice, even at the edge of time itself.

By the time Brodis drew nigh of the preacher's place, the old man and his grandson were already in the corn chopping crabgrass, Lem's white head well visible above the tasseled stalks, the boy a dip of sand-colored hair bending forward to his task. The sun slanted through the deep green patch, a haze of bees droning along the tassels.

Lem spied him and stood up. He waved, tipped back his hat, and headed over.

Brodis didn't mention that his own corn was already laid by. Lem was older. Things took longer. Instead he made out that he'd come to borrow a post maul. Taking down the old shed, he said. He didn't want his friend to think he'd made a special trip just to ask foolish questions.

Lem retrieved the maul from the shed and handed it to Brodis. One eye rested on Brodis's face, the other on the space behind him. "Long as you get it back to me before fall." He picked up his hoe, and Brodis knew he wanted to get back to work before it got too hot.

"I appreciate it."

"Any time." Lem looked toward the sun crawling up the sky, then at the patch where his grandson still labored. Dead ahead, deep between the rows of green, a groundhog sat on his rump, shucking a green ear with his front paws. Brodis started toward it, and the creature speed-waddled into the patch, his fat hindquarters disappearing into the next row. Lem was down on his hands and knees, looking to find the hole.

It was easier to speak to his backside. "Lem, do you credence any talk of women with...powers?"

The man seemed to forget about the groundhog. He came to his feet directly, one eye on Brodis for a long moment, the wrinkles and creases in his face still. "I know there's people do. Why? You seen something?"

"I don't know." Brodis found it difficult to look at his friend. "I'm thinking about it yet."

"Ummm." The old man crossed his arms across the top of the hoe.

Brodis dragged his gaze toward his friend. "I'd just as leave keep it for now."

"Ummm." Lem redirected his two gazes in the direction of the ridge. "Remember that lady used to live up Brush Creek way?"

"I never knew her." Brodis knew the rumors, but he didn't volunteer them because he wanted to hear them again.

But Lem probably knew that. One eye examined Brodis afresh. "Florence Huff. My folks always figured her for a witch."

The bob-tailed syllable jarred Brodis, the brittleness of it. "How come?"

"Said she used to talk to the devil in a enchanted grove." Lem nodded as he said it.

"But how did they know?"

"My mother said it was because she couldn't shed tears and used to talk to animals and dance by her own self in the middle of the night." More nodding.

"That ain't proof."

"There idn't any. Except that I once heard witches had three titties, the third one just a little nip of one between the other two." Now both his eyes met Brodis's. "Course I don't know how you'd know that."

Brodis willed himself to stare straight into the other man's face. "If there's somebody knows, they ain't saying." It was a stupid answer. Any other thing would have been better.

"Well, then there idn't any proof."

"Old women's gossip, most like."

"Might could be." Brodis could see that the other man wasn't finished talking. "It's a few precautions a fellow can take, just in case."

"Well, I don't know will I ever see this lady again."

"Well, then, you don't need to know them."

"What are they?"

Now Lem seemed to relax into the role, fixing both gazes on the blue horizon again. "Now, let's see." His hands wrapped around the neck of the hoe. "Don't make eye contact. She may try to look at you direct, and brazen. She'll try, you know, but you don't let her, because if you do, she'll have a power over you. That's the first thing." Lem tilted his head toward the sky. "And if she was to ask something from you, you don't let her have it, not even a rag or a few apples. You have to understand that if you do, she'll have a power over you all the time she has that object. You don't even have to be there."

"And where does it come from?"

"What?"

"The power?"

"Well, from the devil, just what you said. It's a pact. A witch proffers her soul to the devil in exchange for certain...abilities. But there ain't no going back on the deal. That's how come the meanest ones are the old ones. They get worse as they get toward the end because they know eternity is right up on them." He spat into the earth. "Is this one you have in mind a old one?"

Brodis's eye fell on the maul. "Yeah, old enough."

Suddenly he felt Lem's hand on his shoulder. "Son, the main thing is to remember that you don't have to do everything by yourself."

"I know it."

"Who you talk to is that fellow in Tennessy, the Holiness preacher on the other side of Newfound Gap. Frazier June. He said he cast one out ten, twelve years ago."

"Cast one out?"

"His word."

"In what way?"

"I don't know. I wasn't there to ask."

Brodis was silent.

"Course your case ain't come to that."

"No."

"Because if it was, you'd have to go away up there and ask him."

"If it was." Brodis followed the other man's gaze, and they both stood like that, considering the green tasseled corn.

Then Lem shifted the hoe and made toward the patch. "Real crazy stuff."

Brodis agreed that it was indeed real crazy stuff.

## CHAPTER FIFTEEN

IRENIE WATCHED THE BUBBLES BEADING UP INSIDE the cookpot. The brown flecks hopped from the bottom, dancing and flinging themselves up before falling again to the hot metal, touching quick, and bucking again to the surface, as if trapped in their own fluttering madness.

She watched the boil for a long time, while heat swam from the cast iron and filled the kitchen with its thick and clumsy limbs. After a while it wasn't just the sediment in the pan that waffled, but the pot itself, or maybe it was the stove.

Or maybe it was her. It was the fifth day of drinking tea. She'd started on a Sunday night. And today was... what was today? Brodis was gone, but she couldn't think whether it was for fellowshipping or something else. That would make it Sunday. Sunday was the day he fellowshipped. Or it was Wednesday. But it couldn't be Wednesday. It had to be Sunday because he'd been gone all day. They'd risen in the dark and he'd tied the rolled blankets on the back of his horse and rode up the side of the clearing at the gray edge of dawn. Or perhaps that had been yesterday. Yes, it had been yesterday because today she'd done the milking and rested her forehead against the warm flank of the cow and breathed the hide that smelled of grass and antique bristled fur. Yes, he'd been gone this morning. How come? Because, because…there was a fellow on the other side of Newfound Gap, a preacher. The man lived in Tennessee. That meant Brodis had to spend the night. It was Monday then. Today was Monday. It had to be the…eighth day of drinking the tea. Or it was Monday a week, which would make it eight days and one week. But it couldn't be that long because her monthlies hadn't come. It couldn't be eight days and one week.

She leaned over the stove. You needed care not to touch the cast iron, not to rest your hand nor lean your hip against it. You had to pay attention, treat it as a riled animal. You needed care not to fall, placing your feet, one right in front of the other, flat-heeled, without the weight coming down on the side of the ankle. Now the water in the pan had turned brown, and the flecks at the bottom rolled, and the water folded up and over itself, and steam wrapped her face and soaked it with sweat, not just under the arms, but through and through. And all of that in the middle of the night.

But no. It was daylight. The sun blared into the yard. It was July. It was supposed to be hot. Best to finish the tea before Brodis came in from the field for dinner.

But Brodis was making a trip, where, she couldn't remember. Or he might could have headed back. In any case, she had a secret from him, and she had to guard it. The secret was, it was, it had something to do with the hand that yanked her head and the world that tilted away and the little girl who'd died of coughing.

Or it had something to do with Matthew, whose letters arrived overfolded into tight dense packets in the centers of the envelopes. Like treasure maps. He shared a room with two other boys. Dudley and Luke. Matthew had two desks to himself, one in the classroom and a big one in his dormitory. She had a picture of him there, his head bent over his letter writing, the blond hair falling forward from the crown.

Or maybe the secret had something to do with the piano.

The sides of the piano gleamed with oil. The high keys were the purest, the silkenest, the tickliest…light as fairies in their steps. Not like other pianos. Not like the ones that crashed flat. Instead they were leaf-light, as if they'd drifted cupped and gentle to the ground. Ginny Furman's fingers curled over the keys the way a body held a ripe peach for fear of bruising it. Her hands were small and fleshed like a baby's, and yet here they curled around the piano as if there wasn't a thing in the world as fine as that instrument. She played "Amazing Grace," and the lower register bellied up fat and lush to cushion the melody, the alto of her voice swimming along the top. The notes filled the parlor to the ceiling, and the welter of the piano and their two voices pushed her up, as if she were floating on her back in a pond.

The other women in Irenie's life were like biscuits and butter. They were what you expected, and you needed them to survive, but Virginia Furman was like muscadine wine, something delicious and out of the ordinary that you looked forward to. Ginny knew everything, and had a why for the conclusions she'd drawn.

On the stove, a brown liquid boiled furiously. In front of the window a joree bird yammered at her. *Der-ink! Der-ink! Drink yer teeeeaa!*

The contents of the pot spilled over the edge. It seemed familiar to her and yet not. It occurred to her that it needed moving before it boiled out. But you wanted a pair of hot pads for that. Otherwise you burned your hand. And there they were, on a nail on the wall. She used the pads to heft the liquid to the stove's other eye. And then she remembered. It was for tea. The brown liquid was for tea. She was drinking her mother's tea, and it needed keeping secret.

There were more steps. You put something in the canning jar. Then you shook it up. It was the squaw mint. Three spoons. You put the squaw mint in the canning jar and poured the brown liquid over top. And there it was, the jar, with a mess of crushed leaves at the bottom. She lifted the saucepan from the stove's eye and stopped. Something wasn't right. Something was amiss. It was the canning jar. She had better to set it down while pouring the hot water in. Too much chance of over-splashing. She set the jar on the little table—on the *island*. Then she tilted in the boiling water and the squaw mint. Steam banked against her face, and she couldn't see. She stopped to rest her arm, then poured the rest of the liquid into the jar. The empty saucepan clanged back onto the stove. You had to let the tea steep for thirty minutes. But when she turned away from the stove, the floor tilted toward her, then edged away, and her foot came to rest on nothing, on air, and she fell forward, bracing herself against the end of the little table, which moved under her weight.

Then a sound like the frying of bacon, and steam, and a blade of pain slicing through her thigh and shattering onto her ankle and foot. Hot water puddled the floor, and the steam of it and the air itself seared against her skin, as if the inside part of herself had pushed through to the surface until it was bleeding in the open air.

The mason jar was empty, and it rolled on the floor and came to a stop in a puddle of brown liquid and sediment like mouse droppings and wadded leaves.

She didn't lift her skirt. She was afraid to look.

Instead she stumbled into the July afternoon. The light crashed against her face, and the air burned her flesh anew. The yard was clay baked dry, but there was a branch. She wheeled for the shaded depression of the springhouse, the birches with the cinnamon colored bark. The water would be there coming from the springhouse, and it was, a low trickle in the sand and mud. She sat and scooped handfuls of the cool earth over her legs. The burn heated the branch, and the water that had been chilly turned warm. A red salamander buried into the bank. The cicadas rattled and the branch smelled of wet moss and leaf mold. She lay down on the rocks and the mud, and the trickle was warm—hot—against the back of her hair. Ferns feathered the bank, springy and trembling with distress. Irenie commenced breathing again.

After a spell a dragonfly lit on her chest, its wings a color between blue and green. He waited there on her breast, his back hunched forward like that of a very old man, his big eyes surveying her opaquely.

Her teeth went to chattering, and the dragonfly motored away.

For the first time in many days her head felt clear. Her son had gone to a boarding school in Asheville, but he would be home to visit in October. She was here alone with Brodis. She'd used up her ten days, and more. It hadn't worked. It was time to stop drinking the tea.

Brodis didn't give himself over to the Tennessee service. He'd heard too often that the churches in that part of the country used snakes, and he wanted to be on his toes whenever the deacon loosed them. Besides. The sermon was half message and half carnival show. The preacher Frazier June was a plug of a man with orange hair, red skin, and eyes that glowed cyan blue. When the Spirit was upon him, he looked like someone with the hectic, his eyes bulging as if some pressure boiled within him and threatened to force them clear out of their sockets. His preaching fluctuated between whispers and shouts, and it lasted straight through until early afternoon. By the end, the women and some of the men were falling on the floor and speaking gibberish. When the service ended without any snakes, Brodis didn't know whether he ought to be relieved or disappointed.

Now he waited by the water dipper while a gray-bearded farmer clapped his hand into Frazier June's and beamed at him. Then the fellow said something Brodis couldn't hear, slapped his hat onto his head, and bounded down the three steps to the churchyard.

Brodis felt too large and too serious for the little church. More than one person had cast him a sideways look. But there was no call to live with doubt. You did what it took to find the truth. That was the work of life, not to hurry a conclusion before you had all the information there was to get, especially if you were a man of the Lord. Find out what you could, and then, when the time came, knuckle to the facts.

He stepped forward, cleared his throat, and extended his hand. "Brodis Lambey, Mr. June. I come from North Carolina to see you."

Frazier June took his hand and smiled so wide that his lips split open to reveal a broad swath of pink gums and a crowd of overlapping teeth. But the blue eyes studied him. "Was it worth it?"

"It was some service, Mr. June."

"Everyone's heart leads them here at one point or another, Brother Brodis, but all for the same reason, all for the same ache."

"Maybe not in this case, Mr. June."

Just then a boy of eight or so sidled up and whispered something in the man's ear, and Frazier June bent his head to the fellow's cupped hand and nodded as he listened. Then the boy scooted away just as he'd come, and the preacher straightened. His features were set so close together that his face looked gnomic, curdled.

Brodis didn't picture exactly how he would start, so he just started. "I heard a story that you drove the devil out of a woman under affliction."

Frazier June stopped smiling his gum-thick smile and looked at him. "That is a true story, Brother Brodis, yes, and you're not the first person to find me out and ask about it."

"I'd like to know, what happened...afterward?"

The preacher stared at him.

"After the devil left."

"I see." June's eyes seemed to search for something inside Brodis. "She became a member of the faithful, Brother Brodis, that's what happened. That woman is Cora Stevens, and she's living over by Caton at the foot of the Cross, as biddable as you please."

Despite himself, Brodis was washed with relief. "That so?"

A woman with an infant in her arms passed and said, "Bless you, brother." The preacher waved his acknowledgment.

"Brother Frazier, how did you know the woman was...afflicted?"

To Brodis's surprise, Frazier June gripped his arm as if one of them was drowning. He brought his face within inches. His eyes were so blue they were transparent, like water, and Brodis had the sense that there was no bottom to them. June whispered forcefully enough that he was almost spitting. "*Idolatry. Witchcraft. Hatred. Heresies.*" Each word was a dart.

"Galatians," Brodis said.

Now June lowered his voice even more and bent toward Brodis. "Do you know what a...succubus is?" The word hissed.

It occurred to Brodis that the man might be touched. "Tell me."

"A succubus, Brother Brodis, is a creature that has two forms, one being a human form and one being a animal form."

June's face was inches away. It might be the man was trifling with him. Yet there was some part of Brodis that needed to hear the rest of it.

"You've got your succubus that can take the bodily form of a spirit and travel amazing distances in no time flat, and then you've got them as leave their physical bodies behind and travel like a bird or a cat."

Brodis nodded. The white pillar he had followed the week before had been the form of a human being, his wife Irenie.

Frazier June clasped Brodis's forearm tightly. "I'm guessing you know the story of the girl at the Hendrix mill. Right famous story, that."

Brodis said he'd not mind hearing it again.

"She was riled up, was what it was. Course they all are, them that become witches. They got something they got to prove." He seemed to sense that he had Brodis's full attention and loosed his arm. "Otherwise it's not enough in it for them, not enough motivation, you see. You got to see things from their point of view. What is the thing that's gonna be so powerful as to make them contract their soul away? Got to be something fair size, like revenge. Or it might could be love." June seemed to relax as his story unfolded. "Or pride even. Sometimes a woman just insists on having her way, and she'll do it at all costs. Then you've got your Bell witch over there." He waved his arm, as if the famous hag were next door. "She was mad because that fellow up and let her die without a care, and she might had good reason. Another lady was bent out of shape because a fellow'd not marry her daughter. But that was enough."

Brodis listened more easy now. None of the descriptions fit Irenie.

"Sometimes it's a broken heart." June's eyes augured into his own.

Brodis nodded. "Makes sense."

"Or a dead baby."

Brodis felt a muscle in his jaw jump. That winter it had snowed something fierce. They hadn't been able to bury Hannah right off. She'd spent days in the casket, out in the cold.

Now June opened his lips and reached his tongue over his front teeth to his gums.

When he resumed speaking, the listing was over. "Course it don't have to be a woman, you know. Could be a man. Just happens that most times it *is* a woman because of the nature of the motivation. But it don't have to be, keep in mind."

Brodis nodded in a way that meant attentiveness, but not agreement.

At last the other man moved his face away, as if he had relaxed some. "Now I don't know the exact process. Fellow told me once the woman had to write her name in blood in a book. Another man told me it took going to the top of a mountain at middlenight, turning around three times. Another said no, it wasn't nothing like that. More of a—"

"Yeah, but what do they do?"

"Who?"

"The...witches." The churchyard stood empty now.

"Well now, that depends—on the personality of the woman. She might take something of yourn, a lock of hair, or a old tooth, to get the advantage of you. Don't never loan her nothing. But that right there, that makes them mad too, if you won't let them borrow a churn, or pick from your blackberry patch, or use your saddle horse. That right there gets them fit to be tied, but I'm telling you, don't give such a one any thing you own or she'll have a power over you right straight. You make her mad enough, she can make you or one of your own to take sick. Or she might will just ride you in your sleep till you fall over from pure—"

"*Ride* you?"

"What I said, Brother Brodis. Ride you. Course sometimes they just up and outright kill a person. Cold-blooded murder, like that woman over the Hendrix mill that time."

June was lying as certain as the day was long, but Brodis sensed that he needed to let the rope play all the way out before reeling it back in. "What time?"

"Long time ago, because it was a new mill in the Smokies and wasn't nobody around. It was flat out wilderness back then, and the fellow took his wife out there to live with him where the mill was, but she didn't want to go. She was a young girl, and pretty, and I guess she was wanting to stay in the city where she could get nice dresses and be around people. And instead the man had her living up a creek by a timber mill with the bears and the panthers and the wolves. So after a spell the foremen of the mill died, not a thing in the world wrong with him, just laying there in the morning, goggle-eyed and dead as could be. Didn't nobody know what'd happened. They had to shut down the mill until they had a new foreman."

Brodis nodded. Such stories always began and ended with some-body dead. He gave the rope a little more play.

"Fellow come up and took that job, and the mill opened up again. About the time it did, that fellow up and died too, same way. Went to bed a man in his prime. Next morning they found him just a-staring at the ceiling all wild-like. Mill closed down for good after that, because there wasn't nobody would take the job, see."

June seemed to be waiting for Brodis to cue him, like feeding coins to a gypsy to get your fortune told. "Did they find out who killed them?"

"Oh yeah. They found out. But it wasn't the way you'd reckon. A fellow come in from somewheres else saying he would take the foreman job, but they had to pay him twice what the others was getting. And the owner did, see, because he didn't have no other choice and because they both knowed there would be a third per-son to die. Besides, the owner wanted to see what would happen. Well, this fellow, the new foreman, he had a dog that he kept with him all the time, a bear dog, a redbone that could run like a rabbit and trail a fox and stay with a treed bear like a coon dog and fight too."

Brodis found himself picturing Matthew's dog, Fortune, lean and muscled and alert.

"And this dog had always been with him, a pet, you see. It slept inside with him too. Well, one night this new foreman wakes up to a terrible racket. It's the dog, the redbone, and it's got itself in a ruction with a black cat. Now this was a dog that was used to fighting *bears*, see, so this was a tough dog. And the fellow was amazed to spy his dog, his *bear* dog, having this rumpus with a old cat, and the dog not winning."

Because it wasn't an ordinary cat. Brodis had almost spoken aloud.

"This went on for some time, the cat leaping on the dog's face and slashing with its paws, and the dog growling and looking to get the cat by the throat. The man thought to shoot the cat but there wasn't a clear way of doing it without killing the dog too. Finally, what happened was the dog got the cat's front paw, and the cat wriggled all wild to get away, but the dog wouldn't let go, and the cat lost part of its paw to the dog's jaws. The cat landed on its back and jumped up and leapt for the door. Course the door was closed and it wasn't no way for it to get out, just like it wasn't no way for it to have got in. But that cat, that cat went straight through the crack under the door, just made itself flat and *zoop*, it was gone. The foreman knowed right then that it wasn't no cat doing that. He knowed right then that he had bare escaped with his life. And the dog, well the dog was still holding the cat claw in its mouth, so the foreman took it out and laid it on the table out of the dog's reach and rewarded that redbone right well. After that he went to sleep and didn't have no more trouble.

"What's to say it wasn't just a regular cat with a streak of ornery?" Even as he spoke, Brodis knew he didn't believe it.

Frazier June seemed put out. "Oh, rest assured, it weren't no cat, Mr. Lambey. I ain't finished yet."

"Go on."

"Come morning, the foreman woke up and the cat's claw was gone."

"The dog probably ate it."

"Hold your horses, Mr. Lambey. I ain't finished. In its place was a lady's finger setting there, that had been chewed off at the joint."

Brodis felt a palpitation in his blood, something surging through his veins of its own free will, and though he knew it had come from the story Frazier June had told him, he knew also that his own wife had been the first to set it there. More than anything, he wanted to be rid of it.

It vexed him to realize that June had paused to gauge his response. "Gives you the all-overs, don't it?"

"What happened."

Frazier June regarded him a moment, then took a deep breath. "Well, that foreman was stumped, but he figured the finger to be a clue, so he picked it up and put it in a piece of sacking and took it off to the owner of the mill. They lived in a big house some bit away from the noise of the machinery. The mill owner answered the door and said he couldn't talk long because his wife had took sick in the night. But when the foreman showed him the finger, he said right off, 'That's my wife's finger,' and went straight up the stairs to check. Sure enough she was in the bed just laying there all feverish and he told her to show her hands. Well, she took the one out and showed it but not the other. And he said to her take the other one out. And sure enough, it was missing a index finger."

"What did he do?" Brodis asked in spite of himself.

"Well he got his shotgun right then and there and shot her, that's what."

"*Shot* her?"

"He knew she was the one what killed the other foremen."

"You claimed there to be a *cure*."

"Well, there is, but that one, I guess she was probably too far gone. What with killing two men."

"What if she wasn't? I mean, what if they'd caught her sooner?"

"You have to catch them soon, while they're still conflicted, Mr. Lambey. They have to want to come to God."

"And how did you fix the Stevens woman?"

Frazier June took his time answering. "I just did what the old-timers did. First, you have to be a man of the Lord. Are you a man of the Lord, Mr. Lambey?"

"You wouldn't ask me that if you knew me, Mr. June."

"When?" Frazier June wasn't smiling now. "When was you washed in the blood?"

"July seventeenth, 1924, Mr. June, at three-thirty in the afternoon." The information swam from his tongue of its own accord, but he stopped himself before the rest came out. On the Pigeon River in Haywood County.

"Well, I expect you'll need to know how to do this then. Satan is the hardest working man around, and I don't see him letting up any time soon."

"Amen."

"You know what witch hazel is? It has those yellow flowers in October?"

"Yes." Brodis had seen the spindly bushes on the sunned slope above their barn.

"You take that witch hazel, and you burn it till it turns to black soot. Now you're gonna need a fair amount, so make sure to get you a pile of good branches." Brodis inhaled and nodded.

"Then you take that soot, and you mix it with water, and you draw a likeness of the witch on a piece of paper."

Brodis's disappointment surged. "A *picture*?" It was cock-and-bull as old as the wives' tales it had come from.

Frazier June was quick to reassure him. "Don't worry, it don't have to be a perfect mimic. But what it does need, mind you, is a naming. You got to write the person's name."

Brodis sighed. He let June finish. He had come a long way to hear him.

"Then you take that picture, you see, and you have to bid the Lord Jesus for help at this point, because otherwise it ain't nothing, it's just a picture, and you have to tell Him that your intentions are good, and He'll know. He'll know if you're following your own convictions and your spirit is pure. Because if they ain't, it just flat out won't work, that's all. Then you take that picture, and now this is the part that's dangerous, because this is the time when you're in direct communication with the devil, and he'll be able to see inside you too, and he'll as leave try to get you both than to let go of the one he's already got. Understand?"

Brodis said he did.

"Then you take that picture, and you burn it up, and it has to be at middlenight, you see, because that's the time whenever the original compact with the devil was made, and that's the time when Satan is most... *communicative*."

"And then what? What will happen?"

"The witch will get a taste of the fires of hell."

"What does that mean?"

"Hell will reach up and touch her, that's what. And if she's not too far gone, she'll decide that she don't want that in her future and she'll come back. That's what happened in the case of Mrs. Stevens."

"What if she's too far gone?"

"Fire is a powerful thing, Mr. Lambey. And so is fear. She might die, Mr. Lambey."

"And go to Hell?"

"Well, now, that part's up to her. It depends does she renounce her compact in the final moment or not. You can't control that. That's between her and Satan and Jesus. All you can do is provide the opportunity for her to get out of the bargain. But the main thing is, you got to be careful of yourself. Because the devil is aware of you and he knows you, and he will try to take you too, mark my words. The first thing you better do is look into your own self, Mr. Lambey."

"I can take care of myself, Mr. June. It's part of my job. God said thou shalt not harbor sorcerers, nor anyone that useth divination. Nor an enchanter."

"Nor a witch," Frazier June broke in. "Men wasn't to harbor a witch."

"Or a witch, Brother Frazier." Brodis gnawed at his lower lip and let his eyes fall on the empty churchyard.

"Brother Brodis. You know there's another way."

Brodis made an effort to keep the impatience out of his voice. "What way is that?"

Frazier June paused and looked around the churchyard. "The mill owner's way. Except you'd best to use a silver bullet."

Brodis stared. The man was flat crazy. "That would be murder, Mr. June."

June's response was hair-trigger. "To cut off witchcrafts?"

Against his will, Brodis took a step back.

June took a step forward. "Mr. Lambey."

"What." Brodis planted his feet.

"Remember Exodus 22, Mr. Lambey."

"I know all about Exodus 22, Mr. June," Brodis spat. "But this is the twentieth century, not the Middle Ages."

"Mr. Lambey."

"What."

"Do you mind if I was to ask who this person is? The one that's made a pact with the devil?"

"A member of our church, Mr. June."

"Do you mind if I was to ask which one?"

"I do mind, Mr. June. I mind very much."

That night Brodis unrolled his blanket on Frazier June's porch. The house had darkened, and the family, all eight of them, grown quiet. Brodis double-folded the blanket and set his knees upon the cushion of it. The Lord would sure forgive this one comfort. The night was clear, the stars so precise it had to be the very Heavens shining through the pinpricked fabric of the firmament. The great dipper poured its elixir onto the North Star, and the scorpion crept after the scales without ever gaining an inch. And somewhere away up there his Maker sat watching and waiting, expecting Brodis Lambey to do the right thing.

But the praying was no good. Brodis stood. A communication with God didn't reach up except it was made from the very bottom of humility. This time Brodis set the blanket aside and kneed into the planks of the porch. They were uneven, and the edge of the wood bit his flesh, but the hardness of it sharpened him, and he bowed his head and began in a voice little louder than a whisper. "I know I've been blind. I know that I've jumped to conclusions and credenced that which I've most wanted to believe, I know it. I know too that I've looked on the things in my life and been prideful of the way I've built them because I wanted to believe that I had set the right course and done the things I was called upon to do. But now I see that I've sometimes chose wrong and failed to care for the things I was given to protect. I've stumbled through without knowing direction." The noise of the night chorused him, and his voice rose up and caressed the poplar joists and the metal roof, curled itself against the wall of the house and rolled back to him in the enclosure of the porch. "I'm ready now to hear what you have to say, Lord. Not just to listen but to do. Only let Irenie come back to grace, God. Let her walk in the light again."

He raised his head and opened his eyes. In the clearing in front of him, the outline of a child's metal wagon and beyond that, a rutted road. Come morning he would know what to do. That was the way His guiding worked.

Brodis turned to spread his blanket, but not before the tail of his eye caught sight of a shifting in the window. He looked up. There, inside the house, a darkness dislocated itself from the shadows for a second, perhaps two, and then reabsorbed itself into the murk.


Irenie went for the flour first so as to be toting something when she made her visit to the other place. From the gloam of the grocery store, Hallie Crisp's voice helloed her. His apron showed white, then the rest of him behind it: his face lined but his torso still slim and straight. Her old schoolmate. Years ago he'd married a girl from Burnsville.

Irenie did her best to smile. "I'm afraid I can only stay a minute today, Hallie." She waved her hand vaguely, as if to suggest that someone waited outside in the street to collect her.

"And how is your famous son?"

Irenie blushed. She never tired of the manner in which people asked about Matthew, that same mixture of surprise and curiosity and jealousy. She knew what they wanted to hear: about the things, and the places, about taking the streetcar downtown and sharing a room with a rich man's son, about skyscrapers and good shoes. But for some reason she couldn't oblige. Instead she couldn't get enough of talking about him, of saying his name. "Matthew is taking geometry now. He said it's challenging, but I take that with a grain of salt. You know Matthew." But of course they didn't. Know Matthew. How could they when she herself was forever surprised?

Hallie nodded and thudded a ten pound bag of flour on the counter beside a row of stacked little papers she figured for receipts. The papers fluttered and settled.

"And soda, thank you." She opened her snap-purse and counted out four dimes and a nickel. Hallie clapped a can of Arm & Hammer next to the flour. "You can leave these here till Mr. Lambey comes."

The register banged open, and she pinched the coins into his palm. "I can take them, Hallie."

"Not if I can help it, Irenie." He hoisted the flour up to his shoulder. "Where's the wagon?"

"No wagon, today, Hallie. I believe I have it." She lifted the bag of flour from his arms and set it on her hip, the way she'd tote a set-along child.

"Suit yourself then." The grocer reached for the jingling door, but couldn't resist a gander up the street before Irenie stepped through it.

"Thank you, Hallie."

"I hate that you're packing that load."

"I know it."

"I'll see you next month, Irenie Lambey."

"I expect you will."

She stepped into the bright. The sack was dense and soft like human flesh, and the weight of it on her hip almost felt like the reason she'd come into town in the first place.

But there was more why to it than that. She'd ridden the mule down the mountain and across the bridge for another reason. Perhaps that was the way you did. You put yourself in a situation not out of knowing but out of guessing something bigger might come of it, and that was the way you created possibility. Ginny was probably in her office now.

Irenie turned down a gravel road toward the river, past the smithy's, the whoosh of the bellows and the cooked heat. Tom McCampbell didn't look up when she passed, bending instead to the tap-tapping of iron. She crossed the train tracks and came to a low slung building close to the water's edge made of rounded river stone. The tax assessor had abandoned the place years before on account of flooding. The bridge support rose behind the little structure like an outsized chimney. On the door a steel sign read, "USDA Extension Service."

Irenie shifted the flour sack to the other hip and glanced around for people she knew. Across the river a farmer and a tangled-looking black dog followed a flock of sheep toward the drover's road. Up the street a motorcar slid through the intersection. And across from the smithy's a woman whose name she'd forgotten peered into a shop window. It occurred to Irenie that she maybe looked more suspicious standing by the office than she did walking into it. She knocked on the door.

For a whole enduring minute there wasn't anything. Above her on the bridge, an automobile rattled the planks against the steel frame. What would she say if Mr. Furman was to open the door? Or someone else?

She would ask for Ginny. Say she had a question about the extension meeting.

What would she do if there was no one to answer?

She would walk up Main Street and knock on the door of their home. Returning something she borrowed, that's all.

Just then the door swung in and Ginny Furman stood in the frame looking distracted. But when she spied Irenie, her face softened, and her eyes wrinkled into a smile. "Irenie! What a surprise! Terrific!" She turned into the cool of the office and whipped her arm forward in something like a pitcher's snap. At the same time she called over her shoulder, "You don't have to knock, you know. People are in and out all day, and none of them knock. We'd keep the door open except the sun shines right in."

The inside of the office was dark and cool. Small windows in the thick walls allowed light to pour through in shafts. A fleshy man with bushy mustaches and a thick head of hair looked up from a typewriter.

"This is Mrs. Lambey, Roger, who I told you about. Irenie, my husband Roger."

Mr. Furman stood. He smiled and held up an envelope. "The famous scholar!" Irenie's heart jumped: her son's handwriting, the pages in the envelope folded into a clump in the center. But of course. Her son would be writing to them too. She told Mr. Furman about the geometry class. He grinned and said something that sounded like, "Euclid was the only mathematician I ever liked." He wore denim breeches and a wrinkled chambray work shirt, the buttons straining against the front of the fabric, his galluses unstrapped from his shoulders. Now he extended his hand. "A pleasure to meet you. My wife has enjoyed your company and valued your opinions, Mrs. Lambey." His palm was thick and soft and swaddled her own, his face the kind that let everything he thought show right on through. Right now it showed overmuch interest. Ginny would have already told him many things about her and her son. Irenie tried to tally what those things might be and blushed. Nor could she feature how to tell him she was wanting to talk to his wife alone.

"How's that tobacco doing this year?" he asked.

"Twice as good as last year." She was relieved that the conversation had landed on crops. "Taller than I can reach, and just as thick and green as you're like to see, sir."

Roger Furman smiled as wide as a kid, and there was pride in it too, but not the kind that took over someone else's labor and claimed it for itself. "Delighted to hear it, Mrs. Lambey."

"Couple of days and we'll start the cutting."

If she was still here. On his own, Brodis would have to work twice as long to stake it, twice as long to push the leaves down over the wood. But there was always Clabe Ingles.

"It wouldn't hurt to have some rain," Mr. Furman said.

"No sir. It wouldn't hurt."

"Is there something else I can help you with, Mrs. Lambey?"

"Right now, I've come to talk to Mrs. Furman, sir. On a question of women's medicine."

"Right." He glanced at his wife. "Yes, well I was on my way to pick up a few items at the hardware store anyway." He turned and lifted his hat from the wall, bowed his head through the door and was gone.

Irenic couldn't believe she'd purposed the conversation to come out just so. But now whatever plans she'd made abandoned her. Ginny's face was a mix of curiosity and concern.

"I was wondering...could I tell you something personal?"

"What is it?" Ginny eased her weight onto the desk, and it struck Irenie it was the first time she'd seen her friend sit down slow. Her eyes worried into Irenie's. "Did you get in trouble for the piano?"

"No, it's not that." Irenie searched for the words out the open window, but all she saw was the pylon of the bridge.

Ginny was still watching her. "It's something though. I can tell."

Though she'd already pictured herself saying the words, they caught now in her throat. "What would you think if I was to leave my husband?"

The sound of Ginny's breath was quick and alarmed. "But he's not gonna stand—"

"I know."

"You mean just...disappear?"

Irenie nodded.

"Because if you have legal grounds—"

"Ginny, you know I can't do it that way."

Ginny nodded, and even though she'd only now come to consider the problem, her thoughts seemed two steps ahead of Irenie's.

"There's more," Irenie said.

"What?"

"It looks like I'm gonna have another baby."

"Oh glory…" This time Ginny brought her hand to her forehead and squeezed her temples between her thumb and middle finger, and Irenie studied the top of her dark hair and wondered could the other woman ever feature what it was like to be her. After a long minute, Ginny raised her head. "Does he know?"

"No. I didn't tell him. I looked to start the flow myself."

Ginny blinked and seemed to consider this news. "But it didn't work."

"It didn't work." And there was something about that one admission that carried everything Irenie'd ever done, from the moment she'd stood on this riverbank and first seen Brodis Lambey to the evenings in the dark whenever she lay stiff with a fear that unstopped her. Now the tears that she hadn't cried unleashed, and they were for Matthew's departure and his new life away from her own, and for the darkness of the house in the hollow, but also for the little girl who would have been fourteen this year, and more than anything in the world they were tears for the back grab of hair and the terribleness that followed, for all the years of fear that lay ahead, and for the blue indigo flame that guttered and wept in the dark. "I'm afraid that…" But the ending of the sentence wouldn't show itself.

"Of him."

It wasn't what she had meant to say, but she let it sit. Ginny Furman wrapped both hands over Irenie's and brought them to her lips. "There might be a way." Irenie saw that her mind was traveling down some path away far off from the office they were in. She tightened her grip. "There might be."

It happened like this. You rode into town to buy a bag of flour and the next thing you knew you were walking across the street and knocking on the door of an almost stranger. You left with a name and address written on a piece of paper and tucked into your pocket, one Dr. Potts who lived in a mining town named Copperhill.

For now, Irenie strapped the flour to the mule. Brodis would be back for dinner, and there was plenty to do between now and then.

## CHAPTER SIXTEEN

(

BRODIS DIDN'T PLAN TO CUT THE WITCH HAZEL. HE spun the waterstone, and the beads of moisture kicked up from the trough. He dragged the Kaiser blade across the trembling wheel, angling the mowing edge so that the grain of the rock scrubbed against the steel. It had been three days since his conversation with Frazier June, and he didn't plan to cut the witch hazel. But he'd laid off mowing for weeks, and it was a chore that needed doing. When the stone slowed, he cranked it again, and the beads of water flew up against his fingers once more. After a long while, he lifted the cane knife and peered at it. He dragged his thumb across the cutting edge to check its sharpness, and the blade resisted against the whorls of his skin so as almost to render them countable. He peered at the knife, then in a sudden motion swung it wide and pulled it quick against a limb of forsythia. The branch lopped and laid in the dirt. Brodis reached for the blade's hickory handle, fitted the steel into it, and screwed the two pieces together.

The weeds on the cutbank had come up fast, the Johnson grass and Joe Pye grown higher than his head, the berries on the poke hanging purple and obscene. He reckoned the witch hazel was halfway down. He'd know it when he spied it. For now he commenced the mowing at the top of the drive, slinging the blade wide so that it cleaved into the green, the felled vegetation dropping into the road at his feet, the pith of stems moist, the leaves shivering. The sun came hot on his back, and the sweat that started at his neck spread to his shirt collar and his spine and down his waist. He worked without stopping, the slingblade arcing in his hand like a live thing.

And then he was there. He paused, straightened, and set the implement on his shoulder. The witch hazel was thin and sprawl-legged, each branch shooting from a central root as if the plant grew up figuring to be cut and stripped for switches. In the fall it would star-burst with yellow flowers. In the fall, she would ask what happened and how was it he'd cut the only plant on the farm to blossom in October. He'd say it'd happened during the mowing, and she would shake her head and say she'd always liked the color.

And the blame would rise up between them.

The cane blade sheared through the base of the bush in one slice. Then through the next. And another. Only when he'd cut all three did he stop to consider the spring-legged branches shuddering at his feet.

Frazier June was a zealot with the tinder of insanity lit in his eye.

Brodis left the witch hazel where it lay and continued down the road. By the time the shadow of the mountain inched across the road, he was gathering the felled shrubbery into piles and had near forgot the plant.

Near.

But there it was, the pale leaves like green tufts of hair. The notion of burning it embarrassed him. Not to mention the challenge. The stalks were green and the sap young. A flame would like to never get a hold on it. He left the branches where they lay at the side of the road. The slingblade he returned to the empty nail between the posthole digger and the harrow. Then, as he turned to leave the barn, the color of the red can caught his eye.

He might never have done it, but the gasoline was there and the witch hazel was there, and it'd not take more than five minutes' time, and there wasn't a thing to lose except three or four cents worth of fuel. He would do it and he would be careful to follow directions. That way whenever it didn't work, he'd know that he'd tried everything that Frazier June had suggested.

He set the bundle of switches on the ground and poured the gasoline over top, careful to screw the lid tight on the can and set it far from the pile. Then he bent and dragged a match across a rock and threw it on. Flame whooshed into the air, and the heat of it was a pulsing yellow mirage, and then the wood caught and curled in upon itself in the fire-wave, like fingers shriveling in the heat. The gasoline burned off, leaving weak yellow flames and a pall of smoke so thick and unnatural-smelling that Brodis coughed into his hands.

Frazier June and the story of the cat had tiptoed around his mind ever since he'd returned. At times, it was there in the front, as of something important that needed attending, and he was sure he'd heard the story somewhere before, or several times before, the way a truth shows itself a truth because you keep running up against it. At other times the story of the witch and the cat wallowed with the tales of hobgoblins and fairies that old women told children to keep them out of the woods and hard on their chores, stories about women who transformed themselves into deer or fish or fox. Fairy tales.

The switches burned down to tubes of black ash. Brodis stepped on the remains and ground them into the dirt with the flat of his boot. At any moment someone he knew would come walking up the road and ask him what was he doing.

Fine. It was just ash. All he was doing was making the thing to keep it. It didn't mean he was going to use it. He side-handed the warm dust into a jelly jar, then screwed down the lid and dragged his palms down the front of his overalls. He spit into the jar. When he shook the mixture it came up a black sludge. He shook it again, and the sides of the jar coated gray. He didn't see how anybody had ever written anything with such a mixture. He jammed the container into his pocket until it pulled the fabric of the denim tight against his buttocks and thighs.

Inside the barn, he separated a newspaper across the floor. Images and advertisements from another world spread across the boards: the state of North Carolina allocating money to repair the Eakin bridge, a color movie about slave plantations in Georgia during the War Between the States, a power-hungry leader in Germany. Brodis fished the jar of wet ash from his pocket and twisted off the lid. The metal clattered to the floor. He tilted the container and dipped his index finger in. The ash was hot and grainy against the glass. He stopped and stared at the paper. He didn't know how to start.

Then he did. With his sooted finger, he drew a large triangle in the center of the page. Then he drew three buttons down the front.

But that wasn't right. The triangle was like nothing but a pinafore, and grown women didn't wear pinafores.

But Frazier June had said as how it didn't matter. It didn't have to be a perfect mimic. Brodis dipped his finger into the blackened jar again. Atop the triangle he drew a circle with a long tail of hair, then stick arms and legs that stretched from the pyramid body. The feet pointed in opposite directions. He added eyes like two footballs, a curve of a mouth, a nose like an L. He stopped and stared. It was about as poor a drawing as he'd seen.

It don't have to be a exact likeness. But what it does need, mind you, is a naming.

Brodis wrote the letters at the bottom, carefully dipping his finger over and over in the ashy sludge. Mary Irenie Raines Lambey. He had to make it fair size if nothing else for the sake of reading. Could the devil read? Of course he could. He could read any language. And more than that he had the power to see inside men's hearts. He probably didn't even need the letters. Maybe they were just a formality. Brodis stepped back and evaluated his work, still unsatisfied. A drib of black remained in the jar, and he tilted it and swiped his finger into it. Then, very carefully, he dotted both sides of the face: on each cheek, three freckles.

He set the newspaper outside and stood over it while it dried in the latening sun. Within minutes, it was stiff enough to roll into a loose scroll and secure with a string. He stowed it in the oaken bucket that hung on the loft steps, nestled among the red sticks of dynamite. If she was to find it, well, she would figure Matthew had done it whenever he was a kid.

But the newspaper. It was dated.

He lifted the bucket off its nail, and set it three feet higher, beyond her reach. It could stay there until the day came he decided he needed it. Which was maybe never.

And never might have been okay if he hadn't gone to the camp meeting that Saturday.


It was the same revival he'd attended every year for a decade and a half, the same where he'd met Irenie, the same where he'd first stepped in front of an audience to preach. In all that time, he'd never seen the man before. Other Tennessee preachers, yes, but not him. But on that first evening, come sunset, when the noisy shadow of the tent was crowded with people, and Brodis thought he heard someone call his name and turned to find out who, a man slung an arm around his shoulder and leaned in close to his ear and purled: "Let me know whenever you're ready for help with your...*problem*."

Brodis wheeled out of the embrace and stared into the gnomic face of Frazier June. The man's eyes glowed with a feverish excitement, as if he'd been imbibing, and now he smiled with his pink-skinned gums and his crooked crowded teeth.

Brodis glared. "The problem has settled itself out."

June's eyes bulged. He leaned in as if the two of them shared an exciting, delicious secret. "Oh they never do that, Brother Lambey."

"There've been no more disturbances."

"But I know, and you know, Brother Lambey, that that's just temporary." Brodis couldn't decide was Frazier June smiling or snarling. "There are souls that have familiar spirits, Brother Lambey, and there are those that turneth after them, and go a-whoring upon them."

Brodis's mind drew up short. Whoring? The word was both insult and threat.

But June made out that he'd meant neither. He held up the palms of his hands. "God said it, not me." Like a man whose practice of dishonesty was so regular that it had come to feel to him like straight dealing.

A slow poison gathered in Brodis's limbs and torso.

June must have mistook the pause for something more benign because he dropped his hands and leaned in closer, as if confiding. "He said he'd set his face even against that soul as did the whoring, Mr. Lambey, even against him. And cut him off from his people. Leviticus, Mr. Lambey. See for yourself."

Brodis stared.

June dropped his voice again, whispered. "He shall sure be put to death. They shall stone him with stones."

Now it was Brodis who leaned in, his eyes inches from June's. "What is your point of conversation, Mr. June?" In the dusk, the man's irises were blue as veins. His skin smelled of vinegar.

Frazier June took a tiny step back.

But Brodis grabbed the man's shoulders. He knew he was holding overtight, but he couldn't leave off. His voice came out a growl. "I think it's safe to say, Mr. June, that I don't require any more of your. . .assistance."

June puckered his mouth and wavered his gaze.

Only then did Brodis drop his hands, reach for his jacket and jam his arms into the sleeves. But before he turned, he stared hard at June. "It goes without saying, Mr. June, I'd appreciate you kept this matter to yourself."

Frazier June stepped away, then performed an odd little side-scoot. Only when he was out of Brodis's reach did he call, "Remember Exodus, Mr. Lambey."

For the first time in fifteen years, Brodis left the camp meeting early.


The very same night he woke from the velvet dread of sleep to find her gone, the bedclothes cool in the balmy air. It was early yet, midnight at the latest.

He waited. There was always a chance she'd gone to the privy, or to see about the dogs, a chance she'd heard the shriek of owls too close to the chicken house.

But she didn't return, and this time he didn't ask himself where she was or who she was with. Nor did he hurry. He stared at the blackness out the window. The new moon was invisible and in its place a shroud of clouds. The loggers would have ciphered it to mean a death.

He thought on the newspaper scrolled into a tube in the oak bucket in the barn. In his mind's picture, it leaned against the wall, the paperstring brown and tied in a long bow, the bucket protecting it from mice and other creatures that shredded and chewed at the edges of things. He could retrieve it at any time.

A legion of insects chided from the window, their voices swelling in thick concert. *Katy did. Katy didn't. Yes you ought. No you oughtn't.*

He waited. Five minutes, ten minutes, fifteen. The air in the house was soft as swaddling.

*Yes you ought. No you oughtn't.*

He swung his feet over the edge of the bed and reached for his overalls. The responsibility was his alone, the husband and minister both. He was the only one could open her eyes, could turn her from the power of the devil. It fell upon him.

You have to catch them early, while they're still conflicted.

At the door, he touched the stock of the rifle but left it in the rack. Outside, the breath and scuttle of living creatures trafficked the night. Brodis kicked at the ground. His eye scanned the woods. How long had she been afoot? How long did it take to walk to the top of the mountain? How long did it take to communicate with the Beast that was, and is not, and yet is?

Rhythm pounded around him, an audience of millions. *Yes you ought. No you oughtn't. Yes you ought. No you oughtn't.* In the paddock the horse shifted, and somewhere in the enfenced woods his pigs ranged, wilding through the branch bogs and up the draws, rutting in the warm night air.

And up on the mountain his wife consorted with the one she consorted with.

Outside the air was thick with pent up rain, and his shirt stuck to his back. Brodis entered the barn on the loft side, where cotton blackness and the smell of hay soaked him up. He descended the steps, set the lantern on the floor beside him, and reached above his head for the oaken bucket, feeling along the crossbeam for the nail and the handle. His hand found it, and he brought it down. He set the pail and the lantern at the top of the stairs and kneeled to brush away enough hay to lay out the page. The scroll was lighter and taller than the dynamite, pale in the darkness, wavery with the drying of paint. Brodis unrolled it, but the edges curled in again, and Irenie's likeness wrapped around itself. It needed something heavy to hold it. His eye fell on the pitchfork in the stack of corn tops, and he stood to fetch it. But when he grabbed it, something black curled out from the fodder, and when Brodis jumped back, his foot clattered against metal, and the barn went black. He dropped to his knees and felt for the aluminum bail. The smell of kerosene pinched the air, and his hand touched the cool fluid. Then his fingers came upon the lantern. He set it on the sill of the bay door and reached for a sulfur match.

The wick burned low and fittified. Brodis watched until it evened out, then returned to the pitchfork. He set the implement on one end of the scroll and unrolled the other side, holding it in place with his knee while he reached forward to brush aside the loose hay. The lantern cast a pallid light on the newsprint.

The sight of it embarrassed him, as if its preparation had been a dream he wasn't allowed to admit. He pictured up Lem Thompson's face, and his friend didn't look at the newspaper scroll but held his hand to his chin and stared off at the top of the ridgeline as if he was considering the pooled forces of good and evil. Then Brodis saw the face of Haver Brooks, and the deacon smirked and tapped his index finger against his sweaty temple. He commenced telling a story of Brodis and the newspaper in a tone of voice that suggested yes, it was sure enough true but that he himself considered it all something of a joke. All the while a semicircle of churchmen and farmers tilted their heads and listened, slack-jawed.

"But then," Haver'd say, and pause the way he did to wait for the hearers to kick in with *what*? Haver'd slow down when he described the drawing, so that the others might have time to picture it there, unrolling on the barn floor, the triangle skirt, the arms straight out like sticks, the L-shaped feet.

Brodis brushed the long pigtail with his thumb, and the line of it blurred.

It was only a picture on a piece of newspaper. You burned it or you didn't burn it. Neither Haver Brooks nor Lem Thompson would ever know.

But God would know. He knew Brodis's works, and his patience, and how he could not bear a thing that was evil, and how he had labored for the rule of virtue and had not faltered. But He knew more than that. He knew Brodis had set Him aside in favor of his wife and that Brodis had been neither cold nor hot but lukewarm, that for many years he'd become rich and increased with goods and had need of nothing and had forgotten that he was wretched and poor and naked in the face of the Lord. God had seen it all.

From somewhere in the rafters came the dry scrape of rodent toenails. Brodis reached into his pocket for the box and tapped the end of the cardboard drawer with his index finger. The red heads of the matches showed slantwise. He removed one and pushed the drawer against his leg to shut it. He dragged the red and white tip against the side of the box. But humidity had softened the cardboard, and it tore. He opened the drawer for another. This one he tilted so as to get more surface area. There was a wisp of smoke and the smell of burnt sulfur, but no flame. Then the match, as if changing its mind, sputtered and offered up a tepid yellow light. Brodis held it aloft until the flame stood up and the heat of it warmed him, softening him. God had that effect. Whenever at last you opened your heart to Him, there came an ease that you'd forgot to expect, and you knew then you'd been right to follow your instincts instead of the misdoubt that whined away in the back of your mind.

Brodis lifted his knee and let the edge of the page roll into itself. He held the scroll at one end. The match found the bottom and took, and he tilted it up. The yellow flame climbed up the edge, then bloomed all at once, startling him with its swift life and its friendly-hot burn, lapping easy at the gray newsprint like the hearth fires that had warmed their winters.

There had always been a hearth fire then, before the cook stove, whenever she'd prepared every meal there, bent over the stone, hooking the lid of the iron pot to check the bread, the curve of her back outlined against the square of yellow light, the red braid glowing in the—

This, the woman he was set on punishing. How was it possible?

He shook the scroll before he had time to think it out. But it didn't kill the flame. In place of dying, the fire came back yellower and brighter and Brodis blew out all the air in his lungs and dropped the scroll to the floor where it laid like a burnt up limb, curled in upon itself, wilted, appalled. He crushed the ashed end under his foot. But there was hay on the floor too, and he watched as two straws ignited, then four, then a small pile. He swung his lame foot and stepped forward onto the pile, then another. But his attention came right back to the singed roll, and he bent to reclaim it. Now the page resisted unfurling, the blackened end holding it together. He spread it open in his hands. The bottom was gone, and some of the letters. "Raines Lambey" was gone. So was the little girl's right leg. The rest of the figure was as before, the triangle pinafore, the arms outstretched, the pigtail. Only the freckles had smudged, the little girl's football eyes looking back at him with wide surprise.

He pressed the charred edges between his fingers, ensuring the fire was out. Then he rolled the page again, and tucked it, shorter now, back into the oaken pail.

He would speak to her first. She at least deserved that.

By the time he returned to the house, the katydids had subsided and the whirr of the cicadas had taken over.

In the bedroom, he set the chair across from the door, eased himself into it, and opened the Bible on his lap, the weight of it steadfast against his thighs. He waited. The Lord gaveth wisdom, and out of His mouth came knowledge and understanding. Soon Brodis was dreaming, and in the dream she emerged from the forest with the pale-boned moon behind her, just as she'd done for a thousand years, a creature that had lived in his imagination and nightmare long before he'd ever met her. And as she stepped into the clearing, it wasn't just her, but the wildness of the forest itself come to creep into the world of men. The oaks pressed and spread into the clearing, the saplings sprouted up, and the growth of it reached over the yard and the house until the tendrils and shoots curled and vined and there was no seeing the building. And then, whenever the forest had overspread their home, whenever the house was buried under, his wife emerged from the tangle, unscathed as time.

Irenie paused to ensure being alone. Papered leaves clattered behind her. Could be the unseen rustle of small lives—or could be his game foot swinging wide. There'd be no explaining the drawsack with the fresh change of clothes and the cardboard suitcase that banged against her shin.

He already knew about her wanderings, and he hadn't forbid them, leastways not yet. But there was something dangerous in that too. Ever since he'd discovered her habit he'd come at her strange. He'd yet to ask about the reasons, and she'd yet to proffer them, not because there hadn't been opportunity, but because the explaining would require pulling something naked from her soul and laying it open for him to examine. Instead she kept her eyes peeled for the return of the demon. Instead she tried to be invisible.

And Ginny making out that a woman could turn back time by undoing a wedding vow she'd made before God and the world. It had been Irenie's biggest promise. She'd promised herself and her Maker and everyone she knew that she'd live with Brodis until she was separated by death, and there was no turning back a clock. They said Joshua made time to stand still, but Irenie had her doubts. And what if everyone who married was to cut out whenever they wanted because something ugly rose up between them? There would be no more marriage.

Or maybe this wasn't the way every marriage worked. Her father had said she was accepting the terms of the deal. And by that reckoning maybe it was Brodis who'd been the one to break the promise.

And that view made the decision thinkable. It made the reasons for *can't* look skinny next to the reasons for *ought*.

At the top of the bald, Fortune lifted her nose and sniffed the air. Irenie listened. Nothing. Then she motioned to the dog, and they both descended the western side of the mountain where the laurel and the myrtle and the huckleberry scraggled up between the boulders. Irenie kicked at the ground to notify the rattlers they were coming. As children, she and Lesley and her brother Nichol had riled one just here. Nichol had broken off a sapling to scoop the thing from its crevice. She remembered how strange the animal had looked aloft, its muscles flexing and writhing, its rattling smaller and feebler in the open air.

The overhang when she reached it was black and depthless, the slab of rock beneath her feet cold. Here in the shadow of the cliff she stopped and let Fortune press into the cave's narrow opening. Irenie listened. When the dog didn't come out, she lit the lantern, then crawled after, pushing the suitcase in front of her, her knees scraping along the hard packed dirt. The space widened and the air turned chilly. The rows of glass jars gleamed yellowly. There were dozens of them now, these moments she'd saved. And every one of them, the locks of Hannah's hair and Matthew's first teeth and the gourd rattles Lesley had fashioned for him and the scrolled-up baby drawings, would have to stay put.

She set the suitcase on end and placed a stone atop the draw sack, ensuring it to be there when she returned. She mutched for the dog and turned to go, her mind and body lighter now that she didn't carry the luggage or its incrimination.

There was certain and not certain. When you took the egg from under the chicken it was warm and brown and liquid-heavy in the palm of your hand. And when you cracked it open there was the yolk and the clear and the thin white skein that might could later become a chick. You scrambled that skein into the egg or you fried it, one, along with the rest, in butter in the skillet. There was no chick, not yet, no conjecture that you'd sacrificed the thing before it had reached its age. And maybe that was the way of a baby too. If her courses had started, there would have been no chick, only the skein of the would-be child.

The address Ginny gave her was in her pocket, the ink of it already starting to smudge. Copperhill, Tennessee. She pictured it like that, a great statue of copper that rose from the ground and caught the gleaming red sun. The notion she could choose brought a trill of hope. Maybe she didn't have to follow Brodis, didn't have to lie with him every night for the rest of her life, didn't have to tie her fate to his. There'd been living without Brodis Lambey and there could be again. If she was to choose.

She wasn't a chicken nor a sow.

When she reached the yard in front of the house she stopped, and so did Fortune. Scram and Lacy and Stomper lay awake on their bellies under the porch, paws extended in front of them, ears cocked and tensed. The window glass was dark, but something there held its breath.

She turned to the clearing behind. Nothing. She stooped to unlace her brogans, then unhooked the bib of the overalls and tucked the brass-fitted straps inside the garment so they'd not flap and jingle. The dungarees slid to the floor and she reached down to pick them up. Then, with the denims tucked under her arm and the brogans in her hand, she pulled open the door.

The kitchen was dark as the maw of the cave, but alert. She sock-footed across the threshold, stooping to set the shoes by the door. She swung the bedroom door open without a sound and reached for the cotton nightdress she'd hung there.

But the drag of a match ripped the silence. Her husband's face glowed up yellow, then too the reflection of glass, and the wicker of a lamp, and there he was, sitting in a chair in the middle of the room, a Bible open in his lap, as if he'd been sitting there all along, reading in the pitch dark.

Irenie heard her breath suck into her mouth and on instinct clasped the nightdress against her body.

He didn't speak. Instead he stared at her naked hips and legs with a pop-eyed energy that pinned her to the floorboards. Then, in the least of movements, he pulled back as if seeing some horror, his mouth dropping open. The cliff that was his forehead crumpled down toward his eyes.

Why, oh why hadn't she hoisted the nightdress over her head and let the loose fabric cover her body? Now there wasn't any way to get the garment on without exposing herself to that manic gaze. She might could do it quick, but something told her that the next motion she made would start forth a string of events that neither of them could control. Instead she waited and made ready to react.

Something slow-limbed and terrible edged itself into the room. It stretched its legs, and the air between her and Brodis shivered. Irenie readied her body to move but couldn't do it until the demon did first.

Slowly, Brodis leaned forward in the chair so far that he was sure to come out of it.

As quick as she could Irenie hauled the nightdress over her head and fit her arms into the sleeves. The fabric settled over her legs. She reached for her step-ins.

His left hand folded the book shut. It made a soft clap. "Come. Here."

Irenie shook her head.

"I said come here."

Her legs were trembling. She didn't move.

"Come here, wife."

Her body felt dry and weightless, as if the physical presence of it were not hers to own, as if the woman standing stock against the door frame weren't a woman at all, but the dried up shell of one, like the husk the fisher spider abandoned after squeezing her new self out. There wasn't anything left in the husk to give it free will. A good wind and it would blow away. Irenie's mouth had gone dry, and she couldn't happen to think out what it was she was meant to do. She forced all her planning into the idea of getting her legs into the step-ins.

All at once Brodis sprang from the chair and caught the under-wear in his hand and yanked it from her grasp. It fell to the floor in a limp arc. His right hand grabbed at the back of her hair and pulled steady until her face tilted up toward his. Now his forehead dropped into his brow, and his eyes excavated her face, and for the first time she marked how deep were the furrows running from his nose to the corner of his mouth.

But he didn't touch her body.

Instead he pinched the fabric of the nightdress between his thumb and index finger and lifted it slow. Instead he bunched the garment and drew it up until her legs were bare, all the while searching her face as if he would find something there he'd never seen before. After a long moment, he turned his face toward her legs. They were shaking so much she was sure he could see. Yet he didn't touch her. Instead he picked up the Bible, crouched in front of her, and traced a line down her thigh. The binding of the book was made of the skin of some animal: bumpy, reptilian, and dry. The corner moved from her calf up to her knee then to her thigh. It carried with it a thin line of pain.

"You're burned," he said, without surprise nor pity, the way people told her she was short or skinny or freckled. The way he would examine a diseased crop or a hole in the barn wall.

It was true. A bright crust of red weltered the length of her leg. On her thigh palped a blister the size of his palm. Even her foot was spattered with flecks of red and gray.

Brodis muttered, "Behold." Then she didn't hear any more, only the rise and fall of a person giving his own self advice. "...And He said I stand at the door, and knock." He touched the corner of the leatherbound book into the thin skin of the blister. He didn't touch her with his flesh.

But he saw. He saw everything: the hot water puddled on the floor, the steamed air, the mason jar coming to rest in a puddle of brown, the sediment like mouse droppings, the waddled leaves.

She could say she'd dropped the teakettle, but it wouldn't matter. He knew that she'd laid skirts-up in the mud with the moss and the water against her thigh, knew too the potatoes she'd skinned that day, and the white compress of peelings and beard moss she'd bound against the blisters to draw out the heat.

At some point she noticed how quick her breath was coming. He must have heard it too because he let the nightdress fall and brought the Bible to her chin. It touched the corner of her lips, and she recoiled. "This panting. I haven't heard that on you before."

She shut her mouth.

"Don't do that," he countered. "Open." The Bible touched her lips. "I spied it in the teeth first." His face was inches from hers. The bones below his eyes pushed against the fabric of his cheeks like tent poles.

Irenie looked away.

"Those dog teeth."

Instinctively, she closed her mouth. Her teeth were healthy and mostly even. But she and Nichol were dog-toothed both. They'd gotten it from their father. It was a long time since she'd been sensitive to that particular insult.

"Now, don't do that." The steady pull on her hair drew her head back and up. "Open." The Bible was out of her line of sight now, but she could smell it: sour like sweated clothes, like the fust on his shirts before she dropped them into the iron cauldron to boil. She opened her mouth.

"The canines. They're longer today than they were yesterday."

Again she tried to press her lips closed.

"Unh, unh," he chided. "It's a good half inch, each side." His eyes no longer started from his head. Now he sounded like a man who was looking to puzzle out a question.

All at once he turned and slammed the Bible against the bedside table. The oil lamp jumped. "Woe to the inhabiters of the earth and of the sea!" A pearl penknife fell to the floor. He thrust his face toward hers and switched to a whisper, "For the devil is come down unto you, because he knows that he hath but a short time!"

She closed her eyes.

"Look at me!" he shouted. She did.

His gaze traveled her face, as if searching to unriddle some puzzle. Then his voice changed, nigh on to friendly. "Are you the true wife of Brodis Lambey?"

What did he mean by true? She willed herself not to think on the suitcase she'd packed and stashed in the cave. "Yes."

Loss shadowed his face. "But you hesitate. Even now you hesitate. Prevarication is not in your nature."

Irenie had no answer.

His eyes drifted toward her mouth. "How do you explain your new teeth?" The look he gave her now was hopeful, as if he willed her to supply a story that would explain the canines.

And in that moment she wanted to give him that story, any story that would ease the wound in his face. "Brodis, they've always been this way. Look at the rest of my family."

"The rest of your family. . ." he repeated, as if the idea intrigued him. "What is the name of your least cousin?"

"Brodis." She reached her hand towards his face, and he flinched. But he let her fingers linger on his jaw line. The muscles under the bristle of his coming beard were tight as machinery.

He pushed her arm away. "What is the name of your least cousin?"

It occurred to her that he was testing her. "Lesley."

He launched the next question without pause. "What is the name your mother carried before she was wedded to your father?"

"Little." Her response was automatic.

"What is the name of the child you lost?"

Something in her throat broke then, something she hadn't even known was there until it split, the inside moist and watery and weakly. But she didn't cry. She wanted to pass the test, whatever it was. And she knew on instinct that the crying would disqualify her.

*"What is the name of the child you lost?"*

Hannah, Hannah, Hannah, she wanted to scream. Hannah is the name of the child we lost, both of us, the two of us together, the child that left in the middle of winter because she couldn't cough another cough, Hannah is the name of that child.

His voice bellowed. *"What is the name of the child you lost?"*

"Hannah," she whispered because she understood the anguish that pushed up from under his words. He was looking to find out who she was, looking to learn the part of her that had receded from him so long ago, though he'd not noticed at the time, hadn't noticed all these many years, and the only way in was through the conversations they'd already had. She caressed the side of his face. "Hannah is the name of the child we lost, in the middle of the winter, under the snow and the cold and the drafts. And you laid the boards of the ceiling to save her." She traced her thumb across his brow, brushing away at the fear she saw there. "You remember."

Brodis let go of her hair and let his arm fall. Then he sat down in the slat-seated chair and covered his face with his hands. She didn't know he was weeping until the tears squeezed out between his fingers.

She took a step toward him. The man sitting in the chair was the old Brodis, the one who'd hammered into the middle of the night and sanded Matthew's trunk smooth. Now his elbows rested on his knees and his large body seemed to break. His sobs racked the room. She knelt beside him and touched his thigh. "Everything I've ever done has been for us, Brodis. And for Matthew. But this thing, this one thing, I did for myself."

He groaned as if he were in bodily pain.

She put her hand on his shoulder, and he flinched as if burned. "Get away."

"Brod—"

"Just so came Jezebel to Ahab."

She turned and reached to pick up the step-ins from the floor, then the Bible. Then she laid her body on the bed and listened to the sound of her husband heaving himself from the chair, moving slow as an old man. Then the sound of one knee hitting the floor and then another, as if he were powerful tired. Then the mumble of chanting or prayer. Something about a great white throne that had nothing to do with anything. The voice rose and fell in a lost, keening song.

Irenie stared up at the ceiling, wondering that Matthew hadn't woken, then remembered that he wasn't there.

Brodis's low mutterings filled the room for a long time. "And the dead were judged on those things which were written in the books."

Right now Matthew would be sleeping. In a bed next to Luke and Dudley.

"And the dead were judged every man according to their works."

And the thought of that, of her son asleep in the clean sheets of the boarding school, calmed her. She had done that. No matter what happened, she had that to keep.

"And whosoever was not found written in the Book of Life was cast into the lake of fire and brimstone."

The phrase, that last, caught at her mind. She thought again on the husks of fisher spiders. Whenever Matthew was a child, she and he had collected the empty cases, sometimes two and three inches long, but weightless. Once, he'd set one above the door of the springhouse, to act as the water's guardian. The husk had remained for weeks.

She hadn't thought on that husk in a long time. And she'd never stopped to wonder where the new spider had wandered, having forgotten the shell of her old life. Somewhere else, alive in her new skin.

Did Matthew remember the fisher spider? And what would he say about her now?

Irenie rolled over to give her husband some privacy. She heard something hit the floor that slid off the bed onto the wooden board, something that hit at one corner and then flopped over. A board maybe, or a book.

## CHAPTER SEVENTEEN

)

IT WOULD'VE BEEN EASIER IF SHE'D TAKEN UP WITH
another man. Then he could've lain in wait. He could've brought
the shotgun and a ready-made speech. He could've surprised them
in the moment of their sin and marked the fear in the other man's
eyes and the shame in hers, could've looked for sorrow in her face
when he asked did she take into account the family they'd raised
and the farm they'd built. He could've made her to choose right
then and there. But the evil that had claimed his wife was something altogether different. God himself couldn't contain it. And
now that the devil had seen her, he'd never *unsee* her, never un-
know the curve of her back nor the swell of her buttocks nor the
ankles that narrowed so finely underneath her boots. He'd have already marked that she was straighter and defter than other women,
that she was that rare copper-haired woman with eyes not blue, but
the color of oiled oakwood. And the fiend would have reckoned
her even more of a prize because she was married to a man of God.
None of that surprised him.

But that *she'd* chosen *him*.

It just went to show the consequences of wanting, what happened when a part of your soul longed to embrace that which it was forbidden to have. That was enough to open the door. Right there. Just that. And sure, he had his own wants, would have at one time given up everything just to go back to his river days. Or almost everything. But people weren't meant to live looking backward.

In the morning before morning, when he returned from the milking, she was at the stove and didn't turn. The spatula scraped against the iron skillet. There was nothing to say he hadn't said the night before. The decisions were hers now. Between her and Satan and Jesus. If Mr. June was right, the only thing Brodis could do was give her an opportunity. If she wanted it. Didn't seem like she did. But maybe that was the devil talking, because how much of her thinking was her own and how much the thinking of that other intelligence?

In the yard, the rooster bragged. Brodis made his way to the fields.

Noon dinner was the same, supper quieter still. Midnight couldn't come soon enough.

In the dark, he felt her departure more than heard it, just a shift in the air, the warmth that had once been on the sheets now gone. There was no press of feet on the floorboards, nor lift of the lantern from the nail, nor loose of the latch which he now realized she'd oiled, been oiling, for a long time. The air currented in from the open door, as if she'd evaporated in front of him and wouldn't step back into her body until she was in the presence of the one who'd taken her.

Brodis swung his feet to the floor and reached for his dungarees.

Outside, the moon squatted skinny and horned atop the ridge. A dry wind clattered through the tobacco leaves, and their broad flats were loud as laundry. It would bring rain for certain, and in a few days' time his crop would grow up higher than it'd been yet. A few steps ahead, Scram barked once, a low tentative *whuff*, then again, and Brodis spoke to the animal to gentle him.

He drew the barn door open, and something quick and fittified shot from the darkness toward his head. His arm swung up to protect his face, but the animal had already disappeared into the blackness above. He set the lantern on the sill and climbed up the four steps. The haystack rustled with some vermin too ashamed to show its face in the light.

For the second time, Brodis brought the wooden bucket down and regarded the tube of grayish white among the red. Now, when he drew it out, the end of the paper was damp. He held the lantern above the bucket and saw that a thick fluid had dripped onto the bottom of the oaken pail. He touched his finger to it and smelled. Nitroglycerin. The sticks had begun to weep. He tried to remember whenever he'd purchased the dynamite, but it didn't matter. There was nothing for it but to burn it, the sooner the better. But not in the pitch of night. And not before he'd taken care to do it right.

The newspaper was as he'd left it, a slim roll secured with a piece of paperstring.

Below, the mule stamped.

Brodis replaced the wooden bucket on its nail, then stepped into the night, the scroll held loosely at his side so as not to crush it. Wind wagged the trees, and the shadows reeled across the shifting ground.

He was relieved to enter the house, though its emptiness was both comfort and vexation. Matthew was gone, already, so young, to a boarding school, surrounded by wealthy children, wrapped in cotton sheets and the gentle light that belonged to him alone. Nobody would be able to see it, that light. It had taken Brodis years and years to appreciate it, to his ever-abiding shame. A father who saw too late his son's true spirit, the silver of his soul.

He set the scroll on the hearth next to a jar of upended matches. The time was at hand.

Brodis tapped out a match and dragged it across the granite hearthstone, lifted the globe of the lamp and touched it to the wick. Gold light wavered and pooled around him and lapped at the walls, and he floated in that light until he felt the presence of God widen his breath and his heart. He bent his lame leg and eased to one knee, then both. He closed his eyes until his prayer swam up and washed out of him, eddying and flowing into the gold. "I know that in the past I've said I was ready whenever I wasn't," he allowed, and the knowing of that weakness made him stronger. "That I've flattered myself, and looked to have it both ways, getting everything I wanted in this world at the same time persuading myself that I was doing the best I could for You in the other." This admission shouldered up to the first, and Brodis saw them there, lined up next to his other faults. And there had to be more he didn't see. "I've skipped spring services just to earn a extra dollar on the river, and I've brung money home because I knew it would make me larger in her eyes. I've lusted after her and others even in your own house." He opened his eyes, and the ceiling of the room flaughtered and winked. "I know you've bid me choose, and I've temporized, waiting and hoping that this was not the choice you were asking, telling myself that if I was to do nothing I could keep the people I loved." Outside the wind rattled the palings of the garden fence, hot and dry as breath. "I've figured myself for smart. But now I see that the things I know are as chaff that blows away at the first breeze."

Brodis heaved himself to his feet. The time was at hand. He tried to stand the scroll on end, but it wouldn't balance. His eye fell on the round walnut hole he'd drilled into the stone years before, when their lives had been unblemished, when his son was a boy and dropped the green-hulled fruit into the opening and Irenie hammered it through, the outer leather buckling and splitting to reveal the brown-shelled walnut inside. And when his wife bent forward to pull apart the green-hanging leather, her neck was white in the light of the fire, the freckles spreading below, and when she leaned over the boy, you spied the hollow between her collarbones and the whiteness of the skin there too.

What would she feel when that skin burned?

The blisters he'd gave her ran from ankle to thigh. In time the wrinkled red crust would peel away and leave a scar, smooth and thick like rubber sheeting.

But what if that salamandry skin was to cover her whole body?

What if she was to die?

There shall not be among you any one that useth divination, or an observer of times, or an enchanter.

Or a witch. Any one.

If he didn't do it, the years would pass, and she and he would grow old together but each of them alone. The decades would become bitter with knowing. Then the devil would come to claim his due, and his wife would be dragged into the face of the eternal fire, and that was a burning that lasted forever and ever.

The dogs had eaten Jezebel, and there had been no one to bury her. Her carcass had been as dung upon the face of the field.

He set the scroll in the walnut hole and it stood like a standard. The time was at hand. A scar was skin-deep, the mere showing of a wound. What was beneath was what mattered. God would renew. Brodis closed his eyes against the wavery light. This time he whispered. "You have spoke to me, not once, but many times. I have hardened my heart against the truth. But now I am listening."

He opened his eyes, propped the Bible on its binding, and set his hand against the ends of the pages. Then he closed his eyes again and loosed the pages, trying not to think on Exodus and its particular behest.

Thou shalt not suffer a witch to live.

The pages separated and fell open. Not Exodus. Genesis. He drew his finger down until it stopped on chapter 22.

*And God said, Take now thy son, thine only son Isaac.* Brodis knew the story by heart. The Lord told Abraham to sacrifice his only son, so Abraham fetched the boy to the place God had told him. It took him three days to get there, which meant that he had three days to think on his decision, but nowhere in the story did Abraham ask how come. And whenever he got to the land of Moriah, Abraham split the wood for the offering and still did not ask how come. He told his servants to wait, and at no time did he tell them the terrible mission that God had gave him.

And wouldn't that have been the easiest thing? Just tell them about the command. They'd have stopped him, sure, and he could've said to God, I tried, as sure as I'm standing here. I looked to do the thing that you told me, but no, here are these others who kept me from my duty. And that would have been the easiest thing, sure.

But Abraham didn't do that. He took his young son up the mountain, and when the boy asked him where was the lamb for the burnt offering, he told him that God would provide it. He could have told the boy that no, that this time God had required a human sacrifice and Isaac might could have run away, for sure a boy can run faster than an old man. Then Abraham could have said to God, "See, I looked to do the thing you bid of me, but the jasper got away." Instead he carried his mission in his heart, and it lay heavy there. And he knew what his duty was and he knew he had to do it alone. Just him.

Brodis let the book clap shut. Even now a part of him thought that Abraham was a fool for listening to the words of the Lord. Even now, a part of him believed that he, Brodis, was better off being the one to make decisions, not God.

But the Lord didn't require something of you that you couldn't do. He required only one thing, and that was the hardest thing there was, that you give yourself over to Him without reservation. Jesus didn't leave you in the lurch. It was the other way round. People abandoned Him. You either believed in Him or you didn't. And by doing this thing, this one thing, you made Him real. You affirmed the existence of the Heaven and the Christ. If you didn't do it, if you denied it, you made Heaven nothing more than a wish and the Lord the central figure in a myth, a step above Jack and the beanstalk.

It would either save her or kill her, or both.

He scraped a match against the hearthstone and touched it to the top of the scroll. Right off, the fire reached up and grabbed at his hand, the hungry yellow tongue licking upward ten inches, then more, forking and reforking and sucking up the light in the corners of the room and claiming it for itself, then eating the light from the windows and the stars as well, as if it knew it was the only live thing in the world. Brodis couldn't take his eye from the quickening flame, splitting now and reaching toward him in the wind from the open window like the fingers of divine will, and there in the yellow crest of them breathed a face, and the face was the Son of Man, clothed with a garment down to his foot, and girt about with a golden girdle, his head and his hairs white like wool, and his eyes a flame, and his countenance was as the sun.

Ashes popped and flew, and the fire darted to the center of the room and then seemed to reconsider and draw into its own self, sedate, retiring, leaving behind a lacy black shell that was the scroll. And the scroll wagged forward, as if age had caught up to it at last and the weight of holding itself had become overmuch, and it tipped forward and touched its toes and then fell to the hearth and laid there, the flame extinguished now, the lacework black save for a few glows of red. Brodis didn't touch it nor take his eyes from it. Then came the smoke, pulling away from the hearth. Brodis coughed.

He was cold all over, his shirt soaked through with fear and sweat. When he stood, his knees made a cracking sound.

He collapsed into the rocking chair. He had done it. Outside the wind rushed down the hollow, and the trees and shrubbery furied. But he, Brodis, had stilled because he had done the thing that God had bid him, and it was the hardest thing there was, and his body sank into the surface of the chair until sleep came upon him.

The sound of moaning woke him. The room was spilled in light. The chair creaked when he sat forward, and the house listened. The cow's groan rose again, layered in dread.

He had missed the milking. The dogs whined out their concern. Brodis waited. There was the twitter of birds, the mindless *cuck-cuck* of chickens, but no burble of hot water on the stove, no grate of iron on iron, no smell of sausage nor coffee. He heaved himself up.

The house was empty. He pushed open the front door and stepped into the sun, already brassy on the eastern ridge. The cow moaned, and the flawless bright stretched out before him, and with it something in him too, some recognition that he knew was to come but that wasn't yet provident for him to receive.

In the barn, yellow light sliced through the boards. The cow lowed and rolled her eyes. Her milk was already down, the bag tight and full and blue-veined. He did the job without thinking, then covered the pail and set it down somewhere, maybe the porch, or maybe the springhouse. It didn't matter. He fed the dogs. Lacy turned around once and picked up a mole, dropping it at her feet. He scratched the dog behind the ears, but in his mind he'd already started across the field. He heeled Fortune to him, then on second thought, hereboyed Scram too and leashed them both. Then the three of them set off single file between the towers of tobacco. Some of the leaves had begun to droop, the biggest now spotted yellow, ready to harvest. The rattle of cicadas sweltered up around him.

On the other side of the field, the bees droned at the sourwoods. He started into the forest and up the mountain, the canopy overhead chattering with birds. The dogs looked to him, expecting, but he couldn't bring himself to loose them. Scram stopped and cocked his ears forward. Something moved in the underbrush and then quieted. But Brodis felt it there yet, the eyes of some creature that watched them all. The dog had tensed and stilled.

Brodis unhooked both leads. "Okay."

Scram took off into the heath and after a certain amount of clatter and frenzy emerged from the brush with a rabbit, the body broken at the neck and hanging like a sack. But Fortune had trotted up the path, head up, ears cocked forward in anticipation, as if searching for something in the green, confident about where she would find it.

When they neared the top of the mountain, the path tracked straight into the heath, and the laurely dark pulled them in, the leathered hands of the rhododendron catching at his shoulders and temples. Then Fortune loped ahead into the clearing. Brodis slowed his pace and stopped in the middle of the bald in the exact spot a fellow might stand if he was wanting the fire of God to fork down and strike him dead. Fortune lifted her nose to the air, but there was little wind, only the dull weight of summer. Except for the lines in the turf, the meadow was empty, the grasses yellow and drooped in the heat, splattered here and there with red strawberries and purple flowers and spikes of goldenrod. On three sides, the forest dropped away, the edge of the trees a dark brow of growth. A raven wheeled off the western cliff. There was no sign of her—or him. High above, horsetail clouds wisped against the ceiling of the sky, their hairs streaming to the south and east. Tomorrow it would weather.

Fortune cantered at the eastern edge of the bald, pricking her ears and casting her nose to the ground. She pulled up and whined with impatience, gazing at Brodis with some hidden purpose. Then she lowered her nose again and began searching anew. She stopped, backed up and sniffed. Then she went to casting back and forth over the burnt grass, every now and then lifting her head to make certain he was there.

Brodis watched the dog dully. Wasn't any time now for foxes or raccoons. He kneeled and turned his face to God. But in place of Him it was the white ball of the sun he saw, and he closed his eyes and reached his hands into the noisy light. Please. The word whispered from his lips. But he didn't even know what he was asking for, and he wondered could his Maker know it before he did.

He opened his eyes to a firmament of cauterizing light, and somewhere in that too-bright sky came the voice of harpers harping and hounds howling. Brodis closed his eyes, and lo, a Lamb standing in his mind's eye, and with him a hundred and forty-four thousand men, all with the name of the Father written on their foreheads. The first fruits. The redeemed among men.

An urgent yap punctured the vision. He opened his eyes. Fortune was watching him with impatience. It was she who had barked. Scram was sunk upon his haunches, wailing a long thread of lamentation into the sky.

Brodis got to his feet, and Fortune trotted with purpose to the northern edge of the clearing, where grayback boulders scattered

the slope. He knew the path. It needed hopping from one green-li-
chened rock to the next. The one time he'd chased a deer through
the talus, he'd scrabbled up a rattlesnake.

Now Fortune lowered her nose to the rocks, now stopped and
looked back at him.

He followed. A fellow had to pay attention was all. Soil had collected among the stones, and saplings and poison vine grew in the
crevices. Fortune bounded from one purchase to the next, ears alert
and tongue lolling out the side of her mouth, now standing on a
narrow ledge above a cliff, now scampering around it. After a spell,
she stopped and turned to check his progress.

And then she was gone. Disappeared, though he hadn't seen
her fall, hadn't heard a yelp. He picked his way down to the ledge
where she'd stood. Then he spied the opening. The entrance was
wide and shallow, a low overhang where a fellow could open a
bedroll on a rainy night if he didn't mind the outward slant of the
rock that threatened to pitch him down the mountain. Behind this
shallow indent was a narrower mouth, worn smooth by time and
animals, dark and tall enough for Scram to bound into now. Brodis
crouched at the hole and listened for some sign of struggle from
within. The mouth of the cave breathed a fetid dank. He listened
for the dogs, but they made no sound. He whistled, then thrust
his head into the hole, waiting for his eyes to adjust. After a long
moment he heard excited breathing. He crawled in on hands and
knees, pausing to wait for his night eyes.

His wife's shape caught his breath in his throat, just there, the
outline of her shoulders, the flair of her hips, the arms bowed out in
supplication. But no. The same rose-print dress she'd worn morning after morning at the cook stove. Not her, just her clothes. He
had to lay his hand on the thing to make certain sure there was no
one in it, only the garment spread flat on the tilt of rock, a pair of
pantaloons close by, as if she'd stepped out of the clothes wet and
left them to dry.

Or cast off her human garments to free herself of their
encumbering.

He didn't think why he plucked the printed muslin from the granite, nor why he buried his face in the fabric, the smell of skin and soap and woodsmoke strong enough to bring her to life, so that he was loathe to open his eyes and discover she wasn't there, and even when he kept them closed, something in his chest grew wide as a watershed and his heart knocked against his ribcage and closed up his throat. His tears, in place of falling, choked him, so that when Fortune nosed the clothing in his hands, he didn't have the voice to tell her no. He figured to push the animal away but instead found himself caressing her ears and holding the thick bristled head against his cheek the same way Matthew liked to do. The dog let out an anxious whine and pulled away. Her eyes searched his face. For the first time since they'd reached the bald, the animal seemed at a loss.

Scram commenced to howling again, and the lamentation filled up the narrow space, and the walls echoed the keening as if a multitude grieved from its stony recesses. Brodis rolled up the clothing and tucked it under his arm.

Only then did he spy the fox, or rather, what remained of it. White bone traced against the black earth, small and prehistoric, the head thrust forward, the bones of its spine curled up like the hunched spine of an old woman, the front limbs drawn in as if she'd something to hide, or were rubbing her hands together in anticipation. Brodis heard his breath expel. The triangle of the fox's skull was the size of a leaf, the eye holes enormous, the fitted jigsawed teeth bared in ancient grimace, the bottom jaw pinned to the top by the long curve of the dog teeth.

But there was more. Something that looked to be glass—and was: rows and rows of jelly jars, and mason jars, and battery cases, all filled or partially filled with substances he couldn't lay his mind on. Stones and paper and fabric and tiny animal skulls. Hair. Teeth. Brodis stared and squinted but couldn't bring himself to take one step closer.

The fox, though. The fox had to come home. The bones came up easy, and he laid the larger pieces on the rose print dress. The smaller parts of the limbs and feet separated when he lifted them, but these too he swaddled in the fabric, then wrapped the garment around the skeleton and brought the whole package out of the cave and down the mountain.

He dug the grave in the spice garden, where the herbs lined up in their little designated rows, and the air smelled not quite of cooking, but nigh onto the idea of it. The earth had been spade-turned so often that each thrust of the shovel sank deep. At first the undersoil smelled of garlic and mint and onion, but then it gave way to the red clay below, where the blade struck hard against rock, and he had to lean his shoulder into the job.

When the hole was deep enough to keep away the animals, he set the shovel on the rim of the grave and hoisted himself out.

There was no coffin and no one to help lower the remains, so he set them at the edge and slid himself down once again. He reached for the bundle and unwrapped it. He laid the skeleton in first, the triangle skull and the arched spine. The limbs were a complication, but he set the bigger bones out, then arranged the laced complexities of the feet and the hands. He positioned the spine, stepped back, and then bent to the work again, because it wasn't the shape of the animal as he'd first seen it, wasn't yet the tilt of the head nor the curl of the hand-paws. He rearranged, stepped back, and re-arranged. When he was satisfied, he buttoned the buttons of the rose-colored dress and shook out the wrinkles as best he could. Then he smoothed the garment over the skeleton and straightened the skirt and folded the arms. He stood and hoisted himself out of the hole to regard his work. The garment had her shape. The sleeves met over the front of the bodice, as if in prayer.

The garden wasn't a consecrated churchyard, but he could give her a proper service.

The water buckets sat on the front porch of the house. Two of them were full yet, and he plunged his muddy hands into the sun-warmed water. Then he poured both pails into a tin washtub and refilled them in the springhouse. He stripped off his clothes and eased into the tub, his face turned from the rows of spices, his knees angling up to his chin. When the full weight of his body came to rest on the knobs of his buttocks, the tin bottom buckled toward the ground with a low metallic *pop*. He soaped his body and his hair and last his face, rubbing the grainy bar between his hands and shutting his eyes against the day and bringing his fingers against his brow until the lye burned through his closed eyes and the hot tears finally came and seeped into the dirty water.

At the gravesite, he lifted his face to God, and the sun spread across his cheeks. The black Sunday coat stretched tight against his still damp shoulders, and a patch of sweat under the neck of his clean white shirt crept down the hollows at either side of his spine.

The Bible he carried was not the one he used for community buryings. It was his own personal. He let it fall open in his palms. He expected the pages to part in Ecclesiastes, where the pastoral words surged as old as the turning of summer to fall, but they didn't. This time the pages parted at the end of the book, and Brodis read from the chapters there. "She shall hunger no more, neither thirst more; neither shall the sun light on her, nor any heat." His wife's shape which was not her shape was placid and easy in the grave. In that moment, more than anything he wanted to see the polished gleam of her hair, the shining ribbon of it. But instead there was only the dress, the cedarwood buttons dark and irregular like mistakes. He turned to the book in his hands. "And God shall wipe away all tears from her eyes."

The words were not seasonal and comforting like the words in Ecclesiastes. Instead they were final, in the manner of all things that come to undisputed end.

## CHAPTER EIGHTEEN

IRENIE HADN'T ACCUSTOMED TO THE NOISE OF THE train. Instead of softening into the back of her mind, the clatter and buck of it seemed to louden over time. The first she saw of Asheville was the warehouses stretched out long near the river, then the paved streets crowded with green and red automobiles, the brick and stone factories, and then the streetcars like toys tethered to overhead wires. Two women in fancy hats stared into a shop window, and Irenie watched them until they were dashed from her view. She pressed her face to the glass to search out the school where Matthew was, but there was no school, only a library so tremendous she thought of it there long after the building had passed, its rooms filled to the ceiling with books and gleaming pianos whose surfaces shone like black glass, the chairs cushioned with pillows. And then the train slowed next to a bank built like a tall slice of pie, its windows high and wide, and there, across the street a storybook castle with four tiny turrets and a tower in the center with two windows blue as eyes and a brick path where orange flowers burst upon a carpet of green. And boys and boys of Matthew's age, some carrying rakes or satchels or paper sacks and some just swinging their arms, but none of them him.

The train nudged forward and stopped at a timbered pebbledash depot, and she looked down to see her hand gripping the leather strap of her bag, the bones of her fingers pressing white through her skin. A knot lodged in her chest that was either fear or excitement or something she hadn't known since she was a girl, a kind of freedom maybe, or maybe it was the knowledge that something was about to happen that had never happened before.

The inside of the depot was crowded with worried looking laborers in crushed hats and stained jackets and old women sitting on long benches and gentlemen in suits holding the arms of ladies in fine dresses and another boy shorter and stockier than Matthew with a wheel and a girl with a little white dog pressed against her chest and no one looking at Irenie at all. The mustachioed attendant at the ticket vestibule said, "Morning missus," in a way that seemed to mean let's get on with it. On the wall above his black cap was a drawing of something like a sprouted root, at the center a black dot labeled "Asheville" with four lines sprangling out like suckers from the eyes of a potato. One of them was the A&S, and it traveled north. One was the Western North Carolina, and it branched south and west to Hendersonville and Marion, where it split again to Tyson and Brevard and Erwin and Forest City. The Graham County Line spoked to Murphy, then turned south to Georgia where it divided and forked again. It wasn't a map as much as a plan. Irenie had never seen such a thing, and for a long time after when she thought of Asheville and the school her son attended, she thought of this plan, in this city, where possibility grew errant and thick.

"Missus, please," the stationmaster whined. "Step out if you need more time." But Irenie pushed her money under the glass and said Blue Ridge, Georgia.

Forty minutes later she sat on the train, and the Biltmore Depot and the castle that she now recognized for a church slid from the window. The last she spied of the city where her son lived was empty rooftops, and clotheslines, a blue jay on a telephone wire, and black tarpaper pooling at the bases of chimneys.

The train followed the river west into a thick pall next to low flat buildings like great brick chicken coops. A smokestack rose from the haze, and smaller stacks around it, like rough and blasted children. By the time Irenie figured the town for Canton, it was gone, and before her sprawled a ridgeline that Matthew would have said was the spine of a great sleeping dog, its withers jutting into the sky then sloping down to the head that rested on his paws. The dog's hide had great bare patches in it, and at its paws spread a fair sized settlement, and she knew the town for Waynesville and the river beside it for the Tuckaseegee. Then the mountain shifted, and it wasn't a dog anymore but a hillside with new saplings busting through the weeds and the stumps, and the buildings that crowded up to the tracks were new timber houses that smelled of sawdust. The hillsides were naked, and more naked still when her eye tracked up the high gaps where the skin of the mountain showed red and bleeding.

Scenes blurred across the window, and they were scenes from her own life, the barefoot girl standing at the crossroads holding the hand of a child on one side and a bag of groceries on the other, the boy with Matthew's hair toting the string of trout while guiding the handlebars of a bicycle, the shouted name of a town that sounded like silver, the rows and rows of crops laid flat and bare and naked in the sun, a lone harrow in a field, the unimpressed gaze of horses, stands of corn shifting in the afternoon breeze, purple-green cabbage boiling up from the earth while the red Dominickers twitched through the rows and yanked at invisible worms.

And at every slowing of the train, when the placard with the name of the settlement rolled past, she shrank behind the curtain and looked for a tall mad-eyed man scanning the windows.

In the afternoon, the mountains snugged up closer, their tops wrapped in blue smoke, and the stops here were shorter—Bryson and Bushnell and Forney and Whiting and Almond and Hewitts— but you knew whenever there was a homeplace nearby because of the cackle of chickens and the baying of dogs up the hollow. Then the tracks plunged down into the earth and the hillsides grew up around them, and the train dropped and dropped until it had reached the bottom of a subterranean shut-in gorge, and the passengers stuck their heads out the window and inhaled the cool and the green and the dark. Then her body fell back against the seat, and the train was climbing again, grunting and panting like an old man out of the gloom and onto a knob of earth with a post office that read Topton, then a wide open valley where the dog star had come up with the sun, and after an hour through that spaciousness, the air brakes screamed and hissed, and the train stopped in the town of Murphy.

Irenie wrapped her fingers around the handle of the suitcase and waited, her eyes traveling the crowd to see was there a man standing apart with his arms folded and his brow lowered. But there wasn't, and she bent forward to gather her bag.

Only when she'd set her foot on the platform did she see the other figure watching, an orange-haired fellow she thought she knew, a fellow who sometimes preached in camp meetings whose name was Brother Jude or something like it. For a moment she stared, and he stared back, and his expression was a question with no good answers, and she turned toward the depot so that the side of her bonnet shielded her face from the man's curiosity. She bought a ticket for the L&N going south, into Georgia, where storm clouds mustered over low foothills.

No one she knew had seen her. That morning, it had been Ginny's idea to drive upriver to the next depot where she wouldn't have call to explain to Farris Reid how she came to be purchasing tickets for one person. The two women had driven with the windows open, the coupe spinning noiseless and smooth along the macadam, their bodies buffered in the rush of cool air. At one point Ginny took her hand from the wheel and reached across the platter-shaped hat she'd set on the seat between them. Her fingers were small, padded, and soft, like an infant's. Irenie wondered did her own hand feel calloused and old inside them. They didn't talk.

A single car was parked in front of the river-rock depot. Ginny turned the key and the motorcar chuggered out. Then she drew a deep breath and sighed. But the question she asked was a separate thing, as if she'd just that moment changed her mind. She nodded at the suitcase in the foot well. "Is it heavy?"

"I'll be able to manage," Irenie allowed, making out like she didn't understand the question in the question. The answer was that she'd packed two dresses she'd sewn on the Singer machine as well as her good shoes, the other splint bonnet and the winter coat, the letters from Matthew, the drawsack from the cave, and half of the ninety-seven dollars Brodis had earned on the river that spring. Nothing else was hers to take. Except the attic full of blackberries and cherries and peach preserves and pickled radish, or the jars lined up in the cave. Those things could be figured for hers, the stacks of them waiting there in the darkness for so long. The picture of them pulled at her still. But not enough to face the husband in the middle of the night with the leather-bound book that traced the outline of pain.

Ginny nodded at the suitcase in the foot well. "What all you got in there?"

"A couple dresses, a hat."

Ginny looked frightened. "Woolens? A winter coat?"

There was nothing else to say but the truth. "Yes."

Ginny stared down at her fingers, the tips resting light at the edge of the steering wheel in the same way they'd once been poised at the edge of the piano keys. Her hair hid her eyes. "You're not coming back."

"I figured it best to bring everything."

Ginny nodded without looking at her. And then, just like a child, she took to crying. Irenie was embarrassed. She couldn't remember the last time she'd seen a grown-up woman cry at not having a thing she wanted. She covered Ginny's hand with her own, then took it between her palms and held it in her lap. Some women cried at the coming of the Holy Spirit or the death of their children, but some didn't. Irenie squeezed and looked across the tracks for politeness. The sun edged over the eastern ridge, the light white and opaque. Above, mares' tails trailed across a high sky. Rain, perhaps, in a day, maybe a storm.

"Where will you go?" Ginny asked, swiping at her eyes with the back of her hand.

Irenie handed her friend a clean handkerchief. "It may sound queer to you, but I haven't pre-thought that yet."

Ginny shooed the handkerchief away. "It doesn't sound strange to me." Then out of the blue she added, "There are women working in Asheville, you know, in Waynesville, all over the state. Women working as cooks and secretaries." The thought seemed to cheer her up.

Irenie said that she reckoned that was true. "It seems to me that the first thing is to get myself…unburdened. Then I can figure what to do next."

Ginny looked morose. "I suppose that makes the most sense." She pulled a lacy square of fabric from her pocketbook and blew her nose, and then, without removing the handkerchief from her face, said, "You think he'll follow?"

"I expect he will."

Ginny stared out the windscreen and seemed to study on this new problem. Something in the challenge of it brought her out of her wallow. "Then maybe you had better just get the ticket for Asheville. You can buy the rest of them there."

A pair of silver spectacles in the window of the depot flashed and disappeared. They had sat for too long. This station agent would remember them for certain.

The inside of the building smelled like smoke and oil. The agent was a graying man in an unbuttoned uniform coat, his lenses glinting back and forth between Irenie and Ginny, as if looking to unravel the relation between. He pushed two white squares across the counter toward her.

Ginny followed her down the platform.

Irenie fished into her purse. "Here's what I got." Ginny had written the instructions on the back of a lined page that looked to be torn from a Department of Agriculture ledger.

Ginny wiped her nose, her eyes still red-rimmed and puffed under the rim of her hat.

Irenie read. "Take the Graham County Line from Asheville to Murphy, where it stops. It doesn't go over the mountain into

Tennessee. Then switch to the L&N going south to a town called Blue Ridge in Georgia. Then take the L&N back north on the Tennessee side of the mountains to a town called Copperhill."

The instructions recaptured Ginny's attention, and she nodded at each pause. "Just be ready if the sign says McCays instead of Copperhill. Because you're already there."

Irenie folded the paper. "I will."

Now the old Ginny resurfaced, the one who was already mapping out the next thing. "And be careful. Supposedly the place is full of miners and prostitutes. If you have to ask for directions, ask a woman. Or read the numbers on the street until you find it."

"I will."

"And places like that, there might be cheats and thieves and—"

Irenie grabbed her friend's hand. "I'll pay attention to everything."

A gray smudge showed on the horizon, and a few seconds later the train rounded the bend, followed by the grind of iron and the long hiss of steam.

Ginny raised her voice. "You have my telephone number."

Irenie held up her purse. "Yes." The platform was hot now, the air oil-thick. Irenie was aware of the extra layer of undergarments she wore, the close stiffness of the splint bonnet against her head.

Ginny shouted over the hissing. "And the cash."

Irenie grabbed both Ginny's shoulders and smiled into the other woman's face with a confidence she didn't feel until she spoke. "Yes, and yes, and yes. I'll be okay, I promise I will."

Ginny folded her into her arms, and Irenie remembered Matthew as a child, the way he'd clung if they were to leave him with Mamaw and Papaw—not the studied care of the embrace he'd given her before he'd left for school. Irenie said the same thing she'd said then. "It's gonna be fine." But now she had the fleeting thought that Matthew would never be able to find her, that she was walking out of his life forever. Over Ginny's shoulder, the conductor threw a mailbag up onto the train, then reached into his pocket and pulled out his watch.

"Call me one way or the other," Ginny whispered.

The conductor shouted, "All aboard!" as if addressing a crowd in place of the two of them.

As the train pulled away, Irenie watched Ginny become smaller and smaller in the churned air, a blue china doll, then a jay-colored smudge. Before the image of her friend disappeared, she turned her face. Later she'd remember the moment and try to recall had she turned on account of superstition or grief. Or maybe it had been that she didn't care to see Ginny Furman sucked into the horizon.

The evening came on slow, a turbid breeze pushing through the open windows, the Toccoa River spooling meandrous and thick with silt. Later, she sensed but didn't see the water that shifted near and cool in the slabbed Georgia darkness, marked here and there by the light of a homeplace, no stars.

She dozed.

When the train came to a stop, the sign at the station read Copperhill, Tennessee, Home of the Burra Burra Mines. The darkness cloyed, and the air carried in it the blunt odor of matches. She gathered her things and stepped onto the empty platform. The train groaned and clanged away. Irenie stood under an electric bulb in a weak circle of light. The grind and hiss of the train faded, and it occurred to her that Copperhill, Tennessee, was the quietest place she'd ever been.

But it wasn't. She heard automobiles, several of them, the echoing clatter of wood and cement and metal. There was the sound of a woman singing, and male voices that rose and fell. Town sounds. But the air was naked and choked: no katydids, no crickets nor cicadas nor frogs. No turkey or owl nor the thousand other creatures that peopled a summer night, only the silence and the petrol of automobiles and the burnt matches and the smell of clay in the clotted night.

There seemed only one way to walk, and that was toward the light and the noise of human beings. She stepped from the depot into a street like a narrow gorge, the buildings stacked tall on either side. Doors hung open, and the light from within them silhouetted the shapes of men—young, most of them, their cotton shirts stuffed into canvas work pants that still bore the red dirt of a day's work. Other men leaned against streetlamps and smoked, or sat right on the cement sidewalks and cradled flasks in brown paper sacks, as if they'd sat that way a long while and would continue to be there for many hours more. From a doorway came the sound of banjo music, from another a woman's low-throated croon.

Irenie trained her gaze straight ahead and tried to look as if she knew where she was going. But a voice called *hey there*, and before she had considered, she turned her head to find the speaker. A thick man in a Stetson lifted a bottle at her in happy salute. Then, once he had the attention of the small crowd around him, called, "Excuse me, ma'am," and looked up and down the street as if he were the top-billed character in a theater play.

Irenie walked on past, but the question followed. "Is there a *bake sale?*"

A swelter of laughter.

She knew the comment to be an unfriendly one, but she didn't know why nor how.

The happy voice continued, behind her now. "Is it a church *supper?*"

More laughing. Another voice repeated the phrase appreciatively.

And another, "Apple fritters, Clay. D'ya ever have a apple fritter, Clay?" Another voice shouted after her, "Do we have to go to church first?"

Irenie speeded her pace, but she could tell from the way the voices rose and fell and patted one another on the back that they didn't follow.

Ahead, another group looked the same as the first. She turned into a side street. Here there were no streetlights, only the electric glow of windows and the gagged air, the smothered silence that seemed to follow her from the train station, as if some critical feature more than the insects and the night birds had died. Before her, a cigarette glowed orange above a doorstep, then diminished.

She fingered the snap-purse in her pocket.

The cigarette glowed again. Smoke and perfume hung in the air. The cigarette floated down.

Irenie stopped in front of it. "Excuse me, missus."

A girlish voice answered in no hurry at all. "Well, hey...Are you looking for Theo's?" The cigarette bobbed up, paused, and glowed orange again.

The woman had known without even asking. "Yes. Please."

There was an exhalation and the renewed smell of smoke. "Well, you're almost there, hon. A block and half on the left. Green door."

"Thank you."

"Nothing to it." Then, after Irenie had passed, the voice called thin and wheedly, "Good luck," and Irenie didn't know what to say.

A street lamp burned in front of the little house. There were flowers in a window box, something vivid and red that Irenie had never seen. Next door was the office, just like Ginny had said, the name engraved across the top of the window: Dr. Leonard Potts. Irenie made herself focus on the green door of the rooming house. She knocked.

No one answered. The second-floor windows were lit and shaded. Irenie set the suitcase on the stoop. It hadn't occurred to her that she might arrive too late to get a room. Down the street, a woman and a man walked toward her without seeing her, the man's arm wrapped around the woman's shoulder, her body slung against him like a towel.

Irenie started to knock again, but just then the door swung inward, and a wide woman stood in the doorway, her face soft and unsurprised.

Irenie opened her mouth to explain who'd sent her, and how she'd come to be standing on the doorstep in the dark of the night, but it all seemed very complicated now.

"You here for a room?" The woman tucked a strand of blond hair behind her ear.

"Yes."

"Her eyes dropped to the suitcase. "You know it cost two dollars." Her voice was gentle but down-talking. "You have two dollars?"

"Yes, ma'am."

The woman nodded in a way that said how could it be otherwise, and didn't ask any more questions. "Come with me then." She stepped inside, and Irenie followed into a tight hallway. The walls had been covered in paper, and the pattern was one she'd seen before, though she couldn't remember where it might be, cabbage roses that twined themselves through lattice over and over again. And then it came to her that the paper was the same she'd seen in the samples from the Efficient Kitchen, except faded and curled at the edges now, which was maybe why it was better not to bother with paper, why it was better to keep your roses in the yard to look at whenever you wanted. The big woman didn't turn around. "I'm Iris."

"Oh."

"Just Iris."

"And Theo?"

"My uncle."

"I'm Irenie." She spoke to Iris's back. They passed through a skinny parlor. "Was there a fire?"

Iris stopped and looked at her, for the first time seeming surprised. "A fire?"

"Yes."

Iris studied her face. "No…"

"Oh. I figured…" Irenie wondered what to say without giving offense. "It was a smell back at the station."

Iris's face relaxed. "Oh. Sulfur dioxide."

"Is that what it is?"

Iris stopped at the foot of a staircase. "Funny. I can't smell it. Wouldn't even know it was there except for the out-of-towners. Say it smells like old matches."

"Yes, ma'am, it does."

Iris tilted her head to the west. "The plant's what give it off."

Plant?

"It smelts copper to make sulfur dioxide."

"Oh." Irenie didn't know there was something called sulfur dioxide, nor that there were factories built to produce it. "What for?"

"Sulfuric acid." There was pride in Iris's voice. "Biggest producer in the world. Both my sons work there."

"Oh." It seemed to her she should know the uses of sulfuric acid but she didn't. "My son lives in Asheville. He's taking geometry class in school." It sounded like bragging.

But Iris didn't seem impressed. "Mine did school for a while. Ten years. Didn't turn out to need a bit of it." She started up the stairs, which were tight and steep and so new they smelled of pine resin. "Come on. The only thing I got left is on the third floor." Iris had reached the top of the first set of steps, and she was breathing hard. "It's hotter, is all."

The room was close and stuffy and contained a cot with white sheets and a thin cotton blanket. A window opened onto the street. In front of it, a mechanical fan sat on a crude wooden table with no covering. Iris pressed a button and the fan whirred on.

On her way out, she stopped in the doorway and touched the iron dead-bolt attached to the jamb. "We don't have no trouble here, but I always tell the women to lock up." She closed the door on her way out, then tapped. "Don't forget."

Irenie set the suitcase next to the table and slid the bolt. From the street came the voice of a radio announcer and the rumble of music, something fast and jazzy. The fan buzzed back and forth, every few seconds blowing a warm breeze into her face. From the open window, men's voices punctuated the flabby air, some of them jolly and some of them angry and some of them both.

"...a gal built like a steam engine..."

"Hey, Toots!"

"And I told him I wasn't gonna put up with it any..."

When Irenie laid down her head, the pillow smelled of starch. The people in the street wouldn't be able to see her. They didn't know she was there. The most they might see, if they were to look, was the open window and the little fan. But it seemed strange nonetheless to go to bed in the middle of such wide-awake activity.

"Jesus H. Christ, if you knowed it, why ain't you said?"

"...the stupid bitch arguing about how she ain't never got the money..."

For a long time Irenie'd imagined that the person who'd attacked her weeks before was just such a man, a voice anonymous and rough with anger, a face that bristled with hair and hatred, a stranger so rude he'd let himself in through the window and caught her there in her bed unawares. But now that she heard these voices she knew that wasn't the way it had happened. The man who attacked her wasn't a stranger. It was the person she'd trusted most, the one she'd built a home with, and a life, the husband who'd slept at her side for fifteen years, now the man she was running from. The one who'd attacked her wasn't a thing in the world like these men.

The fan whirred and the unseen voices traveled up and down the street. The sheets were clean. The door was locked. For the first time in many weeks, she felt safe.

## CHAPTER NINETEEN

)

IN THE MOMENT BEFORE WAKING, BRODIS REMEMBERED that his wife was gone. Then he opened his eyes to the pre-dawn. No water boiled at the stove. No pork grease sizzled. No birds sang. The air was a wet towel. The Lord had placed him somewhere in the cycle of days, but he could not determine where.

He set out for the barn, but the sky did not lighten, for God had sealed the world in darkness. The firmament lowered.

He had loved a woman who had trespassed against God and against him.

A fat drop of rain hit the dirt at his feet, and the dust pattered up. The red chickens scolded and ran for the hen house. In his box, the mule pulled a mouthful of hay from the manger and watched the sky. Brodis had scarce set himself down on the milk stool when the next fat drop hit the roof like overripe fruit. *Thwop*. Seconds passed before the next. *Thwop*. Then drops began to pop against the metal like scattered gunfire and in seconds loudened to a roar and steadied into a single sound. Thunder rumbled into the yard so broad and wide it could have boiled up from the deep.

By now, the fresh mound of dirt down in the spice garden would have darkened to mud. By now, the water had begun to filter through the layers of earth.

Somewhere Stomper commenced to howling, a low throated caterwaul that started in his gut and rose up trailing and thinning into a keen of anguish that sliced the morning and curled up into the rafters and pierced Brodis's ears until something that was hid inside him bellied up too, and the sound that burst from his gut battered through his body and filled the barn even to the very rafters. Behold, he cometh with clouds, and all kindreds of the earth shall wail because of him.

The dog keened, and the man sat back and roared, and both voices rose up and filled the barn and shook the metal roof, and Brodis didn't stop until his lungs ran windless. The cow groaned and the rain hammered. Brodis closed his eyes and leaned his forehead into the beast's hot flank. Somewhere under the bristled hide, outsized tubes and muscles pumped and swished and gurgled and moaned.

God rained water on the earth, and it was cleansed.

On the bald, the cloven-hooved tracks would soften and blur. Grass would grow over, and the mountain would heal.

I will show thee things which thou hast seen, and the things which are, and the things which shall be hereafter.

Something brushed his knee. It was Fortune. The dog stopped and shook, broadcasting moisture onto his face. The man stood and stepped to the arched doorway. Water curtained from the sky and sluiced from the roof. The wind had turned brash, and the firmament had shrunk. Rain-slant darkened the compost of dung under his feet, and rivulets channeled into the road. A skinny line of fire flicked down from the heavens and touched the ridge, followed by the fork of another. The earth lightened in a flash of glory. The thunder that followed bellowed through the hollow like the voice of many waters. Fortune followed him and sat now in the archway with her mouth open, panting and nervous, all instinct, all fear.

He that hath an ear, let him hear what the Spirit sayeth.

Brodis stepped out from under the roof and held up his hands. The water ran cool down his limbs and drained into his armpits. Water washed his body and the fields and the mountain and the grave. He greeted it with palms open. His feet carried him towards the fields, and the tobacco rows loomed up beside him, and he reached his hands again to the prince of the kings of the earth who had washed men in his own blood.

And the wind turned cold against his cheek and the rain that bounced from his outstretched hands was no longer rain. Water had turned to stone, and the thousand thousand pricks of it hammered against the roof as the sound of many horses and many chariots charging into battle. A dog whined at his heels and urged him toward the open bay of the barn. But Brodis walked on, and the creature followed or it didn't. The Lord had said it more than once, and Brodis had known it, though he'd just as leave have forgot. He'd said He'd send hail upon the earth, and now the white pellets bounced and collected on the land, and out of the sky proceeded lightnings and thunderings. And voices. The voices of many angels singing round about, and the number of them was ten thousand times ten thousand, and thousands of thousands. The hail bounced against the earth, bigger than before, each the size of a blackberry, and then the size of a grape, then the size of a talent.

All around stretched the rows and rows of tobacco. And Brodis did not blaspheme God for the plague of the hail. He spoke, and the words vanished into the storm around him, but he knew that they found their mark.

Worthy was the lamb that was slain to receive power.

The tobacco stood like soldiers half again as tall as he.

And wisdom. And honor.

The field blurred.

And glory.

Brodis raised his arms to Heaven.

And blessing.

The sun blackened like sackcloth of hair, and the moon was as blood. A line of fire traced against the flinging skies, and the burnt smell of it, its char, boldened him to turn his face to God.

Woe, woe, to the inhabiters of the earth.

But he was not afraid. He heard the voice of many waters, and the voice of mighty thunderings, and he was not afraid. He lifted his arms up. The Lord God reigneth forever and ever. And fire forked down from the sky, and the lightnings and the heavens came down to greet him.

In the little cot by the window, Irenie woke to the grinding of train brakes and the sigh of steam, then another long blast, a pause, and the *shook...shook...shook...shook-shookshook* of the gathering engine. Then the train-sounds shrank into the hills and left behind the strangeness of the city. No redbirds *chenwink*ed. In place of wrens, the voices of human beings wriggled into the room, and iron horseshoes clopped the pavement. Wagons creaked and motorcars roared, and the little fan by the bed blew in the air that smelled of matches.

There were no chores needed doing. Only this.

The doctor's name and credits were etched into the window. Below, yellow curtains hid the inside of the clinic. Irenie opened the front door, and a bell above her head tinkled. The woman sitting behind the desk didn't look up. She was bent to the task of writing, as if that activity required all the attention in the world. Irenie waited and watched, and maybe it was the whiteness of the woman's peaked hat or the springy way her hair rolled back from her unfreckled face or the peach of her lipstick, but Irenie didn't set her suitcase down nor untie her bonnet. She waited, both hands wrapped around the strap, for the nurse to tell her what to do.

Without looking up, the young woman asked, "Can I help you?"

Irenie paused, unsure whether she was meant to begin speaking yet.

Finally the girl-woman looked up. "Yes?"

"Hello, missus." Miss? Ought she to have said miss? But that would have been too informal. "A lady from the government give me this address."

The nurse bent her head to her work again. "Are you here for Dr. Potts's services?" She asked the way a person did when she already knew the answer.

Irenie blinked. All she had to do was say yes. She did.

The woman set her pen down with an air of finality and looked up again. "My name is Mrs. Hayes." Before Irenie could answer, the nurse was regarding her middle and saying, "And how long has it been?"

Irenie shifted. "I missed two monthlies."

"Umm hmmm." It seemed to be the kind of answer Mrs. Hayes expected. "When was your last...monthly?" Now that she'd finished her writing task, she seemed to have too much attention to give Irenie.

"Middle of May, ma'am."

"So ten weeks."

"A lady at the Department of Agriculture said Dr. Potts could bring on the course before it's too late."

The nurse paused. "Department of Agriculture? That's a new one."

"Can Dr. Potts do that?"

Mrs. Hayes nodded her head. "That is the doctor's specialty." Irenie paused, unable to bring forward the question that occupied her most. "How...?"

"How much does it cost?"

"Yes."

The nurse shot the questions fast and precise and without seeming to regard the way they felt when they landed. "Where are you from? What state?"

"From North Carolina, ma'am, up a ways from Asheville."

"And how did you come?"

"From the L&N, ma'am."

"Transferred at Blue Ridge?"

"Yes, ma'am."

The woman didn't ask anything else, but Irenie saw that her attention had again switched to something else. She appeared to be doing figures in her head. Then her eyes sought Irenie's. "In your situation, twenty-five dollars." The figure hung in the air like a challenge.

Irenie blinked. She fingered the roll of dollar bills in her pocket. There were fifty-three of them. "My situation?"

Mrs. Hayes didn't hesitate. "It varies according to a woman's progress."

Irenie took that information and kneaded it, pressed it, rolled it out.

"And how far she's traveled, in your case."

Irenie nodded and opened her snap-purse. Twenty-five bills.

The nurse flattened the ones and touched each with her thumb, then opened a drawer and put the money inside. She paused, and Irenie again had the sense she was making calculations. She turned to Irenie and said to her in a voice so matter-of-fact that it was neither down-talking nor gentle. "Can you read and write?"

Irenie straightened. "Yes."

The woman nodded as if she didn't believe her. She set up a fountain pen and a piece of paper on a little desk by the window. "Just your medical history please." Irenie sat down and for a moment wondered would the woman linger at her shoulder like a schoolteacher watching her make her letters. But the nurse stepped away. Irenie took a long breath and bent her head to the worksheet. But the nib of the pen was old, and the ink bled fat on the page, and her letters were log-thick like the letters of a child. Sunlight leaked through the yellow of the curtains and spilled across the little desk and onto the linoleum carpet. Dust hung in the air, and she reckoned it velveted everything she'd touched in the town, and each breath she'd breathed. By now the fine red powder had settled along her insides, and they too would soon be coated.

But then the window light changed, and a shadow passed across it that was tall and wide-shouldered and hatless. She gathered the edge of the curtain to pull it aside, but by that time the shadow was already at the door, and the latch quivered, and the door swung out, and the little bell made its announcement.

But the fellow who entered had a face the color of coffee, and was carrying an enormous crate of linens. He nodded at Mrs. Hayes and disappeared down the hallway with the box in his arms. From Irenie's lungs came a long release of air.

"Yes?" the nurse asked. "Can I help, Mrs. Lambey?"

"Um, yes please, missus." She held up the pen. "It needs a scrap of paper for blotting."

"Oh...it does that. Just a minute." She opened a drawer and began sifting through the contents.

Just then the little bell on the door jingled again, and Irenie didn't have time to catch up her breath. But the person who stood in the doorway wasn't a man. It was a woman, in a cloud of scent and an offset hat and a broad shouldered suit. Her stockings bared her legs naked, and her feet tilted into leather pumps with tiny brass buckles. Only when you looked at her face did you see how young she was, seventeen maybe, eighteen. Now she paused, just as Irenie had done when she'd stood there, a little suitcase in her hand, waiting to be recognized. The nurse was still rifling through the drawer looking for blotting paper. The young lady glanced once at Irenie, and Irenie turned back to the paper in front of her.

It was at least a minute before there was conversation, and when it came it was low and unfriendly.

The girl's voice: "She said thirty-five."

"That was in the past." Mrs. Hayes' voice turned mulish. "Now it's forty for someone as far along as you."

Irenie made out not to hear. She kept her attention on her papers, even though they were complete, fat ink and all. She fanned her hand over the page.

Then the nurse was collecting the form and putting a clean one on the desk, then writing a check for the coffee-colored man, and Irenie got up and set herself on a chair that gave a view of the front door and the young lady's straight, slim back. The hand holding the top of the page was small and nailbit. She didn't wear a ring. Her suitcase was leather, the color of molasses just before you overcooked them. On the handle was a tag that read "Atlanta."

Irenie set her gaze at her own feet: Sunday shoes scuffed white on the toes and along the sides. Her brown cotton stockings bunched at her ankles, patches of mending beading up like scabs. Next to her, the cardboard suitcase bulged hugely. She touched the ball of hair at her neck and tucked a strand that had worried loose. The splint bonnet hung down her back, the string ties cutting at her throat.

And now the young woman from Atlanta was staring back, and Irenie opened her mouth to say something, but the young lady was already looking away.

The nurse stood up and disappeared behind a closed door. The ceiling fan whirled above them, the beaded chain ticking against the trembling metal housing. The clock dropped its pendulum again and again, regular as beading water.

The nurse stepped back into the room. "Evelyn?"

The young woman from Atlanta picked up her molasses-colored suitcase and her pocketbook and her gloves and was gone. But the picture of the leather pumps with the naked stockings and the brass buckles stayed.

Irenie waited. Time soaked her up. There was no stringing of onions nor shelling of peas, no separating of seeds nor darning nor patching nor quilting. Her hands sat folded in her lap, queer as sleeping cats. The fan whirled and ticked. Outside, the voices of women and children curled past the window, eddied into the little room and around her head and had nothing to do with her. She waited in the cocoon of the clinic, and there was no one to know she was there.

Her name surprised her in its strangeness there. "Mrs. Lambey?" The owner of the voice was a man in a vested suit and a necktie. Again she was embarrassed by the suitcase and the patched stockings. "I can take that for you." He reached for the bag, just as natural as Mr. Crisp down at the store would have done. Then he motioned her into an office that was lined in books. He offered a wooden armchair—"Please"—at the same time he proffered his hand, as if they were meeting at a Sunday supper. "Dr. Leonard Potts." His moustaches were waxed to points, his head covered in a close helmet of brown hair. He smelled of pomade. He didn't seem the sort of man to inquire could she read or did she have two dollars.

"Mrs. Irenie Lambey."

Dr. Potts tilted his head and pulled up a chair for himself. Despite his vest and the hot singed air, he didn't seem to sweat. "Ma'am?"

"Yes?"

He leaned forward in his chair, set his elbows on his thighs, and clasped his hands together between his knees. "Do you mind if I ask about Mr. Lambey?"

Irenie didn't know what to answer. "He didn't come."

"But he's alive?" The doctor's expression was curious, polite, professional.

"He's alive."

"And does he live at home with you?"

Irenie looked at her folded hands, the skin red and hard, the nails cracked. She raised her head and saw in the doctor's face that he was listening, not just to what she said, but also to what she didn't. The attention both appealed and frightened. "We've already had two to be born, sir. And I'm figuring to get a job."

"And your husband?"

"My husband?"

"Does he know that you've come to see me?" The question sat between them, plain and honest.

There was no way to answer it but the same way. "No sir. He don't know about the job yet either."

Dr. Potts nodded, unsurprised. "And you told him you were visiting a sister or an aunt?"

"No sir." Something about the man's attention stripped her. She had the sense that no matter what she told him, he would see the truth. "I'm leaving him, sir."

He leaned back in his chair now, still nodding, though his lips turned down at the corners. "I see. Do you mind if I ask why?"

"Because I am afraid of him." The sentence walked out of her mouth of its own accord, and once past her lips, stood there naked and white and not half as big as she'd figured it to be. It was just what it was.

"I see," Dr. Potts said.

So did she. She braced for the next question. But Dr. Potts was staring at the space above her head, his eyes traveling back and forth as if reading lines there.

Irenie waited.

After a short while, he turned to his desk and picked up a rubber bulb, the kind you would use to water an ailing animal. "Let me explain this procedure, Mrs. Lambey. You see this?"

"Yes."

"I fill it with a solution of potassium soap, Mrs. Lambey, making certain that there are no air bubbles in it."

Irenie didn't know if she was supposed to comment or not. She nodded.

"Then I introduce it to the cervix and into the womb."

She had an idea of the territory he was describing. It wouldn't be so different from a cow's or a mare's.

"Then I pack the area with sterile gauze so that the fluid stays there. The whole procedure takes about ten minutes."

Ten minutes? How many batches of tea had she brewed? How many nights had she rose in the dark to drink the black fust from the mason jar? How many times had her mind swam away from her before she'd slid into the mud at the bottom of the branch? "Then what?"

"Then tomorrow you come back, and I take out the gauze."

Dr. Potts leaned out the door and shouted, "Caroline," then returned to his seat. "Mrs. Hayes will help you prepare. She's done this a hundred times before. She'll give you just enough gas that you won't feel a thing."

Irenie nodded.

Then the pretty nurse with the peach lipstick was at the door and saying, "Follow me, Mrs. Lambey," and Irenie wished that the nurse wasn't so young, or leastways that she would stop repeating her name that way. Both her children had been delivered by Aunt

Annie, who wasn't her aunt, and who never called her a thing in the world but Irenie.

Mrs. Hayes led her into a tiny room furnished with a desk and two chairs and a bed with white sheets. A tower of white garments was stacked on the desk. Mrs. Hayes pulled one from the top—something like a long white apron unfurled—and handed it to Irenie.

"It ties in the back. You'll have to take everything else off. You can hang your clothes here." She motioned to a hook on the wall. "Then I'll be back to do the gas." She sounded uninterested, as if she had already seen everything there was to see, twice.

On the second day Mrs. Hayes didn't give her gas. Irenie stared at the ceiling and tried not to think about the fact that she was lying with her legs open while a strange man in a white coat peered between them. The nurse's upside-down face floated into view and told her she was doing fine, just fine.

The top of Dr. Potts's head was combed in neat oiled rows that reminded her of new-turned furrows. He looked up. "Try to relax, Mrs. Lambey, and take a deep breath."

No sooner had Irenie closed her eyes than something between her legs gave way so suddenly that she wondered had the doctor turned her inside out. She sat up. Dr. Potts's head pulled away. A pair of forceps held something white that looked like quilt batting dipped in blood. It was gauze, and it had come out of her.

"Relax, Mrs. Lambey. You can lie down."

A slow ache that she recognized as her monthly pain set in straightaways, and when a warm fluid pooled under her buttocks, she worried she'd done her business on the doctor's cot. Then she smelled the blood, and a cramp stronger than the first fisted up her womb, and when she closed her eyes, the inside of her lids were red too.

*CHAPTER TWENTY*

THE EARTH WAS WET AND WARM AGAINST BRODIS'S cheek. He didn't see the horsemen, but he heard them almost atop him: the stomping of hooves and the sucking of mud and the jangle of traces. He spied the legs first, the pasterns and forelocks, then the booted feet flexing and loosing in the stirrups, flexing and loosing. The earth grabbed at the animals' hooves, and they high stepped to be rid of it. They were a deep-chested black mare and a scrub-mottled gelding. But there ought to have been four of them: the white and the red and the black and the pale one that was death.

Lesley Raines' voice: "You there! Brodis!"

But Brodis knew better. Lesley didn't ride a horse. He drove an automobile. The horsemen had been given the power to kill with sword, and with hunger, and with the beasts of the earth. And now this.

"Brodis!" The voice shouted now.

Brodis rolled to his side, and the cymbal of the sun crashed upon him. One of the horsemen stepped toward him, and his shape eclipsed the blaring light.

The silhouette spoke. "He's alive anyway."

Brodis was sodden in his clothes and in his boots.

Lesley's voice again. "Brodis Lambey, are you lightning struck?" Brodis couldn't figure what Lesley Raines was doing on his place.

"Hail struck," the other voice said. "Look at them bruises coming up."

Brodis rolled to his knees, hands on the ground in front of him. "Where's the motorcar?" was all he could think to say.

"Where's Irenie?" Lesley countered.

"Road's blocked up with trees," the second rider allowed. It was John Puyette, Lesley's partner at the sawmill. The rim of his hat shaded the top of his face. Behind him and all around was a field of green stalks like poles, most of them hung with something that looked like wet turnip greens. Brodis couldn't place the location. But then he spied the gate where a windthrown tree had fallen against it. It was his gate, his windthrown tree. His field.

His tobacco.

The leaves that had been thick and green-veined and glorious hung shredded and lifeless, row after naked blasted row, the openness so ugly it unstrung him. Bottom leaves hung stubborn from the stalks, but they too were pocked with C-shaped holes. Imprints the size of cherries marked the ground, and Brodis remembered the rain that had bounced white upon the surface of the earth.

Lesley was shouting. "Where's Irenie?"

Brodis answered without thinking. "Gone already." A branch had broken and fallen on the barbed wire fence, and chickens wandered among the ruined plants, pulling earthworms from the ground in long stretches.

Lesley dismounted and stood in front of him now, smaller than him but feet planted wide, hands on his hips, head thrust forward. "Gone where?" Brodis moved to step around him, but the boy-man blocked him. "Gone *where?*"

Brodis turned away. The fields below him had been thrashed. Where yesterday he couldn't see past the next row, today he could see all the way to the Raines' homeplace. He walked in that direction, straight across the rows, the ground sucking at his feet. Lesley strode beside him and shouted meaningless words.

The cornfield was the only thing that stood, the plants vertical and stripped. Brodis wrapped his hand around a nubbin, then opened his fingers to take a closer look. Naked white abrasions splotched the green. He pulled back the scalded leaves of the husk. There were a few brown bruises on the kernels, but the corn would make.

But there was only one patch. Everything else was gone.

Then Lesley was on his horse again, cantering away, the mud and water splashing up around him. He leaned in to clear a fallen limb, turned, and galloped back around the field toward the house. John Puyette took a final look at Brodis and followed. Brodis watched them ride toward the hollow, the grounds between them naked as winter.

The second woe was past, and behold, the third was quickly come.

By the time Brodis began the walk down the hollow, the black horse stood riderless at the side of the house, and the voices of the two men jerked and shimmied up the hill. They were out back, in the spice garden.

Lesley stood atop the fresh grave with his feet splayed, driving a shovel into the new mound. He straightened, turned, and shook the mud and water from the pan. He glanced quick at Brodis but didn't stop the work.

John Puyette sat atop the gelding, watching Lesley dig. Then he dismounted from the horse and stood between Brodis and Lesley. He was a short solid man whose head jutted forward and gave him a thick-witted look. But he wasn't stupid. Now he looked at Brodis a long moment before speaking. "Preacher." His voice chided. "You need to tell the man is she dead."

On top of the grave, Lesley paused the shovel mid-air.

But Brodis couldn't return to the place he'd been the day before, the tin washtub, the formal coat, the Bible that hadn't opened to Ecclesiastes. Instead he raised his voice, and it boomed out the message he hoped was true. "She lives," he announced, "forever and ever."

And then Lesley stepped up next to John Puyette. "Is she *dead*, Preacher?"

Brodis didn't answer.

But Lesley, small as he was, stepped toward him and shouted in his face now. "Is her *body* in this *grave*?" Lesley's shovel came up like a baseball bat, and Brodis recalled that Lesley had played that game whenever he was in school. He had a good stance, feet wide, eyes on the side of Brodis's head. Already Brodis could feel the impact of the implement against his ear, the hard steel *thwang* of it, the crumple of his body to the earth. But he didn't much mind. What could a man do unto him? "Thou livest, and art dead," he told the boy-man who was Irenie's crazed cousin. Then he closed his eyes and waited for the slam of steel.

Nothing happened.

Brodis opened his eyes. Lesley was staring right through him. He lowered the shovel, uttered a blasphemous remark, bent, and commenced digging again. The new-turned earth came away fast, and it wasn't long before a pile of wet mud grew up at the graveside. John Puyette watched both men uneasily.

Brodis left Irenie's cousin to his work and rounded the side of the house. The fence around the vegetable garden was undamaged, even the section he and Irenie had repaired together. He lifted the latch and swung the gate wide. The tally was plain. The tomato plants were finished and the cucumbers ragged, but the rows of potatoes could be dug, and the cabbage that was hard and small might yet grow. Or it could be harvested young. Those were the survivors. Potatoes, cabbage, corn. But it wasn't enough. There wasn't any squash, nor broccoli nor melons nor corn enough to last the winter. Wasn't any pumpkin, wasn't any zucchini. They hadn't planted that way in three years, ever since the tobacco. And now there was only this shred of broken leaves.

He latched the gate behind him. The sun was as hot and bright as ever. Behind the house, John Puyette was rolling a cigarette. Lesley stood in a waist-deep hole, the pile of earth beside him broad and wide. His motions were constant, machine-like: the booted foot on the back of the blade, the thrust of the shovel, the heave, rotation, and dump. And again. Sweat and mud ran down his face, and this particular white shirt would never come clean again. Brodis watched. "The hour is come," a voice proclaimed, and it was his. "To try them that dwell upon the earth."

Lesley stopped mid-dig. He tipped the dirt and drove the shovel into the ground. He rested his right forearm across the handle, and wiped his face with the left. He regarded Brodis for a long minute. "Preacher, you are one crazy fuck." Then he took up the shovel again and bent once more to his work.

Brodis ignored him. "God delivers me from my enemy, and from them which hate me. The Lord is my stay."

This time Lesley didn't turn his head. "Shut the hell *up*, Preacher," he panted from inside the hole. But the last word was feathery and uncertain, as if the boy was crying.

Brodis stepped up to the edge of the grave. The rose-colored dress showed through the soil. Lesley was on his knees, brushing away the dirt with his hands.

"Oh Jesus," he heard John Puyette exclaim. He too had stepped up to the edge. Now he knelt and peered into the hole, the smoke from his cigarette curling thinly around him. Lesley had set the shovel into the earth behind him, where it stood within Brodis's easy reach, the handle still trembling.

The back of both men's heads presented themselves. Lesley's was the color of late summer grasses, the growth whorling around his skull like water in an eddy, and him brushing the dirt with both hands now, and the rose-colored dress beginning to take the shape it had always had. Lesley leaned into the work, and the white of his neck exposed itself, a band of flesh some two inches wide between the swirled tans and browns of his hair and the white collar of his shirt. Brodis had once seen a man's spine cleaved in two just there, above the shirt collar, because another man had raged about a sum of money owed him and swung a peavey at his friend's retreating back. The knobs of Lesley's spine bulged through his skin. A string of blasphemies rolled from his mouth. "Oh, Christ... Oh shit..." He pawed at the dirt in a frenzy. The shovel handle trembled yet.

The rose-print dress revealed itself.

Lesley stopped pawing and peeled back the fabric. He held the dress aloft, and the earth fell from it. Beneath it curled the fox, the bones just as Brodis had laid them. Lesley picked up the animal's head, and the spine came up too. He turned the skull over, as if there might be some clue on the underside. The spine rattled.

By the time he looked up, Brodis had raised the shovel high above his head with both hands. "Put them back."

"What?"

"Do it."

Lesley set the skull back upon the ground.

"Fix it. The way it was."

Lesley arranged the spine and the legs back in the grave. But not the way he'd found them.

"Now the dress."

Lesley held up the garment as if he'd just as leave take it with him, but then he seemed to reconsider and laid the cotton over the skeleton.

"Now the dirt."

Lesley stared up at the shovel, bewildered.

"Even so," Brodis said.

Lesley spoke almost in a whisper, his voice soft for the first time. "Brother, you are plumb bereft." Then he scrabbled from the grave and began pushing the dirt back into the hole with his hands.

Brodis lowered the shovel and drove it into the soft earth. John Puyette eyed him nervously. He didn't reach inside his shirt for the makings of another cigarette.

Lesley touched the handle of the shovel and looked at Brodis for permission. Then he filled in the rest of the dirt.

When he was finished, he threw the shovel far away from him, and it landed in the garden. He brushed his hands through his hair, and clumps of mud fell from his head onto the ground. He put his hat on anyway and turned to Brodis. "She left you." The three words were neither question nor statement but something in between.

"Who?" Brodis asked, though he knew.

Now Lesley untied his horse and shoved his foot into the stirrup, pausing to say it again, this time as fact. "She left you." He swung his leg over the horse, and he and John Puyette rode out of the hollow.

The money jar was high above the drain board and needed standing on a chair to reach it. There, behind Irenie's recipes and special papers. Brodis pushed that box aside and snaked his hand toward the back. The jar was sticky with layered dust. He slid it toward him and tipped it into his hand and as he did so felt that the money was there yet. Green and gray and curling against the inside of the jar.

But something was different. The last time he'd brought money home, he'd had to stuff it down among the other bills. Wasn't anywhere else to put it. Now there was light passed right through the top.

Lesley Raines's voice dismissed him again.

She left you. The pride of your heart has deceived you.

Was it possible his wife had turned away from the flock to venture by herself into the wide world? The USDA lady with the tight suits and the mincy hats had looked at Brodis like a science experiment. His son called her ma'am, and his wife checked her conversation against her approval, but Brodis had let his wife go to the meetings anyway, had continued to let her go, all because of the slow thing that had come between them and because his wife brightened and smiled when she talked about the ladies and because he had loved her most.

And all the while she'd been holding secrets with the woman who'd taken his son, and instead of being *grateful* for the compromises he'd made, instead of *thanking* him for what he'd provided, she'd pushed for more and more. Haver warned him on how he'd

seen Irenie and the woman at the Furman house playing the piano
of all things, and not at the courthouse or the extension office mind
you, but in her own *home*, where it wasn't any call for them to be
at all. And the husband a soft fellow who'd never had real work
except it was to fill out forms and write his recommendations on
a yellow pad or talk about the ways others were doing wrong, and
here were the methods brought on from science, and this is the way
they did it in South Carolina and wouldn't a fellow want to get the
biggest growing from his crop. Always the talk was of yields and
efficiencies and labor saving devices and couldn't a fellow trade for
merchandise just as easy as making everything his own self. *Trade*
for it, was the way he put it, though he knew and Brodis knew that
every time a man spent a dollar anymore the government took a cut
of it. Because the taxes were how they came to afford the paycheck
of a man like Roger Furman. The government sent him out and
paid him a salary to visit each homeplace in the county and give the
farmers who lived there a lecture about efficiency and merchandise
and trading and if the farmer didn't change his ways, well, here
he came the next year again, telling him as how it'd be cheaper to
pen up his pigs and get rid of them sheep and there were people
growing short sweetening in Louisiana or some other dang place so
cheap you might as well not bother with it here. And then, whenever a fellow ignored him, he sent his *wife* into the schools to talk
to the children and into the church to talk to the women, all the
while hammering at the same message about how it was better, it
would be better, couldn't they see it was better to go to this school
or electrify your house or bring in water from the city or fence in
your stock or put up the loom and the cane press and couldn't they
see there was a better life to be had, forget about Heaven because
that didn't matter a whit, forget about the health of a man's soul,
because it was all about making more money in the here and now
and do what the Department of Agriculture tells you because they
have your best interest at heart, and forget about the holy union
of a man and woman who'd built a family and a life, *yea verily*, before the very eyes of the Lord Jesus Christ. Over and over again,

until men who'd been taking care of themselves and their families for generations suddenly up and decided they wanted to, no, they *needed* to change it up and grow a thing they didn't even eat because they wanted to be part of the *market*, and before you knew it the children who wore linsey complained up and down because there wasn't nobody else in the whole school to wear homespun except them.

And God had seen it all and was wroth, and he did fly upon the wings of the wind and make darkness his secret place.

Brodis flung the jar at the floor. It hit the edge of the hearthstone and shattered. The paper money lay in wads. Someone had to have seen her. He would find out who.

And somewhere the beast rose out of the sea, having seven heads and ten horns, and upon his horns ten crowns, and upon each head the name of blasphemy.

Iris smoothed the six dollars Irenie had given her into a metal box. "Leonard said you were good to leave today?"

Irenie took in this new information. Leonard. Doctor Potts. "Mrs. Hayes said today, yes." Or at least, she hadn't said not today. She'd held Irenie's wrist up with one hand and pressed a card flat into her palm with the other. "You have problems, you don't go to anyone else, you understand?" She'd given her the same kind of weighted look Lesley did whenever he talked about his business. "You come right back here," she'd said. "You can call that number any time of the day or night, but you call here."

Irenie hadn't thought of the possibility that she might need to. "What kind of problems?" she'd asked.

Mrs. Hayes still pressed the card and Irenie's hand between her own. Her attention didn't waver. "Pain, even after three days or more. You call here. Not anywhere else. Understand?"

"Yes."

The card instructed her not to take bodily exercise or bathe or have marital relations.

Now, in the foyer of the rooming house, Iris snapped shut the lid of the metal box and fastened it with a silver latch. Then she bent forward to stash the box under the counter. "You're probably wondering about the train," she said from down there. "There's an 11:15 to Blue Ridge." When she straightened, the corner of her mouth turned down with disapproval. "But I can't speak for the connection."

Irenie made her voice casual, but despair leaked into it anyway. "I was thinking of staying and looking for work."

Iris looked up quick. "Oh...Oh, sweetie..."

Irenie nodded.

"I didn't know it was like that."

"No, ma'am. I reckon I didn't either."

At the front stoop, she stopped to tie the strings of her bonnet. Two little girls slapped a rope against the packed dirt road, while a third jumped over the middle, two pigtails flapping against her shoulders. A boy pedaled by on a bicycle, a wooden trailer filled with paper-wrapped foods rattling behind him. A woman with a hat like a bird's nest carried a straw basket in the crook of her arm, and a laborer in a blue denim shirt ran past. They all of them had their place. They did what they did which was what they'd done yesterday and what they'd probably be doing tomorrow and the day after. The red dust settled upon them and on the automobiles at the curb and on every other thing in the town. There was sameness to it, but it wasn't her sameness. Hers was across the mountains, in North Carolina, her chickens and her cow and her mule and her cook shrubs and her cabbages and her tomatoes and her dogs. Her son. And her husband.

And she'd left it.

Irenie followed the woman with the basket. It was the first time she'd ventured into the town in the daylight. The piece of paper Iris had given her said two blocks to the corner of Main Street and turn left. The rooming house would be yellow, and the lady who owned it was Mrs. Ricky Jakes. She might or might not be needing a housekeeper, depending.

Main Street was a bee-swarm of people and trucks and automobiles all crawling between new flat-roofed buildings and—

Irenie stopped. Beyond the row of buildings, beyond the train platform and the spindled telephone Ts rose a hill of bald red soil without a tree nor a shrub nor a blade of grass on it. Rainwater had gullied and branched and striped the skin of the earth until it looked for all the world like a rabbit whose pelt had been peeled away from its fibered muscles. Beyond it rose more hills just as red and just as naked, stretching away in layers. There wasn't a tree nor a patch of green in sight. This was it—this—the queer quality of the city. Here was the copper hill. At the bottom of it squatted a pile of brick warehouses and enormous canister-shaped buildings, their color the same color as the earth, which was the same color as the name of the town. Three chimneys stabbed the sky and squeezed out white smoke thick as ointment.

The burnt-match smell.

On the slantland perched rows of uniform white homes stacked one after the next like boxes, the ones in the upper tiers standing up on stilts. Telephone Ts and electric wires scraggled between the rows. Wooden steps and picket fences carved paths through the naked earth. And atop the hill stood a grand white mansion where at last was a patch of green: three tiny trees wired to wooden scaffolds.

"Hey, *missus*." Irenie turned to spy a plump boy of nine or ten whose hair hung lank in his eyes and whose expression said he'd seen something of the world and had discovered there was much to despise. His voice slid up to her. "Hey, *missus*."

Irenie straightened. "Yes?" His eyes slitted in his sunburned face, and the hardness there was so young she took it to be disappointment. What did his mother have to say about it?

"Do you sell *moon*shine?" His face lit with delight. Except that it wasn't delight at all but a steely-edged excitement. "Are you a *hill*billy?"

She'd never heard the word yet she knew its meaning right off. "Roscoe says you are."

She looked, but before she could lay her eyes on Roscoe, a thick fellow in a denim shirt intercepted the boy and grabbed him by the shirt collar.

"I've got ten hot men waiting on water, boy. Let's get to it."

The child's features slumped into something that looked like obedience, and he stuttered, "I was just—"

The man turned him by his shoulder and then planted a booted foot on his backside. The boy fell forward, touched the ground, regained his balance, and lit out running.

When Irenie turned to the denim-shirted man, he too was gone, or had become part of the crowd of other denim-shirted men, their backs stenciled with the white letters of the Tennessee Copper Company, their fronts dusty and bearded, all of them in a hurry, all rushing forward or past and hollering instructions or greetings or curses.

And above everything stretched the mansion and the copper hill, the white string of road curling into the naked hills with the company trucks hauling ore and acid and sulfur dioxide gas. The earth fissured and cracked and blew down the hill into the town, the same way it would in a week or a year or fifty. No wonder they needed housekeepers. It was a city made of minerals, and nothing in it was growing. The blue-denimed men must have built it without ever looking up. It wasn't that they'd conjured the copper hill in their minds because if they had they might have paused to rethink it. But it had come anyway, rising up lewd and red and spreading its nakedness far as the eye could see, taking hold of the settlement full of men and money and jobs. And the people who lived there never stopped to think it had come to own them.

They'd accepted the terms of the deal.

And maybe the fellow who lived in the house at the top of the hill looked down on the rich and busy town and felt proud of all the people he had say over.

But she wasn't going to be one of them.

The piece of paper with Mrs. Jakes's address was still warm and moist in her hand. She let it loose, and it fluttered to the ground among a pile of potato peelings in the red mud of the ditch. She had once imagined her womb like the center of a mush melon, soft and moist and nutritious, but now it seemed to her that the melon had turned inside out, and the seeds had fallen on cracked earth. And she thought again of the baby that might have been. The doctor had said it was the size of a snap pea, and she figured it that way, a sprout that vined and tendrilled into the cracks of her life and grew and grew until its vegetable needs shut her up inside the house for another fifteen years.

The picture map at the Asheville depot had branches that sprangled in five and fifteen directions. Each was a choice, a plan that stretched before a person and projected the moments of the future. It had a shape that you considered and branches that you chose. She remembered something of that way of viewing the world, back in the days when she'd walked her father's orchard and imagined which of the boys in Eakin she would pick. Only now she wasn't picking a boy who would take her to a future life. She was picking the life.

Ginny had said there were women working in Asheville.

An hour later, Irenie pushed the last of her paper money across the counter at the depot and told the station agent she wanted to buy a ticket to the other side of the mountains.

## CHAPTER TWENTY-ONE

FARRIS REID SHOOK HIS GRIZZLED HEAD, ALL THE while regarding Brodis from beneath the bill of his blue stationmaster cap. "Nope. Mrs. Lambey ain't bought no train tickets." There was a spangle of light in his eye. "Leastways not from me."

Brodis leaned across the counter. He couldn't help it. "Careful, Farris." He wouldn't have to hit the man that hard to knock the hat from his smug head. "You know what the Bible says about letting your heart be glad whenever another man stumbles."

The old man tilted his head, wary, listening.

Brodis gripped the counter to ensure keeping his hands to himself. "Lest the Lord see it, and turn his wrath upon *you*."

Farris pulled his glasses off, set them on the counter between them, and stared up at Brodis. "I reckon I would know did I sell her a ticket, Preacher."

Brodis held the man with his eyes. "You didn't see her."

Farris's gaze broke toward the river, as if searching for something in the rain-swelled water. A pine tree shot past, the root ball aloft, branches submerged in the muddy brown. "I ain't said that. I ain't said one way or the other did I *see* her."

Of their own accord, Brodis's hands snatched Reid's coat and dragged the station agent close: hazel-colored eyes, surprisingly long-lashed, surprisingly elderly. "What is your point of conversation, Farris Reid? Did you or did you not see my wife?"

Farris Reid regarded him with spit in his eye.

Brodis took a long deep breath—incline not my heart to any evil thing—then released the man and slapped the counter between them with both palms.

Reid's posture and voice were stilted. "I spied her right about yesterday, or day before yesterday, early in the morning." He took a deep breath and said with a certain satisfaction, "Right unusual, I thought, before the stores were open. She was toting a suitcase."

"Where?"

Farris Reid's eyes gauged him. "Walking down the street, Preacher Lambey. Walking right down the street. Looked to me like she turned at the smithy's and walked toward the river."

The door of the extension office stood open, a line of farmers waiting outside, their mouths set in grim lines, the cigarette smoke around them sucked clean by the swift river. The men stared at their shoes or at the white-capped waves. When Brodis approached, Bill Rickerson gave a quick tilt of his chin, his face raw with failure. Rickerson had seven people needed feeding, plus another on the way. Brodis stopped and set his hand on his neighbor's shoulder. The flesh through the heavy work shirt was stone. Brodis squeezed, and a pronouncement came through him, but not from him. "He sees." The words rang louder and calmer than he felt. And that was all it took. Right then and there the Spirit rose up so powerful among them that neither he nor Rickerson could speak more. Rickerson fixed a long look at him and nodded.

When Brodis turned away, his eye fell upon the river-smoothed rock that was the building's foundation. Underneath, some night creature had long ago clawed out two holes, now packed hard by the comings and goings of feet.

A man named Clayton stepped aside to let him pass, and Brodis ducked into the open door of the office, half expecting to spy his wife standing there in the dark. Instead the woman sitting there was *her*, the piano player, the lady agent. She was explaining something to a man who held his hat in his hands but whose face was clotted with dirt and anger. Behind her, a half open door led into a darker room, and Brodis peered into the gloom for the outline of another female figure. Only when he stepped up beside the other farmer did Mrs. Furman seem to see him. Only then did her face register surprise, then fear, then the lie of politeness. "Mr. Lambey." She didn't stand. "All of these men were here—"

"Where is she?"

The woman appeared to courtesy the subject. "That, I do not know." Fear visited her features again, but she lifted her face to his. "I only took her to the station. She wouldn't tell me where she was going."

The outline of what had happened took shape in Brodis's mind then, the pretty woman telling his wife that a marriage vow was not a vow, the ride to the station, the letter of reference for the name of a family who would hire her on. And now this same pretty woman sat right here in front of a group of men she and her husband had ruined and told him and all of them lies come straight from the devil.

The gloom of the passageway moved, as if something in the blackness awoke.

Behind him waited the grim-faced farmers. None of them shouted a curse, none of them raised a fist, and none burst into the tight room with a shotgun. They only waited while the fellow on the front of the line proceeded first, and then the second, and the third, and so forth until all of them would drift disappointed and lost into the blighted afternoon because that was the only way the government knew to do a thing. Make one person go away at a time. Though when it came to suggesting changes, they'd been plenty good at doing that wholesale.

Brodis waved at the men lined up behind him and out the door. "Can't you *see* them?" The question came out overloud.

"Mr. Lambey, I'm all too aware of—"

"Can't you *see* these *men*? Every single one of them was living close to the bone before you come. And now they've plowed their fields and set their crops and put every last ounce of their labor into a crop they can't even *eat*."

The last word sliced into the air and stayed. The lady agent stood but didn't come out from behind her desk.

Brodis leaned in close enough that he could smell her store-bought scent. "Because. Of your. *Efficiency*."

Mrs. Furman blanched but didn't move. "There's no need to shout, Mr. Lambey. I'm really and truly sorry for your situation, Mr. Lambey, but you're not—"

"Do you expect they'd be *here* if you and yours hadn't *guiled* them? Hadn't *pleaded* them to get shed of their stock and clear every last inch of land for the growing of a crop they had no *use* of?"

Behind him there was movement, and the low sounds of nodding agreement. The power of that murmur buoyed him and strengthened his words. "*Do* you?"

The woman gathered up every bit of her height. Dispenser of justice. "Mr. Lambey, what is it that you're trying to achieve here?"

Brodis dropped his voice and let his last sentence drop into the quiet. "Pontius Pilate washed his hands, Mrs. Furman."

Right off the woman's features hardened. "*Excuse* me?"

"You heard me. Pontius Pilate washed his hands too. The government, Mrs. Furman. The government. You wash your hands and Jesus goes to his death."

The men behind him were silent now. Even the hang-dog scuffling and the inhalation of cigarettes had stilled. Instead there was a thickness in the air, like ointment, and the words of the argument oozed into it slow.

The woman set her hands on her hips, the fear in her face replaced by something bladed and hammered. All her prettiness was gone. "Does it ever occur to you, Mr. Lambey, that you may not be on the side of the righteous?"

Brodis glared at her. He kept his voice level. "Only God knows the names of those whose names have been writ in the Book of the Lamb, Mrs. Furman."

She didn't seem to hear. If anything, she stood up straighter. "Does it ever *occur* to you, Mr. Lambey, that you might be on the other side? That you might be the person *doing* the crucifying?"

Behind him a quick intake of breath. But the thickness in the air stopped it up. Above them, a motorcar passed, the planks of the bridge clattering and shifting under its weight, its shadow creeping into the doorway and over the waiting men. And in the gloom of the passageway a thing moved, a shape, crouched, as of some behemoth, the big bones of a head, the thick canine neck and muscled slope of shoulder. Something in Brodis's organs loosened in fear. But he made himself to stare at the silhouette of the brought-on Beast because he knew that whenever he looked away he could never look again. Words came out of him and stood firm in front of him, sword and shield. "I shall not worship you."

The creature did not move.

Brodis wielded his words again. "My name is written in the book of life, and I shall not worship you." And he saw that each sentence was a soldier entrenched, so that the more he spoke, the wider the ring of the righteous became. "The time is come and the harvest of the earth is ripe." The creature stirred, but in the darkness Brodis couldn't discern did it step forward or back. Then it turned its head and he knew that it retreated into the gloom. Once more he sent his words forth into the space between them. "And all those who dwell upon the earth whose names are not writ are lost."

The thing in the gloom shrank and was no more.

Brodis turned from the office into the paralyzing light. The faces pasted in the whiteness stared at him, but there was no one said a word.


It was late afternoon by the time he returned to his shredded fields. Stomper lay on his belly watching a groundhog hole. When he spied Brodis, he waved his tail slow and unsure but didn't quit his post. Brodis stepped up to the barn loft and swung open the doors. Blades of light knifed slantwise through gaps in the wallboards, and dust motes congealed in its rays. The oak bucket was as he'd left it, the sticks of dynamite still fanned around the opening. Brodis counted them. There were seven. He examined each. Only two were bleeding. He set those back in the pail and selected a clean dry piece, tucking it under his arm while he opened the knife with his teeth. He palmed the stick in his left hand and with his right inserted the tip of the blade into the soft red wax. The point wanted to slip when it made contact with the dense interior, but Brodis choked up on the blade and worked it slow into the packed sawdust until he had carved out a depression. The blasting cap he fitted into the mouth and secured with cellulose tape. Then he cut a piece of barbed wire, laid the seven sticks across it, folded the ends of the wire around again, and twisted the loose ends tight. Something bit into the pad of his thumb, and the skin of it gave way, and a line of blood trickled out. He brought his hand to his mouth and sucked at his thumb and pressed the pad against his teeth.

When the blood had quit, he wrapped the package in a piece of burlap sacking, then lowered it into a rucksack. On top he placed a roll of visco fuse. If he walked, he could tote the posthole digger over his shoulder. It was safer anyway. He couldn't risk the horse side stepping a hole or getting aggravated by a nest of yellow jackets.

An hour later, he stood on the bridge. Yesterday's storm was forgotten save for the flashing river, angry and brown and rushing into the channel toward the ledge. The five-foot pitch had become an enormous fold of water that wrapped leaves and sticks and trees in upon itself. But the firmament was July blue, the sun easing over the ridge. The town and the evening stretched mild and torpid before him, the courthouse domed and bloated and regal in the center, and the houses of rich men perched on the hill above it. Below his feet, the roof of the extension office bled stripes of rust. The men standing outside the front door were gone. The squat structure bulged at the water's edge like a goiter at the throat of a handsome woman. How much she had glorified herself, and lived deliciously! How much she had said in her heart, I sit a queen, and shall see no sorrow! And the masters of the earth would bewail that mighty city, Babylon, for in one hour is thy judgment come.

But they would stand afar off.

Below him, the door of the office was closed. Perhaps they had shut up for the evening. Or perhaps they were inside. That particular decision was for God, not him. God alone knew the names of the men writ in the book of the Lamb on that day when he was come to set fire to the earth.

Brodis glanced down the length of the bridge to ensure no one was coming, then stepped from the closed-off lane across the street and next to the handrail. He set the rucksack on the planks, loosed the drawstrings, and extracted the visco fuse. He unspooled an arm's length and tied it in a granny knot around the handrail. Then he bound the rest of the coil with the cellulose tape. Below him was the office and an escarpment of beach some thirty feet wide—a big target, but if the spool landed wrong it would roll into the river certain sure. He aimed for the side of the building, and the visco bounced against the wall, fell to the ground, wheeled in a little circle, and came to a stop against the side of the extension office. He checked the granny knot on his end, loaded up the rucksack again, and cinched it. Under him, the wooden planks rattled against their steel supports and he felt rather than heard the vehicle that boarded the other end of the bridge. The motorcar's engine slowed as it approached. Despite the limitations of the one lane, the driver had plenty of room to avoid him. Without turning, Brodis hoisted the pack to his shoulder. The sound of tires slowed to a stop.

"Brother Brodis." The voice was warm, quavery, and familiar. Lem Thompson.

Brodis turned to his mentor. He touched his hat and set his heel on the footboard of Lem's coupe.

Lem's arm rested on the edge of the open window. He indicated the posthole digger with his chin. "Fences down?"

Brodis nodded. He didn't explain how he came to have the implement with him in town.

Lem eyed Brodis and the space behind him at the same time. "Yup." He frowned and nodded, studying him with his left eye. "How much you lose?"

"The tobacco."

Lem nodded again slow, and both eyes stared at the place where the sun had set. "I wondered about that."

"Rickerson too."

Lem sighed.

"You?"

"I got sheep and pigs touchier than blind grandmas, but they'll live. And the corn is stripped, but we'll bring it in and fodder it." He was still nodding to himself, as if embarrassed that the disaster that had consumed so many had only just breathed upon him.

"Yup," Brodis said.

"Yup." The older man sighed and his eyes traveled past Brodis through the railing to the churn of water below. He didn't seem to mark the detonator wire. "God's looking out on all of it Brodis. He knows."

And in that moment Brodis saw the feathered wings that would bear the man into Heaven, and they were broad and sinewed and far more muscular than ever he would have envisioned.

The older man touched his hat and released the brake. Then, as the coupe rolled forward, he turned and shouted over the labor of the engine. "Be careful, Brodis." And the vehicle motored away.

Be careful? That meant something, but Brodis didn't know what. He tucked the posthole digger under his arm and followed the path of the automobile. The warmth of the evening had brought the residents from their homes into the streets. Or maybe it was woe, the oozing kind that thickened a man's walk. The women clustered in groups of two and three, their heads bent together in consternation. The Eakin men smoked on stoops or cudded tobacco, shooting the amber juice into gutters. When someone in overalls passed, they nodded or touched their hats but then straightway looked off in embarrassment. The farmers just stared dead ahead. At the gas station, Willis Darby dropped his eye. "Preacher," he said to the pavement.

A group of women in a doorway broke as he approached, and in the tail of his eye there was the swish of blue that made him think on Irenie's marm, but then the skirt disappeared into Rockland's department store and he didn't look to follow.

It was no matter to him now.

The smithy's shop was battened and still, though the place still leached a pent up heat, as if it too could never be cooled. The saw-mill was closed, the conveyer empty, the rotary blades and steam engines silent, the great arm of the McGiffert loader motionless above the scene like the poised hand of God. Wood dust hung in the air, golden in the evening light.

The extension office sat fat at the water's edge, the rock pylon of the bridge rising behind it like an ungainly chimney. Brodis stepped around the front of the building, passing in front of two eyehole windows. Perhaps they spied him. Perhaps they were sitting at their desks writing up their papers, and in a moment would step out the door and ask him what was he doing. And he would have to explain the predicament he and they found themselves in. That the hour was come and they, like him, hadn't prepared. Neither had they repented of their thefts, nor their beguilements, nor of their sorcer-ies, nor their lies. He surveyed the foundation of the rock building, looking for a place to dig.

At his feet gapped the entrance of the animal lair.

He shrugged out of the rucksack and set it down. Then he un-cinched the top and lifted out the burlap sack. The bundle felt weighty in his hands, and the anticipation was the same he'd known on the river—the jam that affixed the world in one place was about to shift. Time would move forward, and the events that were meant to happen next would happen, and the world would speed itself toward its inevitable end.

Above him beeped the horn of an automobile. He looked up at the bridge to spy a red Chevy truck. Howard Gooch's face was framed in the vehicle's window, concern knitted across his brow. A hand rose next to the face and waved uncertainly.

"Brother Brodis…" The call trailed away.

Brodis gathered himself to his feet, caught himself against the building to steady himself and raised his arm. "Brother Howard," he shouted. "Have you got right with God?"

The old man's face brightened. "And the *risen* Savior! Hallelujah!" He waved vigorously, and his face disappeared into the truck. The vehicle rolled on. Just so had the righteous rejoiced after the fall of Babylon. It'd not bring Irenie back, nor the tobacco, nor the money. But it would hasten the end of time. And the merchants of commerce would weep and mourn; for no man would buy their merchandise anymore.

He retrieved the roll of visco and snipped it to size with the needle-nosed pliers, then secured the remaining roll with a rubber band and set it next to the rucksack. Inside the burlap sack the nitroglycerin was sticky with fluid.

Nor would they buy their gold nor their silver.

With the end of the pliers, he crimped the fuse to the blasting cap.

Nor would they buy their linen, or purple, or silk, or scarlet. He grasped the bundle by the end and lay face-up on the ground next to the foundation. He snaked his hand into the animal den, the back of his knuckles scraping the packed earth. With his feet, he scooted his body close enough that his shoulder snugged up against the opening.

Nor their wine, nor oil, nor fine flour.

When his arm was in as far as it would go, he released the bundle. The sky above him was endless and blue.

Nor the souls of men.


On the bridge, the visco fuse was still tied to the rail. The fragments wouldn't blow that far, most like, but sand would pelt the underside of the planks and shower the smithy's and the mill and the river.

Brodis felt inside the rucksack for the box of matches. Then he untied the fuse and pressed it between the heel of his hand and the steel rail. The match flared, and he touched it to the cord and it fizzed up straight away, and just like the old days he was caught up in the pop and fry of it. He held it up for a few seconds, then tossed the seething end onto the escarpment below, where it lay dead and alive at the same time, the current of the river masking the sizzle but not its orange sparks.

Below him the fuse sputtered and winked. The door of the extension office opened, and an overalled farmer appeared in the

threshold, clamped a hat onto his head and stopped to light a cigarette. From the open door, Brodis heard a man talking, as if explaining, and the speaker was powerful tired. Then a woman's voice
came in smooth and light, as of oil that floats on the surface of the
waters. Then the door closed, and Brodis heard the voices no more.
For a long moment, he watched.

If it came to two, it came to two. The Lord knew them that
had sinned against nature and the world and their fellow man. He
knew they labored on, even though the sun sank into evening and
God-fearing men set their implements aside in rest. And He knew
too that the servants of Caesar could not rest on account of the
treacheries they had wrought. And still He had given unto Brodis
the task that he carried now. Still He had brought him here at this
hour. Brodis didn't get to say.

The fuse had burned and burned, and now the orange sputter of
it crept toward the hole under the office, now disappeared into the
hole. Brodis stepped toward the middle of the bridge where the rain
of dirt and stone could not pelt him and then to be safe he retreated
further still, away from the town and its waywardness, away from
the bloat of its sin. He raised his hands to his ears and swore by Him
that lived forever and ever, Who created Heaven and the earth and
the sea, that there should be time no longer.

He pressed the tips of his index fingers into his ears.

Then the office below him blossomed out like a flower that escaped the bud all in one day and at the same time the steel beneath
his feet lurched up and the suddenness of it jarred his lungs and his
guts and the sound reached him last, the crash of it, and then the
smoke writhed up like a fanged being whose talons sent delicate
tracings of stone into the sky and the fragments that plopped into
the mill pond and the brown churn of the river and the ticking of
the rocks on the bottom of the steel bridge and the air was dust-
thick and white and gray and the smoke purled over the water like
the lake of fire and brimstone, where the beast and the devil were,
and would be tormented day and night forever and ever.

The earth stilled and heat pulsed up and enveloped him. The
building poured in upon itself, and he thanked his Maker for the

steady of his hand and the resolve in his head. The air around him quivered, as if it and the ground convulsed, as if the land itself retched at the corruptions it was forced to swallow.

But it was. The ground was moving. A tremor rose up from the steel and shook his legs and his knee joints. The bridge on which he stood was swaying and weaving like the loose end of a child's jump rope, wood and steel waving in a way he hadn't known it could move, the road falling away, descending down. Brodis backed away, then turned and commenced to edge toward the town, certain of his feet beneath him and the steel rail in his hand, a rail that he held to in case the support below his feet gave way, and he stumbled toward the smoke and the faces running toward the river, their mouths rounded in perfect O's and they were as children though he couldn't hear them. A rumbling had begun around him, and everything tipped, the structure beneath his feet, the rail still in his hand but all of it tipping toward the water. The ground opened beneath him, and he fell in a torrent of dust and wood and rock.

The water was warm and thick and bubbling white through nameless debris, and when he looked up to search out the surface above his head something struck him on the temple and fell away. Chunks of stone and concrete descended around him, searching their way to the bottom. He swept his arms through the water and kicked with his feet toward the light. He pushed up and up toward the bubbles, bursting through the wood that churned at the surface. Even as he gulped for air, he grabbed hold of a shard and held.

The shoreline whipped past, people running, a pile of smoking rubble where the extension office used to be. God was the beginning and the end, the first and the last. Blessed were they that did his commandments.

He felt the ledge before he saw it, the way the current gathered force at the lip of the drop, and he drew up his feet and wrapped his arms tight around the plank. Then he was pitching down and down again, into the roil at the bottom of the ledge, which embraced him and pulled him to its heart. The water turned white with air, and the bubbles rose from all directions, and the plank floated past his vision and the water was all light, and the light was the love of the

Spirit of God who was Alpha and Omega, beginning and end, the first and the last.

He had done it. He had done the thing required of him and by so doing testified to the existence of the Christ. And there would be no more death, neither sorrow, nor crying, neither would there be any more pain: for the former things were passed away, for He had made all things new.

The water pulled him to its heart. The bubbles churned and rose and lifted his spirit. His arms flailed and he opened his lungs and breathed until the water that filled them calmed in his airway, and he saw then the white robe, the familiar face, the golden brown hair and melting blue eyes, the sun reflecting honey colored light in his beard, the skin as soft and smooth as a girl's.

He that findeth his life shall lose it: and he that loseth his life for my sake shall find it.

Brodis inhaled. O lamb of God I come.

## CHAPTER TWENTY-TWO

IN OCTOBER, THE MONARCH BUTTERFLIES SPLASHED the coves yellow, and the spiny-skinned beechnuts dropped, the buckeyes too, their prickly husks splitting away from the brown seeds inside, two to a pod, which courting couples were supposed to divide one to each. Acorns rained from the trees, and the red and orange fruit of hearts-a-bustin' popped from its capsules. Stinkhorn mushroom filled the air with the smell of decay.

Brodis Lambey was dead. Irenie had read the news on the front page of the Asheville *Citizen-Times*: a boy standing on a corner hawking newspapers, shouting something about a preacher in Eakin. And there on the front page was a picture of her husband from his logging days, plaid-shirted, hollow-cheeked and dare-me-eyed, his hair swept from his forehead so that it curled at the back of his head like an old time statesman's, looking like the one man there was who knew how to steer the world.

By the time Irenie had stepped off the train in Eakin, Main Street was alive with county and state and federal policemen, newspapermen carrying cameras like shields across their chests. Only then did she hear for certain about Ginny and her husband. Only then did she hear about the third agent.

The Furman funeral had not been in Eakin. Instead, the remains were sent by train to Asheville, and from there to Atlanta. Meanwhile the roses on the front porch withered and dried, and the knotweed moved in. A month later a grim-faced woman in a shirtwaist dress parked a motorcar in front of the bungalow on Main Street and disappeared inside. People in Eakin said she didn't come out for three days but that when she did, she hired Martin and Hank Hogsed to load a step van with furniture and appliances and boxes. They said the piano went in first, its oiled surfaces now showing chipped in the light, yes, and the little stool with the green-balled feet looking a little too fancy, true. But there was something about it, that piece of furniture, its size, maybe, or the sheen on the wood, that they hated to see go. Few people had seen the piano up close before, but now that they had, its loss was a source of some unnameable grief.

The funeral of Brodis Lambey had been problematic, and if it hadn't been for the influence of Lem Thompson maybe wouldn't have happened at all. Lem spoke of his colleague as a man who cared about good and evil, who tried to do right but sometimes forgot that it was the Lord's responsibility and not his own, of a servant who loved God and his people and tried to shepherd them the best way he knew but was so hurt and angered by his brothers' losses that he'd showed it the wrong way. And sure it was a terrible thing to do but who if anyone would have thought there'd be not one but three agents in the office that late in the evening, and one of them a woman. And the old man, the agent from the next county, had for certain never set foot in Eakin before, and who was to know that there could be three people in that office when it had never happened that way before.

Lem never mentioned the conversation about the witch. And he never asked Mrs. Raines where her daughter had got to the day Brodis Lambey blew up the Department of Agriculture extension office. And even if it had occurred to him to talk to a fellow like Lesley Raines, he wouldn't have been inclined to do it. In the end it would take a third party, an outsider in a string tie and black bowler hat, to bring those two pieces of information together.

In the meantime, everyone living on the far side of the river had to drive twenty-five miles out of the way to get into town. The state approved the repairs, even though everyone agreed what needed building was a whole new bridge. You couldn't go into town for the newspapermen asking questions and stopping the children to ask for poses in front of Rockland's Department store or Eli Watt's feed store. Mostly the reporters stayed right there, taking pictures of the collapsed bridge, its remaining supports standing straight up in the river like the chimneys the old settlers left to mark the first places they'd civilized. Most of the reporters couldn't be bothered to drive upstream to the other bridge, much less to follow the road where it wound in and out of the sunlight among the hills.

But there was one, a Mr. Lamousin. A morose fellow in a black bowler and a bulge in his coat that Irenie knew for a whisky flask, he came to the church, then to the funeral, then to the drover's road. And when Matthew's school let out for harvest break and Lesley fetched the boy home in his motorcar, both of them saw Lamousin's little Austin chugging up the mountain. When the vehicle pulled to the shoulder and the Ford overtook it, Lamousin waved for them to stop and asked did they know the way to the Lambey place. Lesley said he wasn't sure but he thought it was way the hell over to the other side of the ridge.

Two days later, Lesley and Irenie saw the man on the drover's road again, this time leaning against his roadster, smoking a cigar and reading a newspaper, as if he didn't have a thing in the world that needed doing. He tipped his derby at Irenie. "Evening, Mrs. Lambey," as if really that was all he'd ever planned on saying anyway.

"Evening, Mr. Lamousin," Irenie ventured.

"Is there a time when we could talk, Mrs. Lambey?"

"Not today, Mr. Lamousin," was all she could muster.

For the three weeks of harvest break, Irenie and Matthew dug potatoes and rutabagas. They plucked the apples into a wire basket atop a long pole. They wrapped and buried the cabbages, and they braided the long green tops of the onions into ropes. They bleached and dried the apples, strung what beans there were, and put up the sweet potatoes and the turnips. There were no tomatoes. When Lesley and Clabe killed the black and white hog, they hoisted the hind legs up onto the stanchions with a block and tackle while the blood drained out into a tub. Then the four of them lowered the carcass into the scalding water of the trough, and Irenie saw it for the first time: the boy looking around, as if he expected his father to step out of the steam to make sure he was holding that ankle tight enough. She saw it again when Lesley pulled the knife lengthways down the hog's belly, and the coils of entrails slid out, smoking and glistening like bubbles into the pan, and Matthew looked around again, expecting, what? And Lesley saying he and Clabe could handle it between them, and Matthew hanging around anyway, because he knew that was what his father would have wanted.

And by the end of the day, when they'd split the breastbone with an ax and carved the carcass and set the hams to cure, when they'd ground the sausage and rendered the glistening cubes of fat into lard, and his father still hadn't appeared to help, Matthew seemed to grasp that he wasn't coming. And though he and Irenie were both exhausted, or maybe because of it, a kind of spillway opened in him, letting loose more words than Irenie'd known him to use at one time. He talked of everything but his father: a boy named James, and a girl, and Irenie hadn't considered there'd be girls at the school, but there were, and her name was Sarah, and she wore her hair in a headband and the teachers were strict and smart and expected the children to read every night for every subject, and halfway through the telling Matthew stopped, and looked around, as if expecting his father to be there to lean forward over the table and tap a penny.

Her husband's absence was everywhere. At supper, when half the table stretched empty and unused. At the milking, when she sat wide kneed on the crate with the cow's taut flesh between her fingers. In their bed, when she woke at the middlemost bottom of the mattress. For so long she'd counted on the weight of his feet on the floorboards and the smell of his skin on the sheets, and now morning after morning she came into the kitchen and found his not-thereness. And the Brodis she remembered was the young Brodis just off the log drives, the man who wore his hair long and unkept, who noticed her and attended her long before she'd known he could have, the fellow who watched her when she spoke and held her words the way you held an apple to test it for ripeness. The young man with a maul across his shoulder and his head thrown back in laughter. But that was the young Brodis, the one that hadn't existed in a long time. Or maybe he had, and it was her who'd failed to reach him. But that was what she grieved for: the younger Brodis. Her own failure.

But then the witch hazel on the front road didn't bloom, and when she looked closer she saw that the plants were all of them cut low, as if from a Kaiser blade, as if by some last petty act intending to say, no, I meant it when I said not to mourn for me. And she remembered the other Brodis then, the one who surprised her in the dark with his rough-skinned Bible, the one who walked over her plea for the hawks, the one who invited the demon through the window.

Meanwhile an orange-haired preacher from Tennessee had set up a soapbox in town on the corner of Hill and Main and took to warning of witches and the evils of them as had congress with them, attracting every day a small and curious crowd, until one afternoon Sheriff McGill ordered him off the box and picked it up and smashed it against the side of the bank and told him he had better take his preaching back to the other side of the mountains where he'd come from.

And meanwhile a war broke out in Europe. A crazy man was trying to gather every country up for himself. In Eakin, it meant the reporters disappeared, all in one day. All except Mr. Lamousin. Him, they still saw. Him, Matthew talked to here and there.

Then one afternoon Lamousin just showed up. She'd spread out a sackcloth that morning, one section covered in onion seeds and buttons, another in bean seeds and cucumber and squash and sweet potato—she'd even squeezed the small hard tomatoes and yes, there were yellow transparent seeds in them. By afternoon, the sacking had stiffened in the sun, and she sat in the rocker and folded each piece over upon itself until the packet was small enough to secure with twine. Somewhere she heard the dogs barking, but didn't pay it much mind. When she was finished with the tying of the packets, she checked the pepper seeds speckled across a sheet of corrugated tin. Satisfied they were dry, she grasped the metal in both hands and set it in her lap. By the time she settled herself and looked up, there he was, hands in his pockets, the black bowler pushed up on his forehead.

"Afternoon, Mrs. Lambey," he saluted her with his hat. "I hope you don't mind, Mrs. Lambey?"

She didn't get up. Let him think it was the tray of seeds in her lap. With the side of her hand, she swept the white pods across the metal, pushing them into the channels. Then she ran her finger down the first groove, herding the seeds to the edge and collecting them in a jar. "You've overstepped, coming here."

"I realize that."

For the first time, she gave him a good long look. He had a lined and gentle face, neither old nor young. His eyes sagged at the outer corners in a manner some might find pleasing. She had an idea of the kinds of questions he would have, and how he would explain that he was trying to get to the bottom of it all and asking was it a coincidence that she had taken a trip just two days before the massacre took place, and what about the question of the speech Mr. Lambey'd made in the office just hours before the killing. Did Irenie Lambey know anything about that? And now there were some said she'd been friendly with the agent's wife, and could that be more than pure coincidence?

She screwed the lid onto the jar, turned it, and labeled the top. "You might as well sit down."

That evening, after Mr. Lamousin had hiked back up the hill to his car, she remembered the spiders. How long had it been since she'd thought about them? It seemed unlikely that they were still there, if ever they had been. The only way to find out was to go. So she and Matthew climbed to the bald with Scram and Fortune and a lantern in tow. When they reached the clearing, Matthew opened the flame, and the yellow of it turned the wide wide space into a narrow pool of seeing. Irenie brought the light eye-level and held it. It took a moment for her vision to adjust, but sure enough, the reflections twinkled back: dozens of points of light spangling across the ground like secret stars.

The eyes of the wolf spiders.

How many times had she and Lesley and Nichol bent down to search for the secret fragile lives clinging to their strands of grass? And now, after twenty years, here they were again, here they were still, hiding on the bald in plain sight, right now, where they'd been for two decades, all of them watching to see what Irenie and Matthew Lambey would do.

*ACKNOWLEDGEMENTS*

I HAVE BEEN AMAZED AND GRATIFIED AT THE EFFORT
Hub City Press has given to this novel. Betsy Teter has shown all
the passion, care, and idealism I ever hoped to find in a publisher.
Michael Curtis asked the hard questions that pushed the story to
the next level. Meg Reid's wonderful creative vision gave the book
its physical form.

I have also been lucky enough to work with tremendous teach-
ers, including Tim O'Brien, Robert Bausch, Alice McDermott,
Christine Schutt, Michele Wildgen, Tony Earley, Padgett Powell,
Erin McGraw, Luis Alberto Urrea, Dana Spiotta, and Marie Cochran.
And I will always feel a debt to Lisa Bankoff for being the first per-
son in the publishing industry to believe in this book.

So many people have been gracious enough to read my (sometimes very raw) work and mirror it back to me. The more candid
these conversations have been, the more helpful to me—and the more
potentially uncomfortable for the responding readers. These readers
gave generously of their time and took the risk of being honest. I
thank them for their willingness to go there: Carolyn Franks, Reid
Franks, Jim Tibbetts, Richmond Eustis, Rachel Unkefer, Kathleen

Pringle, Mike McGhee, Chuck Franks, and Tom Welander. I owe particular thanks to my trusted writer friends Mark Beaver, Jonathan Newman, and Bennett Spann. Special thanks too to Andrew Feiler, who gave so much of his time and never sugarcoated the truth. Both he and Jim Tibbetts showed such unalloyed enthusiasm for my work that they often dropped everything just to read the next installment.

Lastly, I am impressed, always, by my partner Steve McLaughlin and buoyed by his loving support.

One final note: The story that the character Frazier June tells about the timber mill is loosely based upon the legend of the black cat murders as retold in *Witches, Ghosts, and Signs: Folklore of the Southern Appalachians* by Patrick W. Gainer. Seneca Book, Inc., Grantsville, W Virginia, 1975.

**HUB CITY**
PRESS

**HUB CITY PRESS** is a non-profit independent press in Spartan-burg, SC that publishes well-crafted, high-quality works by new and established authors, with an emphasis on the Southern experience. We are committed to high-caliber novels, short stories, poetry, plays, memoir, and works emphasizing regional culture and history. We are particularly interested in books with a strong sense of place.

Hub City Press is an imprint of the non-profit Hub City Writers Project, founded in 1995 to foster a sense of community through the literary arts. Our metaphor of organization purposely looks back-ward to the nineteenth century when Spartanburg was known as the "hub city," a place where railroads converged and departed.

### RECENT HUB CITY PRESS TITLES

*Minnow* • James E. McTeer II

*Pasture Art* • Marlin Barton

*The Whiskey Baron* • Jon Sealy

*In the Garden of Stone* • Susan Tekulve

*Voodoo for the Other Woman* • Angela Kelly

*Literary Dogs* • John Lane and Betsy Wakefield Teter

*The Iguana Tree* • Michel Stone

*Patron Saint of Dreams* • Philip Gerard

Bembo Standard 11.7 / 14.8